To Paisley & Bella Stay tenacious!

WEEDS OF DETROIT

FROM AUTHOR
MISTY
PAQUETTE

For God and all the Guardian Angels
who took on the gargantuan task
of bringing me home safe.

THIS IS HOW IT STARTED . . .

When I was a kid, I swore I was an angel stuck in a human's body. My mom adored that. She made me tell all her friends when they came to visit, and she hustled me out in front of the relatives to recite my belief at Christmas.

She didn't do that when I told her I'd also be dead before I hit sixteen.

My mother—a staunch believer in ghosts and psychic powers and rocks that make you feel better—flipped. She told me there's no way I could know that for sure, so I should stop saying it. She tried to tell me that I didn't know what I was talking about for years.

The idea of death never scared me as a kid, because sixteen was as far off as a thousand. Even as I got closer to what was supposed to be my last birthday, I didn't worry about it. I accepted it, like that's how things were going to be, and I figured it'd be a quick death because I'd been nice in school and did what my mother asked me to. I was sure that God would go the distance and make my death a * poof * kind of event. A gun shot, a car crash, I'd die in my sleep...something easy.

My sixteenth birthday was tense from the minute I woke up until the minute I woke up again on the morning of my seventeenth birthday. My seventeenth came and went with cake, a new sketchbook, and a metal box of specialty drawing pencils. I like art. My mom gave a tremendous sigh of relief, but she waited to congratulate me until the day after my birthday, when I was officially and solidly seventeen years old.

"You made it. You're not dead," she told me over breakfast. She was triumphant, like she'd won some battle with me. I shrugged with my mouthful of Fruit Loops. I knew what she was getting at.

"Maybe I got it wrong," I told her. "Maybe I'm not supposed to live past my teens or something like that."

"Nope," she said, with one shake of her head and her nose held high. "You always said sixteen, and now you're seventeen. You had your chance. No more dying."

I swallowed my cereal.

Here we go, I thought. Here is where we always went.

"I didn't make it up, mom. I told you, it was just a feeling. Maybe I'm still here because I screwed up, I don't know. Maybe I didn't finish what I'm supposed to do yet, so here I am."

My mother turned a little pale. At that point, we were fighting most of the time, so even on a morning when there seemed to be a semi-truce, it was still a bonus if I could make her miserable.

"What could you possibly have finished at sixteen?" she snapped.

Truce...over.

Every word became a brick I wanted to drop on her.

"I. Don't. Know," I said flatly. "Maybe that's why I'm still stuck here with you."

My mother sniffed with a second, high-nosed shake of her head. "You forget that I've already been sixteen, Lael. I know exactly how it feels, and I can tell you, you don't know enough to have finished anything yet."

"Maybe I'm a little smarter than you." *Oh, that was a good one.* My comment sent a scowl trolling across her face. She deserved it, as far as I was concerned. The score board was finally even, and I knew she hated that more than anything.

We glared at each other across the table until she finally looked away. We finished eating in silence. She made a huge show of ignoring me, so I chewed with my mouth wide open, letting bits of cereal fall out on the table. Screw her. But I knew she wouldn't let it go that easily.

"I was just trying to say," she started in again, "that sixteen is very young to have finished much of anything. You have a lot of growing up to do. That's all." No eye contact.

Yeah. That wasn't some heartfelt Hallmark moment between us. It was said to put her ahead on the argument leader board, and her 'that's all' was meant to cap the conversation, so I wouldn't start another argument.

When I was little, I would get intimidated by the edge in her voice, but I'm seventeen now. Who got the last word was more like gripping up a baseball bat, our sentences like layering fists to see who would make it to the top first, claim the bat, and swing it at the other.

I picture my victory—winding back with my last word bat and swinging at my mother's head like a ripe melon. It comes off clean, sailing through the air, her mouth still moving as I point into the distance. I would be free to round the bases once her mouth was far enough away that I couldn't hear any more of her criticisms.

But there was never a top of that last-word bat, and never, ever, a winner.

"Oh yeah," I sneered at her, "I forgot—you know it all, mom. Seventeen is too young to do anything worth doing. Too young to know anything, according to the wise old cow."

She ignored the insult and raised her chin. "That's not what I'm saying, Lael."

"That's what it sounded like." My hands curled into fists and she glimpsed them.

"You know what?" she said, standing up from the table, "you're seventeen and you're alive. Happy Birthday."

She took her coffee cup and went out on the front porch, letting the screen door slam behind her.

I officially hated her. Walking out was winning in her book, and we both knew it. She always had to win.

"Happy freaking birthday," I grumbled. "Too bad I'm not dead yet."

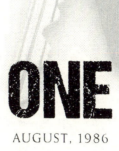

ONE

AUGUST, 1986

T**his one ramps** up before dinner this time. It is a stupid fight, like all of them are. I can't stand the sound of my mother's voice after she's taken a big, fat dose of her nerve meds.

I tell her I wish she was dead.

She runs off crying into her room, howling over one shoulder that she just can't handle it anymore.

I'm the it.

This is how most of our fights go.

This time, when my mother runs away, she leaves the water gushing over a heap of baby spinach in the sink. My step dad, Bob, and I sit opposite each other.

Through the layers of his suit, I can smell Bob's pickled liver all the way across the table. He's a little crooked in his chair, but my mother has tucked a napkin around his neck, and he manages to stay upright. Bob's what my high school health teacher would call a career alcoholic. At the moment, he's a pissed one too.

His bloodshot glare rolls over the table top and lands on me. It's awkward, because neither of us wants the hassle tonight, but we don't know what to do next, in order to stop what is coming. We never know, and it never stops.

Bob gets up, stumbles over to the sink, and turns off the water. He whips back around, his finger aimed at the dead center of my face.

This argument, like every single one, is going to end without being finished. We have not finished an argument since I turned thirteen, four years ago. Instead, Bob will hit me, or ground me, or tell me he's taking away the car that I bought with my own money. That's how it always ends—with a resolution that trails sparks, instead of extinguishing them.

"You had to do it again, didn't you," he says. My mother is not a quiet crier, but I swear she's howling for extra effect now. Every sob cranks Bob's eyebrows down a little lower between his eyes.

"She did it to herself," I grumble.

"She's trying to help you become a responsible adult."

"Help me?" I fire back. "How is being her puppet going to help me? She's a control freak!"

"I think you could use some control." His tone separates us. I am not his little girl anymore. He liked to claim me as his when someone complimented me. But now, glaring at me through his bloodshot eyes, I am not even a step-daughter to him; I am nothing more than an intruder that makes his wife cry.

"I'm not a little kid that you can boss around any..." I start, but Bob's shoulders drop, and I know to stop even before his hands clench into fists.

"In my house, you will follow my rules!" he booms.

"You moved in with us!" I scream back.

My mother's wailing gets louder down the hall. Bob's jaw tightens. He draws himself up. He has no idea what to do with me, or about me, anymore. I've gotten taller, but he's still bigger than me.

"Go to your room!" he shouts.

But I can't let him win. I cross my arms over my chest. "No."

My plan is to flee like my mother did, except I'll jump in my car and get the hell out of here—but even with Bob juiced, he's big and he's between me and the front door. And he ain't moving.

The good news: I have a car key in my wheel well, if I can just get to it.

I gotta try. I step toward the door and Bob gives me a hard shove backward, down the hall, toward my room. I trip on my own feet and throw out a hand to steady myself against the wall.

"Go!" he barks, jabbing his finger at me.

I get my balance and root myself in the mouth of the hallway, shooting him my best fuck you face.

It's a stupid move, and something that I know better than to do to Bob. It sends him into bar-fight mode.

He gives me another hard shove. I stumble backward again, but this time, I go down. I land hard on my tailbone with a yelp.

With one push, he's won this fight the same way he always does: he is stronger than me.

I get to my feet and retreat the four steps back to my room as he advances. Once inside, I slam the door with everything I've got. The walls shake.

I yank a chair from my closet—the green one with the hand painted flowers on the back that my mother used to make me take time-outs on when I was five. I wedge it up under the doorknob. Screw them both.

My mother is still sobbing. I hear her through the wall. Bob's voice joins hers in their bedroom next door. His voice is soft and gentle now, agreeing with her that I am out of control. Agreeing that they need to do something about me. Agreeing that I am the one who is wrong for not agreeing with them.

I let the tears slide out then, but I don't make any noise. I will not sob the way my mother does.

The corner windows in my room that overlook the roof of our garage light up as the sun breaks from behind clouds. The rectangular glow expands and falls on my dingy, baby-pink bedroom walls. Years of smudgy fingerprints and secret crayon drawings show.

I hear my mother sniffle between questions about the cost of tutoring or boarding schools. She thinks the only problem we have is my last report card and that I don't listen to her.

Oh, I listen—I just refuse to be her robot.

It occurs to me that my window isn't just a window. It's a dusty, screen door to freedom. My mom and Bob might hear the floor boards creak if I tried to sneak out down the hall, but they would never expect I'd go out my window.

Window, window, window—door. My mind won't think anything else.

I drag my school backpack from beneath a pile of trash in my closet and empty it on the floor. I travel circles around my room, collecting things that I might need or can't leave behind. My brain won't think in straight lines. I have never packed to leave forever.

I stuff all the money I have in my pocket. I pile in clothes, a couple bottles of nail polish drop to the bottom.

Bob soothes my mother, but of course, she won't stop sobbing. She lives for this.

I wedge my sketchbook inside the pack and stuff my drawing pencil box into the side pocket. Some underwear. An extra bra. A bottle of Bath & Body vanilla bean lotion. Two pairs of ankle socks. My night light, a blanket I've had since I was born. I squeeze in my little jewelry box on top, guarded by a broken ballerina who still tries to spin when I open the lid. It's all that will fit. The zipper teeth strain to close over my mouthful of belongings. I stuff my car keys in my pocket.

4

Balancing on the top of my dresser, I push out the window screen and fling it away. It lands in the grass without a sound.

Now I've got to leave if I don't want to get caught.

If I stay, I'll have to apologize to my mother. Agree that there's something wrong with me every time I don't agree with her. Maybe go to boarding school. I'll have to promise to do everything she commands. But I've tried that and failed.

The only smart thing to do is escape.

I push my backpack out the window.

It tumbles off the edge of the roof and hits the ground with a thud. I freeze, listening to be sure my mom and Bob didn't hear it, but my mother is still sobbing and Bob is still reassuring her that he is going to straighten me out once and for all.

I climb over the window sill, onto the garage roof. The pitch is steep, but the gritty shingles stop me from sliding. I'm sure my skin has just turned fifty shades lighter than I've ever been. I'm scared to death of heights and even though I keep telling myself to jump down—it's not that far, but it's going to hurt a little—I can't.

Our next door neighbor's screen door swings open and I scuttle back, flattening myself against the siding of the house, my ankles slanted on the roof to keep me in place.

The Masnen's door hangs open for a hundred moments, while I hold my breath. Then I hear Mrs. Masnen's sharp voice, "Go all ready!"

I'm positive she is talking to me until Annie, the Masnen's raggedy old Lhasa apso, wiggles out the door, aided by the toe of Mrs. Masnen's house slipper. The door slams shut and Annie pauses on the walk. Through the tangles over her eyes, she spots my backpack, sniffs the air, and barks twice.

Mrs. Masnen shouts at her dog again, "Go!"

Annie waddles off with her tail wagging.

I can't stay up here any longer.

It's not so high up, I tell myself.

Be a spring.

Be a coil.

Be Tigger's tail.

I jump.

The ground comes up fast, but I'm too full of adrenaline to even feel the landing. I splat and hop up, grabbing my backpack and scurrying to my rusty Granada in the driveway. I throw my bag in the back seat.

No one comes running from the house as I start the car. I shoot out of the driveway and then gun it up the street, watching our mailbox get smaller in my rearview mirror. No one rushes out screaming for me to come back.

I'm not sure I feel anything until I'm passing under the expressway signs that guide me into Detroit, but it's then that I start to feel two things.

I feel seventeen.

And I feel scared to death about having no place in the world to go.

TWO

I *flex my foot* against the gas pedal.

At the ramp for the express way, I go west. The cars glide around me like we are caught in the same current. I am swept under sign after sign, all of them leading me into Detroit.

Having been raised on the petticoat fringe of the suburbs, getting closer to the city is terrifying. All my life, I've heard news stories of downtown Detroit. Drugs. Murder. Armed robberies. Whores. The city is filled with lowlifes that don't have the sense to choose anything better.

I grip the steering wheel and follow the gush of cars anyway. I just want to get lost, even though every rapist, junkie, and car jacker within city limits will know I don't belong there, just by the way I push down on the gas pedal at yellow lights, or peer across my dashboard at red ones. At least, that's what my mother would say when we visited downtown and she'd smoosh down in her seat, afraid to look out the window.

My reckless desire to be lost only holds up until I am … lost. As fast as I go, I am barely keeping with the tide of traffic. They fly all around me.

When I see the city water tower, I take the Woodward exit and spill out into Royal Oak. Royal Oak at 11 Mile, has a fairy-dust ambience of safety blown over its artsy streets. Punk rockers and freaks on every corner, the little town is still on the verge—only separated by a flimsy strip of Ferndale from the Arab saturated edges, and solid black blocks, of the ghetto.

But I get out on the boulevard, traveling through the main artery into the inner city. I inch in, mile by mile. I cross over 8 Mile and pass the State Fairgrounds where the news reported people shot during carnivals. Graffiti tags and metal bars spring up on store fronts. Grocery marts are replaced with corner liquor stores, and crumbling motels that blink hourly vacancies like shell-shocked casualties in the broad daylight.

Past 7 Mile, I take my foot off the gas. The cars have to slow down, jerking their brakes and honking at me as I coast toward a red light. The driver behind me lays on the horn and swings her car into the lane beside me. I glance over with a nervous smile and am met with a black woman's furious glare. With a flick of her wrist, she backhands the air over her dashboard. Her nostrils flare as she angrily mouths, "Bitch, GO!" to me before the light turns green and she speeds away.

Traffic is moving too fast and nothing here looks like home. Cars keep honking, drivers gunning it to get around me, flipping me off as they pass. I inch past light after light. I spot a motel on the opposite side of the street. I double back toward the burnt-brick building with the white shutters. A white, wrought iron balcony makes the place look like Scarlet O'Hara's plantation house. The building seems ancient, but the motel sign is one of the only ones I've seen without gaping holes in it. It says *Starlight Hotel* and beneath it is another sign, attached with chain links, advertising free triple X movies with every room. A sign taped in the front window promises reasonable weekly rates and it's not as dirty as the others, so I pull onto the side street and follow it around to the parking lot at the back.

I'm going to rent a room. I'm going to do it. I might be sick first.

I park in the tiny lot and turn off my engine. My mom and Bob will never think to look for me here. They'd be as afraid to come here as I am right now.

I throw open the door.

My backpack slung on my back, I throw open the door to the motel lobby. A shrieking alarm triggers, the sound erupting over my head, as loud and startling as the fire drills in elementary school. But, the moment the door slams shut, the thousand steel pots, beaten with a thousand metal spoons, goes silent.

The lobby is deserted and eerily quiet in the wake of the alarm. The adrenaline pumping through me screams, *get out of here*. My eyes gulp down everything in the lobby, without really seeing it, as I search and sift for imminent danger.

The place is empty, and instead of being seedy and creepy, it's clean and smells like fabric softener. The walls are the color of black cherry ice cream and a spotless, plum runner extends through the lobby like a celebrity carpet, leading to an ascending staircase. A fake fern drapes off the counter, and another leaks from the top of a snack machine. After the string of burnt out buildings on the way here, everything in this lobby is weirdly charming.

On my left is a line of useful machines: a pay phone set in a wood cubbyhole that suggests, but would not provide, privacy; a squat little box of an ice machine with a lopsided crown of plastic buckets. A fake fichus tree punctuates the line up, its branches smashed against the tall pop machine beside it. The fern-topped, snack machine is at the end, right before the stairs, with rows of metal, curlicue fingers clutching snacks behind glass.

To my right, one look at the counter, it's obvious that this is a counter that means business. As impenetrable as a highway guardrail, the monster takes up the entire right half of the lobby. Baked-bean brown and marbled with black veins and flecks of gold, it stands as high as my chest near the lobby door and only slightly lower at the payment window. The very center of the beast's back is embedded with a deep track, from which bulletproof glass, at least a half-foot thick, extends all the way up to the vaulted ceiling. The office is wedged like a foxhole between the bulletproof barrier and a wall of tall windows that looks out at the oil change shop next door. Room keys, hung on a peg board inside the office, shiver on their hooks as heavy footsteps clomp down the stairs behind me.

"You just usin' the phone, or you lookin' to git a room?" A woman asks from above me. I step away from the counter and peer up the staircase to the first floor landing.

A black woman, more bottom than top and dressed in violet hospital scrubs, stares down at me. I'm frozen by her stare, although my blood is pulsing.

Her eyebrows rise. "Well?" she asks. "Whuch'ya gonna do?"

"A room...I think."

The woman sidesteps down the stairs. One foot goes down, the other joins it, and that's how she gets to the lobby floor. Once she's there, her nostrils flare like an exhausted horse. She drags a ring of keys from her purple cotton pocket and unlocks the office door. Once inside, she locks the door behind her, like I'm a criminal.

"So, okay," she wheezes. "Whu'chu wanna do?"

I stoop to speak into the trough.

"How much are the rooms, ma'am?" My eyes slide up to meet hers and the returned stare is stony, one eyebrow cocked over it. I can't tell if she is annoyed with, or confused by, me. Maybe I was too loud or not loud enough. Still hunched over near the trough, I raise my eyebrows, wondering which it is.

"You ain't gotta do dat." Her eyes flick to the trough. I scoot back and stand up straight again. She taps a round vent over the trough.

"This one here's fo' talkin'," she says. "Rooms is twenty-eight a night; eighteen fo' a short stay." Her eyes sweep over me and I assume she sees my confusion again because she adds, "Short stay's three hours. You don't want no waterbed, do ya?"

"No," I shake my head. "I thought your sign said you rent by the week? How much is that?"

"It's one fitty a week."

"What does that include?"

"Include?" Her head swivels back, her whole face puckered. I've said something wrong again. "It includes housekeepin' once a week...towels, a bed, soap...whuch ya wan' it to include?"

"I just didn't..." I let the words fade as I shift from foot to foot. "I'll take it, okay?"

She rolls her eyes, blowing out a sigh. "Ahright."

I stand there, not knowing what I need to do next, figuring renting a room is probably like going to the doctor's office. She'll probably give me papers to fill out and I wonder how she'll get them through the metal trough hole if she does. When I look up, she's staring at me.

"You gotta pay fo' it," she says flatly.

"Oh. Okay." I swing the backpack up from off the floor and unzip a front pocket. I wish I had more common sense to know what I was supposed to do, instead of always having to be told. I pull out my money, folded over so it looks like a thick, green wallet. Everything I've got equals about two weeks rent, maybe two and a half.

The woman's eyes dart to the door, then the stairs, and when her gaze returns to me, she looks angry.

"Ain't you got no sense, girl?" she hisses. She's leaning in toward the round slot now, so her voice is louder. "Put dat money back in yo' pocket. *Right now.*"

I do what she says and this time, my face feels as dark plum as the runner beneath my feet. I look up at her, wondering why she's mad and how she expects me to pay for the room with the money in my pocket.

Her expression is a little softer with the money hidden away, but she's shaking her head again. "You don't go flashin' no big stacks a' money roun' a place like dis! Ya only take out whachya need and *da's it.*"

I nod my understanding. This time, I reach into my pocket and use my thumb and index finger to peel back bills, trying to count them as I do it. My eyes travel up the bulletproof glass to where it meets the ceiling. When I think I have the right amount, I pull out the money, keeping it in my palm like a magic trick. I nod to her, to let her know I have it, and she lets out another long sigh with another eye roll.

"Well, go on." She taps the shiny metal trough. I pass the green wad of bills through, clenched between my finger and thumb, but hit a glass partition in the center. It stops me from being able to just pass it straight across to her and it seems impolite to just push the stack over the top and let the bills spill out all over the desk on the other side. I don't want to make any more mistakes with her, so I wedge my wrist into the opening and crook my arm so that I can thread my fingers up over the center lip and pass her the bills pinched between my fingertips.

Once the money is bulging out on her side of the partition, the woman just stares at it, and then at my arm, wedged awkwardly through the slot.

I smile at her and wiggle the bills so she can see that I'm making an effort to be helpful. My arm is starting to ache.

Her lips pull into a silent, sour whistle before she reaches out and takes the wad. She counts the bills I've given her in plain view.

"I need aotha' twenty," she says and shuffles through the bills again, so I can see that I'm short. I pull out another twenty and pass it to her, but this time I let the bill drop once I get my fingers over the partition. "An' a license."

I can't give her that. It won't read the right age. I blush as I lie to her, "I don't have it on me."

"Mmm," she eyes me knowingly as she flattens the bills into a drawer beneath the desk. "How old are ya?"

"I'm...uh...I'm eighteen," I tell her. She only glances back up, but I'm sure she can see the lie engraved on my head in bold, black just-turned-seventeen block print.

"Huh," she says as she takes out a pen and a wide, spiral-bound book. "Fine. It don't make no difference ta me. Jus' gimme yo' name." She sighs, spreading the book open on the desk.

"Lael," I say.

"Lael?" she repeats under a quirked, not-buying-it lip.

"Like...snail. Or fail," I tell her. "My mom's a hippie."

"Da's yo' firs' name? I jus' need yo' las'."

My hands are sweating. "Wallace. My name is Lael Wallace."

"Ahright," the woman says with a long look before she puts it on the paper. "Weeklies stay on da third floor. Complimentary room cleanin' is included. See dat lounge ova' there?" She points the pen straight out the side door of the office. I look in the direction she's pointing, but have to walk around the corner to see what she's actually pointing at.

There is a walkway I hadn't noticed at the end of the counter. In the middle of it is another staircase leading down to a bottom floor, and just past it is an opening into the room she's calling the lounge. I follow the walkway and look in.

The lounge has a saggy couch on the outer wall and a fridge and microwave across from it. At the far end of the room is a door to the boulevard with a red bar across it that says EMERGENCIES ONLY. Paper signs are taped over the windows, advertising triple X movies, cheap rates, clean rooms, new management.

I'm pretty sure I've seen everything I was supposed to when I hear the woman clear her throat from behind the office door. I return to the counter and she is glowering at me from behind the thick glass. I've screwed up again.

"I saw the lounge," I tell her. She stares at me like she's trying to wrap her head around what I'm saying. I let my shoulders rise and fall in a loose shrug, unsure what I've done to disappoint her again.

"Yeah, ya did," is all she says. "Weeklies can use the fridge and microwave ova' there. Mark yo' food, but we ain't respons'ble for anythin' dat go missin'. Clean up afta' yo'self too."

"Okay," I say. "Thank you."

That seems to throw her. She rolls her tongue in her cheek.

"Where you from?" she asks and then, just as quick, she shakes her head. "Neva'mine. You welcome." She takes a key off the pegboard behind her. "I'll show ya yo' room."

"Okay." I say and again, "Thank you."

"Uh huh." It doesn't impress her this time. She takes the key in her palm and unlocks the office door, steps out, and locks it up again from the outside. She tries it once and when it doesn't open, she stuffs her ring of keys into a pocket where I am surprised they fit.

As we climb the stairs together, the woman is quiet except for her labored breathing.

"What's your name?" I ask when she pauses on the second landing to catch her breath. The landing extends further out, creating a little alcove that is blocked by the stairway rail. A fake fern droops over the edge of the jutting ledge and if I lean a little over the rail, I can see the entire length of the lounge below.

"Name's Lavina," the woman pants. "I clean da rooms. And don't go leanin' on dat rail too much. Ain't nothin' too sturdy roun' here."

It starts sinking in that I'm really staying here as we reach the top floor. A tingle of anxiety shivers my spine. I rented a room for a whole week. I'm not going home. Part of me wants to race down the stairs and back to my car, but the other part just wants Lavina to hurry up, so I can see my first 'place'. However, Lavina goes up the stairs the same way she came down, so it takes a while to get to the next level, which opens to the third floor.

Electric romance-lighting flickers from wall sconces, turning the deep plum carpet the color of a seasoned bruise. Lavina waddles down the hall in her purple hospital scrubs, her thick hips swaying like a violet hippo, to the very last door on the right.

"If there eva' a fire, dat door there is da emergency stairs." She waves a hand to a recessed door across the hall. "It goes down ta tha groun' floor. I'd jus' use the reg'lar stairs if I was you though. Them emergency stairs ain't lit good and God knows what's walkin' round in dat stairwell at any minute."

Deep in the recessed hall, I imagine the dark ear of a shadow pressed to the other side of the emergency door, listening to us right now. The shadow waits for Lavina to turn away, so it can reach through the door and pull me into the stairwell, quick as a spider. Another shiver rolls through me, and this time Lavina sees it. She flattens out her brow. Her glare wipes all the shadows from my imagination, and for a second I'm more afraid of Lavina than what could ever be hiding in a stairwell.

"Jus' stick wit' the reg'lar stairs," she says. She rattles the room key into the door knob and swings the metal door open. She shuffles into the pitch-black room while I stand frozen in the hallway like a moron. She pops on the bathroom light and calls over her shoulder, "You comin'?"

Years later, I'm sure I will think of this room as a very standard room, but at the moment, in my mind, it's my first apartment. I have paid the rent and, from wall to wall, this place is all mine for now. Well, at least for a whole week. Being mine stretches the four walls so much, this room is a mansion to me.

Lavina flicks on the bedroom light and I step inside.

The bathroom to my left is pristine. It is white, with white walls and a white tiled floor, a white bathtub, and a white shower curtain, a white counter, and a white toilet and sink. White towels and washcloths are stacked on a slatted, silver shelf. Besides the silver faucets, mirror, and shelf, everything else is blindingly white.

"You done in there? I got thin's dat need doin'." Lavina's voice is impatient.

"Sorry. It's just so..." As I come into the bedroom, I can't control the grin spreading across my face.

"What?" Lavina asks.

I throw out my arms. "It's beautiful!"

"Pshh..." She rolls her eyes.

The bed is huge, compared to the twin size I have at home. The thin bedspread is tucked around two pillows at the head; it reminds me of my boobs in a tube top. There is a dresser on the wall opposite the foot of the bed, with six wide drawers and a huge mirror on top. It's screwed to the wall. I run my hand over a drawer handle, wanting Lavina to leave so I can inspect my new 'home' by myself. A television set is attached to a high wall platform and slanted so the best view is from the bed.

Lavina goes past me to the window, pulling a silver chain that opens the blinds. As the slats scoot open, the motel sign looms right outside. I could probably reach out and swing the Triple X sign that dangles from the bottom on a chain.

"If dat sign botha's ya any—" Lavina starts.

I cut her off. "It doesn't."

She doesn't need to know I'm afraid of the dark. She really doesn't need to know how carefully I packed my night light and that it is slung over my shoulder right now, along with my ratty receiving blanket and a box full of jewelry that turns my skin green if it gets wet. All she needs to know is that I'm a grown-up who just rented her very own room.

I look down on the boulevard from my new castle view. All sorts of garbage is blown up against the curb. Cars race by, sending discarded burger wrappers and sheets of shredded newspaper flying like tattered fairy wings. A woman dressed in a ratty, winter coat pushes a rickety grocery cart filled with garbage bags and returnable bottles down the cracked sidewalk.

I suck in a breath. This is my home for the next week.

I am Rapunzel now, with short hair.

"Dis one's tha *on* button fo' da TV," Lavina begins, but I'm barely hearing her instructions as she explains the TV remote and how to use the phone.

I shake off the vision of the dirty street outside and the excited tingle returns. This place is mine. I want Lavina to leave so that I can open all the drawers and put my stuff in them. I have to fight the urge to dump out my backpack on the bed while she's still talking.

She says something about the coffee pot downstairs and when I have to pay rent for the next week. Rent. I'm a girl who pays rent.

She opens a metal flap on top of the metal box beneath the window and says something about the dials and I nod, but don't hear a word. It is like listening to Bob talk about tire pressure after I'd just got my first set of car keys in my hand. I just want Lavina to leave so I can jump on the bed.

"There's three locks on da door," she goes on, bustling over to the door. She demonstrates as she instructs. "Da knob locks up on it own, but ya gotta turn tha dead bolt yo'self, and there's a chain ya slide inta dis track here at the top..."

"I'll figure it out," I say with a grin and she smirks.

"You fo' sho' now, aren't ya. Ah right, then. I'm roun' if ya need anythin'."

The metal door clangs behind her. I am almost dizzy with the joy of it, my own place, my very own. I put my forehead on the closed door, my eyes shut. No one can come into this room and tell me what to do, when to do it, what to say, or what not to say. I can eat in bed, I can watch TV whenever I want, I can make a person leave. And I want to remember the very first moment that I turn around, open my eyes, and see my very first place.

I take a deep breath and slide my forehead across the door, ready to turn for that first look. But I brush up against something that moves.

Images of fingers and spiders shoot through my head as I gasp and push myself away from whatever touched me. I open my eyes to the chain, dangling off the door frame. It swings like a hangman's rope, or like it is trying to throw itself into the empty artery of the lock.

I take the cold end of it in my hand. The chain makes a gritty sound as I push the worn nub into the track. I turn the deadbolt with a heavy clunk. I wonder if I will ever get used to locking all these locks when, at home, we never bothered to lock our front door.

This is my home now. Behind three locks and a metal door.

I clear my throat. The sound doesn't echo, it falls. The dark carpet eats it whole and then there is only the hum of the florescent light from the bathroom. I flatten my back against the icy door of a place that already seems much smaller than it did moments ago. It smells like vacuumed carpet.

Instead of running and jumping on the bed, I sit down on it with my backpack nestled between my ankles as where I am sinks in. I think I'm going to be sick.

I try telling myself that it will not be too dark at night.

I remind myself that there are three locks on the door.

I tell myself that I am an adult now.

I can do this, I say.

I repeat it out loud. Twice.

Then I hunch forward over my knees and cry.

I put my clothes in the dresser drawers while a thousand disconnected thoughts spill around my head.

Why didn't I bring my pink shirt?

If someone knocks on the door, do I answer?

Where am I going to get a job?

What about my Senior year of high school?

Are the police going to come looking for me?

How many people are going to be raped or murdered in the city tonight?

Will I hear it happen?

Am I absolutely positive the locks are all locked?

Do my parents even know I'm gone yet?

The concerns flow in a stream, but gather in a flood that waterlogs me. Each fear bounces to the surface, then pushes aside to make room for the next. My optimism sinks, dragging my heart down with it.

Why didn't I grab that pink shirt?

I pick up the remote and flip away from the news. I click past a dopey sitcom and land on channel three. A woman screams from the speaker and I nearly drop the remote. On screen, a naked man spreads the woman's legs wide open. She's not exactly screaming in pain. She throws her head back and grunts as the man mounts her. She talks about the size of his penis as it slides into her, center screen. Porn. On the TV. The remote bounces off my foot and onto the carpet.

I've never seen porn before. At seventeen, my mother always explained me to friends as a 'late bloomer'. I even overheard my mother's friend refer to me as 'shielded'. I thought all their labels made me sound clueless, but I've read books, and had health class, and I've even had boyfriends. I've been kissed. I've been fingered. But all the movies I've seen always spotlight how important it is to the guy that the girl is a virgin on their wedding night. It's romantic. I'm saving myself for the right one.

Yes, it's all that. And I'm scared to death of actually doing it.

Even though I'm blushing, I can't look away from what's happening on the TV screen. How it's happening. None of the books I've read could detail what it's like the way this does on the screen.

The man drives his penis into the woman. She stops screaming and starts cooing like he's singing her a lullaby instead of pounding against her so hard that her hair bounces. She seems to like it. The shot switches from their full bodies to a close up of his penis, stiff as a baseball bat, ramming through her pink folds.

I get hot between my own legs.

They change positions. She's on top of him now, pointed out toward the camera, her heels balanced on his thighs, her legs spread open like butterfly wings. I can see everything.

It's embarrassing.

And hot.

I have no idea what to do about the pulsing ache between my legs. It's as if my heart has slipped down between my thighs and is running for its life. I've felt that before—that pounding beat—but I've never been able to relieve it.

I switch off the TV.

And turn it right back on.

I stare at the screen. My buttons just aren't pushable, it seems, but this pulse is going to kill me.

I switch off the TV and drop down on the carpet beside the bed. I do 300 sit-ups without stopping, until my tail bone aches and my burning abs calm the drumming between my legs. Wet with sweat, I change into my pajamas—a tank top and shorts.

I lay there until my heartbeat finally returns to normal. My stomach rumbles. I didn't eat dinner before I left home.

It's dark outside and the hotel sign kicks on, illuminating my room with a glow through the open blinds. I close them and it blocks out the sign pretty well, but it leaves the room spooky dark. I turn on the lights and my stomach growls again, like it's chewing on itself.

I'm afraid to unlock the three locks, but I'm starving and there were vending machines in the lobby. I take the room key Lavina left me, dig three bucks out of the backpack I've hidden under the bed, slide the chain out of the track on the door, and unlatch the deadbolt with a clunk.

Before I can get the door open, a man in the hall shouts, "I ain't fightin' with you no more!"

I twist the lock back to where it was, thunking it into place. My stomach growls again and it makes me angry. I go to the bed, sit on the edge, and pick up the phone. I can't remember what Lavina told me, so I press "0".

"Front desk," a man's voice says. I kind of expected Lavina, so I stammer a minute, scrambling to find words.

"I...uh...I wanted to make a call."

"Press 5, and then 1, if it's long distance, and then the phone number." The guy sounds bored.

I nod, like he can see it. "Okay, thanks."

"Uh huh." He hangs up.

I dial 5 and 1 and punch in the number which has always meant home. My mother answers on the first ring.

"Hello?" Her voice is high and stringy, not like she's been crying, but like she's annoyed.

"It's me," I say.

"You better get home right now, young lady. You think it's okay to jump out a window? The things you said to me were unacceptable!"

"Bob pushing me around isn't acceptable either."

"You have ten minutes to get back here!"

"Or what?" I say. She puffs and chuffs on the other end. Ha. I really got her. She has no idea what to say and she doesn't know where I am. Ten minutes? Yeah, right. It would take me 45 minutes and that would only be if the streetlights were green all the way.

"You're already grounded," she bristles. "Don't make this worse than it already is."

"We're sending her to fucking boot camp!" Bob shouts in the background.

"Tell Bob he can go fuck himself!" I shout into the mouthpiece. "I'm never coming home."

I slam the receiver down on the cradle, hoping it will ring in her ears all night long. I grab my room key and without bothering to put my shoes on, I go to the door, flinging open the locks.

THREE

I **stomp down the** empty hallway in my bare feet, the carpet coarse beneath my toes. Thieves, rapists, murderers, and every other criminal I've ever seen on the news...they could all be waiting for me outside my room. And I don't care.

I shoot down the stairs and the landings fearlessly. In the back of my head, I'm almost hoping that I run into trouble, because nothing can hurt me with all this adrenaline pumping through my blood. I'm sure of it.

On top of my roaring heartbeat, what's pounding in my brain is how my mom said I'm already grounded. Like I'm still the little kid she used to shove into the time-out chair. I'm vibrating with how I told her that Bob could go fuck himself.

I should've told her they both could.

I step onto the lobby floor like I own the place.

"What the hell do you think you're doing down here like that?" a man barks from the office. It's muffled by the bullet proof glass, but the startling sound of him drains every drop of adrenaline from me as I spin around to see who's talking.

A guy in a grungy plaid shirt glares at me from behind the high edge of the counter. His face is a round, rotted squash, with angry, red acne scars pitted in his cheeks. From the looks of the harsh furrow in his brow, he probably spends a lot of time scowling.

I stop dead. "Are you talking to me?"

"Who else would I be talking to?" he growls, standing up from his chair. His eyes straggle down my body, stalling on my boobs. "Lavina told me a little redneck from the sticks moved in here today. Guess she wasn't kidding, huh? You must be Lael Wallace, room 46. Paid in full. I'm Ned." He leans toward his side of the glass partition, eyes plunging into my cleavage best they can. He grins.

I cross my arms over my chest. My pajamas suddenly seem scandalous. The spaghetti straps too flimsy, the shorts too short. I notice my nipples rubbing against the fabric and my face heats.

He glances at my face. "You want change for the vending machine?"

I stand there, staring back at him, clutching my dollars in my palm the way Lavina told me to—my second magic trick of the day. Were all those insults his way of joking? I can't tell, now that he's softened his tone. Maybe I misunderstood him. Maybe making me feel like a roach was his way of being funny.

When I don't move, he jabs a finger toward the metal trough. But his brow has smoothed out. Either he's really bad at joking, or he thinks I'm stupid. Maybe it's both.

"Well, come on then!" he says. "I don't got all night. Put it in already." He half-laughs, flicking his fingernails against the glass like he's bored.

My stomach snarls as I step closer to the counter. I don't twist my arm into the slot this time, but shove the bills in, up and over the lip in the center, letting them spill out on his side.

He picks up the crunched roll of singles, pulling them apart and smoothing them out.

"Sweaty," he notes with a creepy grin. He deposits the bills in the drawer under the desk, and counts out three bucks worth of quarters. He drops the coins, one by one over the lip, but as they hit the trough, they roll out in all directions and roll across the counter. I try to catch them before they go off the edge. A couple hit the floor anyway and I scramble to trap them beneath my bare feet so they don't roll under the machines. When I stand up with eight coins in my hand, I catch Ned with his forehead pressed against the glass, staring down the sagging front of my tank top.

I slap my hand holding my room key over the center of my shirt, trying to block the pervert's gaze.

He waggles his wiry eyebrows at me, dropping the last of my change through the slot. "No bra. Niiice."

I block the coins from rolling away this time, slapping my free arm down on top of them, but I have to fit them all in one fist because the other is still shielding my boobs. Once I've got them, I glare at the guy behind the glass.

He chuckles, like I'm a lame joke and he's being generous.

I turn my back to him and shove the quarters into the machines. My butt and legs are on fire as if his stare is a magnifying glass aiming a laser of sun on them.

A can of Coke drops into the chute with a thunk and a cellophane-wrapped package of Suzi Q cakes drop into the bottom of the vending machine. I squat to open the door flap, scooping out the cakes as the office door knob jiggles behind me. Ned is coming out.

I grab my Coke and shoot up the stairs, taking the steps two at a time. I am already on the second landing when he shouts up, "You dress like that around here and the least you're gonna get is stared at!"

I sprint down the third floor hall to my room, my heart racing like the white rabbit racing down his hole.

I fight the key into the knob and drop my Coke as I fumble to get the door shut. I lock all three locks.

Breathing hard, I back away from the door as a sob struggles up through my pinched throat. The cellophane cake package is stuck to my fingers, the cakes smashed in my fist.

FOUR

I **wake every hour** throughout the night—when a door slams, when a woman howls, when a car honks on the boulevard, and when nothing happens at all. I wake up and stare at the red-numbered alarm clock, bolted to the side table. The hotel sign outside my window illuminates the room with a murky glow.

The room is sweltering hot, but I'm still too freaked out to get out of bed and turn on the air. I figure if I don't make a sound, no one will know I'm even here.

As the sun finally rises, I am triumphant. I'm still here. I'm tougher than I thought and my courage builds, the brighter it gets outside. The sun takes over and snuffs out the hotel sign. I re-check the door locks once more and change into my other pair of shorts and a fresh t-shirt. I wish I'd brought more clothes.

It's after eight now. Thursday. That means my mom and Bob should be at work, which also means I might be able to sneak home and get some of my stuff. They might be standing guard or have already changed the locks, but it still might be worth a try.

I'm starving again. That feeds my bravery too.

I could take Ned on now in the bright shine of the day. Lavina's probably here too, and I don't think she's going to be very happy knowing how he treated me. She seems protective like that—like this is her hotel and I am her customer, even if she is just the maid. I'll bet she gives Ned what and for when I tell her what happened.

But the thing I'm most proud of, what is singing in my veins, is that I made it through the whole night. The monsters that shouted and slammed doors, groaned and banged headboards all night—they must all be sleeping now.

I pull open my room door like nothing can cut me down. And just like I thought, the place is a morgue. I make my way down to the snack machines in dead silence.

Breakfast is two packages of neon orange crackers with a smear of fake cheese between them, and a can of root beer to wash it down. Lavina startles me before I have a chance to grab the pop out of the machine chute.

"Well, good mornin'," she says. She's wearing slate blue scrubs today and continues on her way, bustling past me and side-stepping down the stairs toward the lobby. Over her shoulder, between pants, she asks, "Was yo room good?"

"No," I say.

She pauses, but I'm not sure if it's to talk to me or to catch her breath. "No? How's that? What's wrong wich'ya room?"

"I guess it's not the room, it was the guy at the front desk last night."

She gives one nod and continues down the stairs. Still clutching my can of root beer, I follow her down to the lobby and then down the steps leading to the basement level. I want her to know about Ned. She turns down a dark, narrow hall on the left and waddles off into the shadows. I don't follow. It's as black as a cave.

A naked light bulb clicks on and I glimpse Lavina taking a left into another dark room. Another light pops on.

The smell of fabric softener billows up as I follow down the hall and turn the corner, into a laundry room. Three washers and four dryers— non-industrial, just like ours at home—line the walls, and at the far end, towers of folded towels and sheets are stacked on top of a wood board suspended on cinderblocks. Lavina goes to a unit of raw, metal shelving filled with bottles and cans of cleaners. "Now who was it give you trouble las' night?" Lavina gives me a long, knowing look. "Or is it jus' that you homesick? This is yo firs' time out, ain't it? You missin' yo' mama?.."

It strikes a nerve. Deep. I expected her to be on my side, to be fired up and ready to kill Ned, but she's acting like whatever happened was just because I'm a child.

"No," I snap, "I'm not a baby. My problem was with the guy behind the desk. Ned."

"Oh yeah? What he do now?" Lavina asks, but she's not all that interested. She's busy sorting through the cleaners on the shelf. When I don't answer, she doesn't ask. She doesn't say anything until she's got her bottle of blue liquid in her hand and is making her way toward the laundry room door where I'm standing, blocking the exit. "Well?" Her eyebrows peak. "You gonna say what he done to ya, or you just gonna stand there an' keep me from doin' mah job?"

I move and she walks past. I scramble to follow her once she turns off the light and the whole laundry room goes black. All I want to do is explain what happened with Ned, how he was looking down my shirt and kept tossing the coins through the window slot so they'd roll away. I want her to be on my side. But it all sounds like tattling now that she's accused me of missing my mother.

"Ned's rude." I tell her.

Lavina goes up the steps to the ground floor, across the lobby, and up the second flight without a word. I follow behind her, listening to her breathe. Her nostrils flare like a bull.

"He's really rude," I repeat.

"He rude," she puffs. "I heard ya."

Why am I still following her? She doesn't seem to care what I'm saying at all. But there is nothing for me to do but go back to my room and sit alone. Maybe watch porn again. I could do that.

"So...what'd he say to ya?" Lavina stops in front of her cleaning cart parked in the middle of the hall. She grabs a roll of paper towel and goes into the room beside it. "I swear, girl...talkin' to you's like pullin' teef!"

"He's a pervert," I say, leaning in on the doorway frame. She squirts window cleaner all over the dresser mirror. The bed is messy, but otherwise, the room looks clean. The mirror was already spotless. "He dumped my money in the slot so it rolled out all over the floor and he could look down my shirt."

After a moment of thought, she nods. "Yeah, that sounds like Ned. I'll talk to 'im. Pro'lly won't do nothin' though. He got a nasty way 'bout 'im sometimes, but if he don't listen, I'll be sure to talk wit' Clive too. That make you happy?"

Kind of insulting, but yeah. "Who's Clive?"

Lavina pauses at the mirror. Stares at me like I'm an idiot. "Jus' the owner of dis' hotel." She huhs and goes back to wiping the glass.

Was I supposed to know that?

Lavina shifts gears and changes the subject. "So how come a white girl like you's lef' da country to live down here and live in the ghetto?" Lavina asks just as the lobby door alarm goes off. I flinch at the screech, but Lavina just pulls away from the mirror and throws down the soggy paper towel on the dresser top.

"Ain't nobody kin come in while I'm still downstairs, now ken they?" she grumbles. I jump out of her way, so she doesn't mow me over walking out of the room. She goes down the hall, her enormous hips cycling like mammoth bike pedals.

With nothing else to do, and her interest in me finally showing, I decide to follow along behind her again. She harumphs her way down the steps, but Lavina groans the minute she hits the lobby floor.

"C'mon now...not you ag'in!" she says.

A *giant woman* is standing in the lobby, wearing a cornflower-print dress with a frilly bodice that reminds me of my grandmother. So do the woman's beige, thick-soled heels. The difference is that this woman is at least six foot three, with skin as dark as a Friar plum and red-blond hair that seems to shift when she turns her face toward Lavina and me.

I gape the minute I get a good look at her.

She is not a *she* at all. *She* is definitely and unmistakably, a *he*.

A thick, five o'clock shadow conceals his cheeks, although it's only about nine in the morning. The wig slapped on his head drips synthetic curls down his temples and over the top of his wiry, black sideburns. I've never seen anything like this. Back home, a man dressing up in old lady clothes would be carted off to the hospital for treatment.

"Lavina! Baby!" the man squeals beneath his trembling wig. His voice is as deep as a well, but he delivers his words like a woman would. I can't stop staring.

Lavina isn't caught up on the details of him the way I am. She just scowls at him.

"Donch'ya baby me, Yolanda," she scolds as she rises up on tiptoes to look out the front door at the parking lot. When she goes flat again, she turns and glances over her shoulder, up the stairs. The scowl is still firm when she looks back at Yolanda. "You know you ain't s'pose to be in here when Clive could catch ya!"

"I didn't see his car," Yolanda explains, raking her long fingers through her wig. I'm shocked it stays in place. "So he in't here, is 'e?"

"He could pull up any second," Lavina growls, yanking the office keys out of her pocket. Once she's in the office with the door locked behind her, she leans close to the speaking vent in the glass. "So whuch'ya want, Yoyo? A night? A week?"

Yolanda's snaggle-toothed smile is grisly, but his reply is sweetly feminine. "A week, please, darlin'."

"An' you know you gotta stay outta sight," Lavina adds the reminder, still holding tight to her scowl. Her eyes dart to the front door and back.

"I know, baby," Yolanda says.

"Donch'ya fo'git now, this could cos' me mah job, if he catch you."

"He ain't gonna catch me again, sweetie, I promise you that. He bust off my tooth that las' time, remember?" Yolanda opens wide, pointing to the jagged, half tooth in the front of his mouth. "And I still din't tell him it was you who got me that room, now did I?"

Lavina sighs, motioning for Yolanda to send the money through the slot.

He glances out the front door again before pulling a wad of cash from the frills guarding his cleavage. He licks his finger, smearing it with purple lipstick, and fingers through the bills gingerly. It ends with a frown.

"Hang on now," Yolanda murmurs and then hikes his dress up to his hip, fishing around in the elastic waist band of his panty hose for more cash. I can see his shiny, purple panties and the thick club of his penis wedged in them. It's compressed against his body. He catches me looking and flashes me his gap-tooth, busted up smile as he drops the hem of his dress back around his knees.

He passes the cash to Lavina through the slot and flicks his stubbly chin in my direction. "This one a friend of yours?"

Lavina barely glances up. "She a new weekly."

"Oh, a neighbor!" Yolanda squeals again and sticks out his hand for me to shake. "Nice to meech'ya, honey. I'm Yolanda."

I'm not sure what to do with Yolanda's extended hand. I've seen news stories about junkies, car jackers, hookers, and murderers and all I know about Detroit is that the news, and my mom, and Bob, and our neighbors, and everyone I know says the same thing: Detroit is full of dangerous criminals and freaks. Bob always says the people here would kill you as soon as scratch their head, so I'm not sure what Yolanda's going to do once he gets ahold of my hand. I don't really want to touch him; I don't even know what he is.

But he towers over me, and as his hand hangs there and his smile fades, what my mother taught me overrides everything else in my head. She taught me to always be polite, no matter what.

I put my quivering hand in Yolanda's, sure he's going to feel the tremor of my nerves. I hope he doesn't kill me for it. Instead, Yolanda's smile breaks wide open as he nearly crushes my bones. He shakes hands like a big man too.

"What's yo' name, sweetie?" he asks, still gripping my hand.

"Uh...Lael."

"Lael? I don't think I ever heard that name before." His eyes wander out the front door and scan the parking lot one more time.

"I know," I say. "It's a weird name."

"Naw, not weird. It's pretty." Yolanda shoots me a gap-toothed grin as

Lavina drops a room key in the slot. It's only then that he lets go of my hand.

"Rememba now," Lavina shakes her finger at him, "stay outta Clive's way, or boda us is gonna be in trouble, an' I ain't 'bout ta lose my job 'cause a you."

"You ain't gotta tell me twice, girl." Yolanda plucks the key from the slot. He brushes past me, heading up the stairs. He doesn't have any luggage. Over his shoulder he says, "I don't need no more busted teef."

I'm standing, mesmerized by Yolanda, when the door siren wails again and another customer throws open the front door.

A white woman, stick thin and tiny, comes in first. A black kid, only a thread shorter than her and with messed up glasses, trails behind. She holds the door for him, the alarm screeching as she curses and barks, "Jesus Christ, get the fuck in here, Will...now."

When the kid finally fumbles over the threshold, she mumbles good boy and lets go of the door. I think she's the mom and he's her son.

I can't help but stare at the two of them. Side by side, they are strange, sharing almost the exact same height and weight, but one is black and one is white. I've never seen that before. She has a delicate nose, he has a broad one, but their eyes and lips are the same, even if his look ten times larger behind the thick, glass lenses. She's weathered and pale, with blond hair that is so dry it looks fuzzy. He is a sallow brown, with kinks of black hair shaved close to his skull and glasses bandaged all over with tape. He chomps a hunk of gum with his mouth open.

The woman pauses at the edge of the counter while the kid sticks to the opposite side of the lobby, sliding his shoulder against the front of the machines until he reaches the wide window of the snack vendor. He flips over, pressing his back against the machine. He stands there, working over his juicy mouthful of gum, only pausing when he has to gulp down the sticky overflow of saliva. He's got way too much gum to do anything but chew like a beast. When he sees me watching him, all the joy in chomping escalates. He chomps and swallows and smacks his lips even harder.

Lavina's eyes settle on the woman after a quick glance at the kid, and she tips her chin only just enough that I think she's telling me to pay attention to the two newcomers. I step back toward the stairs, making room for them at the transaction window.

The woman steps up to the window and dumps her loose, liver-shaped purse on the counter. I could probably stare at them all day, since the boy seems delighted in me noticing him and the woman seems oblivious to it.

"How much is a room?" she asks, leaning toward the window vent on her tiptoes. I see now that her mascara has had time to drain off her lashes and onto the puffy pillows beneath her eyes. She pushes back her hair, but her bangs stick to her forehead.

The kid inches closer to me, squeezing into the space between his mother and I. He pivots toward me on a dirty sneaker and when I meet his gaze, he freezes like a mannequin—one arm up and bent at the elbow, the other at his waist. He stays that way, his dead stare fixed on my forehead.

He holds steady until I look away. From my peripheral, I see him quickly change positions, widening his stance and slumping his torso to one side. His body is rigid, but he lets his arms swing at the elbows like a busted robot.

"Fo' how many?" Lavina asks.

"Me an' my kid," the woman says. "He's ten."

"Twenty eight a night fo' tha single. Thirty fo' tha double. Thirty-six fo' a waterbed," Lavina tells the woman.

The woman feels through her pockets, all of them, one at a time and then back through the cycle again, as if she can't find her money. "How much for a week?"

"One fitty," Lavina says.

"We want a week." The woman drops her hands from her pockets and reaches for her purse, unzipping it and poking around under the surface.

I glance at the kid again. He's still swinging his arms.

"Quit the robot shit," his mother snaps when she sees me looking. He falls out of it into a stoop, but keeps pumping his gum as his mother pushes the money through the slot to Lavina. "I'll pay the single rate now and bring you the rest tonight. I can do that, right?"

Lavina shrugs. "Sho'. Long as you git it ta me 'fo you s'pose ta check out tommor'ah." She puts her hands on her thighs and pushes herself to her feet. "Check out's eleven tomorr'ah mornin' if you ain't paid the rest. An' I'm gonna need a license."

The woman doesn't even look in her purse.

"I don't have no license. Can you use a Food Mart card?"

"It got yo' name an' face on it?" Lavina asks. When I told her I didn't have a license, she just wrote down my name, but Lavina seems determined to have more from this woman.

"No. Just a name."

"Whuch you got wit' yo' name and face on it?"

The woman groans as she digs through her bag. She comes up with a blue, plastic coated card. "I got a MovieBuster card. That's it. There ain't a picture on it, but it's me."

"I need somethin' wit' a pi'ture."

"I don't have nothin'." The woman waves the card in the air. "I swear it's me, alright? Can't you just take that?"

"I ain't s'posed to fo' weeklies." Lavina lets out a long, annoyed sigh before tapping the tips of her fingers into her palm, signaling the woman to pass the card through the slot. "C'mon. Give it here."

"Thanks." The woman shoves the card through the slot. Lavina takes it and turns it over twice in her palm as though she's still not sure.

"It's me," the woman insists. "Penny Grayson. I swear it's me."

"I believe ya. It's one fitty fo' da week," Lavina says, but her expression says she doesn't believe any of it. She takes a pen from the desk and writes down the woman's information in the big spiral book as the woman passes the bills she's counted twice through the payment slot. The kid scoots over toward the snack machine, punching all the numbers and checking the coin return.

"He a retard?" Lavina whispers to the mother. Lavina keeps her chin dipped toward her chest, just like the tone of her voice, but the boy turns from the machine as soon as she says it.

"You a fat nigger?" the kid asks her, shoving his glasses up on the bridge of his nose.

Lavina stares at him so hotly, I expect the kid to burst into flames. He doesn't. He stands there, staring back at her, his eyes magnified as big as tennis balls behind his taped-up, paper-clip-rigged glasses.

Lavina's gaze switches to the kid's mother. "You let yo' chil'ren talk like dat?" she says.

"He can talk however he wants to anybody that come at him like that. He didn't call you retard."

Lavina doesn't touch the bills in the payment slot. "That might be, but you wanna rent a room from me. Not tha otha' way 'round."

The woman's chin juts, her teeth combing her upper lip. She turns to her son. "Will, don't you call this woman a nigger. If she calls you a retard again, you just call her a big, dumb bitch, but don't you call her a nigger. That ain't nice."

Lavina reaches forward and takes the money, straightening the wrinkles out of the cash before she slips it in the drawer. She drops a room key into the trough.

The woman grabs it and swings around, heading for the stairs, hoisting her purse over her shoulder. She doesn't call for her kid to follow, but stomps as she goes up.

I meet Lavina's gaze just as I hear the pop can I'd left sitting in the chute behind me being lifted out of the machine. I turn to see the kid holding my can of root beer.

"That's mine!" I say. The kid's mother is already up on the third floor. The kid slinks toward the stairs holding my can with both hands.

"Hey!" I step toward him. "I paid for that!"

The kid turns around and stares at me with his empty, mannequin face. He feels for the step behind him with the toe of his filthy, flapping sneaker. When he locates the bottom step, he puts his foot on it and backs his way up the stairs.

"Are you deaf? I said that's mine." I say again, pointing to the drink in his hand.

The kid just shakes his head at me, expressionless, as he retreats up to the third step.

"I found it," he says.

"This ain't no treasure hunt," Lavina shouts to him from the office. "You foun' it 'cause she jus' bought it. That don't make it yours."

The kid freezes on the step, staring at me. He's got a weak chin that dangles so I can see the enormous wad of gum stuffed in his cheek. His hands stay tight on my pop can. I know he's not giving it back to me. Not if I can't catch him and I know I can't. From the looks of him, I assume he's got a history of being fast.

I sigh and sweep him away with one hand.

"Just take it."

The kid doesn't wait for me to say it again. He turns and shoots up the steps with my root beer clutched to his chest.

"You could've said thank you!" I shout after him, but all I hear are his sneakers making a fast get away. They sound every bit as fast as I expected too.

I look back at Lavina. Her lips are pursed.

"Now what'd ya go an' do dat fo'?" she says.

"I wasn't going to get it back."

"He a punk kid! You jus' gonna let 'im steal yo stuff like dat?"

"I was trying to do something nice."

"Dat wasn't doin' somethin' nice! Dat was plain ol' givin' in. Watch now, 'cause dat kid's gonna cause you all kinds'a trouble 'cause he knows you jus' gonna let him. Jus' you watch."

"He probably never gets anything like that."

"Naw, dat ain't all there is to 'im. He a thief."

I hate how she's talking to me like I should know better. I turn away to roll my eyes and head upstairs.

Rounding the corner to the third floor, the kid is squatted on his heels outside Room 36's closed door. Arms hanging between his knees, he's drinking my root beer with both hands around the can. The second he sees me, he pauses as if I'm going to try to wrestle it away from him. When I don't, he goes back to it, gulping it down as he stares at me over the rim of the can.

"I hope it's good," I tell him. I'm even angrier with him since Lavina barked at me.

He keeps on drinking.

I'm a few feet down the hall when I hear him hum his response behind me. "Mmm mmm!"

I just ignore it and keep walking. At my room door, I do the careful, ritual look over my shoulder to make sure no one's standing in the recessed hallway behind me. There's never been anyone there, but it always feels like there is. I glance at the kid down the hall.

He's standing now, with my empty pop can lying at his feet. He's dangling at the waist like a busted robot again. His forearms swing like dead men hung from trees.

I go into my room and lock the door behind me.

I've made it through another night, but I'm exhausted in the morning because I still couldn't sleep with all the strange noises outside my room. It's like groundhog day—I get crackers and pop again from the vending machines and find Lavina on the second floor again. I watch her clean a couple rooms. I sit with my back against the wall out in the hallway, staying out of her way.

She's good at what she does. She doesn't short-sheet the beds, skip any toilets, or forget to check all the drawers in the dressers. Her system is to start off in a bathroom, working from the sink to the toilet to the shower, then she checks under the bed, in all the drawers, empties the garbage can, makes the bed, dusts, and finishes it all off with the vacuum. She could be a crime scene specialist, she's so thorough, and every room smells like lemon cleaner when she's done.

"How long have you worked here?" I ask when she drags out her vacuum and shuts the door.

"I bin here jus' 'bout every day since Clive bought de place, two years ago."

"Do you work every day?"

"All 'em but Sunday." She pushes the cart down to the next room. I get up, pull the vacuum along with me and leave it beside her cart before I slide back down the wall to my sitting position.

Lavina doesn't thank me for the help.

Instead, she shoves down the pile of soiled sheets that are barfing over the edge of the cart bucket. She's ruthless, cramming them down with a determined grunt. When she comes up for air she asks, "How come you wanna watch me clean all day, anyway? Ain't you got no place to go?"

"I'm going home today," I offer.

"For good?"

I tap the back of my head against the wall. "No, just to pick up some more of my stuff."

"Where 'bout's home?"

"The country." I don't want to give her the exact location. I still don't know if she would try calling my mom. Or the cops.

It seems unlikely she'd do either when she shrugs and grabs a stack of fresh towels from the middle cart shelf. "You live in a nice house?" she asks as she goes back into the room.

"I guess," I say.

"Well, you here 'cause yo' daddy beat you?" she asks.

"I have a stepfather. He doesn't beat me—just pushes me around a lot."

"Huh," she says, carrying out and dumping a wad of soggy towels in the front bucket of the cart. She pauses for a breath. "He leave bruises on ya?"

"No," I say.

"He touch ya where he shouldn't?"

"No." Ew, yuck.

"Yo mama beat ya or touch ya?"

"No."

Lavina leans over the edge of the cart, staring down at me. "Then why da hell you here, girl?"

I shrug and look away. Her smirk is a slap in the face, minimizing all the reasons I left home. Bob's drinking. His shoving. My mom's need to control my every move.

But Lavina doesn't stop. "How come you not sleepin' on yo friend's couches? Why you wanna be here?"

What I want to say is: because I don't have friends and my mom and Bob won't come looking for me here. They're too scared of people like you. But I keep my mouth shut. I don't need Lavina getting insulted and mad enough to report me.

I shrug her question off again, but decide it'd be better to end the conversation altogether. I slide up the wall, my back flat against it and my thighs burning as I push myself to my feet. The lobby alarm sounds and my escape is delayed by a man's husky shout from the lobby.

"Lavina! Where you at, girl?"

"Glory days! You see what I mean?" Lavina says to me as she throws down her cleaning rag. "Do everyone gotta wait 'til I'm busy to need somethin'?" She turns her face toward the stairs and bellows, "Jonah! Secon' flo'!"

Heavy footsteps clomp up the stairs and a man in navy blue pants and shirt appears around the corner, walking down the hall toward Lavina and me. He's holding a zippered, blue vinyl bag that looks like a pencil pouch.

"I got your change from the bank," he says, waving the bag at her.

I look to Lavina, expecting her to yell at him for announcing and waving around his money like that. It should be in his sock or something.

But she doesn't say a word. She only smiles at him. "Thank you! I appreciate that."

I look back at him and catch his gaze traveling up my thigh. It takes a second for him to reach my face, but when he does, faint lines of amusement break out around his eyes and his broad smile nearly glows against his skin.

I'm sure plenty of women would find him attractive. He's got the high, fine bones of an African warrior and skin the rich color of a wet, wooden spoon. Meticulously groomed, his hair is trimmed close, with three, fine lines shaved from one temple and reaching just past his ear. The lines remind me of the ones drawn in cartoons to show that a character is running fast. Thick enough shoulders, solid boots.

If I was into black men, who knows.

Lavina takes the bag from him and starts for the stairs. He doesn't move. He's too busy staring at me, smiling. And kind of blocking my way from following Lavina. My toes carve dips in the soles of my shoes as I wait for him to move. I don't know what he wants from me.

"Lavina," he calls over his shoulder, "you gonna introduce us?"

He's got to be ten years older than me at least.

Bob would call this man a porch monkey or a jungle bunny. He always says it is *them people* that ruined the city because none of them knew how to keep a job. Bob says black people are all savages. I think Bob should look in the mirror.

But Jonah, in his grease-smudged uniform and heavy, well-worn work boots looks like most of our factory-working neighbors back home. His uniform actually looks a lot like Bob's. The way Jonah talks doesn't sound like the way Lavina does, but more like the people back home.

Lavina glimpses back with a wave of her hand. "Dat's Lael. She a new weekly. Country girl. And dat dere's Jonah. He da manager next door at da oil place nex' do'."

"Lael," Jonah says my name like it's hard candy. "That's unique."

The way he stares right into my eyes makes me think maybe he's a savage after all. I am paralyzed until he looks away. I scoot past him— he's at least a head taller than me—and catch up to Lavina. I can feel the heat of his eyes on my back. Well, maybe a little lower than my back.

We follow Lavina down to the lobby. She locks herself in the office, so I'm left out in the lobby with Jonah. I back up against the ice machine, jarring it and sending the plastic buckets tumbling all over. Jonah laughs and grabs the buckets that roll off onto the floor.

I blush.

God, I'm just useless.

Jonah restacks the buckets, moving closer to me. I back away until I'm flat up against the pay phone cabinet. He lets me retreat with a soft chuckle, and turns back to Lavina when she says his name.

"Thanks ag'in," she adds.

"Sure thing," he says. "Anything else you need outta me, Miss Lavina?"

"Dat oughta do it. I kin git to da bank mah'self tomorr'ah, thanks."

"Glad to be of help," Jonah's voice drops to such a deep octave, I feel it in the pit of my stomach. He raises a hand in a parting wave. "Lemme know if there's anything else ya need."

"Yep, thanks." Lavina steps out of the office, locking the door behind her. She doesn't give him a second look as he leaves, but Jonah's eyes pause on me, and he grins, the high cheekbones underlining his almond eyes.

"It was nice meeting ya, Lael," he says.

I dredge up a smile and shoot past him to climb the stairs behind Lavina. The door alarm goes off and the door shut after he leaves.

"Look ta me like Jonah's got eyes fo' ya." Lavina gives me a smirk once we reach her cart again.

"Oh, I'm not into black guys," I tell her.

"You not? Well, da's good, 'cause ya oughta leave 'em ta us African Queens who kin handle 'em." She pulls a couple towels from her cart and carries them into the room, talking over her shoulder to me. "But lotsa black men wanna chase you white girls 'stead'a keepin' wit' their own. And I think Jonah the chasin' type."

Lavina's words might as well be stirring the neon orange crackers in my stomach with a dirty spoon. Jonah's a lot older than me, practically an old man. He's black. He's a guy and I'm not looking for one of them right now.

"Well, I'm not the catchin' type," I tell her.

"How old is you ag'in?" she asks, dragging out a pile of soggy, dirty towels. She doesn't wait for my answer. "Don't matter none. Every girl's da catchin' type. Dat is, 'til she bin caught once or twice."

FIVE

I *didn't pay any* attention to the oil change shop next door when I first came here, but now that Lavina's said she thinks Jonah likes me, I'm self-conscious. I don't want him to. But when I walk out of the hotel an hour later, the blaring door alarm makes my stomach tight.

I peer across at the open service bay doors, and there is Jonah, smiling and waving to me. I give him a fast wave and jump in my car. I focus straight ahead and don't even give the shop a sideways glance as I turn onto the boulevard and head back home.

But heading home, my guts knot up even tighter. I don't know what's going to happen when I get there. Bob and my mom might be sitting there, waiting to ambush me. Or they could've changed all the locks.

The drive takes 45 minutes from the hotel to my driveway, but I do it on auto-pilot. It seems like I blink and all of a sudden, I'm pulling into my driveway. There's no sign of Bob's rickety old Dodge or my mom's battered, LeSabre. Thank God.

My house key works.

No one is inside.

It's weird to walk into the house with no one there, the ghosts of our last argument still filling up the room. Creeping down the hall, just in case, it feels as though Bob's hands are still at my back, pushing and shoving me through this. The air conditioning kicks on from the window unit in their bedroom and the whine from the fan reminds me of my mother's whining the day I left.

I open the door to my room. All closed up, it's stifling. The time-out chair has been pushed off to the side of the door, the window now shut, the screen still missing.

I move fast. It doesn't feel like my house anymore, even though less than a week has passed. I collect my clothes by the armful and finally snag a box of garbage bags from the kitchen to load up my stuff. I drag bag after bag out to my car, stuffing them into the truck and backseat, the floor and front seat too. Annie, the Masnen's dog, is the only soul that notices I'm here and she only gives me one short bark. It's more like a greeting and not enough to raise any alarm.

By the time I shut the front door and lock it up, my car is stuffed with trash bags full of my belongings, as well as my mom's plug-in electric skillet, and two brown paper boxes full of canned food from our pantry. My mother will be fuming when she sees I cleaned out her stock of spaghetti rings, ravioli, tuna, and saltines, but she'll be furious when she finds out I also took the hundred dollar bill she keeps taped to a box of spinach in the freezer for emergencies—like when Bob drinks up his paycheck and there's not enough left to keep the lights on.

I just hope Bob is drinking less since I'm gone. That'll buy me some time before I have to pay it all back. I close up the house and lock the door, but there's a weird shiver in my heart. If my mom's not waiting for me to come home, she might not be in any hurry to come looking for me at all. Disappearing hasn't been hard to do at all.

Jonah steps out like a dark apparition from one of the bays and waves to me the moment I get out of my car.

"Need help?" he shouts over as I open my trunk and heft out one of my bags.

"No thanks, I got it," I shout back. It'd be weird if I accepted his help, schlepping all my personal belongings up to my apartment/*bedroom*, but it's nice that he offered.

He retreats into the office. I have the feeling that not much gets past Jonah.

Yolanda is getting a Coke out of the machine in the lobby when I lug in the third garbage bag over my shoulder like Santa Claus. I have four more bags to go. That kid—Will—pops up from the basement stairs.

"What're you doin'?" he asks.

"Yeah, what you got in that bag, honey?" Yolanda asks, poking the plastic with one of his purple, claw nails. He doesn't seem as scary now that the initial shock of meeting him has worn off.

"Dead body," I tell Yolanda. I ignore the kid.

"Well, it shore ain't the first time I helped drag aroun' one 'a those," he says. "You need help?"

My mind scrambles for an excuse to refuse the help. "No thanks. Clive might catch you."

Yolanda puts his can of pop on the counter. The kid's eyes are rooted on the Coke.

"Ain't you thoughtful?" Yolanda hits me with his grisly smile. "Lavina tole me that he ain't due back tonight, so we ain't got nothin' to worry 'bout."

"Where is Lavina?" I ask.

"Down foldin' towels," the kid says from the stairs.

"I appreciate the offer, but I think I've got it," I tell Yolanda. I decide to return the favor of kindness and nod to his pop can. "You better watch that. Cans go missing a lot around here."

Yolanda cocks her head, confused, but Will scowls at me as I start up the steps.

Up and down, up and down, I'm huffing and puffing each time I pass Yolanda and Will, still standing around in the lobby, as if they're old friends. I also turn down Yolanda's offer to help every time.

I wish I was finished when I catch another glimpse of Jonah at the shop across the street. He doesn't wave this time, but I see him in one of the bays and I just can't help but think of what Lavina said about him. He's a full grown man, nothing like the guys I went to school with, only a few months ago. And he might be a savage, just good at hiding it, like Bob always said—all these people might. It makes me want to hide.

I lug up another bag and when I return to the lobby, Yolanda says, "How many more?"

"Just a couple," I say and this time, Yolanda follows me out the door.

"Look, sweetie, lemme help. I ain't doin' nothin' but waitin' fo' mah man, an' you gittin' sweaty haulin' up all yo' stuff," he says. "It ain't no problem fo' me ta give ya a hand."

He's so sincere, and even though I assure him I have it, he still follows me out to my car. I pop my trunk and there's the last bag and the last box full of canned food—the biggest one. It was hard to lug it out of my mom's house when I was still full of adrenaline and hadn't already hauled a half dozen bags up three flights of hotel stairs. Now, just looking at it makes my shoulders ache.

Yolanda hitches up the waist of his pantyhose beneath his dress. "Oh, I got this," he says and he reaches down and scoops up the box. With one fluid movement, he hefts it up on his shoulder, crushing the frills at the base of his neck and pinching the curls of his wig so his whole hairdo slides off to one side. I don't say anything about that. I can also tell Yolanda's not going to put the box down, so I grab the last bag and resign myself to being helped as I slam the trunk shut.

"You don't have to do this," I tell him again as we walk into the hotel, under the screaming alarm. The can of pop he'd been drinking is gone off the counter, but Yolanda doesn't seem to notice.

"Ain't no problem, honey," he says as we climb the stairs. Will darts up ahead of us and I nearly trip on him. Yolanda laughs. "That one there's busy," he mumbles about Will.

As we round the second landing, I can hear Yolanda start to puff.

"I should've just brought the cans up in two trips," I say, readjusting the trash bag over my shoulder.

"Oh no, honey, it's fine," Yolanda pants. "Look like you got enough food here to last a couple weeks at least, huh? Maybe you could gimme a couple cans if you got extras? Ya know...ta say thanks for the helpin' hand."

"Sure," I say, but now I wish he would've let me carry it up myself. Those cans are all I've got for as long as they last and I know it's greedy, but I don't feel like I can spare any of them. And now I'm going to have to.

"Meant to say, them is some cute shoes you wearin' too," Yolanda says.

"Uh, thanks. They're just my old sandals."

"Oh no, they cute!" Yolanda says. "What size'r you?"

"My shoes? Tens. I've got huge feet."

"Naw...they's perfect! I seen you was bringin' in a buncha clothes and shoes. If you wanna sell anythin'...you jus' let me know, alright honey? I like yo' style and I be willin' to pay cash."

"Okay," I say, because I don't know what else to say. "Thanks."

Will is waiting on the third floor. I step into the hall and he shoots across my path and down the hall toward my room. I stumble backward, startled and trying to avoid him, and fall against Yolanda.

"Damn it!" I shriek.

"Now da's en'uffa that!" Yolanda shouts at Will. His voice is deep as a kettle drum and it even scares me. "If you wanna help, you kin do dat, Will, but ya damn near knocked my girl here down the stairs!"

Will comes to an abrupt halt, turning back to us. I think he's going to be a little snot, like usual, and say something awful, but instead, he lowers his chin to his chest.

"Sorry," he says.

"Holy crap," I whisper. I can't believe he was actually able to shame Will.

Yolanda snorts a little laugh. "*Now* you gonna help us, Will? You take Lael's bag there, so she can git her door open."

Will comes trudging back and actually takes my bag. As we walk down the hall, Yolanda says to Will, "Lael pro'ly give ya some of these here cans for helpin' her out, jus' like she givin' me some. Ya see now why you should help yo friends instead'a scarin' 'em half to def?"

Yolanda may be like nobody I've ever met before, and he may have just promised away some of my food, but he's no savage.

Bob wasn't right about everybody.

In my head, I like to think of my room as an apartment.

The end of the dresser is my kitchen. My mother's electric pan sits on top, her canned goods still stacked in the box beside it. I had to give Will two cans of spaghetti rings, and Yolanda took two beef stews and two cans of tuna for their help, but once I dump a can of ravioli in the electric pan and the smell begins to fill the room, it erases my disappointment.

Now, I'm just a grown-up in her apartment, cooking dinner.

While I wait for the ravioli to heat all the way through, I empty the garbage bags. The deep top drawer of the dresser houses two settings of stolen silverware, dishes, bowls, a cup, a mug, a can opener, spatula and ladle. I nestle my clothes in the other dresser drawers, put my shampoo in the shower, my pillow and fuzzy blanket on the bed, and I drape a couple necklaces from the edge of the mirror. The last dresser drawer, beneath my kitchen utensils, holds my pencils and sketch books, a couple of my favorite books, nail polish, and my busted jewelry box which contains the money I stole from my mom's freezer.

Once I'm finished unloading, I sit back on the bed with a bowl of bubbling ravioli and flip on the TV.

The news is on. The reporter looks into the camera lens as if he can see me on my bed as he talks about a rape that happened just a mile down the boulevard from the hotel.

The next story is about a crack house in the very heart of the city. It burnt down with some junkies inside it. The bodies haven't been identified.

A man broke into a liquor store a few miles away and gunned down the cashier.

A teen was shot, walking on the sidewalk, by a drive-by shooter.

I put down my bowl and pick up the phone. I don't know why I do it, except that I know how freaked out my mom gets when she watches the news. As much as I hate her, I don't want her to worry.

"Lael?" my mother says the minute I say hello. I release the breath I've been holding. She says, "Where are you?"

"I don't want to say. I just wanted to call and tell you—"

"You better say, or I'm hanging up and calling the police right now."

I suck in that breath I just released. "Fine. I'm living at a hotel in Detroit."

"Living there? Oh, I don't think so! I cannot believe you are in Detroit...and at a hotel. Have you watched the news tonight? Do you even understand how dangerous it is where you're at?"

"Nope. I'm totally stupid," I tell her.

"You're in a war zone!" Her tone is the one that makes my soul feel dark and disconnected. It's full of furious shaming and you should know better. I sit up straight against the headboard of the bed. I have to be prepared, alert, if I want to fight back and win. Her voice narrows. "Who is with you?"

Bob's in the background on her end of the phone, answering for me. "Some pimp, I bet. She's probably got herself in trouble with drugs, just like I said! Why else would she be down there? Jesus, LuAnne, you knew this was gonna happen!"

Some people expect their children will grow up, go to college, get a good job, have a family. Mine have always expected me to get hooked on drugs and find a pimp.

"I saw that you were here today. That you stole from me."

"Borrowed," I say into the receiver. "I'm going to pay you back as soon as I have the money."

"You will bring back my belongings immediately, Lael." Her voice is tight. She is trying to hold all the quivers in her voice together, clutching them in her throat like balloon strings in a damaging wind.

Ultimatums. I'm used to these.

It makes it easier on me when I know exactly where I'm at on our battlefield, and now I know we've reached ultimatums. I settle back against my pillow. The smell of ravioli steams up from the bowl beside me as I loosen my grip on the receiver. I twist the curly phone cord around my finger. Ultimatums are easy enough to handle. I balance the receiver between my jaw and shoulder, pick up my bowl, stir it, breathe it in.

"Did you hear me?" I can hear her clutching at the strings. Hanging on so hard, she has to take a breath between each word. "You will bring it all back tonight."

"Nope," I say.

I smile as she explodes on the other end. She's lost her grip completely as she bellows, "Don't you dare act like this is no big deal!"

I put the ravioli back on the nightstand. We're moving into accusations. Those are always a little trickier. I have to beat her to the punch.

"Oh, like how you act when Bob is pushing me around?" I hope she can hear my shitty smirk.

"This isn't about Bob!" she screeches. "It's about you stealing from your own mother!"

"Oh well." I sing-song my response.

Bob starts shouting, "Gimme the phone! Gimme the phone, LuAnne!"

"You're going to do as I tell you," my mother insists, but she's starting to cry.

Game over.

"I'm not coming back," I say. "If you want it, come get it yourself."

Long, heavy pause. The silence is a flat-lining heart monitor and I'm waiting for the next beep.

"I'm ashamed of you," my mother finally says. Her tone is as limp as a leftover funeral lily.

"And you're the mother of the year," I grumble.

The game is over, but now we have to try to revive it with shaming. It takes less than a heartbeat for my mother to dig in.

"Bob and I have done nothing but give you a roof over your head and clothes on your back and this is how you behave?"

"Is that the best you've got?" I fire back.

She's absolutely right. They've done nothing but the very basic that was required of them. I know I'm nothing more than an annoying toilet flush at night to them. Another plate to fill. Space in a room they could use for a den. In short, her attempt to shame me has totally failed.

"You've done nothing," I repeat my mother's words, hoping it will crush whatever's left of the quivering bouquet in her voice. "You got that right."

In fact, I've just done them a huge favor by leaving, except that now they have to explain my absence to the neighbors and their friends and any family that still shows up for holidays. Oh yes, that's the real issue here.

The embarrassment.

But it's only August. I'm sure they can come up with something by Thanksgiving.

"So help me, God, Lael, if you don't come home tonight, you're never stepping foot in this house again." I can hear her set her jaw. It juts forward when she's really furious...which is usually when she knows she's lost the fight.

This should be where I do my victory dance, but instead, the sound of her sticking out her chin makes me uneasy. How did she lose? Something's not right.

She could easily win by calling the cops and having them bring me home...but instead, she's just threatening that I can't come home and she's setting her jaw like she's lost...

Oh.

She hasn't called the cops.

She's not going to.

She's relieved that I'm gone.

Oh.

"Go ahead and try to make me come home, control freak. I'll just leave again." I snarl through the receiver.

She's not going to bother.

"You're not getting another cent from me, I want you to know that." She laughs. This is what she wanted. She wanted me gone so she could tell her friends that I was uncontrollable, that they did everything they could for me, that this was my fault and not theirs. It's only cost her one hundred bucks, an electric skillet, and a box full of canned food. "And Lael? I'm cancelling your health insurance and taking you off our car insurance tomorrow morning. If this is what you want, then you got it! You're on your own, baby!"

I hang up on her.

SIX

My stomach shrinks at the smell of the ravioli.

I hate her. I hate her in deep, dark ways that should make me ashamed.

The trouble is, I'm not sure if I hate her more for saying she'll make me come home, or knowing that she won't lift a finger to make it happen. I shouldn't be unhappy—I'm where I want to be.

I get up and close the blinds on the glow of the motel sign. The air kicks on. The gust hits me in the face.

I'm miles and miles away from her, a whole different world, but I can still hear her. She's cutting me off like a lame arm.

I click on the TV and flip away from the news channel. I don't need to hear how bad things are. I already know.

I click past a sitcom and a moan races into the room. I've turned to channel three, the hotel's streaming porn.

I've been a good girl, just like my mother expected me to be. I've never had sex before, and have never seen it happen, until the other night. And now.

It's a different couple than the ones I watched the other night.

This woman is an Asian girl. She's sliding her tongue down a man's penis, her eyes cast upward, gauging his enjoyment as she does it. And she seems to love doing it.

The scene vaporizes the fight I just had with my mother. I focus instead on how the man reaches down and grasps the woman's nipple. She gasps like she enjoys that too.

She takes hold of his penis in one hand and grasps his hand with the other. She draws his fingers to her mouth. Her tongue moves over the ridge of his fingernail, slips into the valley between the two fingers, and rises up to the tip of his middle finger.

The camera cuts to his face again. Eyes glazed, half closed, he's mesmerized. So am I.

Then we're following her hand gripping his as she moves his slick fingers down her chest, gliding them over her belly. She guides his hand to her mound. He bends down and slides his fingers into her as if he's sheathing a knife.

The camera switches to her eyes as they close. She breathes like she's just run the track at school.

Another moan. The lens roves away...to another couple.

Another couple! In the same room!

He's black, she's white.

I turn the volume down in case anyone outside can hear what I'm doing. I check the locks on the door.

Then I undress in my cold room and slide between the cool sheets, pulling them up around my shoulders.

Breathing through my mouth, I move my fingers against my body and try to make myself feel better.

I wake up on my bed, half naked, to someone shouting in the hall. I sit up straight, my heartbeat stalling in my ears, but a long, heavy silence is all I hear. My nerves settle back down in my skin. It must have been the tail end of a dream that woke me...

"HELP ME! HELP! HELP!"

It's that kid, Will—I can tell by the sound of his voice. I bolt out of bed, pull on my pants, and shoot to the door. My heart is sitting on my tongue as he screams for help again. I fumble with the locks.

Once they're undone, I throw open the door and race into the hall.

There's nobody out there but the kid. He's standing at the opposite end.

The moment he sees me, he grabs his scrawny belly and doubles over, laughing.

"What the hell are you doing?" I shout at him.

"Look at your hair!" he squeals as he falls onto the carpeted floor and rolls from side to side, guffawing. Like he should talk about hair. His stringy, albino mop is sticking straight out over one ear.

"Are you stupid?" I roar at him. But I'm the one who really feels stupid. Nobody else fell for his joke. All the other doors are still shut.

His room door opens a crack and his mother hisses at him, "Will! Knock it off and get in here!"

He gets to his feet, but instead of going to his mother, he resumes his robot stance like before, head tipped to one side, his dead face staring at me. His arms swing from the elbows like synchronized pendulums.

"Stupid kid," I mutter, turning back to my door. It's closed. Latched. Damn it. I don't have my key.

Will turns and sprints to his room door when he sees me coming down the hall toward him. It's satisfying to watch him pound on the door, terrified, as he watches me advance. His door opens and he slips inside, slamming it behind him, before my bluff is called. Good. I hope he's plastered to the other side, trying to catch his breath.

I go down the stairs, stomping down each step and gritting my teeth. I'm going to have to ask Ned for help. I feel sick just thinking of him coming upstairs to open my room door.

I step up to the lobby window, ready to puke. But there's an older Arab man sitting back in the office chair, not Ned. The guy there is super old, probably my mom's age at least. He's got a nose thick as a light bulb at the tip and it dangles over a squirrel's tail of a moustache. He also has dark circles under his eyes, but he smiles the minute our eyes meet.

"I help you?" he asks. His lips draw up and get lost in the squirrel tail. When he says you, he throws a trailing w on the end.

I nod. "I locked myself out of my room. Can you open my door?"

He jumps out of his chair. "I help you," he says. I wonder if that's the only English he knows. He turns to the key rack on the wall and drags a finger in the air along the rows, finally settling on a silver loop strung with half a dozen keys, from a bottom hook.

When he comes out of the office, he doesn't scoot out quick like Lavina does, but casually strolls out and takes his time securing the lock behind him. He turns to me when he's done and extends his arm so I can lead the way.

"I help you," he says again and we trudge up the stairs. I don't like being in front of him. He walks a little too close, so I keep my face turned to the side and watch him from my peripheral. It's unnecessary, though. He's too busy yawning and rubbing his eyes to notice how creeped out I am.

Halfway up he pieces together the opening of a conversation. "I Sam.

Night desk watch."

"I'm Lael," I tell him, even though I keep climbing stairs. "Weekly, third floor."

"Good," Sam says. We're quiet the rest of the way to my door, where it takes him two tries with two different keys before he pops the lock. He holds the door open as I skitter past him. The smell of him—heavy cologne and a little B.O.—wafts up my nose. My stomach flips, worried he's going to follow me inside, but when I turn to him, Sam just smiles. He hasn't moved.

"Good?" he asks.

"Thanks," I say, and with a nod and tired grin, he lets go of the door and it bangs shut, locking him out.

I wake for the second time that night, to another shriek in the hall. But this time, I sit up and rub the sleep out of my eyes instead of springing from my bed. I know better now.

The alarm clock says it's one in the morning. I wait for the next shout and when it comes, my throat squeezes shut. It's not the dumb kid down the hall. It's a woman.

"He got a gun!" she screams. "Somebody call the cops! This motha fucka's got a gun!"

The fear climbs in her vocal cords. She starts pounding on the metal doors, kicking them. My own room fills with the sound as she beats on my door.

"Somebody call the po'lice! He gonna kill me!"

My stomach tightens. My limbs tremble and I can't settle them down. I roll off the bed and hit the floor, banging my nose on the bed frame. Sparks of pain shoot through my skull, but I still can't get control of my quivering bones.

"Get back in here, bitch," a man hollers. There's no waver in his voice at all. It's angry and sharp as broken glass.

I scoot under the bed frame, burying my nose in the carpeting. I breathe in dust and cover my ears.

"Both you! Hey!" I hear a third man shout. I remove my hands to hear more clearly. I think it's Sam, the night clerk—I recognize the accent, his trailing w.

The man I think is Sam yells, "Lady, you come down, but you...go in room! Cops is coming!"

There's a scuffle and a door slams. That's it. Everything goes quiet, except my hot breath blowing into the carpet. The dust chokes me now, but I can't move.

I'm frozen until I hear cops in the hallway. They rap on a door down the hall and announce, Come out of the room! Police!

My muscles relax. I knew a lot of cops back home. I went to school with Dave Marsh, whose dad was an officer and came to our classroom once a year to talk about drugs. He brought suckers for everybody who answered his questions or got a question right.

Lindsey, who lived at the end of our street and went to private school, had a dad who was a cop too. Even though her parents were divorced, her dad still drove his cruiser down our street to visit her. Sometimes, if he saw one of us neighborhood kids walking down the street or hunting bullfrogs in the ditches, he would activate the sirens and say hello through the car's bullhorn speakers.

After about five minutes of nothing but calm talking, I crawl out from under the bed and go to the door. With my ear pressed to the cold metal, I can hear the discussion. Grabbing my key and ice bucket, I open my door.

There are two cops in the hall. As much as I've been scared of the cops finding me, this time, I exhale at the sight of them in their beige uniforms. Nobody's guns are drawn and when I step out of my room, nobody yells at me to go back inside. They're too busy to really notice me much at all.

They've got a black woman in the hall—the one who must've been screaming. Her mascara has drained off, streaking all the way down to the base of her chin, but she's not crying now. She stands with one hand on her hip, swiveling her head as she talks. Her afro is flat on top and bushy at the sides, like an unraveled scarecrow.

She thrusts out her chin at the cop who is taking notes on a pad of paper in his palm. "I tole you, my boyfr'en ain't done nothin' wrong."

"I wouldn't say nothing," the blond cop with a heavy forehead disagrees blandly. He's doesn't even glance up at her while he speaks.

"Naw, it was that sucka at the front desk," the woman argues. "He come up here with a gun and started wavin' it all aroun', sayin' he was gonna kill me!"

"He's on his way to jail," the first cop assures her with a dull sigh.

Are they talking about Sam?

The second cop, an older guy, stands in the threshold of an open room door. His hand is resting on his holster, but other than that, his stance is so relaxed, he could be having a beer at a barbeque.

Clutching the empty ice bucket, I walk down the hall slowly, peering into the open door as I do. A man, dressed all in black, stands inside the room, hands at his sides. His glare says none of this is my business.

But it's like I'm invisible anyway. Neither of the cops look up at me either, even though I try to catch their eyes. I want to tell them what I heard—that Sam came upstairs after the woman was yelling about a man having a gun.

The barbeque cop reaches down and picks up the garbage can at his feet.

"You've got about ten used needles in here between the two of you," he says. "And all this," he holds up a palm full of itty, bitty baggies, "is going down the crapper."

The man in the room doesn't respond. The barbeque cop disappears from the doorway and the toilet flushes.

"I know what happened," I mumble to the younger cop with the notepad. I don't look at the woman with the afro, even though she's staring right at me. "I heard a woman screaming, she was saying he has a gun and beating on my door. But that was before Sam even came upstairs."

"Did you witness the event?" the cop says. His face is so stoic, figuring out whether he's annoyed with me or angry or interested is like trying to climb a rock wall that is smooth, flat, and a thousand feet tall.

"I heard it all. She was pounding on—"

"But you weren't in the hallway to actually see what occurred," the cop cuts me off.

"She don't know nothin'," the woman says, smoothing away the edge of her afro with the back of her hand.

"No, but I know you were yelling—"

"Wa'n't me," the woman says.

"She was screaming about someone else before Sam—"

The cop's eyebrow darts up. "The night clerk?"

"Yes," I say. "He came up and told everyone to get back in their rooms. He said he called the police."

"But you weren't in the hall," the cop says flatly.

"No, I wasn't." I drop my eyes. The woman dismisses me with a *mmm hmm.*

The old cop gives the man and the woman a warning, that if the police are called back here, they're both going to go to jail. Then, the cop walks out and the woman goes into the room, shutting the door behind her.

The cops go down the hall. I follow behind them a few steps, but then they stop and let me pass by.

In the lobby, the cop with the heavy forehead doesn't bother to address me, but turns to speak with Ned.

"I don't think they'll be causing any more trouble tonight. If they do, they know we'll be back, and they'll be going to jail."

"And Sam's downtown?"

"That's right," the cop nods. "It's against the law to draw an unlicensed firearm, so he'll be down in the holding cell until he makes bail."

"My boss is on his way down there now." Ned rolls a pencil between his fingers like it's a poisoned dart. The cop leaves and Ned, on one side of the bullet proof glass and me on the other, both watch the police car exit the parking lot through the door.

Once they're gone, Ned throws a pencil down on the desk. "Can you believe that bullshit?" he says. I guess he's talking to me. "Sam just goes up there to calm stuff down and they throw him in jail."

"They had drugs up there too," I say. I can't believe I'm talking to Ned like he's a normal human being, but I am. I heard what really happened upstairs and Ned agrees. It's us against them. "The cops just flushed it all."

Ned chuffs a laugh, completely ignoring what I said. "You know, Sam's got five little kids and two other jobs. He ain't coming back here to work after all this, which means Clive's gonna squeeze me to work double shifts until he finds some fool to work midnights for him." He picks up the ledger folder and slams it back down on the desk. "I'm fucked!" he shouts.

I slip away, up the stairs, the moment he looks away.

SEVEN

I *hear Lavina's cart* squeaking around in the hall. The alarm clock says it's eleven in the morning.

I grab my ice bucket. I never fill it up, but it gives me an excuse to go out and talk to Lavina about last night.

She looks up when I step into the hallway and bunches up her nose. She jingles her ring of keys, picking out one for the door lock across the hall, rapping on the door before opening it up.

"House cleanin'!" Lavina shouts through the opening. No one answers, so she swings the door wide. "Heard there was some excitement up here last night."

"A woman went nuts!" I spill the details, dropping my ice bucket to my side. "There were three guys and a girl—"

"I know, I rented 'em the room."

"Well, she was running up and down the hall screaming that one of the guys had a gun."

I stand in the doorway as she pops on the bathroom light. No soiled towels, just a messy bed. Lavina pulls the covers back and a soggy washcloth falls on the floor. She makes a face, but leaves it on the floor as she pulls the sheets off the bed. "You seen which one it was?"

"No way. I was under my bed!"

Lavina laughs at me as she scoops up the sheets and the washcloth. "I got a question fo' ya."

"Yeah?"

"What you do fo' money? I ain't seen you go to work. You hookin'?"

"No!" I shake my head wildly.

"Make no dif'rence ta me. So whuch'ya doin'? You thievin'?"

"No!" That's pretty insulting. This is what she thinks of me? "I've got some money saved up."

"And whuch'ya gonna do when it all gone?"

The edges of my lips dive. This is like talking to my mother. And the thought of having to go home makes me sick. "I'm going to start looking for a job tomorrow."

"Well, tha's what I wanna talk which you 'bout. There a job avail'ble downstairs, if you don't wanna go too far." She piles the sheets into the back bucket on her cart.

"What about Sam?"

"Sam ain't comin' back. He got two other jobs and five little ones. He don't need to be gettin' hi'self shot, runnin' 'round wit' a gun like he did. Clive lookin' for a new clerk. You might wanna talk wit' 'im."

I squeeze the ice bucket so the opening looks like a smashed mouth. "But I don't want to get shot either."

"You ain't gonna get shot." Lavina makes a sound from the side of her mouth that I think is meant to let me know I'm stupid. "Sam should'a never come outta the cage, 'specially wit' dat gun."

"The cage?"

"The office," Lavina clarifies, as if I'm a foreigner who can't speak the language. She carries sheets into the room and starts making the bed. "Clive put dat gun in da drawer, but I don't know why. It ain't got no bullets. What's he think we gonna do? Throw it atta crim'nal? Sam should'a knowed dat if you gonna wave a gun aroun', you sho' better be ready ta use it." She tucks in a corner. "But you...you be fine, so long as ya don't leave da cage."

I walk into the room and lean against the edge of the dresser. I need money. Working at the hotel would be way better than trying to find a job in one of the places with the bars on the windows.

"How much does it pay?"

Lavina kicks something at the edge of the bed. "Rent plus some, I think." She bends down to retrieve whatever is on the floor.

"How little? I have to pay for my car and food and..."

Lavina pauses mid-bend. "It's a desk job, not a trus' fund. If ya want it, we'll talk ta Clive when he get in."

Lavina squeals and jumps up from the side of the bed.

I stumble backward. "What? What's the matter?"

Lavina laughs and kicks something from her side of the bed. A thin, glass cylinder rolls across the floor and hits the bottom of the dresser with a thump.

"What is that?" I step closer and peer down at the object. It's knobby, cloudy, solid glass.

"It a dildo!" Lavina shouts. I reel back from it and she explodes with laughter as she hustles past me into the hall. She grabs a can of Lysol off the cart and sprays her hand with it, front and back.

I'm glad I'll be working as a clerk instead of a maid.

My phone rings as I'm flushing my leftover spaghetti rings down the toilet for the third time. Without a fridge in my room, there's no way to keep leftovers, but the rings keep floating back up from the pipes like little targets.

"C'mon downstairs," Lavina says when I answer the phone. "Clive wanna talk to ya."

"Okay," I say and she hangs up. I guess I've been given my orders.

I'm walking down the hall when Will pops out of his room. He shoots out like a flash of lightening, slamming against the wall across from his door, as if he's been thrown. Except that nobody threw him. He rolls across the wall, shoulder over shoulder, until his back is flat against it and he's staring at me from behind his stupid, broken glasses. He just stares his creepy, dead-eyed stare.

I try to ignore him as I head for the landing.

He snorts. Like a hog.

I stop and turn back to him. "What is your problem?"

Suddenly, he's alive again.

"What's yours?" he asks.

"I don't have a problem...except you."

"My mom's fucking Samson," he says.

"What?" I stop dead. Where did that come from? And this kid is like ... what did his mother say ... nine or ten? And he just said *fucking*. I glance at his closed room door. "You should watch your mouth. Your mom would probably kill you if she heard you talking like that."

"She's fucking him," he insists again. "Wanna see? I can open the door. I took the key." He lifts his hand and just like he says, the room key ring is dangling from the tip of his index finger.

"No, I don't want to see! Gross!"

Will blinks his eyes like a little brown owl behind the thick glasses. He seems hurt that I don't want to take him up on his offer, which is even weirder.

"His dick is this big," Will continues, holding up his hands and leaving enough space between them to indicate that whoever Samson is, he's pretty hung, as if that means anything to me. Or changes my mind about opening that room door.

"I'm going to tell your mom what you're saying, if you don't knock it off," I tell him. The truth is, I want him to stop talking because he's freaking me out. I've never heard a little kid talk like this and I don't know what to say to him, except to tell him to shut up. His mom's as weird as he is, so I don't know if she'd care what he was saying, but I don't know even what I'd say to her. Your kid wanted me to watch you having sex. Ewww.

Will pushes his shoulders off the wall and follows me onto the landing and down the stairs.

"Go away," I say.

"I can do whatever I want," he says. He speeds up, hopping down each stair so he can step on the heels of my shoes. He nails it and I stumble, pitching forward but catching the rail, so I don't break my neck falling down the stairs.

I cram my heel back into my shoe and whip around to snarl at the kid, "What the hell is your problem? You could've killed me!"

He jumps back and freezes on the step above me, staring like a dead fish from behind his ridiculous glasses. He tips at the waist, dangling there and letting his arms swing. The robot...again.

"Ugh...whatever," I say, swatting the air before I turn away and head down to the lobby.

Will's feet patter down behind me, but I hold the railing just in case he tries to kill me again.

Once I reach the lobby, I forget all about Will. Lavina's in the cage with a stout black man who is working over a toothpick between his lips. His round face makes him look innocent, but he's got a glimmering gold tooth that says otherwise, and a sideways glare that reminds me of an irritated tiger.

I step in front of the payment window and plaster a broad smile on my face, so I look friendly. He doesn't let up on his glare.

"This her?" he asks Lavina. I guess that's just the way he looks.

"Yeah, da's her." Lavina says and I drop the smile.

"Hey, kid," Clive says to Will. Will is working his way through the coin return slots of the vending machines, but he stops, looking up when Clive addresses him. "If you ain't got money, get back up to your room. This ain't a place for you to play."

Will doesn't give Clive that crap about being able to do whatever he wants. Instead, he bolts up the steps and disappears.

Clive relocates the toothpick to the corner of his mouth, reaches back and unlocks the office door. He swings it wide open and gestures for me to come in with them, even though there isn't much room with him and Lavina both in there.

The office is shaped like a piece of pie. There is a wood shelf with a TV and VCR wedged into the very tip and a lower counter running beneath the payment window counter, with stacks of movies on one end, the ledger book, and a panel of buttons and lights with a time display at the center and phone receiver on the left side.

Clive backs up and stands in front of the TV. Lavina has her back against the windows on the outer wall of the office, but her rear end is like a shelf and the space is so narrow, the front of her nearly touches the counter beneath the payment window. I step in, but I'm not sure there's enough room to close the door.

"Don't worry 'bout dat," Lavina says when I reach for the knob. She flicks her chin at Clive. "He got a gun."

My stomach turns over. I think of Yolanda's missing tooth.

"Lavina said you want a job?" He scans me up and down. He narrows his eyes and I don't get the feeling that I measure up.

"That'd be great." I crack open my smile again. I can't help it. I smile when I'm scared...especially when I'm terrified that I could be shot if I don't answer right. My cheeks ache.

Clive's toothpick twitches as he speaks. "The pay is forty bucks a week, cash, under the table, plus your rent. It's midnight shift, from eleven at night to seven in the mornin', when Lavina comes in. If you got to work a little over though, there ain't no overtime."

I'm a morning person, up with the sun and the roosters usually. Except during drug busts that happen down the hall from my room. That wakes me up, but I don't know if I'll be able to stay up all night. But forty bucks and my rent paid?

"No problem," I say.

"Nobody comes in the cage during your shift, and you ain't allowed to leave it either." Clive says. I wonder what I'm supposed to do when I need to use the bathroom, but I don't say anything. I'm sure he doesn't mean I can't use the bathroom. Besides...forty bucks, plus rent.

"Night clerk keeps the movies playin', checks people in and out, and answers the phones." Lavina points to the stack of movies and the intimidating board full of lights and buttons beneath the payment counter, as Clive goes on, "An' I want ya ta keep the bums outta here. They come in and look through the fridge, drink up the coffee. This ain't a homeless shelter. And the she-its—men that come in here dressed up like women," he says and Lavina shoots me a keep your mouth shut about

Yolanda look, "we don't rent rooms to freaks like that neither."

I flash him a smile so wide, he could count my molars if he wanted to. There was a dope head waving a gun around on the third floor last night. Freaks seems a little picky, considering where the hotel is located, who I've seen in the halls, and what I've heard through the walls during the past few days.

"Ain't nothin' ta learn da phones," Lavina says. "Any fool kin work that board and do check-ins."

I hope I'm not the one fool that can't do this job.

"You interested?" Clive asks.

Forty bucks plus rent. I don't have to go home. And forty bucks? I could eat off ten, I bet.

"Yes," I say. "I am. Thank you."

Clive's eyebrows lift with one puff of a chuckle, as if I've just shocked him.

"You're welcome," he says, plucking the toothpick from his mouth. "You got Sunday nights off. Lavina'll go over everything with you and you can start Monday night."

Sundays off. Only Sundays?

Forty bucks a week and rent is paid.

The edges of my lips feel like they're brushing my ears. "Sounds great," I say.

I hope I don't end up in jail like Sam.

EIGHT

L avina's training lasts all of ten seconds. It's like my mother's wedding rehearsal when she married Bob. Bob's sister told me where to stand and what to do and expected me to remember everything, even though she only said it once and all at once. I couldn't remember anything the next day, so I winged it.

It worked then. I sure hope it works now.

Ned calls and wakes me up at a quarter after ten. "You comin' down here or what?"

I sit up and rub my eyes. "I don't start until eleven."

"You start your shift then, but you've got to sign off on the cash drawer first and it's gonna take you a half hour to count it. Didn't Lavina tell you to come down early?"

"She said I was supposed to count everything up at shift change."

"Riiight," Ned drawls, like I'm trying to pull something over on him. "And your shift starts when mine ends at eleven, so come down here and let's get this done."

I'm kind of excited about starting this new job, so I don't argue. I tell him I'll be right down and he hangs up before I can say anything else.

I tromp down the stairs, my hands full of stuff to eat and things to keep me busy if I'm bored. I can already tell that this is going to be just like my mother's wedding all over again. I'm already winging it and I'll probably screw up a lot too, but I keep thinking of how my rent will be paid and I'll get a paycheck on top of it. I'm living just about as high on the hog as I could've hoped.

Ned is slow getting up from the office chair once I'm standing outside the cage door. He reaches around behind me, as I scoot in, to lock the knob. The toe of his boot hits the edge of my flip-flop. His face is inches from mine and his clothing smells like it sat in the wash too long. I catch my breath and hold it. His hand is near my butt as he fumbles with the lock on the knob. Is it that hard to lock the door? All he does is smile as I try to shrink out of his way a little more. I finally exhale with the snick of the lock.

He withdraws his arm from around me and tips his head toward the desk. "You want to count out the drawer, or you want me to do it for you? I'm fast."

"You can," I say, since I don't have any idea what procedure we're supposed to follow.

He sits back down on the office chair. I move further into the cage and stack my stuff on the other end of the sprawling desk top, beneath the counter. My supplies for the night include my sketchbook, my book of fairy tales, a can of pop, and a box of saltines from my mom's pantry. When I set down my pouch of drawing pencils, the top flap opens up and my pencils roll out like a logging operation, spilling out on the floor.

"Jesus," Ned says as I stoop to pick them up. He doesn't move, but stays where he is, his legs spread wide so I have to lean over his knee like a sick Twister game if I want to pick up the pencils. I snatch one from near his foot and he grunts an mmm hmm under his breath. I decide to leave the rest until he's gone.

He pulls out the cash drawer and drops it on the counter so all the coins jump in the tray. After that, he rifles through the bills so fast, I can't keep up. He jots down the numbers he counts on a piece of columned paper that says, Till Sheet, across the top. It doesn't help that he's got some of the bills mixed together in the drawer.

"Wait," I say, "was that a twenty or a ten? I think it was only ten, but you counted it as a twenty."

Ned turns his head toward me, although his squinted eyes rest on my crotch instead of my face. "Because it was a twenty," he snaps.

"Are you sure? I thought it was—"

"I'm sure," he says with a groan. "Look, we can recount the whole drawer ten times if you want, but if you wanna do that, you better come down here at ten o'clock, not ten thirty. I'm not staying and working your shift too, just because you can't tell a ten dollar bill from a twenty."

I point to the clock read out on the main phone board. "It's only ten twenty-nine now."

"And I'm not done yet," he replies sourly. "I still have to finish the tally and then I have to catch you up on the rooms with morning calls."

"What are morning calls?"

"Wake-up calls, genius, for the people who requested them."

"Oh."

He grimaces. "Yeah, oh. Now, if it's okay with you, I'll finish counting your drawer so I can leave when I'm supposed to."

I stay quiet so he can count. He marks down everything and hands me the till sheet.

"Sign here," he says, pointing to the bottom of the columns where he's tallied up the total. It's 10:35 p.m.

77

I sign my name. Really, I just want him gone.

Ned picks up a spiral bound pad and drops it on the desk in front of me. "Room 21 wants a wake up at five forty-five, and room 250 wants one at six thirty. Keep the movies going and don't fall asleep. Especially, don't forget those wake-up calls. Got it?"

"Yes."

"Alright then, I'm out of here," Ned says. He scoots around behind me to unlock the door. His front presses up against my back. The ridge of his pants slides across my rear as he opens the door. I'm frozen in place until he goes out the door, the alarm wailing with his exit.

I wish I could go upstairs and shower.

What I notice about the people who come into the hotel is that they bring all kinds of things with them. Some bring briefcases, even though they don't look like business men, and sloppy Casanovas bring bottles of wine in brown paper bags. Mediocre Romeos bring six packs. Men go out and come back with bags of fast food, crinkly drugstore bags, more brown bags with bottle necks pushing out the top. Every once in a while, somebody brings in a candle, or a camera, or a bag that buzzes like a hornet when it's knocked against the counter. Rarer than all these things is someone carrying in flowers. Rarest of all is luggage.

The job itself turns out to be super dull. There is nothing to do in the cage but sit and wait for the next customer to come in and rent a room. The TV is on, but muted. Clive said the TV screen and the volume both have to stay on, so I'll notice when one triple x movie is done and put in another. He said it's important to keep the movies playing. I'm not supposed to let a tape rewind in the machine either—that takes too long. There's a special rewinding gadget on top of the TV for that.

I keep the TV muted even though it's against the rules, because it's way too weird when customers come in to rent a room and there's a chick on the screen belting out moans, and a guy's tongue between her legs. The first couple of times that scenario happened, I thought the amount of blood rushing to my face could cause a stroke. So now I just keep the sound off and an eye out for Clive's car to pull into the lot.

The ice machine rattles and kicks on. I'm so bored I can't take it anymore. I've drawn, I've watched the porn on TV (not a good idea) and I've chewed through an entire sleeve of saltines. My mouth is dry and my pop can is empty. The lullaby of the ice machine's motor sends me into a hazy fade. My chin hits my chest and I jerk it back up. Twice. Thank God, the phone rings.

I answer all official, "Starlight Hotel, can I help you?"

"Lael? Is that you?"

Oh my God. It's my mother.

"Mom?" I answer. "How did you get this number?"

"Why are you answering the hotel's main phone line?" she counters.

"Um, I work here?" I hit her with both blazing barrels of sarcasm, then lock and reload with the flat question, "How did you get this number?"

I can hear her bluster. "You're working there?"

My pride swells. I've only been gone five days—almost six, according to the clock on the phone console—and I've already got a job and a place to live. Two things she never thought I was capable of doing.

"A hotel isn't a home," she continues.

"It is to me," I say, leaning back in the office chair.

She draws a deep breath. "Fine. Then, if you're going to be an adult, then you better start acting like one. I want all my things back that you stole from me today."

Stole.

She's my mother. At least, she was once.

Maybe it wasn't right to take her plug-in pan or to run away from home like I did, but it wasn't right either that she looked the other way every time Bob gave me a shove, or that she kept me on strings that she jerked whenever she felt like it.

"I've got to go," I tell her. "I'm working."

"Not before you tell me when you're going to bring my things back."

I leave the phone lying on my shoulder, listening to her breathe. I don't have an answer for that.

"When I have money to buy my own, I guess."

"And when is that?"

"I don't know, Mom. I just started working here."

"Well, that puts me at ease," she snaps. "And what about everything else, Lael? What are you going to do about school? Or car insurance? You know, living on your own isn't cheap. What are you going to do if you need to go to a doctor? You don't have health insurance anymore, you know."

I didn't, but I do now. And I'm healthy. Ha. She can kiss my ass. "Good thing none of it is your business anymore."

"You are still my legal responsibility until you're eighteen." Her voice is as hard as a lead shield.

"So...responsible means cancelling my insurance. Yeah, that sounds totally responsible." That shuts her up. For a second.

"Food, clothing, a roof over your head...you have no idea what it's like to be an adult—"

"But I'm doing it," I say solidly. "I'm living on my own, taking care of myself without your help...and there's nothing you can do about it."

She slams the phone down in my ear.

I'm wilting and it's only midnight. This is hell. I droop in my chair and pull myself back up when my head hits the desk. My forehead throbs.

I finally cross my arms on the desk, swearing to myself that I'm only doing it to prop myself up, but when my head drifts down onto my forearms, they feel softer than any pillow I've ever had. All I think of is floating. I'm drifting like an angel caught in a draft.

A shrill ring cuts through my bliss and jolts me awake.

My cheek is wet with spit. The phone console is lit up and flashing like it's going to explode. The clock says it is 1:55 a.m. More lights, indicating calls from rooms, ignite across the board as I wipe off my saliva. I pick up the phone and press one of the buttons.

"The damn TV went off!" a man barks from the other end of the line. "The screen's just snow!"

I glance over at the TV to confirm it. The guy's right. The screen is a blizzard and the finished, rewound tape juts from the slot.

"Sorry," I say. "I'll put in a new movie right now."

"Thanks," the guy growls and hangs up.

I put in a new tape and the moment it kicks on, the phone panel goes dark as if I've unplugged it. I settle back down on the chair, but the adrenaline, from getting hollered at, is still going strong. At least I don't feel like sleeping anymore.

I pull out my sketch book and all my pencils, including the ones I retrieved from the cage floor, and open up my copy of Grimm's Fairy Tales. My sketch book is full of wolves, long braids, and gingerbread houses, stunted little men that are part frog, and princesses in long, flowing capes that would trip them up in real life.

"What's that?" a boy's voice says.

I stretch up on my chair to look over the payment counter and peer around for that rotten kid, Will—it sounds just like him—but there isn't a soul in the lobby. I turn and peek out the cage door window at the lounge, but there's no one there either.

I'm really tired. It must've been the ice machine rattling around that sounded like a kid talking.

I flip through my fairy tale book and find a picture of a man wearing a bearskin when I hear, loud and clear, "Are ya deaf? I asked ya what that is!"

Will's voice fills the office like he's hiding under the desk. I even check to be sure, but he's not there. His giggle sounds like it's behind me, but there's nothing behind the chair but the vertical blinds and the outer window. I jump off my chair, turning in a circle, looking for him.

"Where are you?"

His laughter explodes, coming from all directions. It bounces off the cage's bulletproof glass, as if I'm in a fun house.

"You don't know! You can't find me!" He's pushing his voice to be spooky, but he can't stop giggling.

There's no trace of the little brat. Finally, I sit back down and snatch up my pencil. I exhale to calm myself down and slowly begin to sketch a man's feet, with a bear skin and claws over the top of them. It's one of the worst sketches I've ever done, but I don't pick up my eraser.

"Look at me!" Will shouts gleefully.

I ignore him, mostly because I can't find him even when I try.

"I said, look!" His tone is stretched tighter than new rubber bands on braces.

I just keep on plucking the bear's coarse fur from the pencil lead in tiny strokes.

"Look up here, dummy!" Will growls, losing at his own game.

I glance up at the ceiling and—what do you know—I spot something I never expected. The kid's head is stuck through a hole in the wall, which is about the size of a small TV screen, at the very top of the cage ceiling.

Above the cage door, the wall extends, not to the very top of the hotel, but to the landing between the second and third floors. I never thought to look up there before, probably because there was never any need to. When I study where the hole is, I realize that the kid is standing on the ledge with the fake plant—the jutted lip of the landing outside of the flimsy hand rail Lavina had warned me about.

I tip my head back further to look at him. "Get off there before you fall! Ain't nothin' around here too study!"

"You sound like that fat asshole bitch nigger," the kid says, even though his voice drops with the last insult.

"You better watch your mouth." Back home, everybody knew better than to use that word, and having lived at this hotel for less than a week, *I* know saying stuff like that can get you killed. Even if Will is black. "Where's your mother?"

Will probably does too, because he drops it. "She's getting ready for Samson to come," he says.

Oh yeah. Samson. I don't know if I can ever forget how Will offered to open the door while the guy had sex with his mom.

"What're ya doin'?" Will asks.

"Why don't you come down here and talk to me like a normal person?" I make a few more strokes on my drawing. I don't hear anything, so I tip my head back to look up at him. "It's pretty rude to just sit up there and spy on me."

He jerks his head back through the hole and vanishes from sight. I wonder how long he's been up there eavesdropping on me. The ice machine rumbles again, kicking into another cycle. The kid's bristly black hair, framing the edge of his forehead, pops through the opening again. Once his glasses appear, and he sees that I'm still watching, he yanks his head back with the swiftness of a sewing machine needle, but it's awkward, as if he gets his chin stuck. He does this two more times, disappearing in a flourish each time our eyes meet.

What a little snot.

There is another scuffle and the fake plant that was up on the ledge comes crashing down onto the lounge floor, about five feet from the cage door. A shabby sneaker comes along with it.

There's a lot of scuffling overhead and I think of the kid up there in an all-out panic, seeing his shoe on the floor, and knowing how close it is to the cage door, and not having any easy way to retrieve it.

Now I'm the one that giggles.

"Hey," I call up to him. "Your shoe is down here, dummy! If you want it back, you're going to have to come and get it!"

The ice machine completes the cycle and lapses into a steady hum. Stretching up on my chair, I peer over the edge of the cage door window. The shoe is still laying sideways beside the fake plant on the floor. It's a grimy canvas high top, camouflage green, with a dingy bubble toe. The sole looks slippery, most of the treads gone.

It's five more minutes before Will creeps down the steps like a wary cat. I watch him out of the corner of my eye, as he slinks down, staying close to the railing. When he's three steps from the lobby floor, I look up from my sketch book and our eyes meet. He's blinking so fast behind his glasses, it looks like he's about to have a seizure.

I'm hit with a surge of sympathy. He is a jerky kid in filthy clothes with screwy glasses. But he's just a kid.

I fold my arms on the desk and smile at him. He drops his head suspiciously to one side, looking for a trap.

"Your shoe is over there." I tip my head in the direction of the spilled planter. He's frozen, except for his rapid-fire eyelids. "Over there," I repeat, pointing.

He rises a little out of his crouch, keeping his back to the railing and slips down the last three steps. On the floor of the lobby, he stops, glancing between me and the location of his shoe, sizing up his odds. I haven't moved one millimeter.

He's sweating so much, his face is as shiny as the bottom of his sneaker and his glasses slide down his nose. He shoves them up with the heel of his hand.

I try to remind myself that this kid stole my pop, and that Lavina has warned me about him being trouble, but I kind of feel sorry for him. It's probably another mistake in my long list of mistakes.

"How many times do you want me to say it?" I ask. "Your dang shoe is over there."

It is maddening how long it takes him to inch into the lounge. By the time he's makes it past the edge of the counter, I have to fight the urge to throw open the cage door, snatch up his raggedy sneaker, and beat him senseless with it.

He hunches down beneath the lip of the counter, out of my sight.

I ease up onto one knee on the chair and peer out of the cage window.

His hair appears first, sprouting up like a wiry little weed from the bottom edge of the glass. The tiny stalk of hair grows as he rises, thickening into a meadow of bristly, sprouting buds all over his crown, followed by his broad forehead. Finally, his brown eyes blink behind his smudgy, busted-up glasses. The thick frames are have new tape in the middle.

The second our eyes meet, he plunges himself back down, out of sight.

I stifle my laugh.

The kid shoots across the floor and snatches up his sneaker. Once he's got it in his mitts, he darts past the cage and up the stairs, bounding up them two at a time. He stumbles before he reaches the landing, falling with a humiliating thunk, flat on his face, sprawled on the steps.

I can't hold back. The laughter spills out of me.

The kid scrambles to his feet and lunges out of view. I laugh so hard, tears run down my face.

Once I settle down, all is silent for the next ten minutes and then I hear the squeak of the metal railing upstairs pulling against the screws that hold it to the floor as Will climbs over it onto the ledge again.

"Be careful!" I shout up to him. "You could kill yourself if you fall from up there!"

He reappears through the hole, a scribble of his hair first, and then his entire face. What a dorky kid. I smile up at him. He does make me laugh.

"I could spit on you," he says.

My smile goes flat, just like any sympathy I just had for the little snot. "Don't," I tell him.

I'm sure we both know—there's no place in the cage where his spit can't reach.

The alarm goes off as the front door jerks open. A fat man in a purple, velour sweat suit totters in. I rent him a room, fumbling through the entire process—I can't remember what ID to ask for, forget to offer the waterbed rooms downstairs, and only get his last name in the ledger—but he seems too distracted by whatever's out in the parking lot to notice how terrible I am at my job. Once he's passed the money through the payment slot, he leans back from the counter and signals out the front door.

I drop the key through the slot in the Plexiglas and he scoops it out of the trough as a thick woman in chunky glass heels and a vinyl dress sidles in. They're a weird pair. He looks like he just came from smoking a pack outside a gym and she looks like she dressed for a sleazy Halloween party. Even though her stilettos jack her up so high, he manages to throw his arm over her shoulders and the couple wades up the steps, murmuring to one another as they go. He has to keep a step ahead of her, so they're the same size.

I think they're going to disappear, but once they reach the second floor landing, they give away the kid's position.

"Whuch you doin' there, little man?" the man asks Will.

"Nothin'," Will grumbles.

"Hey—girl down there in the office!" the man shouts down to me. "You know there's a kid watchin' you on the ledge up here?"

"Yeah, I know it." I shout back. "Thanks."

The couple's footsteps fade away and Will's head appears through the ceiling hole again. He makes spitty noises, like he's gathering saliva to rain down on me.

"Better not," I say without looking up.

"Then tell me what yer doin'," he says.

He wins. "Drawing."

"Looks like a stupid pi'ture."

"You think that because you can't see anything through your dirty glasses."

He grunts. "I don't wanna see yer stupid pi'tures."

"Then stop looking."

My pencil lead breaks. I groan as I pull out the garbage can from beneath the desk and hold my cheap pencil sharpener over it. I twist my pencil until the shavings curl out the top and drop into the black liner. By the time I finish sharpening the pencil, the kid is standing on the third step up from the lobby floor again.

"You're just a copy cat," he says, gripping the railing. "You ain't drawin' your own pi'tures, yer jus' stealin' 'em out of that book."

"Is that what you came down here for? To be a stupid little jerk?"

He doesn't answer. Instead, he just stares as he pulls a pack of bubble gum from his stained front pocket. I'd be afraid to put anything that came out of there in my mouth, but he unwraps piece after piece, loading down his jaw with it. I flip through the pages of my sketchbook, looking for the best stuff I've drawn, so I can prove that he's an idiot.

He inches down a few steps as I do. "You got more?"

"Yes," I say. I don't know why I want to impress some dumb kid, but I do. "Come over here by the glass and I'll show you."

He narrows his eyes. "Show me from here."

"Nope. If you want to see them, come over here. You can't see anything from over there."

"I'm gonna spit on you," he says, sucking up the excess saliva his gum creates.

I roll my eyes. "Through the glass? Good luck."

"No, from up there." He points to the second floor landing.

"You know what? Shut up about spitting. If you spit on me, I'll tell your mom and you'll get kicked out. How's that? I'm trying to be nice to you, but if you keep saying that stuff about spitting, you can just get out of here."

In response, he drops his torso loosely over one hip. He dangles his arms and swings them, all the while staring at me with a blank face.

"What are you supposed to be, anyway?" I say.

The kid keeps swinging. He closes his mouth, swallows his bubble gum juice, and then lets his lips fall back open.

"Robots don't breathe, if that's what you're trying to be," I tell him.

"They don't swallow either. And you don't even look like a robot. You look like one of those mannequins at the store...the kind they put dresses on."

Mid-sway, the kid's arms go rigid and he snaps himself upright.

"I ain't no girl."

So that's one of his soft spots. My smirk jabs it a little.

Will crams his gum into his cheek and shouts, "I ain't no girl!" He stomps down into the lobby and up to the window. He thumps his fist against his chest. "I'm a boy! I got a wiener! Girls ain't got wieners, ya stupid pig!"

I smile at him and he stops dead. The awareness of where he is standing breaks across his face and he can see that he's been had. Before he can retreat, I push my open sketchbook up against the bullet proof glass. The book blocks our faces from one another, but I can see him frozen in place from under the bottom edge of the book cover.

"I drew that," I say proudly. He doesn't answer. My hand gets tired holding up the book. "Can you see the picture or what?"

"I see it." he grumbles.

I'm not going to ask him what he thinks. I lower the book slowly. The kid is still standing right in front of the desk, like a zoomed-in lens, blinking at me as he works over his glob of gum. This time, I think we are both shocked that he is so close.

"I ain't no girl," he says, sucking up another juicy breath. He wipes his mouth with the back of his hand.

"And my pictures aren't stupid," I tell him.

We glare at each other a moment. "What's your name?" he asks.

"Lael."

"That don't even sound like a girl's name. That's a ugly boy's name."

I shrug. "It's my name. I didn't pick it."

He pauses long enough to catch his breath and when he exhales, the breath races out in a roar, along with his gum. The glob hits the bulletproof glass with a juicy thud and drops onto the counter. He looks at me all wide eyed, but I can tell he's not going to pick it up.

Before I can yell at him, the kid turns on his heel and speeds up the stairs on his slippery soles.

A tall man in a brown suit that nearly matches his skin, wakes me by walking into the lobby and tripping the alarm at three thirty in the morning. I jerk up my head. My tongue is fat, like I've been gagged with a wad of cotton balls.

The man doesn't even glance at me, but continues toward the stairs. I think of letting him go, but I didn't check him in and don't know what he's doing here. Lavina said nobody goes up, unless I know where they're going. She also said peoples git shot that way and nobody wants ta clean that up.

"Hello?" I call to him. He stops, his foot on the first step, and turns slowly toward the cage. His hair is cut close to his skull in a meticulous fade and the moustache on his upper lip is so thin, it looks drawn on. I smile as best I can as I rub my eyes, one at a time. "Can I help you?"

He steps off the stair and comes to the counter. The directness of his gaze makes me shrink in my chair. He's got startling silver eyes that are so foreign to his skin color—to anyone's—that they make him look like he's part machine inside. The longer he stares down at me, the more I wish to God I'd never said a word.

"I'm here for Penny Grayling," he says. "She said to come on up to room 36."

"Okay," I say. His stare sends spikes of glass through my veins. I don't even care if he's here to shoot Penny. I just don't want him to shoot me.

"You seen a girl come in here? Asian chick, black hair down to about here..." He takes a step back and holds up his hand like he's cutting the hair off at the top of his butt. "Real pretty girl. Name's Saturn?"

I lift both shoulders and drop them. "It's my first night. I haven't seen anybody like that."

He steps close to the counter again and leans his elbow on the marble, resting his chin on his fist, against the little ledge of his palm. "Is it now? Well, I believe you. And now that Penny's livin' here, I'm sure we'll be seein' a lotta each other. What's yo' name?"

I don't want to tell him, but being the clerk, I think I have to tell him. I suppose it doesn't matter too much, since I'm lodged behind this bunker of bulletproof glass. "Lael."

"That's a real pretty name for a real pretty lady," he says.

I cringe. My mother's a lady. "Thanks."

"Womens, like yo'self, call me Samson." The quick flash of his wink appears like a spark.

Samson. The guy that Will was talking about...with the big thing.

He glances over at the TV screen and shoots me with another wink. "Be sure to keep those movies running tonight, will you, Lael?"

"Sure." My name on his tongue feels like a violation.

I peek at the clock on the phone board. It's almost four a.m. I've only got to stay awake until seven, when Lavina gets in. I can make it.

Madden, or Samson—whoever he is—has already disappeared up the steps.

NINE

All I remember was the digital clock numbers got blurry.

Next thing I know, somebody's pounding on the glass over my head again. I jerk up in the chair and come eye to eye with Lavina's furious glare.

I'm instantly awake. And sick to my stomach.

"What you think yer doin'?" she says as she waddles around to the cage door. She hits the glass pane with one sharp knuckle. I unlock the door and she comes in with all kinds of exhales that make me feel like I just fell asleep in the middle of brain surgery. She pushes past my chair, smashing me against the desk, and dumps her bag of lunch on the desk near the TV.

"I'm sorry," I stammer.

She turns to face me head on. "You got one job here. Da's it. Jus' one. You gotta be awake. Check folks in and out, switch out movies, and do mornin' calls if there's any. But ya gotta be awake to do ya job, girl! If Clive'd come in here and seen you sleepin' like dat, you know what'd happen?"

"He'd fire me." My throat squeezes around the words.

"Damn right he would! And pro'ly me too, for tellin' 'im you could do dis job!"

"I'm sorry." My vision floods. The cage looks like it's at the bottom of a fishbowl. Another minute or two of Lavina being angry at me and I'll be nothing but a sobbing glob of tears and snot lying at her feet.

She must see it, because she drops her arms at her sides with a heavy sigh. If I could disappear into my shoes, I would.

"Move aside now," she says and I mold myself to the closed door so she can sit down at the desk. She pulls out the cash drawer and the paper Ned had me sign at the beginning of my shift. She exhales long and slow. "Look, ya jus' cain't be sleepin' at the desk, ya understand?"

I nod. My throat stings like I've swallowed a box full of bees.

"It Monday," she says with another sigh. "An' Mondays ain't never good. I come in here and know I ain't gonna have time to eat that lunch I brung, 'cause Clive ain't got nobody ta cover mah one day off'a week. Day of rest mah ass. I gotta work twice's hard today 'cause he too cheap ta hire somebody fo' Sundays. Ya know what I mean? Today gonna be shit."

She turns her brown eyes on me, and I'm surprised at how soft her gaze is. I guess this is her way of apologizing for yelling at me for sleeping. We both know I shouldn't have been doing it, but I think she feels bad. It helps soothe the sting in both my throat and eyes.

I smile at her. "I could help you with the rooms, if you want."

She smirks. "Oh, 'cause ya so well rested now, ain't ya."

I jump as the door alarm sounds and Jonah, the guy from the oil change shop next door, walks over the threshold.

The moment his eyes meet mine, he breaks into a sunbeam smile that changes the climate in the cage.

"Mornin' Jonah," Lavina says sweetly.

"Good mornin', ladies," he says. Ladies, the way Jonah says it, with his brilliant smile, makes the word sound sweet and friendly and delicate. He holds up his blue canvas money bag. "Did you get to the bank, Lavina? It's Monday, and I figured you always got too much happenin' on Mondays, so I got extra change if ya need it."

The chair squeals beneath Lavina as she sits back on it, but her smile is as genuine and bright as Jonah's. She laughs. "You's so thoughtful, Jonah. I could use that change fo' sho'. Ya know, I din't even get no bre'fast this mornin', I been so wound up. Clive still ain't hired no back-up maid, and it make Monday turrible, knowin' how much I gotta do t'day jus' 'cause Clive draggin' 'is feet."

She motions for me to unlock the cage door, but then, with Jonah blocking the way out, the only thing I can do is back into the cage and stand by the TV. Jonah's eyes flick to my crotch and away, but then I realize he wasn't looking at me. He saw the porn on the screen. I don't know which makes me blush more—the idea of his eyes between my legs, or on the porno.

Lavina takes the bag of money from him. "Kin ya gimme a minute ta count da drawer?"

"Take your time," he says, and when his gaze rises to mine again, I'm the one to look away.

"I can count it out for you," I offer. "Ned told me we had to do it together, an hour before shift change."

Lavina grunts. "Girl, he fuckin' wich you. He know he s'pose ta tally da drawer at the end'a 'is shif'. He playin' you. I count my own drawer."

It makes me feel like a thief. After several minutes of awkward shifting and leaning, and Jonah the whole time leaning on the doorframe looking at me and smiling, and Lavina counting the bills twice, she finally looks up at me. Her expression is flat.

"You wanna count it? Yo' ten short," she says.

My brain stammers. "What do you mean?"

"Yo' ten short. Whuch ya think it mean?"

"Ten bucks?" My mind flips back to Ned counting the drawer too fast for me to keep up. "Ned miscounted it. Last night, he counted a ten as a twenty, and I told him—"

Lavina runs her finger over the till sheet, dragging her fingertip down to my initials.

"This yo' initials?" she asks.

"Yes, but—"

"That yo' initials," she repeats flatly. "Ya signed off on it."

Both Lavina and Jonah are staring at me. The amount of blood in my face makes the rest of my body feel cold.

"He counted a ten for a twenty," I whisper.

"Yo' drawer is yo' respons'bility." Lavina's eyebrows raise with her every word. "Ya wanna pay it now, or ya want me ta tell Clive ta take it off yo' paycheck?"

I shake my head. A dark storm churns in my stomach. Ned stole ten bucks from me and I just let him do it.

"I'll pay it, but I've got to go up and get the money from my room."

"Ahright. G'won and git it then." Lavina says.

I square my shoulders, grab my stuff, and squeeze past Lavina. Jonah moves out of my way. I climb the stairs to my room. If I see Will on the ledge, and he pulls any of his stupid, little kid shit, I'm going to rip his head off.

By the time I reach the lobby again, I'm not humiliated anymore. I can't decide if I'm more furious, or starving, or exhausted. Jonah's still standing there, leaning against the counter with his canvas bag under his armpit. I go to the open cage door and hold out the bill to Lavina. She takes it, eyeing me hard.

"You okay?" she asks.

"I just sat up all night to lose ten bucks," I tell her, watching her slip my ten bucks into the drawer. "I'm going to go eat and pass out for a few hours."

She closes the drawer with a big sigh and uses the counter to leverage herself onto her feet. "Sho' wish I'da got mah bre'fast."

Jonah stands up straight. "I was gonna head down to Red's and get somethin' for the crew next door. You want me to bring you back a little somethin' too, Lavina?"

"I could shore use some food." She reaches right into her shirt and fishes some money from her bra. She gives Jonah a five dollar bill. "Gimme some eggs ova' easy, wit' some bacon; hash brown, done crispy; an' I want biscuits instead'a toast. Two. Tell 'em there's two pieces a' toast, so I want two biscuits. Las' time they tried ta short me. An' grape jelly. Get me extra of that and some whip butter too. Extra of it. They neva' put nu'ff on the hash brown, and ain't neva' any on the biscuit."

Jonah turns to me. "Wanna come with me, Lael?"

Listening to Lavina give her order makes cracking open the last can of spaghetti rings sound even less exciting. And pretty soon, it's just going to be tuna.

"I can't," I tell him. "I just gave Lavina my last ten bucks."

It's not really a lie. I have a few more bills in my jewelry box, but not enough to pay for my car and to give my mom her money back, so she'll leave me alone. There's not a dime extra. Especially if Ned keeps stealing from me.

"It's my treat," Jonah says. "I'll buy if you help me carry back all the take out boxes."

Lavina turns her gaze to me—the expression of a bored hound—as if to say, don't you tell me you're gonna turn that down.

I'm more hungry than tired.

"I'll carry back everything," I tell Jonah.

"Alright then," he says, slapping his hands together and rubbing them, "let's go get some food."

It's unnerving to walk down the sidewalk, away from the hotel. It was one thing, when I was driving into the city in my car, but it's something else to be going in further on foot. And with a stranger.

The store fronts we pass are mostly boarded up. Tall buildings with empty apartments on top, and short, hollow buildings with broken window glass swept to the edge of the sidewalk. Some places the boards are falling off, and some don't need any boards at all, because fire has eaten them from the inside out. The brick building on the corner is streaked with wide, burnt ribbons. They run all the way up to the roof, like long, black screams. A few businesses are open, but they don't look like it. They huddle behind heavy bars on their windows and doors.

"How old are you?" Jonah asks.

"Eighteen," I lie. "How about you?"

"Twenty-seven."

"Wow," I say.

"Too old?" he asks.

Too old? Does he mean that the way it sounds? Then, ew, gross. And yes. Way, way, way too old.

But he's buying me breakfast, so I don't want to be impolite. "I just thought you were younger," I say.

"Yeah? Well, thanks." He tucks his hands in his pockets as we walk.

The little gesture puts me at ease. I don't want him to think I want anything other than whatever this is—I'm carrying boxes in exchange for breakfast. "So, how come you're living at the hotel, Silver Spoon?"

"What'd you call me?" I glance at him, cocking an eyebrow so he'll explain.

"You know...born with a silver spoon in your mouth. You look like one of them pretty, white girls that lives in one of them nice houses." He's smiling, but I can't tell if he means it as a compliment or an insult.

"My family isn't loaded, if that's what you mean."

"You gettin' angry? I'm just playin' with you!" He nudges my arm with his elbow.

"I know," I lie.

"Well, anything's more than what I had growing up," he says with a laugh. "I grew up in the ghetto. More like I grew up with a dirty spoon in my mouth." I wince at the image and he laughs again. "So how come a girl like you is livin' in a Detroit hotel? I don't see a lot like you around here."

"I moved out." I shrug like it was a casual decision. "This was the first place I saw, and I wanted to live in the city."

"Huh," he says. "At a hotel?"

"Yup." I stick my hands in my pockets and press my lips shut. "Where is Red's?"

He lets it go. "It's just a little ways up...see it?" He points to a diamond-shaped sign peeking out from the edge of another vacant cinderblock building.

A man turns onto the sidewalk, walking toward us. Before I can answer Jonah, the man breaks into a jog. Jonah takes hold of my wrist and pulls me behind him to make room for the jogger. At least, that's what I think is happening until the man slows down a few steps from us.

"How much she goin' fo'?" the man asks. There are brown spots in the white parts of his eyes, like his irises are leaking. He rolls his tongue up inside his lips and then pokes it straight out, thick and bright pink like the tip of a tentacle.

"Sorry, man, she's not workin'," Jonah says.

Working? A deep tremble tightens my muscles to my bones. Does this guy think I'm a hooker? I'm still wearing the wrinkled tee I wore all night long and shorts. Sneakers. Not leather and stilettos. I stay behind Jonah, thankful that he's bigger than the other guy, who keeps swooping around to get a better look at me.

"C'mon, broda," the guy pleads. He pushes his hand into his pocket, picks out some lint, inspects it, and shakes it off his fingers. He plunges his hand back into his pocket again. "I jus' need a little. There's a hotel down that way—we'll be in and out. You won't even miss 'er."

The tremble inside me builds. My feet shake in the soles of my shoes. The tips of my hair even quiver at the corner of my eyes.

"Sorry, brother, she's not what you're looking for. She's a good girl."

"None'a dem's good," the guy snorts, his tongue pushing out of his mouth again.

"This one is." Jonah's voice is so soft, a feather would crush it. It sounds like he's sorry for letting the guy down, but not that sorry.

"Ahright," the man says, with three hard and fast nods. "Ahright, then. Ahright. Sorry, man, my mistake."

"No problem." Jonah raises one hand, but the other he keeps slightly behind him, like he's keeping me corralled where I am. We stand there until the guy stops nodding and finally walks away. Jonah exhales and his arm drifts down to his side. I step out from behind him.

"You see why you don't walk around by yourself out here?" he says. "This ain't the country."

I take a deep breath. "You were so calm."

"Losing your head can only get you in trouble and there's already enough of that around here," he says. I notice Jonah's sharp, quick glimpses as he scans all around us, making sure the man continues walking in the opposite direction. He did it before, but he did it so casually that if that man had never approached us, I would've never thought Jonah was watching everything as intently as he actually is.

"Should we be running?" I whisper to him.

He looks down at me, his lips splitting into an amused grin. "You really are from the country, aren't you, Silver Spoon?"

We got a window seat at Red's, which means a brown, vinyl-covered booth that sucks at the back of my legs when I move. We both ordered our breakfast, along with cups of steaming hot coffee. The brown mugs sit in front of us, diluted with a couple white, plastic tubs of half-and-half. The first sip relaxes me so much, I look across the table at Jonah and feel like we really could be good friends.

Red's is an oasis, flanked by the littered boulevard and a street full of abandoned and burnt-up houses. But inside the restaurant, the booths are almost all filled. A thick cloud of cigarette smoke sits on top of the scent of sizzling bacon. Murmurs of conversation and the scrape of silverware are punctuated with the waitresses shouting their orders back to the kitchen. Nobody seems to want to kill anybody else in here.

"Everybody is so...normal here," I say.

"Compared to the people at the hotel? I bet!" Jonah chuckles. He points to the man sitting on a high stool behind the huge, antique cash register. "That's Red, right there. He's been shot four different times just trying to make a living. See that gun on his side? The cooks all have 'em too. Nobody better make any trouble in here, less they want some for themselves. And you see how big that register is? Red done it on purpose. You couldn't drag that thing outta here if you tried. And Red's willing to die before anybody else gets it open."

"Wow," I say, staring at the knobby end of the gun at Red's side. When the owner sees me looking, I look away fast. I don't want him thinking I'm a problem.

"Can I ask you something?" I say. "Something kind of personal?"

"Sure," Jonah says.

I grip my mug. "Why don't you talk like Lavina?"

Instead of getting angry, Jonah laughs. "Whuch ya mean by that, girl? You tryin' ta say Lavina don't talk normal?" He sits back and takes a sip of coffee, despite his smile. "Is that what you mean?"

I nod. I'm pretty sure I'm supposed to be embarrassed to ask, even though I'm not exactly sure why. It's not an insult. I just wonder why he doesn't.

Jonah relaxes back on his side of the booth. "My mother insisted that I be an educated black man," he explains. "She was worried that there aren't enough of us around. Lavina probably didn't get the chance to go all the way through school. A lot of the kids I knew didn't, and the ones that did stay in and finish school, a lot of them weren't there to study."

I brighten. "What college did you go to?"

He only flashes a grin. "I meant high school."

I look into my mug, embarrassed now that I asked.

"Sorry," I say to clear away the awkwardness, but I think it just makes it worse.

Jonah takes a drink of his coffee, adds another tub of cream. "Lavina came from a family like most people 'round here. No money, lotsa kids. It's tough trying to grow up without money. Lavina was working young.

The way I understand it, she married young and had her boy, Tavon, young too. He works Saturdays as the relief clerk for everybody's day off."

I just stare at Jonah, gaping. "Lavina's got a kid and she's married?"

"Her husband was killed in a drive-by shooting when Tavon was little."

"How old is he now?"

"Twenty-six," Jonah says, taking another sip of his coffee. "She just bought him a birthday cake last month."

"That's weird. She never said she had any kids."

Jonah grins, knowingly. "Lavina don't say a whole lot."

The waitress returns and sets down our plates of food. I have two. A platter with the eggs, bacon, and hash browns, and a smaller plate with two pieces of toast and tubs of jelly. I hover over the top and breathe in the steam of the browned butter and the bacon, my mouth watering. I've never appreciated breakfast as much as I do now that I haven't had anything all week but bowls of canned raviolis, spaghetti rings, and saltine crackers smeared with peanut butter.

"Smell good?" Jonah whispers across the table. I open my eyes and am looking into his. Maybe it's the eggs and bacon, but Jonah, makes me feel peaceful.

"So," he says, poking his eggs with his fork, "tell me about who Lael is."

But I'm too hungry to talk. I grab my fork and scoop a pile of hash browns into my mouth. Once that happens, all I can do is moan softly as my eyes roll into the back of my head. It's like I've never tasted food before. The eggs are buttery, the bacon melts on my tongue.

"You got a good appetite, I know that," he says. "You can talk with your mouth full if you want. You just got to tell me about this mystery girl that can eat like a man."

Poor guy. I can't stop wolfing down the food, but between swallows I tell him whatever he wants to know.

"Boyfriend?" he asks with a raised brow.

"Nope, not even looking."

He takes a drink, watching me over the edge of the mug. "Maybe the right one ain't convinced you to look."

I gulp a glob of hash browns and grimace as it goes down sideways. Jonah scoots my water glass across the table. Once the hash browns are dislodged, I tell him, "I just want to have fun and figure out what I'm doing."

"And what's that?"

It sounded like a good answer, until he questioned it. I shrug. "I want to make it on my own."

"Oh, so you're Miss Independent," he teases.

"Yup, that's me." I cram another heap of eggs in my mouth. I wish I could order another plate full, but he's paying and it would be rude, but God Almighty, this food is the best I've ever eaten.

"You're exactly what you should be." He taps the table with one finger with an admiring gaze tractor-beamed on me. "No woman should want to rely on a man. You're young. No babies, no wedding rings. You're making your own cash and doin' your own thing. You're a strong woman, Lael. More of 'em should be."

"That's what I want to do." I joke, swabbing my plate with the toast. He makes me feel so good. Capable.

He salutes me with his fork and I smile even though there's probably bits of breakfast speckled in my teeth. He gets me. I think Jonah and I are going to be really, really great friends. Jonah signals the waitress to bring more coffee.

After everything is eaten, I sit back with the leather cradling me, my coffee mug in both hands. The long shift finally catches up with me once my belly is full.

Jonah keeps asking questions, about where I lived, if I have siblings, what my mom and Bob are like, who I've dated, what I like to do. I tell him more than I think he really wants to hear, but since he keeps smiling and asking questions, I keep heaping on the answers.

Unfortunately, my eyelids feel thick and they get heavier and heavier as I sit in the booth. My brain isn't gripping my thoughts any more. Thoughts sail through my brain like they're on castors and I have no idea how I'm going to walk all the way back to the hotel, when I all I want to do is curl up in this booth and sleep for a year.

"Our order for Lavina and the guys is ready," Jonah says and I snap my head up, realizing I'd nodded off.

"I'll carry it," I slur. "I said I would. I meant it. For breakfast."

"Nah, I got it, Silver Spoon. Let's get you back to the hotel, so you can get some sleep."

I wake up to my phone ringing. Sitting straight up in bed, I don't recognize my room because there's a hotel sign outside instead of our garage roof. The phone rings again and I remember this is my room. The clock beside the bed says it's 9:30.

I pick up the receiver. "Hello?"

"You're going to be down here at ten, right?" It's Ned. The second-to-the-last person in the world I want to hear from right now. The first is my mother.

"No," I tell him. "Lavina told me we don't count the drawer until shift change, and you did short me, just like I said. You owe me ten bucks."

"I don't owe you nothin'," he snaps.

"You counted a twenty as a ten," I say.

"The drawer was square. You signed off on it." There's an impatient tap tap tap on his end of the line, like he's bouncing a pen on the counter. "So are you coming down here at ten or what?"

I hang up on him and settle back against my pillow. My eyes just close when somebody knocks on the door. He must've sprinted all the way up the stairs. He can't be serious.

"Go away, Ned! I'll be down at eleven!" I shout from the bed.

"It's Will. I gotta talk to you."

Ugh. The kid. I groan, but he sounds kind of desperate, so I get up and drag myself over to the door. I undo the locks and open up. It's not just Will in the hallway. The he-she, Yolanda, is standing out there too.

"I seen Will knockin', so I thought I'd come visit too, an' see if ya got any of them bags unpacked yet." Yolanda says. He's got his nails done today—long, blue claws that glitter. They match the eye shadow he's got painted on, all the way up to his eyebrows. It almost works with the purple spandex and the black tee he's modified so that it drapes off his broad shoulder. And he's wearing pink house slippers on his enormous feet.

"I'm sleeping! I'll talk to you two later," I grumble. I drop the doorknob and stagger back to my bed, but Yolanda pushes her house slipper in the crack and shoves the door open. I watch the whole thing with one eye open.

"You had a little too much of somethin', sweetie?" Yolanda asks. She plants a hand at her waist and pushes one hip out. Then she spots my little kitchen set-up at the end of my dresser, along with my disappearing stack of canned food. "You're all set up in here, aren't ya?" She turns back to me on the bed and leans down so my one eye is level with both of hers. "So which is it, honey pie? Tricks or treats?"

"What are you talking about?" I moan. I just want them out.

"She means are you a hooker or a junkie," Will says. He opens one of my drawers and takes out a bottle of my perfume, spritzing it in the air and sniffing like a hound.

That's it. I sit up, slide off the end of the bed, and snatch it out of his hand. "Get out of my stuff!" I growl at him, throwing the bottle back in the drawer. And then, to Yolanda, "I'm not either one, for God's sake! I'm clerking the midnight shift downstairs in the lobby and I'm tired!"

Yolanda presses his lips flat. He looks like a duck.

"You ain't gotta get pissy, honey," he says. "We was just bein' neighborly. You said you was interested in sellin' some of da clothes you din't want, but you ain't in the mood right now. I feel you. We kin talk wich you when you feelin' better."

And now I feel bad for yelling at them. Well, at Yolanda. Not so much Will, especially since he's back in my drawer and lifting out my jewelry box. I snatch that away from him too, throwing it back in the drawer and slamming it shut. He glares at me, as if I'm being rude.

"You were out eating with that loser from the oil shop." He says it with eyes crushed to slits, as if he's accusing me of robbing a bank.

"So what?"

"Oh! A date!" Yolanda squeals. It's the least girly thing I've ever heard in my life.

"Are you gonna fuck him now?" Will asks and Yolanda pulls in a shocked gasp, his blue claws splayed across the bodice of his dress.

"Which one?" Yolanda asks. "There's some goo't lookin' mens over at that oil shop! And Will, do your mama know you talk like that? I bet she don't!"

"She don't care." Will swipes a finger across his nostrils like proof.

"I've met her," I tell Yolanda. "She doesn't."

"Scandalous," Yolanda sings, turning to look at the now-empty wall in my room where she'd helped deposit my garbage bags from home. "So you had a date!" He arranges himself gingerly on the edge of my bed, his chipped smile gruesome. "Tell us everythin'! This is betta' than watchin' the stories! We want to hear everythin', don't we, Will?"

"You're datin' a son'a'bitch," Will grumbles. He's got my perfume bottle again.

"It wasn't a date—" I insist, tearing it out of his hands and slamming it down on top of my dresser. "And you don't even know him, so why do you think he's a sonofabitch?"

"I can jus' tell," Will says, turning his head with his nose in the air. He follows it to the bathroom.

"Stay out of my stuff," I tell him, but when I glance back, my perfume is gone.

"So it wasn't a date." Yolanda smoothes back the frayed strands of her wig with two claws. "Then why don't you show us the clothin' you're lookin' to sell? I pay cash an' everybody kin use a little mo' money, ain't that right, lamb?"

I wish they'd both just get out of my room.

I start counting Ned's drawer at eleven o'clock on the dot. I've done it the last three nights, and he hovers over me every time. Tonight he's especially trying to hurry me along, but he's ten short again.

"No way am I signing off on that," I tell him. "We can sit here all night."

At ten after, I still haven't budged, so he yanks out his wallet and throws ten bucks on the counter. I pick it up with a smile and stick it in the drawer.

"Thanks," I say.

He slams the cage door behind him and shoves open the front door, the alarm shrieking in his wake. I already know I'm never going to see the ten he stole from me the other night. The best I can do is never let it happen again.

I settle into the office chair, still uncomfortably warm from Ned's butt. Putting my head back, I don't see Will on the landing tonight. If he is, he's silent and I'm not going to stir up anything.

By 1:30, I'm fading out again. I struggle to keep my head off the desk, but I give up when the clock won't flip the last digit and let even one more hellish minute pass.

The next time I open my eyes, it is because of the sharp rap of knuckles on the glass over my head. The clock says 2:43 p.m. and I smell smoke.

I lift my soggy cheek off the desk and cock back my head. A tiny woman with matted, white-blond hair stands on the other side of the counter, her forehead to the glass as she peers down at me. As I sit up, she backs away, almost tripping on the bed sheet she's got wrapped around her like a toga. Her eyes are only half open, her cigarette dangling from her fingertips.

"The movie's off again," she mumbles.

Oh, I do know her. It's Penny, Will's mom.

"Sorry." I stumble to my feet.

"I pay a lot of money to stay at this hotel." Her voice is soft, and disconnected, a thought, rather than a complaint, and her eyes loll from side to side as if they're on a wave-tossed ship. "I thought maybe there was something wrong with the TV, but then I come down here and you're taking a snooze on the job."

I'm assuming she's annoyed, but she sounds more amused than angry. Her eyelids don't open up the whole way, and they don't focus on me, so it's hard to tell for sure.

If she's mad, I'm ready to tell her how her kid follows me around being an idiot all day and I put up with it. How he took my perfume. But she just stands there, trying to find her mouth with the tip of the cigarette. All that seems to matter to her is that the porn isn't playing.

"Good thing it was me that caught you and not the boss, huh?" She blows out a line of smoke and tries for a smile, but her lips work like stretched-out rubber bands. I think this is her, trying to be nice.

I grab Cowgirls at the Cucumber Farm from a cardboard sleeve on the desk, remove the tape from the machine, and pop in the new film. When I look back at her, Penny's mouth is slack. She sees me looking and wipes the back of her hand over her lips, which closes them.

"All set," I tell her.

She snorts a laugh. "You think you can handle staying awake for your shift?" I think she's actually concerned. Or making a joke. I can't tell.

"Yeah. Sorry."

My head is still foggy enough that I can't tell if she's trying to do me a favor or threatening to tattle to my boss. When I manage to tug a grin onto my lips, I just hope it appears either appropriately apologetic or completely indifferent. Whichever fits.

The TV screen bursts to life with girls rolling around on a hay floor. Insects buzz and dart in front of the camera lens. Credits flash in between snippets of dirty scenes.

Penny works her mouth like she might have something to say, but she doesn't. She finally turns away, stumbling on her trailing sheet up the stairs.

I sit down again, and within minutes the haze that hasn't fully cleared is back. I put my head down on the desk and before I can even consider staying awake, I am already surrendering to the soft, sinking feeling that pulls me toward a dream.

I am flying. Dipping and rolling in nothing but air. I want to go up. The second I think it, I am launched like a rocket, pushing through the invisible boundaries of the sky. My body pops through the blue air of the Earth into the deep night of outer space. There are no stars, no planets, and I don't even care. I float like a tiny cloud, misplaced in the dark basin. Weightless in the beautiful blackness, every inch of me relaxes. I spread out my arms and soar through the void.

"Hey!"

In an instant, I'm yanked from flight and dropped back onto the chair in the cage. I fall into myself, eyes popping open, level with the desk. A stack of movie tapes sits a foot away from my face. A pen lies on a pad of paper. I pull up my head and the shrill ringing from the brightly lit phone panel rushes into my skull. I squint at the clock. 3:04.

My thoughts organize themselves. I am where I started again.

Someone is pounding a fist on the counter this time.

I raise my head a little higher. Will is there, his eyes stretched open so wide, they seem to touch the top and bottom rims of his glasses. He is on his tiptoes, struggling to pound the glass over the wide lip of the counter. Once I see him, he stops pounding but keeps jerking his head back and forth, between me and the staircase.

Change the tape!" he shrieks in a whisper.

"What?" I hear him perfectly, but his words tumble out of order in my head. He flaps his hands toward the TV as he watches the stairs.

"Put in a new movie! Hurry!"

"Alright..."

"Hurry!"

"Alright!" I growl over one shoulder at him.

His panic is aggravating. I glance at the empty staircase as I pull myself to my feet. I don't see or hear anyone coming. I figure the kid is having a great time putting me on, after having caught me in a dead asleep at the desk. It doesn't matter anyway. He's actually done me a favor since the last movie is sitting in the mouth of the VCR and who knows how long the phones have been exploding. They silence the minute the TV pops to life.

But, even with the new movie safely churning in the VCR, the kid is still wound tight. He stays hunched down, frozen in front of the counter with his eyes glued to the stairs. He watches as though he expects a grenade to come rolling down.

I yawn at him. "Why are you freaking out so much?"

"My mom's with Samson!" he whispers desperately over his shoulder. "You gotta keep the movies runnin'!"

I hear light footsteps and Will shoots away from the counter. He scuttles down the stairs leading to the ground floor. He hangs onto the banister with his neck straining upward as he tries to peek through the gap in the layers of floors overhead.

The drowsiness drains out of me as the footsteps grow louder. I lean across the desk, waiting to spot the grenade or the ghost or the end of the world that is coming down the steps at a steady pace.

With my face nearly pressed flat against the protective glass, the first thing that appears is Samson's shiny black oxfords. He is so tall that he gallops. Both hands are lined with gold rings like brass knuckles.

"You sleepin' again, Lael? Is that what they're payin' ya ta do?" He holds his decorated hand to his chest, caressing his baubles with the opposite fingers.

"Sorry," I say.

He smiles like I've agreed to something.

"I just started a new movie," I offer.

111

He taps his pinky, its fingernail as curved and brown as an old banana, in the deep shadow beneath his cheekbone. From my seat in the office chair, his downward gaze makes me feel small.

"This is a tough job for you, isn't it honey?" he asks softly. His voice thrums, but it has the wrong effect on me. It makes me squirm. He doesn't seem to care. "Maybe it's time you looked into a different line of work. Somethin' more fittin' for a beautiful young lady."

"I like it here."

His left iris has the shape of an upside down horseshoe, lying in the bottom of his dark eye. The center of it is as shiny as the scale of a black fish and it beats with his pulse.

"I just wanna be sure that you're on it tonight, sweetheart. So we get what we're payin' for," he purrs. I'm hardly listening to him. I am fascinated by the hypnotic throb in his eye. "No sleeping on duty, now, 'cause me and my woman's got a little gettin' to get to, an' I can't have you fallin' asleep and ruinin' a good thing for me. Get it? You know what I mean now, don't ya? Be a good girl an' keep them tapes runnin' for me, all right?"

"I will," I say, trying to move my focus from the vibrating center of the horseshoe. Samson chuckles and breaks my gaze himself by sinking his eyes to my lips and then further down, to my chest. I shudder and with one blink his eyes are back on mine again as though I'd only imagined that they'd left.

"It's all good then." He raps on the counter twice as he moves away from it, the rings glinting. "Thanks again."

"Yup."

Samson glances around the lobby as he moves to leave it and catches sight of the staircase leading down to the first floor.

"That you, Will?" Samson asks with a good-natured grin. He peers into the shadows.

"Yes," Will squeaks.

"Me an' your mama is partyin' up there." Samson's voice hardens as he speaks. "It's no place for you, got it? You stay away for an hour and I'll make sure you git yourself a new fishing pole or somethin'." Samson puts his ringed, right hand into the front pocket of his slacks and jingles some coins. "You wanna fishin' pole?"

"What's it for?" Will's voice wavers from the shadows.

Samson turns back to me. "How come the lights down there ain't on?"

"Oh...uh...burnt out, I guess." I shrug.

"Maybe you could change a light bulb instead'a sleepin'." A muscle flexes in the side of his jaw as he glances at Will. Samson rattles the change in his pocket again before looking back at me. "And watch that little bastard when you do. He pro'ly stole your bulbs. He's a little fuckin' thief. He steals money out my pockets all the time."

Samson turns and goes up the stairs, whistling. The sharp pitch sticks in the air, but the tune finally disappears with the distant slam of a door from the third floor.

Will is still frozen at the bottom of the staircase.

"He's pretty scary, huh?" I say when I collect myself enough to speak.

Will creeps up into the lobby, his eyes on the stairs. "I ain't scared of 'im."

"He scares me," I say.

"He's a liar."

"Don't worry. I don't think you'd steal light bulbs."

Coins, definitely, along with perfume and cans of root beer...but not light bulbs.

Will stands in front of the payment slot, still watching the stairs as he runs his fingers over the front counter, following a tiny vein in the marble pattern.

"I'm gonna be rich someday," he says.

"Oh yeah?" I lean my elbows on my side of the counter and put my chin in my palms. "Sounds like you're going to be a fishing pole richer, if you just stay down here for an hour." I feel bad for him about that— having to stay out of the room so Samson and Penny can get busy.

"He can't tell me what to do," Will continues. "I don't want no fuckin' bastard fish pole."

For his age, this kid's got a mouth like I've never heard. He says fuck as much as I say the, but I'm starting to see why.

"Then ask for something else," I say. "I'd stay out of his hair though. It sounds like all you have to do is let him hang out with your mom alone for an hour, and he'll buy you whatever you want."

Will shakes his head. "He ain't hangin' out. They're fucking."

TEN

T*he phone is* becoming my alarm clock.

11:03 p.m.

I almost think it's a mistake, or that it's eleven in the morning, but then I pick up the phone and Ned shouts at me from the other end, "Where the hell are you? I've got places to go! If you're going to be late, it's five bucks every fifteen minutes. My time's worth money!"

"Sorry," I say, jumping up and stumbling in circles, disoriented. "I'll be right down."

"You better be. You already owe me five bucks..."

I hang up on him, grab my back pack, and load it up. Fairytale book, sketch book, pencils, nail polish, three bucks. I sling it over my shoulder. The phone rings again, but I know it's Ned, calling to yell at me some more, so I don't answer. I just stuff my key in my pocket and head downstairs.

Before I make it to the landing, Will's door opens, but it's not him that steps out. Samson locks eyes with me.

"Hey there," he says, closing the door behind him. "Good to see you, Lael."

"Hi," I say, trying not to be rude, but trying not to slow down either.

Ned's probably dialing my phone like a lab rat.

Samson reaches the doorway to the landing first, blocking my way.

"Sorry, I don't have time to talk," I say. I'm not really sorry at all, but relieved that I've got someplace to go. Samson gives me the willies.

His fingers are on the middle button of his suit coat, and his smile looks like he just took it out of a can.

"We haven't had a chance to talk yet and I've been meanin' to do jus' that, Lael." His voice is soft as a baby's blanket. I cringe inwardly at the sound of it.

"I've got to get downstairs," I say. "I overslept, and Ned's been blowing up my phone. He's pissed that I'm late."

I try to side-step him, but Samson drifts along with me. I step back and so does he, like we're dancing. Come. On. His smile is a little too intentional.

"They work you hard here, don't they?" he says, tsking beneath the thread-like line of his moustache.

Up close, Samson's skin is a rich, flawless cocoa. It looks more like a brutal tan, than heritage. He doesn't have the thick lips or wide nose of a black man either, but his hair shows the black branch of his race. His wiry curls are coated with oil, the slick waves pressed meticulously against his skull. I think it's whatever he puts in his hair that makes him smell like no man I've ever smelled before. And it's this smell, forever more, that will remind me of this moment.

I'd feel so much better with a few inches of bulletproof glass between us.

"Ya know, if you were my woman...I wouldn't even let ya work. You too fine for that." He adjusts his body, gliding into my personal space, his large, brown hands winding around my wrists. They feel like moist handcuffs as I pull back and he tightens them.

Samson moves closer and I stumble back against the wall. He's angled so

I can't slide out and slip through the door to the stairs. The stuff in my backpack is lumpy and jabs my spine. Samson's breath smells like turpentine.

"Listen, just listen to what I got to say," Samson whispers, but his hands squeeze my wrists so hard, my pulse stops. His black eyes are the size of whole planets. "Girls like you, I just want to take care of 'em. I can feel you shakin', but I ain't the man you need ta be afraid of. I'm the man who looks out for ya. I kin make your life so much easier. I kin give ya a job where you kin make all the money ya want."

My heart rebels, throbbing to rush into my hands. The sound of its trapped beat floods my ears.

Ned shouts something from downstairs and I hear Will call back, "I'll go see if she's comin'!" Seconds later, Will shoots through the door onto the third floor, rounding the corner and aimed for my room. He comes to a skidding halt at the sight of Samson, pressing me flat against the wall.

I mouth help to Will, but the kid turns away as swiftly as he came. He races back to his own room door and pounds on it with his fist.

"Hey," Samson barks at him, but it's too late. Penny swings the door open and steps into the hall, first looking at Will, and then she sees Samson smashed up against me.

"What are you doing?" she barks as Samson lets go of my hands. But she's not talking to him. She's talking to me.

"I've got to get to work downstairs," I squeak.

"Yeah, you better git downstairs," Penny barks.

"I was jus' havin' a talk with Lael," Samson explains smoothly. He pivots and I slide away from him. "Ain't none of your concern, Penny."

Free, my adrenaline takes over and I dart away. I shoot around the corner, onto the landing, and race down the stairs. When I hit the lobby, Ned leans off the office chair and opens the cage door. I nearly bowl him over to get inside.

"What the fuck, Fail?" Ned snaps. I slam the door behind me. "Fifteen minutes late! You think I got nothing else to do but sit around and wait for you all night?"

"I'm sorry," I stammer, but I'm trying to keep quiet enough, as if I can hide in plain view. "It wasn't my fault. Samson stopped me on the third floor—"

"Like I give a shit," Ned says from the office chair. "I counted the drawer, all you gotta do is sign off on it."

I try to steady my breathing. "Let me just count it real quick—"

"Look, I have to get out of here and you're late fifteen minutes late," Ned says. "You should've been down here when you were supposed to be, instead of making me call you and wake you up. Now my whole night is fucked."

"It's only fifteen minutes," I say. "And it was a mistake. I'll come down fifteen minutes early tomorrow. Just give me a minute, and I'll count it really quick."

"Fine." He stands up, knocking over the chair so it clatters on the floor. "Count the fuckin' drawer. But just so you know? I've got to say somethin' to Clive about this. I don't get paid to work my shift and yours!"

I feel like he's scooping out my heart as he talks. I haven't even worked here a whole week, and if Clive knows I was late, I might lose this job. I'll have no money, no rent. I'll be homeless.

Samson struts down the stairs. The moment I see him, I turn my eyes back to the desk top. He says hello to Ned as he passes the cage. Ned says, how you doin' buddy, to which Samson answers by continuing out the door. The alarm screams and when the door closes and it is quiet again, I glance over my shoulder through the blinds that face the side street. Samson's beat-up, white LeBaron cruises past, toward the boulevard. My heartbeat slows to a jog.

"Don't just sit there," Ned complains. "Count the fuckin' drawer."

"Forget it," I grumble, grabbing the till sheet. "Just go. I'll sign off. Just leave."

"You should trust me, Lael," he says in a calmer, softer tone. "I counted it twice."

I nod. I should be able to trust him. He's my co-worker. Maybe his mistakes have been as honest as mine. Maybe my eyes were playing tricks on me. Or maybe it was my mistake and I didn't charge enough or count back the right change.

Right now, even being the pervy guy he is, I feel a thousand times safer with Ned in the cage, than I did on the stairs with Samson. I'll take any pity Ned's willing to shell out and be grateful for it. I'll give him four cans of ravioli and show up early every day for the next two weeks if he wants.

And right now, I'll give him the faith that he's counted the drawer and left it square.

I sign the till sheet and Ned grabs the doorknob.

"See ya, Fail," he says as he goes out. "And ya better be here at least fifteen minutes earlier tomorrow, with the drawer square by the time I'm supposed to leave, or I'm saying somethin' to Clive for real."

Despite wanting to trust Ned, I count the drawer once he's gone, just to be sure. I count it all out four times to be absolutely sure. The last stack of bills flutter out of my quivering grasp.

I'll have to sneak up to my room later and bring down twenty bucks.

I pick up the phone and set it back down, twice.

Twenty bucks.

My first thought is to call Lavina and tell her about Ned. And Samson. I'm scared to leave the cage to get the twenty dollars, because I don't know if Samson's coming back. But if I wait until Lavina comes in and counts the drawer, I'll have to let her know face-to-face that I fell for Ned's manipulation again. It might be easier to hear her tell me how stupid I am over the phone. And I deserve to hear it. I just let Ned walk out of here with my money again.

I stand up and knock over the office chair, just like Ned did. It clatters against the cage floor, but it doesn't make me feel any better. My eyes well up.

I pick up the phone to dial my mother. Maybe we can work things out with the insurance so I don't get pulled over and thrown in jail. The dial tone goes to the busy signal, as the receiver rests on my shoulder. I can't get my mom's spinach money out of my head. She's not going to work anything out with me. She'll love it if I call…it will give her a chance to be all high and mighty, laughing her condescending laugh that she does when she knows I'm in trouble and have nowhere else to turn. I'll be giving her exactly what she wants—the upper hand—so she can smash me under it like a bug. The busy signal on the line goes dead. I drop the receiver back down on the cradle and tip my face up toward the ceiling.

"Will," I whisper.

Nothing.

The loneliness is like itching powder inside my veins. I pick up the phone again and dial Lavina's number, written in faded pencil on a sticky note located behind the phone console. I bite down on my fingernail, wincing at the clock as the phone rings on Lavina's end.

Four rings and a man answers.

"Hi, this is Lael," I say right away. "I'm sorry to call so late. I work with Lavina at the Starlight hotel."

"Uh huh." Whoever he is, it doesn't sound like he cares who I am.

"Whuch'you want? She sleepin'."

"Oh, um...who am I speaking to?" I ask.

"That ain't yo' bi'ness. You call't me," the man says. "Whuch'you want?"

"I just wanted to talk to her. About a short in the drawer."

"In her drawer?"

"No, mine."

"An' how's that her problem?"

"It's not," I say.

"Ahright, then I'm sho' she'll talk ta you tomarr'ah." He hangs up.

I pull my heels up on the office chair and lay my cheek on my knee.

"Will?" I whisper again.

There' still no answer from above.

The good thing is, I'm too terrified to fall asleep in the cage. I imagine Samson finding Will's tiny hole in the ceiling and somehow scaling down into the cage on a bed sheet. I check the door knob to make sure it's locked about a thousand times. The cage door is so flimsy compared to the solid barrier of the counter and the bulletproof shield that reaches the ceiling. A bullet wouldn't make it through the glass, but I think the door is a whole other thing.

Around midnight, the front door opens and the alarm yanks me out of my trance. I stand up from the chair, the kinks in my back and legs nearly crippling.

A fat, little, white man, with white hair and a beard to match, waddles into the lobby. He's got a long, stained pillow case slung over his left shoulder like a ghetto Santa, but instead of a red suit, he's wearing a button-down shirt with wide, yellow rings around the armpits, and a salmon pink, sleeveless, pullover vest.

He hurries through the lobby like he's late for Christmas. By the time the front door closes, he's already passed the vending machines, slipping a grimy finger through each coin return as he goes.

I watch through the cage door window, but Santa has no interest in me.

He goes into the lounge and dumps his filthy, stuffed pillow case on the last cushion of the couch. He takes a seat beside it, reaching down to pull off his duct-taped boots and line them up carefully, their heels touching the edge of the couch. Punching down his lumpy pillow case, he swings his legs onto the cushions, rolls to his side, facing his shoes, and goes completely still.

What am I supposed to do now?

What am I supposed to do now? Clive told me I better keep the homeless out, but he didn't say how I was supposed to do that. Then again, all Clive seemed worried about was that they'd drink the coffee or rummage through the fridge, but Santa hasn't even given that side of the lounge a second glance.

I'm afraid to even approach the man—he could be crawling with bugs, or rabid, or nuts. I've never seen a homeless person up close, but I've heard they're all vicious and crazy. I think they'd have to be, to live on the street. I remember one news report where a homeless guy, who was sweet and harmless at first, snapped when he couldn't get the money for his booze. The bum killed a guy who brought him breakfast every day.

I watch Santa laying motionless for a few more minutes. I'm not positive, but I'm pretty sure he's already snoring. I could sneak over there, scare him awake, and tell him he has to leave. And Santa might jump up and kill me. Or, I can drift back down onto the office chair and let the guy sleep.

An hour later, I've abandoned all thoughts of going to the bathroom, or retrieving the twenty bucks to balance the drawer.

Will shows up on his perch overhead. He hangs his head through the hole and immediately launches into a million questions about the guy on the couch, as if I'm an authority.

"Why's he here?" Will whispers.

I shrug. "I guess he needs a place to sleep."

"He ain't got no room?"

"Nope."

"Then he's a bum, Lael, and anybody can't jus' come in here and sleep! My mom says bums are filthy fucking retards."

I tip back my head to glare at him. "Don't talk like that."

He glares back a moment and then gives up and looks away, probably back at Santa again. "Lavina's gonna fire you."

"Lavina's not my boss."

"Yes she is. She's gonna yell at you, and then you're gonna get throwed out."

"No I'm not." I rub my temple. He's probably right.

"She's gonna fire you 'cause you let bums sleep wherever they want to, and they're dirty. You're making it all dirty around here."

"Have you looked at yourself?" I ask him. "If we had to throw everybody out who was dirty, you'd be the first to go."

Will squinches his nose. "But he stinks."

"I bet you stink worse than he does, and you can take a shower whenever you want."

"I'm telling Lavina on you," he says.

"No you won't. Lavina scares the crap out of you. Besides, I'll tell her you broke that vase that used to be up there on the ledge. And then I'll tell her how you steal stuff off her cart too."

I've caught him, more than once, stuffing handfuls of tiny soap bars in his pockets.

"You're a big, fat brat that lets bums stink up everything," he says.

"Why don't you come down here and do your stupid robot pose for him?"

"Shut up, always-sleeping-at-the-desk Fail!"

"Jeez, you're such a brat. I'm done talking to you." I grab my backpack from the floor. The tip of my brown nail file pokes me, so I slide it out and begin to scrape my nails with it.

"Stupid," Will says again.

I keep filing away, in silence.

"I said, you're stupid," Will says.

Still, the only response I give him is the gritty scrape of my sandpaper stick.

"I'm gonna spit on you. Hear me?" he says. "I'm gonna spit right on you, and then I'm gonna spit on that fucking filthy bum too."

I don't look up from my nails although I'm worried that he might actually do it this time. I don't think he could launch a goober as far as the couch, but I know he could definitely hit me. Still, I keep filing.

"Stupid retard...you're so dirty and stupid..." Will taunts from overhead. "Lael's so big and fat...you're a big fat stupid, filthy, dummy retard..."

I take out a bottle of Lilac Sparkle polish and put a thin coat on each nail. I blow across my fingers to dry the paint. Will keeps up his chant.

Will shuts up every time people come in, so I rent three rooms in luxurious silence, even though I smear my wet middle fingers in the process. Once they're gone, Will starts up again. I ignore him and try to fix the smudges with more polish.

After a few more choruses, Will's chant tapers down into a yawn. I blow across the fifth coat of Lilac Sparkle in silence as I hear him climb over the rail and scurry up to his room.

Santa is gone when I wake up the second time, but looking over at the empty couch makes me feel the same way as when a spider would get loose in my room back home. I'd think I clobbered it with a shoe, but no. It scuttled away and hid, regrouping to pop up someplace else...maybe even on me.

I shiver, wondering if Samson snuck back in while I was napping too. My neck is stiff, probably from it lolling on my chest or falling back in my sleep. At least there weren't any wake-up calls that I missed.

I rented six rooms, all under weird circumstances.

The first was to a man and woman who paid me with stacks of quarters for a short stay.

The second room I rented was to someone Yolanda brought in—a surprisingly handsome bald man who wore sunglasses, even though it was two in the morning and pitch black outside. He rented the room and Yolanda, giggling wildly, acted like he'd never seen me in his life as he clung to Mr. Sunglasses's arm.

The third was to a man who kept peering around the lobby as if someone was going to jump out at him. He wanted a corner room with no one in the room beside his. Since I don't know the room numbers really well, I made a guess about which room might be on the end and when he didn't come back to exchange the key, I figured I got it right.

The fourth was to a woman who had a dog collar around her neck. The man that joined her in the lobby never said a word as she rented the room—only picked up the short leash and jerked it toward the stairs once I'd given her the key. I heard her barking, all the way down in the cage.

The fifth room went to a woman who stood silent, her hands at her sides and eyes on the floor while the man with her complained to me about room rates and how I better keep the fucking movies running. Evidently, it wasn't his first time here this week, or maybe Ned fell asleep sometimes too.

The last was to an old, white guy who asked for a three hour short stay and wanted extra towels sent up to his room. It was three in the morning. I told him the room had towels, but he shook his head.

"I want extra," he insisted.

"Well, the maid won't be in until seven a.m." I said.

"There's no maids working?"

"Not at night."

"Why don't you just bring them up then?" he asked.

"I'm only a clerk. My boss insists that I stay at the desk. I think there are four towels in the room already."

The guy bristled a little. "How come you don't have a maid for the night shift? There was always maids before."

I shook my head. There are four towels up there. What's he doing? Making a dress?

"That must've been the old management."

"Better management, if you ask me," he grumbled, but reached into his back pocket for his wallet again. "Well, then, I guess I'll pay for the whole night."

I took his money and made a note for Lavina to deliver towels.

"Oh, sir?" I called after him as he headed for the stairs. "Will there be someone joining you? I'll need a name if they want to go past the lobby."

That was one of Clive's rules. Nobody goes up the stairs without a key or a name of the person who rented the room. Lavina said to call the cops if anyone ran up on their own, but that hasn't happened yet.

The guy turned on the stairs. "For Christ's sakes, just send up the towels."

It's 7:40 now, and the thought of the twenty bucks has weighed on me all night. It's got to be in the drawer before Lavina comes in.

I press my face to the window in the cage door, surveying the lounge (empty), the lobby (also empty), and the basement stairs (too dark to see past the last step—creepy). I hurry out of the cage, lock the door behind me, and shoot up the stairs to the third floor. Glancing at Will and Penny's door, I sprint down the hall as fast and light on my feet as I can, fumble the key into the lock on my door, and finally get inside with my heart battering my ribs.

I snatch a precious twenty out of my broken jewelry box and race downstairs as fast as I came up. I hate Ned.

My heartbeat returns to a semi-normal beat but as Lavina's ancient brown Cadillac pulls in, it starts thumping again. She's going to ask me about the phone call so late last night. Now that I've put the twenty in the drawer, and counted the till three times over earlier, I'm not going to even bother telling her that Ned shorted me again. I don't need the lecture.

But when Lavina comes in, she brings Jonah right behind her, carrying a brown box with cleaning supplies in it.

Oh no. I really don't want to talk about what happened last night in front of both of them again. Especially when she made me feel like such a dummy last time.

"Thanks for da help," Lavina tells Jonah as she rounds the counter for the cage door. "If ya don't mind none, I'd sho' 'preciate a han' puttin' that box on the shelf down in da laundry."

"No problem," Jonah says, flashing me a smile as he passes the cage.

"Ya know, Clive keep puttin' more re'spons'bilities on me, but he ain't payin' me no mo' money," Lavina complains to him as she side-steps her way downstairs. "He got me workin' five days a week! Ned threatened ta leave, so Clive jump right to it! He got Tavon as a back up for Ned and Lael's days off, but Clive still ain't lifted a finger to git another maid ta help out wit' mah load."

"You too good at what you do," I hear Jonah tell her.

When they come back up, I unlock the cage door. Lavina's puffing, but Jonah isn't even winded.

"Your son is taking over my shift tonight?" I ask. I remember Jonah mentioning it.

Lavina blows a gust of air from the corner of her mouth. "Whuch'ya think? Clive gonna stop rentin' rooms 'cause you need'a day off? That man'd work ya all seven days if 'e could. My boy, Tavon, comin' in. He gonna earn a lil' extra."

Tavon. That's probably who I talked to last night.

"And how are you doin', Lael?" Jonah asks as Lavina gets out the drawer. She goes as silent as a 300 pound mouse as she starts counting. I'm ecstatic that she's not asking about the phone call last night.

"I'm good," I say. When he doesn't take his eyes off me, I start babbling. "Just tired. I was awake all night, you know...graveyard shift. But it was pretty busy. I kept the movies going—" I jab my thumb at the TV behind me. "And I rented six rooms. Four short stays, two overnights. Oh, yeah, Lavina—the guy in Room 22 wants extra towels. A lot."

"Whuch you mean a lot?" she asks, pulling back the edge of her lip.

"He said he wants extra towels. He was really annoyed that there was nobody to bring him more towels even before he went up to the room."

"Oh now," Lavina smirks. "The man's up there by his'self?"

I nod. Lavina turns to Jonah. "Jonah, you do me one more thing? You bring that man up there 'is towels? I have a feelin' it ain't towels he's wantin' on."

I blush as I realize what she's implying.

"I can take them," Jonah says. He goes down to the laundry, brings up two fresh towels and two washcloths and goes up the stairs. He trots back down a few minutes later, grinning, as he enters the cage. He motions for us to stay quiet as the man from Room 22 stomps down the stairs and rushes out the door, cursing under his breath.

Once he's gone, Jonah shakes his head with a laugh. "You called it, Lavina."

"He din't want no towels, did 'e?" She laughs too. "Dat dere was one'a da ol' hotel customers," Lavina explains to me. "He want his'self a woman. Dis place used ta be fulla hookers. Dem peep holes on da basement floor doors was so da hookers could see when da cops was comin'. Them women would crawl out da windows down dere an' run 'way, down da sidewalk. An' da mens that come in here, orderin' towels, it was dere way ta say dey wanted a girl up in they room. Hand towels was fo' one thing," Lavina slides her fist up and down to signal a hand job, "towels was fo' 'nother, an' everythin' meant somethin'. Dat way, nobody in the hotel heard nothin' but da girls goin' up ta deliver towels to da rooms."

I blush hard with Jonah standing beside me.

Lavina holds her stomach as she laughs. "What'd he say to ya, Jonah?"

"He said Lael talked him into a full night stay and 'that white girl didn't bring up no towels!'" Jonah pats my back as he laughs. "He was hot that I was the one standin' outside his door with towels. Cursed me out for playin' 'im."

Lavina throws her head back with a guffaw. "Ohhh! I bet he was hot after waitin' all night ta git a little an' nothin' come up but a big ol' Jonah!"

Lavina continues to laugh as she puts away the money drawer and signs off on the till sheet.

Jonah looks over the top of Lavina's head at me. "You hungry?"

"Me? Uh," I scrape the back of my leg with the front of my opposite foot. I stopped thinking about Jonah since I haven't seen him in a while. "I'm super tired. I think I'm going to go upstairs and get some sleep."

"I'm starvin'," Lavina pipes up. "I could go fo' some egg an' biscuit."

Jonah hasn't looked away from me. "I could really use some help carrying back the boxes."

"You carried them all last time," I pointed out.

"Then you owe me one," he says.

"I'll come," a voice says from overhead. All three of us crane our heads back and look up at the ceiling at Will, his head through the hole. It looks like there isn't any more of him than a head and spindly neck.

"You up on dat ledge?" Lavina shouts at him. "Dere ain't no rail up there! Get offa dere 'fo ya kill yo'self!"

Will disappears with a frown, but two seconds later he's downstairs, teetering off the third step as he hangs onto the rail like a skydiver.

"I'll carry the boxes for ya," he offers Jonah. I hope Jonah lets him too. Otherwise, Will is going to be down in my room trying to mooch a couple cans of food from me.

"I don't think your mama would want you goin' to breakfast with a stranger," Jonah says.

"She don't care," Will insists. "She ain't gonna wake up 'til afternoon anyway."

"Yo' mama okay up dere, lil' man?" Lavina asks. Her voice is surprisingly gentle and Jonah cocks his head at Will, the two of them seeing or hearing something in what Will said that I don't.

Will pumps his head up and down. "Her and Samson was up partying late, so she said to get my breakfast someplace else, 'cause she's sleepin' in." Will pumps his muscle man arms for Jonah. "I'm strong. I'll carry all the boxes for you, I swear."

Jonah looks Will up and down. "Looks like you could use a little bacon 'n eggs."

Will just stares back at him, his huge eyes boinking behind the glasses, but as I look at Will too, I start to see the whole frail boy swinging back and forth, holding the stair rail. I've never really noticed how much Will's pants sag on him. Were they sagging that much a few days ago? His face is always filthy, but it's not just dirt that makes his cheeks look so hollow—it's that they are. I realize that it's why his eyes look so big— because the rest of his face is made up of that sharp jaw and pointy cheekbones. The ridge of his nose is too thin and that's probably why his glasses are always sliding down and he keeps shoving them back up. Not just because they're broken.

Will yanks up his pants as we stare at him. The cuffs are a couple inches too short, but the ankles that stream into his sockless, filthy shoes are just bones.

My God. I was worried about giving him a couple cans of tuna.

Jonah rubs his chin as if he's on the fence as to whether or not he'll take Will.

"Me and Will can both come," I say. "If you need more help carrying boxes."

Jonah lights up at my offer. "I suppose I do. Now I've got all kinds of help this morning," he says to Lavina.

She chuckles, handing him a five dollar bill for her breakfast. "At leas' you gittin' whuch'ya payin' fo'," she says.

I slide into one side of the booth at Red's and although I think Will is going to sit beside me, Jonah knocks knees with me instead. Will has the whole other side to himself and he's so small, it looks like he's sitting alone in the middle of an eight-man life raft.

"How you like your eggs?" Jonah asks him. He's been talking to Will the whole way here, which has taken all the pressure off me.

Will raises his bony shoulders. "I dunno. All I ever had is scrambled."

"Scrambled is the best," Jonah says. "You like pancakes?"

"Yup." Will nods like there's a spring in his neck.

"You want bacon or sausage?"

"Can I have both?"

"I think it comes with one or the other." Jonah glances at me from the corner of his eye. "But we can get you more, if you can eat it all. How's that?"

Will's spring-loaded nod goes off again. "I can eat it. I can eat a whole plate of hash browns too. Two plates, even."

Jonah's smile is a little strained. "Sure," he says. He knocks me with his shoulder. "You're quiet."

"Just tired," I tell him.

I am, but I've also been listening to how Jonah's been talking to Will during our walk to Red's. Jonah's voice was deep and tender as he asked Will all kinds of stuff about himself, like what superhero Will likes best (he's got a Spiderman pillow) and how old he is (ten—wow, I thought he was a lot younger by the way he acts and looks and talks) and where he and his mom lived last (a different hotel). Jonah was really listening too—his eyes were on Will the whole time, instead of flicking back and forth between us—which would've been a dead giveaway that he was trying to earn brownie points by being nice to the kid in front of me. But I don't get the feeling that Jonah's like that. He seemed genuinely interested and laughed when Will said something funny.

Jonah might actually be a genuine guy. He asked me to come to breakfast, but it doesn't seem like there's a catch. He's barely looked at me and hasn't said much to me the whole way here—it's been all about

Will. To be honest, I'm starting to miss some of the attention, as the two of them continue to laugh and talk without really including me.

"Samson's your mom's boyfriend, isn't he?" I ask Will.

"Uh huh," he says.

The waitress brings coffee for Jonah and me, hot chocolate with an elf-hat glop of whip cream on top for Will. Will attacks it, sucking it down and makes a face when it burns his tongue. He grabs a tub of creamer the waitress brought for our coffee, rips it open and pours it on his tongue. He swallows it down, rips open a second one, then a third, then a fourth.

"Don't drink all that! You're going to get sick," I tell him.

"I won't," Will says, a dribble of cream running out of the corner of his mouth. He wipes it away by sliding his whole lower arm across his face.

"So who's this Samson?" Jonah asks me. "And why you want to know about him?"

"'Cause him and Lael was gonna fuck in the hallway," Will says cheerfully.

Jonah's gaze turns razor sharp as I gape at Will.

"We were not!" I whisper-shout across the table. "Samson attacked me!"

Will seems shocked. "That's what I said."

"No it's not!" My coffee sloshes over and burns my hand as I set it down. I curse.

Jonah scratches his eyebrow. "What happened, Lael?"

"It was...he was—" My face grows hotter than the coffee burn on my hand. I don't want to explain. I wasn't smart enough to avoid Samson, wasn't strong enough to get away, or even brave enough to face him again.

Jonah waits for me to answer. Will tops off his cocoa with tub after tub of cream until it's all gone.

"He pushed me up against the wall," I finally say.

"He was humpin' her," Will adds.

My throat feels stuffed full of wet mittens.

Jonah sits back, his coffee on the table in front of him. A tiny muscle jumps in his jaw and I feel like I've done something to upset him. I'm not sure why I feel the need to say I'm sorry, but I do.

Will scowls at Jonah. "It wasn't Lael's fault."

"I didn't say it was," Jonah says. He blinks as though clearing his mind and turns his soft, brown eyes back on me. "Stay clear of that guy. I'll be keeping an eye on the hotel a little closer now. You let me know if you have any more trouble, understand?"

Oh. My heart is light. It's the way I used to feel when I was little, swinging on the swing set. I would kick up and lean back, pulling hard on the swing chains, until I'd finally rise up so high, for a split second it would feel like I was floating in the sun like an angel, or a piece of dandelion fluff. Jonah, saying he's going to watch out for me makes me feel even lighter than that.

The waitress brings our food and Will forgets me completely as he dives into his platter the same way I did on the first day Jonah brought me here. And Will eats the same way he looks: like he's starving. I'm ashamed again that only an hour ago, I was thinking of hiding in my room all day just so I didn't have to give the kid a lousy can of tuna. I can hardly eat.

Jonah orders Will another plate of pancakes and I ask the waitress for a box. I figure I can give it to Will when he's hungry later.

When the pancakes come, Jonah places the order for Lavina and his co-workers and orders Will an extra side of sausage before he turns back to me. It's a lot like when the sun pops out from behind the clouds. He's looking right at me with an easy smile slipping across his lips. He's got straight, white teeth, and for the first time I notice how handsome Jonah is. He's thick and broad in the shoulders, long and lean in the waist. It's taken all this time for me to see how his eyes are so deep and insightful.

"Watch anything good on TV lately, Lael?" he asks.

Will's busy stuffing his pockets with the sugar packets, butter and jelly tubs that the waitress brought. I focus on him instead of answering because my mind is swimming in guilt, as if Jonah could know that I've been watching channel three every afternoon, lying naked on my bed beneath the sheets. As Jonah waits for an answer, my tongue twists, imagining that there's a hidden camera in my room somewhere.

"Let me guess," Jonah says.

My face is on fire, I can feel it. Don't let him guess, my mind shrieks, not in front of Will and a whole restaurant of people trying to eat breakfast!

"I watch the news," I blurt.

Jonah laughs. "The news? Why would a girl like you be interested in the news?"

"I don't know," I stammer. "I want to know what's happening, I guess."

"Around here?" He chuckles, blowing on his coffee. "Nothing good, that's for sure."

He scans the restaurant like he always does, and when his eyes return to mine, I smile at him. Jonah makes me feel safe. I float as Jonah returns my smile.

Will kicks me under the table. Hard.

"Ow!" I suck in a breath and glare at Will. "What'd you do that for?"

"Nothin'," Will mumbles, glancing at Jonah. "It was an accident."

"Well don't do it again!" I tell him, reaching down to rub my shin. I look back at Jonah, but the moment is gone. My hair almost falls in a dimple of syrup on the table, but Jonah catches it and tucks it behind my ear as I continue to rub at what is probably going to be a bruise. "Jonah," I grimace, "do you know where there's a grocery store around here? Someplace not too far?"

"Not too far?" He thinks out loud as his eyes rove away, out the window. "There's a Shop 'N Eat in Royal Oak, off Washington. It's not a big place, but it's pretty good."

Will perks up his head, a few pieces of hash browns still hanging from the corner of his mouth like straggling roots. "I'll go with you."

"Maybe," I say. Yolanda's taught him that help equals free food, but I don't know if I can afford that much help.

There is nothing like being stuffed full of food and exhausted at the same time. I leave my Styrofoam box of leftovers on my dresser, climb over my mattress, and collapse on the pillow. In the soft, warm sheets, I turn thoughts of Jonah over in my mind.

He paid for my breakfast and Will's. He made Will carry most of the boxes of food back, but when I told him it looked like Will couldn't handle it all, Jonah bent down and whispered to me, "It's to make him feel like he earned his breakfast. He better burn off some of it too, or he'll be throwin' it all up. Did you see all that cream he drank down?"

I also saw how Jonah asked the waitress for extras of all of it, even after Will had already filled his pockets. It warmed me that Jonah understood. When we left the restaurant, Jonah held the smaller bag out to Will and said, "These are for you, buddy."

And the whole way back, Jonah watched out for us, scanning the sidewalk and the corners, always looking, always watching. He didn't miss one word I said either, asking questions to keep me talking and hanging on my every answer. When a car rumbled by on the street, hitting a pot hole with a bang, Jonah's arm shot straight across the front of me, scooping me behind him. His work clothes smelled like fabric softener. Jonah laughed when he realized it was just a car that made the noise, but I really believe that if anyone on the street tried to cause us trouble, Jonah would wrap his tall, brown body around mine and become a human shield.

Whether I mean to or not, I'm starting to love how Jonah makes me feel when he's around.

ELEVEN

*I*t's *been four* whole days and Jonah hasn't come to take me for breakfast again. I'm a little ashamed that I'm craving warm eggs and bacon so much that I've convinced myself that I'm craving Jonah's company too. I can't take anymore orange crackers and root beer from the vending machine, that's for sure. My clothes are getting loose.

I roll out of bed around noon and drive down to the store Jonah told me about, nervous as a bag full of cats and watching for cops until I pull into the parking lot. I don't know how the cops know if you don't have insurance or if you do, but I know if they find out I don't, I'm in trouble.

By the time I make it back to the hotel, I am exhausted. I have two grocery bags full of food. Jonah waves from one of the open service bays across the street, but he doesn't come over to help me carry in the bags. With my arms full, I can't wave back, but I want to. I haven't seen him and...I kind of miss his big, bright smile.

I thought all the way to the store and all the way back about how I would tell Jonah all about my adventure—how I couldn't find anything in the aisles, and had to go up and down the rows about forty times, and how I gave up on finding the tuna, which I don't like anyway. In my head, when I imagine myself telling Jonah, it's all funny and charming and he laughs at all the right parts.

But Jonah is too busy working to give me a hand. I juggle the bags to throw open the front door of the hotel.

What wasn't charming about grocery shopping was how much everything costs. My mouth watered when I smelled the rotisserie chicken churning in the deli, but it was $5 for a whole chicken. I couldn't have eaten the whole thing in one day and putting stuff in the community fridge downstairs—Will would probably take it, or lick it, or sneeze on it. No thanks.

The food set me back $22.74. I didn't expect that. The money I'm earning is going almost as quick as I get it. The spinach money seemed like a fortune until I started paying for gas, and food, and toothpaste. I bought seven cans of ravioli, a jar of peanut butter, a jar of jelly, a marked-down loaf of white bread, a box of a dozen Ramen noodle packages, packets of drink mix and sugar, two bags of chips, a box of Twinkies, a box of Oreos, and a box of saltines. And the toothpaste. I had to put a magazine back on the rack because it was too much.

I lug up my bags, depressed. Money, money, money—it's all I think about now, and how Jonah didn't come running to help me.

I hear Lavina arguing with Clive before I even reach the third floor. They're standing outside the room next to Will and Penny's and when I step off the landing into the hall, it doesn't slow them down one bit.

"I cain't keep workin' these hours, Clive, I tole ya that!" Lavina's standing next to the cart, her finger moving like a windshield wiper under Clive's nose. The toothpick between his lips twitches. It seems to incense Lavina. Her head slides back and forth on her neck as she gives it to him, both barrels. "What you think I am? A machine? Ya like ta say I keep dis place a'float, but I cain't keep workin' like I been! I been doin' my job, plus orderin' all da cleanin' supplies, checkin' folks in and out, an' doin' all the laundry. You got me runnin' up an' down like I some teenager! I come in sick, I come in on holidays, I work six days a week, an' I work double da day after I got a day off 'cause there ain't nobody ta keep it all caught up, but me! How much you think one person kin do?"

Clive pulls the toothpick from his mouth. "You can take an extra half day off like I tole you to!"

Distressed is an odd look for a man like Clive, with his golden tooth and gaze that could scare lions, but that's exactly how he looks right now. He looks like he's found the end of the rope and is losing his grip.

"Take it off?" Lavina snorts back at him. "Din't ya hear what I said? I got three times da work ta do when I come back! It like I neva had no time off at all! You gotta fine some mo' help. I cain't keep on like this!"

"I been lookin' fo' somebody, but ain't nobody been right." Clive rubs his brow. "Don't know what else you want me to say."

"You bin lookin' for two months! I wanch'ya ta say ya foun' somebody! An' how you been lookin'? You been lookin' at da TV screen in yo' room? Or lookin' 'roun yo' dinner table? Lookin' on da sidewalks as ya drive in?"

"Careful now, Lavina," he says, his index finger in the air.

"Ya gotta put ads in da newspaper! Do interviews! Ya ain't gonna find nobody jus' askin' 'roun da poker table."

"You're runnin' me ragged," Clive says, turning away from Lavina and waving to me. I think he'd welcome any distraction from Lavina's glare. Clive's toothpick rolls from the front of his mouth to the left corner of it. "Lael, I'm thinkin' of switchin' you from clerkin' to house cleanin'. Whuch you think 'bout that?"

I set my bags of groceries on the floor by my feet.

"No," Lavina says, planting her fist on her thick hip.

Clive looks back at her. "Why not? You shoutin' at me for help and I'm gittin' you help! It's easier to find a clerk than a maid."

"You heard what happened down the street," Lavina says, her voice dipping downward, along with her chin. She looks up at Clive from beneath her flat brow.

"Don't you start wit' that now," Clive says, thrusting the toothpick back between his teeth.

"That maid was kill't wit' an ice pick! You won't let that door stay locked whiles I'm up here cleanin'. It ain't safe for nobody, let 'lone a girl from the country!"

I gulp as soon as she says it. Ice pick? Killed? No way am I being a maid.

"I got ya an alarm on the door!" Clive argues.

"Whole lotta good it'd do me! 'Sides, you only put that in so I wouldn't miss any customers. Don't ya keep spoutin' how it *fo' security*!"

"Ahright, Vina, ahright." Clive shakes his head. "I'll put an ad in the paper tomorr'ah."

"Good." Lavina grabs a tiny bottle of shampoo and a thin square of soap.

Clive picks up another bottle from her cart and frowns. "Why'd you get the premium kind? Folks here don't care if it premium or generic."

"If I'm doin' da orderin', den you git whuch you git," Lavina says. A long look hangs in the air between them and I'm more than a little surprised when Clive breaks into a smile. He shakes his head and turns for the stairs.

"You right, Lavina," he says with a chuckle. "You always right."

He disappears down the stairs and Lavina turns to me, eyeing the bags of groceries. "Out spendin' all yo' money?" she asks.

"Jonah told me where to find the grocery store."

"Dere's one in Royal Oak, on Warshington."

"That's where I went." I heft my bags back up, into my arms. "Have you seen Jonah? Isn't he bringing you change anymore?"

She screws up her face. "Whuch ya mean? He still bringin' it every mornin'." She pauses, a smile spreading on her lips. "Oh, wait now. Ha'come ya lookin' fo' Jonah, Miss I-don't-date-no-black-men?"

"It's not like that," I say, drawing back my head with a scowl, like she's crazy. I know how she feels about black men dating white women and I don't need her needling me about it. Sometimes she reminds me of my mother. I'm not about to tell her how often I've started to think of him. "We're just friends, that's all."

"Jus' friends?" She studies me closely. I guess I pass her inspection, because she gives up quick and picks up some disinfectant spray off the cart. "Well, that's smart. So why you lookin' fo' 'im? You wantin' a 'nother brea'fast?"

"No," I shift my bags for emphasis, to show her I have my own food. "I was going to ask him about my car," I lie, but as I think of it, I realize it's actually a great excuse to speak to him. "It's making a noise."

"Oh," she says, swatting me away with a swipe of a green rag in the air. "Ahright, then. G'wan an' put them bags away. They look heavy."

In my apartment, I open up a bag of chips, sit on my unmade bed, and dig in. This would've made my mother's head pop off. An unmade bed? Shameful. Working my way through a bag of chips by myself? Gluttonous. I can hear her nagging in my head: you should be eating a real lunch...that mess of a bed is embarrassing...I can't believe you're living in a hotel like an addict!

I stuff down another handful of chips, the crumbs falling all around me until my bed look like a crime scene stencil.

Someone knocks on my door.

I hope it's Jonah, until I stand up and bits of chips rain down on the carpet. My bed's a mess. I throw the covers over the mattress, pounding out as many crunchy wrinkles as I can before stuffing the chip bag in my dresser drawer that houses my kitchen utensils. I wipe my face with one palm, then the other, and I unlock the door. I open it with a smile.

"Hey, girly girl," Yolanda says. I'm relieved for about as long as it takes him to tromp into my room in his enormous kitten heels. He's wearing a blue, scoop-neck leotard and hot-pink sweat pants bunched up at the knees. "I was jus' wonderin' whuch you up to?"

"Not much. Just hanging out."

"Well, if you got time, how about them clothes you wanted to sell?" He digs into the neckline of his leotard and pulls out a twenty dollar bill.

Almost as much as I just spent on groceries. And Ned's short in the drawer.

My gaze goes right to the small line up of shoes I have beneath the thermostat. I was just thinking about the pair of brown wedges parked there, and how I really don't have much that goes with them. Except the skirt with the huge pocket on it, which I absolutely hate. I open my drawer and pull out the skirt, along with a rayon blouse that is wadded up so bad it might never unwrinkle again.

"I have a few things," I say.

Yolanda doesn't waste a second. He picks up the clothing, one piece at a time, with a squeal for each. When I dump the wedges on the bed, Yolanda lets out a whoop that I think will interrupt the entire floor.

"How much, darlin'?" he asks.

"Well, these were thirty," I say, my fingers on the wedges. "The skirt

I got for twenty, the blouse...it's really wrinkled...I can't even remember how much it cost."

"Got any jewelry?"

I open up another drawer and pull out the broken ballerina jewelry box. Popping it open, the rest of my mother's spinach money is right on top.

"Uh, uh, uh!" Yolanda yelps. "Where'd you git all that money, lamb? You didn't say you was rich!"

"I'm not," I tell him, digging into the bottom of the box and pulling out a clip bracelet. I also take out a pair of earrings that always pull down my earlobes too much. Yolanda towers over me, peering into the box. I clap it closed and put it back in my drawer, piling my underwear, bras and socks on top before kicking the drawer closed with my heel. "That's all the money I've got," I mumble, as if I have to justify the cash. "I've got to pay for everything myself now."

Yolanda's watching me with a smirk so high that the right corner of his lips almost touch his nose. "You ain't got nuttin' to worry 'bout from the looks of it."

"It's not enough," I say, but I let the list of things I have to pay for trail away.

"So how much for the clothes?" Yolanda asks.

I feel guilty asking for anything now that he thinks I'm rich. At least, I'm richer than he is.

"Would ya take fifteen?" he asks.

"Yeah," I say. It's not twenty, but I feel guilty for having money that he doesn't.

Yolanda's smirk disintegrates into a frown as he holds out the twenty dollar bill. "You got change, baby? This's all I got right now."

"I don't," I say.

"Kin I pay ya tomorr'ah then?" Yolanda asks as he gathers up the jewelry, clothing, and shoes.

Now I'm frowning too. I didn't think he would be taking my stuff without paying for it first. "Tomorrow?"

"I ain't got no change is all, lamb," he assures me, clipping the bracelet on his wrist. It doesn't quite fit, buckling on top. "I can get this bill broke and give ya cash in the mornin'."

"Lavina can probably break it now."

"Oh, she a busy, girl!" Yolanda says, swatting away the idea. "I don't wanna go down there and tear her 'way from her work jus' for this! Don't tell me ya don't trust me, now!"

No. I don't. Last time I spoke to Yolanda, he was staggering down the hall, wasted, and he wasn't even making sense.

"C'mon now! I'll bring it to ya firs' thing tomorr'ah. I promise."

I can tell he's not going to do this any other way. "Alright. I guess…"

"Good!" Yolanda says with a clap, squeal, and a tiny hop. He heads straight for the door. "Alright, sweetie, I'll have the money for ya tomorr'ah. Or by the end of the weekend at the very latest, okay?"

Wait. What?

The phone rings.

"You get that, baby," Yolanda says. The phone rings again. "I'll have yo' money to ya soon! Thanks, lamb!"

The door slams shut.

I go around the bed and pick up the phone. "Hello?"

"Lael?"

Oh my God. Of course.

It's my mother.

It's like she has a red light that pops on, making her rush to the phone and call me whenever I'm having the worst moment ever.

"It's me, Mom."

"Oh. Good. How are you, Lael?"

"Fine," I say.

"Anything new?"

Her asking as if she's sincere is new. "I'm dating someone. His name is Jonah."

"From the hotel? Are you sure you want to date someone from a place like that?"

"I'm from this place now. And he's incredible."

"But someone from that area..." Her insinuation trails away.

"If you're trying to ask me if he's black, he is." And fuck you, Mom.

"Lovely," she adds with a sarcastic sigh. "And how old is this fellow?"

Oh brother. "He's twenty...two."

"Does he know you're still a minor?"

"He doesn't care."

"I think he would definitely care, if anything between you two happened. He could get in a lot of trouble..."

"He doesn't care," I repeat stiffly. "He's a better adult than any of the other ones I know."

Silence.

"Well, I'm calling to let you know," she says in a voice so pointy, it jabs me in the eardrum, "you no longer have car insurance or healthcare insurance."

No, this isn't why she called, although she does love to grind it in. But she already told me she was cancelling those, so here we go. Again. Always.

"Sounds good," I say dully. That will jab her back. Nothing raises her roof more than not being able to get to me. "Thanks for letting me know."

"We've also changed all the locks on the doors, so your key won't work any longer."

I stuff a handful of chips into my mouth, crunching them down in her ear. "Super."

There's a long pause, with just the sound of me chewing and swallowing.

Then, in a very small voice, my mother says, "Why, Lael? Why did you leave like that?"

I stop short. This is new. She sounds vulnerable, but not in the pity me way she usually does. She sounds like she's actually interested in knowing what went wrong. I'm going to have to circle this conversation with extreme caution. Guard my flanks, keep my guns ready.

"It was because of Bob, wasn't it," she rasps.

No. Bob was only part of it. He was the trailing muffler on a rusted car with a bad engine and leaking tires.

This all started with her ignoring me, because she was busy falling in love with Bob. It gained momentum when my mother realized Bob wasn't the prince she'd thought and, since she couldn't fix him, her focus turned to fixing me by picking apart every inch of my life—you could stand to lose a little weight, Lael; B's aren't good enough, Lael; you don't need to be dating, Lael.

And then, she started keeping track of everything I put in my mouth. She insisted on checking over every homework assignment I had. She had excuses why I couldn't go out with friends from school or on dates with boys—family dinner, chores like Cinderella, grounding me for my grades.

But, I know my mother. No matter how much she says she wants to know why I left, how this happened...she'll never accept that it began with her.

Still, I'm going to tell her the truth. Maybe I'm still annoyed that Yolanda just walked out of my room with all my *shit*. Maybe it's because my mother just opened this whole conversation with letting me know how she cancelled all my stuff and changed the house locks. Whichever it is, I'm going to give her the truth canon-style, because, if nothing else, it's going to result in great fireworks.

"No, it wasn't Bob," I tell her. "I think Bob made it worse, but—"

"I know you thought you lost me when Bob and I got together."

"No, mom, it wasn't—" I start again.

"I was falling in love, Lael, and I thought you were old enough not to be so needy anymore."

Uhm, fuck her.

"I wasn't," I say flatly. "Jezus, if you'd stop talking for two seconds, Mom, I'd tell you—"

"Bob's drinking got a little out of hand, and we both had to deal with that," she puffs.

I shut my mouth. We've only had this conversation eight hundred million times already, and my mother is already so far down the old rabbit hole, I can't even grab hold of her ankles to pull her out. She wants to blame Bob and she's not going to settle for anything less than that. Still, I'm not going to agree with her when it isn't the truth.

"It's not about Bob!" I shout into the phone.

"Of course it was," she sniffles. "When you grow up, you'll understand how hard it is when someone you love has a problem with alcohol."

"No, Mom, it wasn't Bob! And I'm grown up enough now to tell you—it was you! You want to control every move I make and every thought I think!"

"I do not," she says with an indignant sniff.

I drag my point right back to the center of the conversation. "Yes, you do. Just like you did just now! You've been correcting everything I say that you don't like, but it's still what I think, Mom!"

"So you just want me to sit here and not say a word? That's what you want?" she says and then the line goes silent.

Here is where we always go, and I'm so, so, so tired of it. She's not going to say another word. I can rant all I want and at the end, I'll blow up because she's not talking and she'll say, I thought I wasn't supposed to say anything.

But this time, I'm not going to play the game.

"I've gotta go, Mom," I say.

"I thought you were going to tell me what you think?" she says. The snark in her tone has me itching to make her cry, but this time is going to be different.

"Nope," I say. "I'm at work and I can't stay on the phone. Talk to you later."

"Lael!"

Oh no! She's losing her hold!

I smile as I hang up, gently laying the receiver on the cradle. In my head, I take a bow and whisper a sublime, fuck you.

"*Ya need a* hobby or some'pin," Lavina says when I park myself opposite her cart on the third floor. I've got my sketchbook and pencils, and I'm drawing a wolf from my Grimm book. I'm sure Will would be hanging over my shoulder if he and Penny hadn't gone out to the store.

"This is my hobby," I tell her.

"Maybe ya need ta go out wit' friends."

"You're my friend." It's embarrassing to say it, like I'm asking her permission to be sure it's true.

"I'm talkin' 'bout men friends."

I get closer to the paper as I sketch out the wolf's ears. "Are you talking about Jonah?"

She leans on the cart. "Why yo' mind go right to Jonah?"

"You said men and Jonah's the only man outside this hotel that I talk to. Unless you meant Ned."

She raises an eyebrow. "You think I'd eva' tell anybody ta go out wit' Ned? C'mon now. An' I don't know 'bout Jonah neither, but you bin hangin' 'round wit' 'im?"

"Nope. I haven't seen him in five days."

"Huh," she says, taking towels from the middle shelf of her cart. "You certainly is countin' da days."

"No, I'm not," I say, making extra pencil strokes of fur down my wolf's throat.

The door to Penny's room opens and I stiffen at the sight of the foot that steps into the hall. Samson. The only thing that makes me okay with seeing him is that Lavina is here too. Even though she's in the room and I'm in the hall, I know she's close and won't let anything weird happen. I still cringe when his gaze falls on me.

Lavina's name rises in my throat, but I can't get it past my teeth as Samson walks toward me. A grin spreads like a disease beneath his thin moustache.

"Hey there, sweet thang," he says. His gold-ringed hand snakes into the pocket of his tan slacks as he comes to a halt, hovering over me. "Where ya been, Lael?"

Lavina's humming in the bathroom as her name just sits on top of my tongue. I can't shove it out. My eyes flick to the open door, but Samson slides right in between, blocking my gaze. He peers down at me, tossing change around in his loose pocket. My head is almost in line with his crotch. The sound of his coins jangle my nerves.

"We got interrupted last time we was talkin' and I don't know that I got my point 'cross correctly." He smells so heavily of hair gel that my stomach flips like a runny pancake.

150

My pencil is frozen, my body won't do anything but breathe.

"You need somethin', suh?" Lavina asks sharply from behind Samson.

He turns to her, gluing a wider smile to his face, but he removes his hand from his pocket. Lavina's fists are balled at either side of her waist.

"Just talkin' to my friend, Lael," Samson says.

"Lael," Lavina doesn't take her eyes off him, "you friends wit' dis man?"

"He's Penny's friend," I say. No way is he mine.

"That sound mo' right ta me," Lavina says, eyeing Samson up and down. "Man yo' age usually ain't friends wit' lil' girls."

Samson rattles his change. "Don't know how any'a this is a maid's bi'ness."

Lavina glances at me. Her lower lip crushes up against her upper one. She looks away, picking up a bottle of glass cleaner. "Nah, you right, it ain't. But this girl works here and she s'posed to be helpin' me wit' these rooms, not sitting 'round talkin' to friends." Lavina looks back at me. "Well, git up!" she barks. "You gittin' paid ta work, not sit dere drawin' pi'tures!"

I jump to my feet, stepping on my pencils. "Sorry," I say. I rush into the room and Lavina swats my thigh with the rag as I go past her.

"Sorry ta haf ta interrup' ya, suh," she apologizes to Samson, but she also shuts the room door behind both of us. Lavina and I both wait until the front door alarm announces his departure. We peek out the window and watch his LeBaron pull out of the lot before Lavina turns back to me.

"How you know him, really?" she grills me with a bristle-brush tone. "You bin talkin' to him?"

"No!" I say.

Lavina squints at me. "Well, good. Stay 'way from 'im. That man's been in here b'foe, an' he ain't nothin' but trouble."

Lavina opens the door again, but I stay in the room, leaning on the wall while she runs the vacuum.

As Lavina coils up the vacuum cord, a woman appears, knocking on the metal door frame with one knuckle. She's a gorgeous black girl with Asian eyes and glossy hair. I recognize her immediately. I checked her in last night with a skinny, red-haired white guy. She's hunched over a little and clutching her side.

"Can I help ya?" Lavina asks.

The woman's smile quivers. "You got any free aspirins on yo' cart?"

Lavina shakes her head and the woman grimaces.

"You okay?" Lavina asks.

"Got a busted rib or two, I think," the woman says. Then, "There was a man up here a minute ago. Either of ya know 'im?"

"His name's Samson," I say.

Lavina shoots me a look as she asks the woman, "You know 'im?"

"Not any more. We used ta date, so now I stay outta his way." Her way of saying date sounds nothing like the dinner-and-movie kind of thing. The woman winces as she changes position. "If ya ain't lookin' to date 'im, you should stay clear'a him. He rough on his dates, if ya know what I mean."

"He a pimp," Lavina says flatly. She hooks her chin at the woman. "You stop workin' for 'im?"

The woman nods. She's a hooker? Was a hooker? I checked her in, but I assumed the guy she was with was her boyfriend. She looks like she's not that much older than me, but then, the guy didn't either. I thought hookers always dressed in leather, with horrible make up—like some of the ones who have come in. The only ones I've been for sure about at the front desk are the ones who come in with old, gross men. Now I'm assessing every couple that's come in for a room.

"Goo't fo' you," Lavina says.

"He ain't none happy 'bout my bein' gone, so don't go tellin' him that you seen me, ahright?" the woman squeezes her side. "I kin come back from a couple broke ribs, but I cain't get outta dead."

"We neva' seen nobody." Lavina carries her cleaners out to the cart. "I think I know ya. You been in here b'foe, right?"

"A couple times."

"Wha's yo' name?"

"Saturn."

"Yeah, I thought so." Lavina says. "I tell you what—I might have some asp'urn down in the cage. I'll go down an' check right quick."

"Thank ya," Saturn says.

Lavina leaves Saturn and I standing in the hall. I have no idea what to say to her, but she takes care of it.

"How long you know Samson?" she asks.

"I don't, not like that," I say.

"He tell you how he gonna treat you if you was his yet?" Even shifting the tiniest bit, she winces.

I nod, but she shakes her head.

"Nah, I don't think he really did," she says. "'Cause he didn't tell you he was gonna beat ya, did 'e? Or that he was gonna take all yo' money? Pro'lly din't tell ya that, did 'e?"

"How do I get him to leave me alone?"

"Worse fo' you, if he want you," Saturn says, pinching her waist.

"You need to go to a doctor," I tell her.

"Ain't got no money to go ta no doctor." She puffs a laugh, followed with a deeply pained grimace. "Ain't got no money to go home, neither, and my baby girl's wit' my neighbor. She gonna be wonderin' where I'm at, but what kin I do?" She looks at me then, hard, like she's trying to place me. I shuffle my feet, her gaze is so heavy. "Ya know," she says with a tiny, sharp inhale and a wince, "you remind me of my lil' sister. She sweet like you. She gone now, though. One'a her boyfriend's took her out—kinda like this one tried to do me today."

"I'm so sorry," I say, putting a hand on her arm.

"Me too. She was a good girl. Shouldn't'a been in this kinda job. We all jus' do what we gotta, right? I do it for my baby girl, ya know? Ain't nobody else gonna feed 'er."

A surge of pity overtakes me. "How old is your baby?"

"Boo's jus' seven months. She a lil' chunk." Saturn's smile is small and sad. "She know how to say mama now too. She says it every mornin'. Not like that son'a'bitch that busted me up and din't leave me a penny to git home." Her eyes fill and her gaze falls to the floor. "Boo gonna be lookin' fo' me and I ain't gonna be there."

"I'm sorry," I tell her.

A grin zaps across her lips and is gone. "Too bad sorry don't get me a cab ride home."

I think of her little baby at a neighbor's house, waking up and not having her mama—her broken mama that can't afford to get home. It stirs me up.

"Hang on." I tell her, putting one finger in the air. My heart feels lighter, thinking of what I want to do. "Just stay here, okay?"

"I cain't go nowhere else," Saturn says blandly.

I shoot down the hall to my room. I open the door and go to my dresser, lifting my jewelry box out of the clothes piled on it in the bottom drawer. There's hardly any thought in my head but one: I'm going to do something good for that little kid that wants her mama.

I know it's a stupid thing to do, considering the cliff between me and financial security is crumbling away pretty fast. But I can't seem to change it, so at least I'm going to do something that will make me feel good. I take out five bucks. It won't get her too far out of the city, depending on where she lives, but it should get her wherever she needs to go within it.

I put my box back into the pit of my drawer and go down the hall to Saturn. She's got one hand on the cart, but is still gripping her side as Lavina comes around the corner with a plastic cup of water. Saturn drinks down the aspirin as I reach them.

Saturn tosses the cup in the garbage pail on the cart.

"Here," I say, holding out the five dollar bill. Lavina's eyebrows raise. "To get home to Boo."

"Who's Boo?" Lavina asks, looking between us.

"My baby," Saturn says, snatching the money from my hand. She squeezes her side. "I best be callin' that cab. Cain't wait ta see 'er." She looks at the bill. "This might be 'nuff to get me close to home, but I don't think it'll get me all the way. You got any more?"

That's not the response I expected. More? What she got is already more than I can actually spare.

"Uhh," is all I can get out of my mouth as my eyes dart back and forth between Saturn and Lavina. Lavina looks sour. "That's all I've got," I finally manage.

"It'll have ta work," Saturn says. It's like I've insulted her and our new found sisterhood. "At least it'll get me some'a the way."

Saturn shuffles back to her room and opens the door without another glance back at us. The metal door slams shut and blasts a cold draft on what was my helpful mood.

"You got money ta be throwin' away, you should'a said so. I could use a bucket er two." Lavina says closing the door on the finished room and pushing her cart down to the next one.

"She's got a baby and she couldn't get home," I explain.

Lavina unlocks the next door, rolling her eyes at me. Rolls her eyes!

"What?" I say, following her into the room with her toilet bowl cleaner and brush. "I was trying to help somebody else out! Why's that so awful? The guy she was with broke her ribs and left her without anything so she couldn't even get home!"

Lavina chuffs. "Weeds figure out a way ta grow, don't they? They do it with water, an' they do it when ya jus' leave 'em 'lone too."

"You don't think I should've given her anything to get home? I was just trying to help!"

"Help's somethin' that girl's gotta do fo' hu'self. She pro'ly got money stuft in her bra, or down in her boots where it oughta be. Ain't nothin' you gonna do gonna change 'er. She be right back here tomorr'ah, makin' money the same ol' way she always do. But you—you's gotta start lookin' out fo' yo'self. You ain't got money for every weed that spring up."

It sounds like—and feels like—every time my mother chewed me out for doing something wrong. My stomach gets heavy, even though I've hardly eaten anything in a couple days, and I get hot all over. Maybe I'm going to throw up.

"I was just trying to help!" I argue, my tears stinging like peroxide as I try to hold them in. My sniffle only seems to annoy her more.

"Now listen here," Lavina snaps. "City's fulla people like that one. Some of 'em's good and some of 'em's not. They'll take ya for everythin' you got, 'specially when yo' willin' to jus' give it to 'em. Ain't they fault. They all tryin' to survive—that's they job. But da's yo' job now too. Peoples in Detroit is jus' like weeds. No matter how much poison gets poured on 'em, no matter how much they get stomped down. And girl, don't you pity 'em none. They's damn good at survivin'. That's what weeds do."

I'm crying now, streams of tears running down my cheeks and off my chin. I can only pull in tiny breaths, my lungs aching. Lavina ignores me, dropping her toilet brush on the cart and snatching up a rag and her sink and tub cleaning solution. She goes into the room and I hear her spritzing as if she's putting out a fire.

When she comes back out of the room, she takes one look at me and slams her cleaner down on the cart.

"You gonna have ta g'won and go cry someplace else, Lael," she says. "I don' mean ta upset ya, but ya gotta learn, and fast, if you gonna live in a place like this. Betta you hear it from me, rather than gettin' kilt fo' not knowin'."

I nod and escape to my room.

I'm not going to answer the knock at my door, because I think it's Lavina.

But I should've known better. Lavina doesn't give a crap that she's bashed in my feelings.

"Lael, you home? Open the door and see what I got!" Will shouts from the other side.

I have cried myself dry. I open the door a crack.

"Look!" Will shoves a plastic bag in my face. I get a glimpse of two water guns, one blue and one purple, before Will pulls them away. "Let me in!"

God. Whatever. I open the door and Will spills in, stumbling over the flapping sole of his shoe. He's too excited to really notice my puffy eyes.

"We was gonna get my glasses fixed today, but Samson took our money, so we didn't go." He pushes up the taped center of his rickety, messed-up glasses.

"He took it all?"

"No. My ma always keeps some in my pillow case so we can git food."

I guess every mom hides some spinach money.

"But since we couldn't git my glasses done, we got tacos and my ma took me to the store for a sorry present."

"What's a sorry present?"

"Whenever we miss a appoin'ment, I git one." He holds up the package of squirt guns, shakes it. "And we missed one today!"

I swipe the bag out of his hand. "How many appointments could you have?"

"Whenever we go to the doctor's. For my Uncle Lodgist."

"What are you talking about? Who's your Uncle Lodgist?"

"My cancer doctor," he says, ripping the package open.

Cancer? He flashes into the bathroom.

I follow him, stopping in the doorway. "You have cancer?"

"I dunno," he shrugs, holding the blue gun under the faucet. "We don't go no more." He plugs the gun, lifts it, and shoots me in the face.

"Hey!" I shriek. He darts past me out of the bathroom and pulling open my door.

"Bet you can't find me!" He uses the door as a shield, his scrawny arm poked around the side as he sprays me again with a pin point stream of water.

There's nothing I can do but defend myself.

The door slams as I scoop the purple gun out of the sink. I fill that sucker to the hilt. With my key in my front pocket, I dash out the door.

Will's not in the hallway, but Penny is.

"Hey!" she says. She shuffles toward me in an unintentional serpentining line. This is what high looks like, even though I'm not sure what she uses to get this way. All I know is that it looks like she's going to fall asleep, but she's still moving. "I wanna talk to you."

"I was just looking for Will."

"Come here." Penny swipes her hand like a bear claw through the air, in an awkward motion for me to follow. She opens up her room. I don't want to go in there, but Penny says, "Hurry up!"

I step inside and the smell hits me like a truck. Samson. Then, the stink of crusty feet. I don't go in any further.

Their room is trashed. Empty fast food bags and cups litter the dresser and overflow the little trash can. The floor is speckled with bits of paper and trash and dirt. A pile of soiled clothes sit in a mound in the corner. The bed sheets are swirled all over the mattress, and there's a ratty Spiderman sleeping bag on the floor with a dingy, matching pillow, as flat as an empty wallet, tossed on top.

"Does Will have cancer?" I ask. The stink of Samson is suffocating.

Penny rounds on me, her half-closed eyes moving like marbles on a short, sea-sick track. "I don't think so," she says. "But I wanna talk to you 'bout Samson. You know we're dating?"

I put my hand up to my nose, pressing the edge of it against my nostril to block the stench. "I guess—"

"Well, we are," Penny snaps. "And I don't need any other girls sniffin' aroun' for 'im."

"I'm not!" What the hell? "I don't want anything to do with him! He caught me in the hall when I was going down to work—"

Her mouth sets in a grim line. "He said you called 'im over to talk with 'im."

"If I never talk to him again, that'd be fine with me!"

She considers it, and I think she's trying hard to focus on me, but her eyes keep rolling away. "How come?"

"Because he scares the crap out of me!" I tell her. I don't mention Saturn and what she told me and Lavina. Best to keep my mouth shut on that. "I don't want anything to do with him. Ever."

Penny tips her head back and tries extra hard to focus on me. Her mouth flops open. After a couple seconds, she smacks her lips and looks away.

"Just stay away from him," she mumbles.

"Not a problem," I tell her as I head for the door. I can't wait to breathe fresh air. "I've got to go find Will."

"Okay," Penny says, sitting down on the edge of her messy bed. Her eyes roll and she whispers, "Okay."

I let myself out, gulping the air in the hallway. Will peeks around the doorway to the landing.

"What'd she want?" he asks, scratching his cheek with the barrel of his water gun.

"To tell me to stay away from Samson."

"Oh," he says and he lifts his gun and fires, hitting me right in the face. Before I can even wipe off the water, he races down the stairs.

Everything else—Samson, Penny being high, Lavina yelling at me, if Will has cancer—it all disappears as I sprint down the stairs after him. He's a whole flight ahead, giggling hysterically, and he jumps off the last three stairs to the lobby floor as I'm rounding the second landing. I grab the rail and race down, but when I reach the lobby, I freeze.

Jonah is standing at the payment window, his elbow on the counter.

"C'mon Lael!" Will shouts from the basement, but I slow down, brushing the hair out of my eyes and gasping for breath, embarrassed to be caught playing. I swing my hand with the water gun behind my butt.

"Hi," I say. Jonah's changed. Something about him is different, even though I can't detect what it is. His eyes look deeper—both the color and the way he gazes at me. His skin is as smooth as marshmallows melted in deep chocolate. He's not wearing his work uniform, instead, he's wearing jeans and a short sleeve button down. He looks sharp. I've missed seeing him.

"Lael!" Will shouts again from the basement level. "Lael, I'm down here!"

"How ya been?" Jonah asks. I peer into the cage, but Lavina's nowhere to be seen. How long has he been standing here?

"Are you looking for Lavina?" I glance at his hands—no blue canvas money bag either.

"No," he says, tipping his head. "I got off work early and I came to see you."

"LAEL!" Will screams.

"I'm not playing anymore!" I shout over my shoulder at the basement stairs. Then, turning back to Jonah, "What did you want?"

"I was wondering if you're working tonight?" He shuffles his feet. He's still wearing his big, black work boots that he always does.

"I'm waitin', dammit! Dammit, dammit dammit!" Will chants from downstairs.

I ignore him, consumed by the short distance between me and Jonah. I feel it like a loss and I don't like it anymore.

What's happening to me? Jonah's a black guy.

But as I look into his eyes and he stares back, I don't see anything but *Jonah*, the one person who always wants to make me feel good.

"I've got to work at eleven," I tell him.

"Would you be up for dinner before your shift?" he asks.

His gaze gives me flutters, but I slide backward in my excitement—I really like Jonah, but getting into his car? I don't know if I trust him that much yet. But if we don't go out, the only other option is to invite him up to my place. The only furniture I have is my bed, so that's not happening.

But I don't want him to leave.

Will pops up from the stairs. "She don't wanna go nowhere with you!" He goes back down just as fast as he came up.

"Shut up, Will!" I snarl at the stairs.

"Oh, wait," Jonah says, pushing off the counter.

"No, it's not that I don't want to go out, it's just that—" I squirm, unable to tell him. I don't know how I can feel so drawn to him and still so scared of him at the same time. My gut isn't giving me any clear direction.

"You do want to go out with me, don't you?" He dips his head down while looking up at me, so his eyes are even larger. They swallow me whole.

"Yes," I say.

"No she don't!" Will hollers.

I stomp to the stairs and rain my whole reservoir of water down on Will in angry shots. He shrieks and runs from the bottom of the steps, tripping on his flapping sole. I hear him splat on the floor and curse. I walk back to Jonah.

"I swear, it's not that I don't want to go out—"

"I know you don't want to go far 'cause of work," Jonah says with a wink. "Don't worry 'bout it. I got an idea."

"What?" I ask, his grin jumping to my lips. His voice is so soothing, my gut settles. I know by just his tone that everything is going to be okay. Somehow.

"I'll be back for you at eight." He taps two fingers on the counter before turning for the door.

"Where are we going?"

He flashes me another grin from over his shoulder. "You'll just have to wait and see."

My stomach flutters with a cup of excitement and a pinch of worry.

Jonah goes out the door and I'm immediately hit in the temple with a stream from Will's gun. I turn and race down the basement stairs after him.

TWELVE

*J*onah's a half hour late and I've been sweating since 7:45. I've gone downstairs twice—once for ice, and this second time for a Coke—hoping that Jonah would walk in and catch me, so he wouldn't have to come up to my room, knock on the door and have to be invited inside. I especially don't want Jonah coming in when I'm not downstairs, because Ned's at the front desk, which makes waiting downstairs awful too.

"Plannin' on gettin' laid tonight huh, Lael?" Ned says from the cage. A blush shoots up from my neck like a feverish thermometer.

"No," I snap. "I'm going out with a friend."

"Friend, huh?" Ned laughs. "You always put on the whore paint that thick for friends?"

"Shut up," I tell him. I knew I shouldn't have used the bright eye shadow. I thought it looked exotic, but maybe I just look like a hooker.

Ned snorts. "I could erase your whole expression with a trowel."

"Her skirt ain't short enough to get laid," Will shouts down from the second floor landing ledge. I think that's his version of help.

Ned tips back on the legs of the cage chair, staring up at the hole overhead.

"What the hell you doin' up there?" Ned says.

I can't see him, but I can imagine Will does what he always does. Disappears.

It's confirmed when Ned says, "Where'd ya go? Hey, kid!"

"Whu'dya want?" Will hollers. I'm sure he's poked his head back through the hole again.

"What do you know about getting laid?" Ned asks.

"None'a your bizness!" Will says.

"You said her skirt wasn't short enough," Ned argues. Still staring up at the hole, he stands up from the chair. "See, as a dude, you gotta know that every skirt is short enough! You gotta know how to grab it at the bottom edge and whoop! Ya flip it up over her head and..." Ned grinds his pelvis, staring at me as he does it.

"I'm gonna spit on you," Will says.

"You do that and I'll come up there and throw your fucking ass off that ledge."

Ned's behind bullet proof glass and still, nobody feels safe.

I'm going to puke. My heels are pinching off the circulation in my toes. I buy the Coke and go up the stairs.

"Don't talk to Ned," I tell Will as I hobble past him, squatted on the ledge. "He's not fooling around."

"He's a fucking cock puke," Will whispers. Then, "Don't try to get laid, okay?"

"I'm not going to get laid!" I shout at him, stomping up the steps to the third floor. Every step is excruciating in the heels.

"Yeah ya are," Will grumbles.

"NO, I'M NOT!" I shout as the front door alarm goes off.

"Hey, man," I hear Jonah say down in the lobby. "How are you doin'?"

"Good," Ned says and then, hollers, "LAEL! Hey kid, is Lael still up there?"

"She's comin' back down!" Will reports.

The sound of Jonah's voice is like a titanium shield against Ned and Will's comments, but I quickly rub my palms on my face to remove as much make-up as I can. I try to steady myself on my heels despite my numb toes.

"She's been running up and down the stairs, waitin' on you for the last hour, man," I hear Ned telling Jonah.

Idiot.

"Yeah, I had to get a few things done." Jonah says. Heading down the steps to the lobby, Jonah comes into view. He catches sight of my legs and follows them up as I come down.

All I can think of is my skirt and if it's too short. Or if Jonah knows how to grab the hem, like Ned said. The heat in my face spreads from my cheeks, down through my chest, and into my arms. I'm on fire.

Jonah's eyes finally meet mine and his smile explodes. He doesn't have to tell me I'm pretty—his face says it all. So does his appearance. He looked good before, but irresistible now, wearing designer jeans and a navy shirt that clings to him. He's left a sexy hint of a shadow on his jaw and as I reach him, I smell the faint scent of lemon that instantly relaxes my nerves.

"Ready to go, Silver Spoon?" he asks.

I nod. I'm not crazy about him calling me that, but the way he says it, with a quick wink, I don't bother telling him. I'm going to get in his car, if that's what he has planned. I trust him.

"Don't forget your shift starts at eleven!" Ned shouts over the door alarm.

I don't answer as I step outside, trying to keep steady on the heels. They're too high—I know that now—but Jonah offers me he is arm like I've seen men do in the old black and white movies. My heart flutters in sync with my stomach as I loop my arm through his. I have the urge to caress the muscles in his arm, which I think would weird both of us out, if I did it.

"Where's your car?" I ask. Looking around the parking lot, I know most of the cars, but I don't see Jonah's brown Century.

"You didn't seem too excited about going out, so I did somethin' a lil' different." Jonah layers his hand over the one I have twisted through his gentlemanly arm. He's so close, his face brushes my hair. "Damn girl! You smell almost as good as you look." I beam, until he tugs me gently toward the street. I wobble to a stop. "Where are we going?"

"To the shop," Jonah says. "I got something set up for us."

I'm not sure this is better. Going to a crowded restaurant suddenly feels more secure, but I let him lead me across the street to the shop door. I can trust Jonah. I can. And if we don't go to the shop, he's going to think I want to go back to the hotel.

To my room.

My room with my bed.

Jonah slips his key into the grate over the door first, then he unlocks the dead bolt on the inner door. He lets go of me in the customer area, blocking my view of the alarm with his broad shoulders as he disables it. The place smells like working men: oil, grease, gasoline, cleaners, and even a touch of cologne. With the alarm off, he turns to me again.

Oh, that grin. It's silky on his lips. I can't believe I'm falling for this man.

"Come with me," he says, holding out his hand. I take it. He lifts the hinged part of the counter, holding it up like a drawbridge so I can walk beneath it. He guides me past the organized clutter of the front desk, to the door leading into his office.

"My space," Jonah says as he pushes open the door.

It's a tiny room with an old tanker desk against the wall, a chair wedged in front of it and behind it. There's no room for anything else.

Shelves bolted to the walls are crowded with thick manuals and some boxes of parts. The desk has a brown phone on it with a mismatched green receiver, a lamp, a grease-spotted brown paper bag, and three, short, white candles.

Jonah takes a lighter down from the shelf beside the door. His arm brushes my shoulder. There's no way it couldn't in an office as small as this one. It's intentional but my eyes flutter with the feel of his skin. He lights the candles, one by one, and places them at the edge of the desk, before he reaches past me and flicks off the florescent ceiling lights.

We're washed in the dim flickering of the candles. Jonah reaches over and pulls the front chair away, as much as he can, from the desk.

"Have a seat," he says. It's enough for me to slide in. My toes throb, but it's good to be off my feet.

Jonah takes the opposite seat. He pulls the bag close, reaches in, and unpacks two Styrofoam boxes. The dim light catches on a small scar on his face I've never noticed before. It's like I've uncovered a hidden clue to Jonah, and seeing it makes me feel as if he belongs to me a little more because I know something about him that most people will never even notice. The thought warms my insides, just like the luscious scent of Mexican spices.

"Hope you like burritos," he says, opening up the first box and sliding it across the desk toward me. The smell of the smothered burrito hits me. My stomach growls.

"I've never had a girl who loves her food the way you do." Jonah laughs.

"Look at how pretty it is," I say. It's speckled with diagonal cut green onions and bright red chunks of tomatoes.

Jonah hands me a plastic fork and knife wrapped in a paper napkin before opening his own box.

"This is from Verde's," Jonah says. "Best Mexican restaurant in the city. Go ahead. Try it. The way you love breakfast, I can't wait to see what you're gonna do with this."

I saw off a small piece. If I spill on myself, I'm done for, because the only way I've found to clean my clothes is by taking them down to the laundry room during my shift and sneaking a couple loads of laundry through the machines. But after what happened with Samson, I've been afraid to leave the cage and now I'm running out of clothes.

I slip the little chunk of the burrito into my mouth. I close my eyes and only pop them back open when I hear Jonah chuckle.

"You know how to enjoy your food like no other woman I've ever known," he says. "I love it."

But my appetite dries up with the sight of him. The flickering light dances across his cheeks as his eyes take me in. I could sit here all night, being absorbed by Jonah, until there is nothing left of me. It would feel so good to be a part of him and his world.

Oh my God. I'm falling for Jonah.

Me.

Falling for an older, black man.

Well, ten years older. It doesn't seem like that much. And when we talk, it doesn't seem like anything at all.

And black...the word isn't even accurate. It doesn't do any justice to how gorgeous his toasted brown complexion is, or how it's become my new favorite color just because it is the color of Jonah.

I smile across the desk at him. He smiles back and looks down into his box.

I am totally falling for him.

"So," he says.

"So," I echo.

"Verde's is my favorite place, but I'm not all that hungry now that I got you here. I don't wanna waste a second eating, when I could be listenin' to what you have to say."

"We'll talk with our mouths full, how's that?" I say, scooping up a forkful. Between chews, I say, "Okay...what do you want to talk about?"

He gets a big mouthful too. A tiny piece of lettuce falls out of his mouth as he says, "Everything."

Even with his mouth full, I never realized his voice could be so tender. I want to tell him everything—anything—whatever he wants to know.

"Tell me about the kind of men you've dated," he says, wiping his lips with one of the paper napkins.

"I haven't dated any men." I laugh. "I've dated a couple guys from school, but I wouldn't call them men."

"Huh," Jonah says, poking his burrito with the tines of his flimsy fork.

"What kind of women do you like to date?" I ask.

"Oh, well," He moves chunks of burrito around in his tray. "I like the kind named Lael, I know that."

I grin into my burrito tray like a big dope. "So, you aren't...attached?"

"Attached?" he says, his soulful gaze bolted to me. "Right now I am."

My grin gets even dopier.

Jonah and I talk about my mother. About Bob. I kick off my heels beneath the desk.

I tell him about going to the grocery store and getting lost in the aisles. He laughs. He asks how I've been cooking up in a hotel room, and I tell him about the skillet I stole from my mother.

"That's pretty clever," he says. He's got the longest eyelashes I've ever seen. It knocks the wind out of me. "You'll have to invite me over for dinner sometime."

"Maybe I will," I say breathlessly.

"You're one hell of a tough woman, coming to a place like this and making it work like you have," Jonah says. "Independence looks good on ya."

I shrug.

"What?" he laughs. "You going to try an' tell me you're not?"

"I have to be," I hint. At some point, Jonah's going to find out that I'm seventeen, not eighteen, and looking into his eyes, I don't want him to ever think I'm a liar. I want him to understand why I had to lie to him about it.

"How come?" His voice lowers, his tone heartbreakingly tender.

"I've been lying to you," I whisper.

"You have?" His eyebrows creep into his hairline. "About what?"

"Can you keep a secret?"

"Better than anybody you'll ever meet," he says, laying his hand on top of mine. His palm is smooth and silky, while mine is probably leaving a foggy, sweat ring against the desk.

"Don't be mad, but I'm not eighteen," I tell him. Before he can open his mouth, I barrel through my explanation. "I'm seventeen, but I'll be eighteen next July. I'm supposed to be a Senior in high school this year, but I had to drop out when I ran away from home because my stepfather is an alcoholic and I couldn't live there anymore. But my mom knows I'm here and she's mad about it, but she's not reporting me or anything. She just cancelled all my insurances, so if I get sick, I can't go to the doctor, and if I get pulled over, I might go to jail, which is why I don't go a lot of places in my car—"

"Slow down," he says with a chuckle. I hear the candle wicks crackle. Jonah lets out a long exhale from across the table and then he squeezes my hand beneath his. "Is that it?"

I glance up at him. "It's pretty bad," I say, but I'm already feeling better about it. "I'm a drop out too. But I plan on going back...when I make enough money so I can. I want to do something with my life."

"Aww shoot," Jonah laughs, leaning back in the office chair so it squeaks. "That's what you're worried about? Whether or not you're gonna be something?" My eyes fall back into my lap, but then Jonah's fingertips are under my chin, coaxing it upward. I meet his gaze and his eyes are so anchored, I let myself free fall into them.

Being looked at this way, I feel naked. But there's a slight smile on his lips that also makes me feel encouraged and that is enough to make me cry. The tears rise up and I bite the edge of my lip, trying to hold them back with more pain.

Jonah stands up and moves around the edge of the desk. The candle light casts giant, jumping shadows of him on the wall that look like him, and then look like some distorted monster looming over me. He collects my hands and pulls me to my feet, so we're standing chest to chest and I'm breathing in the faint lemon scent of him.

"Look at me," he whispers.

I tip my head back slightly, raising my eyes to his.

"You are way beyond somethin' already," he says. "If you're never any more than this, Lael, you should know it's way more than enough. You're a beautiful woman. You're independent. There's nothing better than that."

His premise seems flawed, but his eyes are so soft and it's the first time anyone has said I'm going to be fine. The encouragement overwhelms me and I cover my face with my hand, so I don't bawl right in his face. I'm so *fucking* needy, I can't stand it.

He leans over and grips my arms gently, right above the elbows, gathering me to him. I tuck my head against his neck and breathe him in.

"You can tell me everythin'," he whispers and it breaks me. My tears spill out, a whole bucket of relief-grief soaking into his shirt as he rubs my back.

Once the ugly part of my cry is all over, I pull away, embarrassed, but Jonah doesn't let me go. Instead, he pulls me in close and his lips meet mine. The small kisses come first, like ripples in a pond, lapping at my skin, tugging gently at my lips.

I place my hands on his waist, his leather belt beneath my fingers. I inhale lemons and taste the tang of the burrito he was eating. I kiss him back, opening my mouth slightly, sliding my tongue across his lower lip like I'm sealing an envelope. His arms bind me, his breath scribbles across my cheek.

My fingers trace the muscles in Jonah's chest. He roots one palm at the base of my neck. I draw back for a breath and he plants small kisses around my mouth, cultivating my lips for a deeper, more sensuous kiss. What I return to him is as good as any love letter, and between every line, he sows another kiss, the thought blooming within me: he wants everything I will give him and more.

Jonah is like no one I've ever dated. He doesn't ask permission to kiss me, or swab his tongue over my face, or try to reach under my shirt to unhook my bra. His hands don't dive for the hem of my skirt either, thank God.

Instead, Jonah's hands are steady. His grip on my arms is firm, but not unpleasant. Every movement of his jaw is leisurely and tender. He kisses me like there is nothing else in the world to do, and that there is no other goal than to savor my lips as thoroughly as he can. He kisses me like a man.

I'm a different story. When I can let go and flow along with him, I'm great. But when I think of what's happening, I get sucked right back into my head. I don't know where to put my arms. I step on his feet. Finally, I clunk foreheads with him.

We both draw back with an ouch!

"What's wrong?" he asks. "Why are you movin' like that?"

"Because I don't know what to do!" I blurt.

"Oh," he says and then cocking his head to one side as he studies me, "Oh." He pulls me forward, erasing the step I retreated. "It's alright. I'll show you," he says.

He leans in and kisses my forehead, lingering there, placing the warm velvet of his lips to my skin as if he is transferring the tenderness. His soft, slow kisses move to my temples and spread down my hairline. I don't hear the kiss, but feel it, brushing against the sensitive, knobby lobe of my ear.

The full length of him presses against me. He rubs his cheek against mine, his breath moves the hair beside my ear. I turn up my face and he kisses me harder this time, crushing my lips beneath his, thrusting his tongue into my mouth. I can't catch a breath.

I squeak.

Jonah pulls back. His arms soften, release. "I didn't mean to do that," he says. "You just felt so good, I lost my head for a minute."

I feel like a child. I reach for him, run my fingertips down his arm to his wrist, but he drops his hand. Steps away.

"I'm sorry," I say. "I just…"

He shakes his head, nah nah nahing under his breath. "It's on me. I just got carried away."

I want him close again. I want his forgiveness for my lack of skill.

"No, it was me," I insist. "I'm so sorry, I just…"

He steps forward then, sweeping me into a more delicate embrace. "Stop saying you're sorry, Silver Spoon."

I sway back with a tense smile. "I wish you wouldn't call me that."

"Silver Spoon?" he asks with a playful grin. "It's my pet name for ya."

"It makes me sound like a rich brat." I laugh a little to soften the truth.

"You are definitely not a dog."

"But I'm not a fancy snot either," I mumble.

"Don't be mad, I'm just playin'." Jonah backs up, glancing at his watch. "Whoa. I've gotta get you back. It's almost eleven."

Jonah walks me back to the hotel.

"Hey man," Ned says as he pops the cage door open for me.

Jonah stands at the counter, leaning on it in front of the payment window. I go into the cage, kind of wishing Jonah would just leave, since things have gotten awkward since I said I didn't like the nickname he gave me. He snuffed the candles and we walked back over here in silence.

"Hold on." I grab Ned's arm before he can scoot out the cage door. "I've got to count the drawer before you go."

"You've got three minutes." Ned pokes a finger at the clock on the phone board and pulls the door closed with a slam.

Whatever. I take a seat and pull out the drawer.

"It's all there," Ned whines, reaching for the door knob again. "I'm going."

"I swear," I snap, "I'll call Clive and Lavina right now, if you leave here before I count it."

Jonah smirks, tipping his chin down and eyes up. Our eyes meet and he gives me a wink. It melts me. I'm overreacting to the whole nickname thing.

"Clive can suck it, if he thinks I'm waitin' around for you every night. Half the time you're late and I can count faster on my toes."

I ignore him and start counting. Ned leans on the counter, his balls right next to my head. I'm sure that's on purpose, but a glimpse from the corner of my eye and I notice Jonah noticing.

"You work next door, huh?" Ned flicks his chin at Jonah.

Still chin down and eyes up, Jonah glances at Ned with a slow nod.

"Can you get me a discount on an oil change?" Ned asks. His balls are still at my cheek level, but I know if I react to it, Ned will just take it to the next level. Instead, I ignore it.

Jonah, however, stands up straight, still watching. "Bring it over," Jonah says blandly. "We'll see what we can do for ya."

"Cool," Ned says as the front door alarm goes off.

I peer over the counter to see Yolanda stomping in. Tonight, he's wearing a copper wig, purple eye shadow up to his eyebrows, and red lipstick swabbed over with so much gloss, his lips look like they are bleeding metal shavings under water. Yolanda checked out the day after he bought all my stuff and I haven't seen him since. And he's wearing my bracelet.

"I told you, we don't rent to she-its." Ned sneers at him from beside me. Yolanda ignores him.

"Hey, sweetie lamb," he greets me.

"Hi," I say stiffly. Not only am I trying to concentrate on counting the drawer, but he still owes me money.

Yolanda sweeps his eyes up and down Jonah, automatically lowering his lids. The lipstick is a glamorous freak show curtain, pulling away to reveal the dental nightmare of Yolanda's smile. Some teeth are missing, some look too long. The rest are all huddled together, waiting for their turn to rot out of his mouth.

But it doesn't detour Yolanda. He puts up a limp hand and swaggers toward Jonah. "Now, who you belong to, honey?"

"This is Jonah," I say, still trying to count. "My friend. He works over at the oil shop across the street. Jonah, this is Yolanda."

It's hard to introduce Yolanda, with his five o'clock shadow and six-foot-plus frame, in a periwinkle dress my grandmother might've liked. Jonah just smiles and tips his chin, leaning an elbow on the counter again.

"Oh, he's yo' friend," Yolanda says turning his attention back to me. "Sugar pie, do ya got'a room fo' me tonight?"

I glance back at the key peg board. It's Friday night and—no surprise—there aren't any available rooms left, but I can't say I feel sorry for him. Not after he split without paying me and isn't bothering to bring it up now.

"No," I say. "We're full."

"Fuck," Yolanda says. "How about shorts? Got any shorts about to leave?" He slides the tip of his long, fake nail between his grisly front teeth.

"It don't matter," Ned growls. "Clive said no she-its."

That's the wrong thing to say to Yolanda. His feminine tone slips away. "How does a uni-browed fool like you keep a job anyway? You look like a fucked up Pekinese and I bet ya ain't got the IQ of my last shit."

"At least I know what I am," Ned says.

Yolanda answers with a hair flip. "I know what you is too—a dumb shit."

"Fuck stick." Ned mumbles shoving the drawer with his knee. "God damn, Lael, are you done with the drawer yet?"

Jonah stands up straight on the other side of the bulletproof glass.

Ned pretends not to notice Jonah drilling him with a glare. But I see it.

"By the way, three regulars told me you ain't been keepin' up with the movies either. Clive'll fire you if he hears that, so I'd watch it if I was you. Besides, you should be taking notes, Lael. I'm sure your man here would appreciate it if you took some notes!" Ned nods to Jonah, but Jonah doesn't nod back. Ned leans back and cranks up the volume on the TV. The man on the screen holds a woman by the jaw as he crams his junk down her throat. She gags, the sound of it spilling from the cage.

My face goes up in flames. The moans and slurps and gagging is one thing, but Jonah can see exactly what's on the TV from where he's standing too. Glancing at the screen, there's a man pulling on a woman's nipple like it's made of bubble gum, while he thrusts into her mouth.

I put my head down and grit my teeth, re-counting the stack of bills I just lost count on. I should just let Ned leave, but I can't afford it.

"What? It's not a secret, is it?" Ned hoots over the blaring porn. He points to Jonah. "Brother, you know you're dating Snow White, don't ya?"

"I ain't your brother," Jonah says flatly.

"No, he ain't," Yolanda adds.

I try to bury myself in balancing the till. I need to concentrate so I can get this done and get him out of here.

I wince, glancing up at Jonah. He's not smiling. His jaw is tight and his eyes aren't on me at all. He is following every move Ned makes. And Ned's such a tool that he's not even paying attention.

The guy on TV unsheathes long enough from the woman's drooling jaw to allow her to gasp a breath and beg for more, even though it doesn't sound like she really wants it.

"Yeah!" Ned shouts, pumping his fist over his head as the guy on TV assaults the woman again. "That's what I'm talkin' 'bout!"

"Ugh," Yolanda rolls his eyes, one bloody lip spiking over a ragged tooth. He leans toward the slotted vent in the window and yells through it, over the moaning. "Lamb pie, how 'bout ya rent me a short stay later? Can ya hole one fo' me?"

Ned throws his hands on the counter, leaning over me to shout through the vent, "How many times do you gotta hear, hell no, ya stupid tranny?"

I shove him away. Whatever's between me and Yolanda is nothing compared to what I think of Ned right now.

"Yeah," I tell Yolanda, "come back in two hours."

"Thanks, lamb baby." He glares at Ned as he says it. "An' if you kin fine me a all-night stay, I'll put in a extra ten fo' you."

Ned shakes his head. "She ain't on shift yet. It's still mine until she counts that fuckin' drawer. But, I'll tell you what, freak show, I'll give you an all-nighter if you throw twenty in for me."

"Twenty extra? I can get two rooms down the street for that."

"Then go down the street." Ned shrugs. "No sweat off my balls, Meat Fairy. But if you wanna stay here, it's an extra twenty. Lael ain't rentin' nothin' to you, or else Clive'll be here scoutin' rooms for you."

"There aren't any available to rent," I tell Yolanda with a scowl.

"Twenty?" Yolanda repeats. Ned nods. I don't know what he's doing—there's no rooms available. Yolanda throws up a hand and waves him away like a gnat. "Fine. Twenty fo' you, Ned. We got a deal then?"

Ned isn't even paying attention to her. He's encouraging the woman on the TV again, while he pumps his hips in unison with the man. When the scene changes, he turns back to Yolanda.

"Come back in two hours," he says. "And leave the twenty with Lael."

"Unless you're coming back to change the sheets, I'm not skimming for you," I say.

"I'll throw you a fiver," Ned offers.

"I'm not even supposed to leave the cage," I say.

"Oh yeah! Because Clive don't want you gettin' raped for free!" Ned says with a smirk. "He's gotta make his cut!"

"Hey," Jonah barks.

Yolanda adds, "You disgustin', Ned."

"And your daddy shoulda pulled out," Ned tells Yolanda.

He acts like Jonah's not even there, but I don't know why Ned isn't factoring in how he's got to walk out of the cage and past Jonah if he wants to get to his car. Ned keeps on going, popping gun fingers at Yolanda.

"You probably heard that a helluva lot when you were a little boy, huh?" He slaps his own cheeks with the palms of his hands, making the oh no face, and then he turns back to the TV. Ned clenches his tiny, under-developed bottom lip between his teeth and pumps his hips to the sound of the woman shrieking. He grunts along with the motion. "Take it baby! Yeah! Take it! Take it!"

Jonah folds his arms rigidly over his chest. It catches Ned's eye and he zeros in. I think he's lost his damn mind if he's going to pick a fight with Jonah.

"So you gonna be the guy to do the honors and pop Fail's cherry?" Ned asks. Oh my God, he's actually going to do it. Jonah's glare is so focused, I expect Ned to split in half, but he just keeps talking. "Or did that already happen earlier?"

"Why don't you come out here and ask me about it instead?" Jonah says.

I'm going to puke, but Yolanda giggles.

"Oh, Ned's too much of a pussy to do that." he tells Jonah, pushing the strands of his wig off his forehead.

"Pussy," Ned throws a hard laugh in Yolanda's direction. "Somethin' you know nothing about!"

"I got more balls in mah purse than that one's got in 'is whole family tree," Yolanda says to Jonah. "'Cept maybe his mama. From the looks of 'im, maybe she a she-it too!"

All the fun Ned was having vanishes. "Fuck you!" he roars at Yolanda, slapping our side of the bulletproof glass with his palms. "Fuck you, ya cockless tranny freak!"

"Why don't you watch your mouth," Jonah says between tight lips.

"Hey, fuck you too." Ned snaps at him.

"Just stop, Ned." I say.

"No lamb, let him run his mouth off," Yolanda says with a grisly smirk. "Somebody's gonna have to open the cage door some time, now ain't they? Yo' man out here...he's a big'un, swee' pea!" Yolanda's almost singing through the vent. "Aww, Ned...I sure wouldn't wanna be you. All small like you is—havin' to open up that door to a big fella like dis one! An' one that wants ta beat ya senseless like dis one does too! Huh...I'm glad I ain't you, Ned. I know that fo' sho'."

I scrawl my initials on the till sheet. The drawer is—shockingly—square.

"You're all set, Ned. You can go," I say.

"Call off your boyfriend and your fucking hermaphrodite, first," he says, "or I'm tellin' Clive you been skimmin' and rentin' to she-its."

Yolanda puffs at him from the vent. "You so ignorant, boy."

"And I'll be over here to tell him the truth," Jonah says.

Evidently, Ned doesn't realize who Jonah is, how close he is to Lavina, and how Lavina has Clive around her little finger...well, except when it comes to getting extra help. Huh. Maybe she doesn't have the pull I think she does. Maybe Ned does has more pull than I realize.

"You're an asshole." I say. I turn with the cash drawer, ready to slide it back into its track beneath the desk, but Ned steps forward and I clip his leg with the metal edge.

"What the fuck?" he hollers, cupping himself. "You almost got my nuts, ya crazy bitch!"

Jonah moves to the cage door. "Open up, Lael," he says. His tone is so sharp, it could be an ax.

Yolanda leans into the vent again. "Ohhh, you 'bout ta get yo' ass kicked good, Ned. Yup, yup...here it come."

"You open that fucking door and I'll get you fired," Ned says as I reach for the knob.

"C'mon, lamby," Yolanda coaxes me through the vent. "Open it on up. It gonna be worth it! You so young and pretty, anybody'd hire you! Go on and open up that door, honey lamb. It'd do us all right ta see Ned get a good ass whoopin'.'"

"Who's gonna hire you?" Ned fires back, his head swinging between me and Yolanda. "Samson?"

"Stop," I say and I hold my hands up like I'm stopping on-coming traffic. "Ned, you're square. You can get out of here."

Ned folds his arms against his chest. "I said I ain't leavin' until all your friends clear out. And if it ain't soon, I'm callin' Clive and tellin' him you got your friends here to kick my ass. He's just down in Greek Town tonight. He'd love that. I'm the one who covers all the shifts and bends over backward for him! He'll be back here to fire you and toss ya outta here faster than you can blink."

"Sweet thing," Yolanda whispers through the vent, "just unlock the door and let's git this ass kickin' over wit'."

"Hey...thing...don't you got somewhere to blow?" Ned sneers. "You should get right on that."

Yolanda laughs mechanically, holding her stomach. Her wig slips down over her eyes and Ned howls.

"Oh, you ain't that clever on yo' own, Ned," Yolanda says, pushing the wig back in place. "Somewhere to blow...who's boxers you scrape that one off of?"

"Fag," Ned says.

"Bigger fag," Yolanda shoots back.

"You wish you could suck my cock."

Yolanda's voice goes full-on dude. "God, I wish you wasn't such a pussy and would unlock that door, Ned, that's all I wish. My cock would be up yo' ass so high, you'd be eaten it fo' bre'fast, lunch, an' dinner!" Yolanda steps back, takes a deep breath, and fluffs out the bottom of his wig. He smoothes his hands down over his lumpy chest, recollecting himself. His more feminine voice returns as he aims for the door. "Well, chil'ren, mah parole off'cer would be pissed if I kicked this lil' stain's ass mah'self. Wish I could stay and see how Ned looks wit' a busted head, but I got thin's I got ta do t'night."

Ned grumbles something crude about what that might be under his breath. I wish I could kick him. Yolanda reaches over and gently squeezes Jonah's bicep.

"You is such a big, strong man, now ain't ya! Yo' jus' all full'a muscle! Aww, Ned, I wish I could stay, 'cause this one's sho' gonna hurt!" Yolanda presses his mouth to the glass in front of Ned, leaving a thick, red, smeary set of lips that looks more like a gruesome bug splatter. Yolanda turns to Jonah. "I'm too much of a lady ta do it mah'self," he says, "but you go on and fuck up that lil' white boy real good, okay, sweetie? I'll give ya fitty bucks next time I see ya, if ya make sho' the lil' sonofabitch cain't have no mo' like 'im."

Jonah smirks.

Ned runs his finger down the ledger as if he's not listening, but the color has drained from his face.

Yolanda does a little *ta-ta* wave and goes out the lobby door. Ned flinches at the sound of the alarm.

Why he didn't think through his exit plan before shooting off his mouth is beyond me. Why he didn't factor in that Jonah works across the street and could kill him at any time is another mystery.

All I know is that Jonah becomes more incredible to me with each passing second. He can call me Silver Spoon all day long.

The porno finishes and the TV screen goes to snow.

Jonah cracks his knuckles.

Ned pops in a new video tape. He isn't going to leave until Jonah does. That Jonah wants to beat him is really sweet, I absolutely adore the idea, but it will probably just get me fired and I don't have enough money to make another move.

"Jonah, can I just talk to you tomorrow?" I say. "Ned's never going to leave with you here."

"You okay?" Jonah asks.

"I'm fine," I say before Ned can open his trap and start it all up again.

Jonah thinks on it a moment, gives me a small nod, and with another heavy glare in Ned's direction, goes out the door.

Ned whips around, pushing aside the vertical blinds on the back window. He watches Jonah cross the street, get in his car, pull out of the oil shop and, finally, turn onto the boulevard. Ned lets go of the blind.

"See ya, Fail," he says, as if nothing just happened, but he rushes out the cage door and bolts out the front door to his car. He roars out of the hotel parking lot before the echo of the door alarm has even silenced.

It's over. I sit down on my chair and let out a deep breath, but I wish Jonah had stayed.

Will pokes his head through the hole over my head a couple hours later, but I'm in such a crappy mood, I don't talk enough to keep him happy.

"How come you're bein' such a stupid head bitch?" he asks. He says that stuff like it's not insulting.

"I'm not a bitch," I tell him. "Don't call me that. I don't feel like talking right now."

"I'm gonna spit on you," he threatens, but when I don't respond and just keep doodling in the corner of the ledger, he finally disappears for good. I change the movie before the credits start rolling and the phone rings.

"Starlight," I say.

"Lael?" It's Jonah's milky-smooth voice.

I settle back against the office chair, pushing a lock of hair behind my ear as my smile spreads like a rumor across my lips. "Hi," I say.

"Hi." He chuckles on the other end and the sound slips deep into me, warming my belly. "Ned gone?"

"Right after you left."

"Good," he says. "I didn't like how our date ended."

"Sorry."

"It's not your fault." He chuckles again. "But I want a do-over. That okay with you?"

I squirm happily on the chair, leaning forward, my elbows on the desk. "Sure."

"I haven't stopped thinking about you since I left. In fact, I can't sleep. Mind if I come to see you?"

"Right now?"

"I don't think I'll be able to sleep the rest of the night unless I do. I'm on my way." He hangs up.

I swear I've swallowed a jar full of lightening bugs.

I wait for Jonah, positioning myself on the office chair. First, I pull a knee up to my chest, resting my foot on the seat. After a minute, I pull up both. I tip my head to the side so my hair falls over one eye and just my profile is visible from the door.

After a couple minutes, my hips ache.

The door opens, but it's the guy from Room 24. Wine run. The guy flashes me his key and holds up a brown bag before shooting up the stairs.

I brush my hair off my face and stand up. Try again. I open the ledger and lean over it, business-like.

That lasts for a minute. Jonah still doesn't come.

I take a rag and dust off the desk top, the TV and the VCR with long, graceful swipes.

No Jonah.

I cough out the dust I've stirred up, go out of the cage and wipe off Yolanda's lipstick prints from the glass. An hour creeps by.

The phone rings.

"Lael," Clive says on the other end. My spine goes stiff. I can almost hear his lips juggling a toothpick over the background noise of a busy restaurant. "I just spoke to Ned," he says and I groan inwardly. "He said you told him that I said you ain't s'posed to leave the cage ta clean short stays. Not sure how you got that idea, but—"

I want to say, It's real simple, you told me not to leave the cage.

But what I say is, "You told me not to leave the cage. When you hired me, you said don't leave the cage because of what happened with Sam."

"You didn't hear me right then, 'cause them short stays is my bread and butta'. What happened with Sam was 'cause he was wavin' a gun 'round when he didn't have no business doin' it. So, we straight now? Go 'head and change the sheets and tidy up after each short, so we can rent the room ag'in. That's yo' job."

"Alright. Thanks for letting me know."

Clive hangs up.

Ned's an asshole. But that phone call proves it—Ned has more pull with Clive, and it could get me fired. I shoot upstairs and close the room door while I change the sheets when the first short stay checks out. There's nothing gross in the room, except the smell of funk. Otherwise, it just looks like an unmade bed, but it's still creepy to walk into the empty room, knowing what just happened in here, and strip the bed like I'm getting rid of crime scene evidence.

And I rent the room ten minutes later.

Still no Jonah.

By 3:00 a.m. I've just given up on Jonah completely, when I catch the shadow of a vehicle twisting past the vertical blinds. I'm not sure it's Jonah, but I throw myself down on the chair and yank up one knee again. My heel slides off the edge of the seat as the door opens. I am so anxious and hopeful that I ruin everything, bouncing onto my feet before whoever-it-is, in case it's Jonah, even gets to see my sexy, leg-up pose at all.

A skinny black guy stands in the frame, holding the door open, alarm shrilling, motioning for whoever's with him to come in.

"Hey, how much for a couple hours?" the guy shouts from the door way.

The constant shriek of the alarm kick-starts a headache right over my eyes. "Sorry," I try to shout back, "we don't have any rooms available for another couple hours."

Less than that, but I don't need a couple goozing all over each other in the lobby for another hour, waiting for the last renters to leave and me to change the messed up sheets.

The guy shouts something out the door and a woman shouts something back, about how they need to find a place now. He finally lets loose of the damn door and leaves.

I curl up in a hard knot on my chair, rubbing my temple with one hand and scrawling mean little poems about cowards on the back page of the ledger. Cowards that call bosses and get good people bitched out. I record my venom in words that don't rhyme right, but I don't even care. I've got my pen stuck in my mouth, the capped end pushing my lip into my nostril, when the alarm blares and I glance up and see Jonah standing right in front of me at the counter.

I nearly fall off my chair.

The pen drops out of my mouth and the cap goes skittering somewhere under the desk as I scramble to my feet. I snap the ledger closed and throw it under the overhang of the counter. Straightening my knees with a hard snap sends the chair scraping away and banging against the wall behind me. For all my careful planning, he had to come now. Now, when my pen is nearly buried up my nose.

Instead of saying anything, he smiles. It's not an I-caught-you smile either. It is a happy-to-see-you smile. It relieves me, makes me feel like maybe he didn't see the pen after all.

"Hello," he says.

"Hi," I say.

"I'm glad that pen didn't punch a hole in your brain," he says.

My face burns like the core of a bonfire, but Jonah holds up a cardboard tray with two cups nestled in it, in one hand, and a greasy bag with a smiling donut on the side in the other. He grins. "I thought maybe you'd like somethin' sweet."

I know I'm not supposed to let him into the cage, but it's 3 a.m. and Clive hasn't come in. I don't think he's going to, if he hasn't already.

And the only thing I want is to talk to Jonah.

And kiss him.

I pop the door and Jonah drags in a folding chair he finds leaning on the lobby wall. He takes the space closer to the TV, turning down the volume before putting his back to it so we're not sitting there watching porn together.

"Can you still see the screen?" he asks. "I know we gotta remember to switch the movies out."

"I will," I say, turning away as my cheeks heat up again. Partly from the porn, mostly from the we.

"At least, now I know what Ned's all about." Jonah takes one of the cups out of the cardboard holder and slides it across the counter to me.

"Yeah, about that...I have to be careful with Ned," I warn him. "He could get me fired." I tell him how Clive called here and changed the rules on me.

"What's he thinkin'?" Jonah shakes his head. "He's gonna have some pretty little thing up changing sheets at midnight? Is he crazy? I bet Ned's only fixin' up the beds so he can skim a couple short stays for himself. How's Clive to know if he got one short stay or five?"

"Ned was cheating me on drawers when I first got hired." I add, flipping the plastic coffee lid on the desk top. The TV flashes, goes to movie credits. I hop up. "I've got to switch the movie," I say.

"It's easier for me," Jonah says, reaching for a tape. "This one good?"

"I...uh, you have to see which one's next in the rotation. On that paper there." I drop my voice to an ashamed whisper as I point to the sheet. "If you play the same one too much, they'll call yelling about that too."

Jonah skims down the list with one finger, chooses a different video, re-checks the title, removes the old tape and slides the new one into the machine. He waits for the opening credits, which happens to be a woman's butt cheeks splayed upward like a fleshy peach pit. When he turns back to me, I'm fuschia all over again.

"Why do you flush over this stuff? It's just sex," he says softly. "Ain't nothin' to be embarrassed about."

That seems like a stretch when the next screen is a snippet of the guy folding the woman in half and drilling her like an oil well. Since I can't make the blush disappear, Jonah uses his broad shoulders to fill up the space between me and the TV again. My own shoulders finally drop.

"Would you like a donut?" he asks.

"Sure," I say. I would say anything not to have to talk with him about the porn anymore, even though the moans and sticky sex noises continue on, almost like a twisted, hotel version of elevator music, beneath our conversation. We talk about what donuts we each like best, funny customer stories, and how I spend my days when I'm not working.

"I just hang around my room," I say.

"Or with Lavina while she's cleanin'," he adds. His pager goes off and he glances at it, but dismisses the call and clips it back on his belt. He picks right up where he left off. "There can't be a whole lot to do in your room all day, is there? I noticed you don't go out much. Your car's always in the same spot."

"Since my mother cancelled my car insurance, if I get caught by the cops, they might throw me in jail and my mom's not about to bail me out."

"You won't go to jail!" Jonah says. "Then again, you're a white girl. You might get a ticket, but I don't think most folks aroun' here have car insurance to start with. Most of 'em can't hardly afford their cars," he says. "One thing to know: niggas usually have nice rides and they always dress fly, but when it comes to the rest of it, they ain't got money for that!"

I gasp. "I can't believe you use said that!"

"What? Nigga?"

"Yes!"

Jonah laughs. "Don't you say it, now. If you say it, all the sista's would be on you and beat you down before you got another breath out. That ain't for white folks to say. Jus' my people."

"But you can say it?"

"It's like callin' your brother stupid. You can say it 'bout your own, but let somebody else call my brother stupid and I'll tear that fool down!"

"I don't think anybody should say it."

"That's cause of where you come from, Silver Spoon."

I don't like that he's drawing a line between us, and I don't like that we went from us to his 'people' and mine. I stiffen up a little, pulling up my chin. "But you can call me Silver Spoon and you think that's okay."

"You don't like it 'cause you've had years and years of black people oppressin' you?" he asks, but his grin is playful. "Look—givin' you a nickname—I'm just tryin' to show you how I feel about ya."

And just like that, whatever discomfort was between us is gone. I feel a little guilty that I still don't like the nickname he's chosen for me. It's just him being affectionate and I don't know why it bothers me, considering it's coming from his heart. I'm such a big baby.

He kicks up his boots on the counter and the TV is in direct view again, a huge dong in my peripheral, then an overgrown bush springs into view, when I look in Jonah's direction. I can't help but glance at it, but Jonah captures my gaze when I flick away from the screen. He turns his head toward the screen too.

"Just two people, havin' a good time," he says lightly, as if we're watching some sweet old movie, or ice dancing.

"Uh huh," I agree, but I let my eyes move to his boots. It's horrifying to have porn playing, because even with the sound down, we can still hear the awful music, along with every sharp slurp and slap and squish.

"The thing about watching porno that nobody ever talks about," Jonah tries again, his tone still light and conversational, rather than sexy, "is that people never think of it as educational. But if you watch it, you can get a real good idea of what you like and what you don't. Look what he's doing now, he's just kissing her neck. Look." His tone rises, like he wants to prove himself.

I glance up. A fresh scene is just starting up, the couple kissing, the man's lips moving up her neck, the woman craning back, already in a state of bliss.

"See?" Jonah says. "I love kissing a woman's neck. It's an erogenous zone for both men and women."

I don't even know what an erogenous zone is, but in this context, I think it's synonymous for target. Hit the zone and you get instant sex, that's what I can put together from what Jonah's saying and what's happening on the screen.

I glimpse his neck, the smooth skin and the way it curves around his ear. He doesn't have much for earlobes, they're incredibly compact and kind of perfect. I wonder what his response would be if I kissed his neck like that.

Jonah moves his boot and my eyes shoot back up to his.

"Do you like being kissed like that?" he asks softly. He licks the middle of his bottom lip with one slow, smooth motion of his tongue.

I shrug, but I mean yes. That soft spot, under the ear lobe, the sensuous trail down the side of my neck...yes, I've been kissed there and I've more than liked it. I think of Jonah's lips, how they would feel on my neck, and I can't help it when my eyes flick to them. He licks them again, the insides of his lips a vibrant, silky pink against the deeper pigment of his skin.

"If nobody's kissed you there yet, you need it." His gaze sweeps down my neck to the base and then his gaze glides slowly back to my eyes as if he's been drugged. By me.

There's something powerful about enchanting a man. Especially this one, who has had a lot more experience than I have, and must have a lot better idea of what he likes and what he doesn't. And he is all about me. The surge between my knees is like standing in the front row at a concert, the moment they turn the speakers on. I squeeze my legs together.

"See? It's not so bad to watch," Jonah says, "if ya just look at it like bodies doing what they do. Nothing shameful in that." He lifts my fingertips off my knee. "Is it okay if I hold your hand?"

Under the circumstances, it should seem creepy, but it's exactly the opposite. It's sweet, comforting. I reach out and take his hand. He rubs his thumb across my skin and it's softer than a flower petal and blows all the love me not's away.

The first porno is just scenes that get right to it, one after another and no breath in between. It's only about a half hour long and Jonah doesn't talk, but switches from rubbing the top of my hand with his thumb, to making soft, slow circles in my palm with his fingertips.

The second one has a plot, if you can call it that—just a corny story stringing together flimsy reasons for screwing. Jonah talks through all of them, making fun of the scenes, mentioning what he likes and what he doesn't. I'm pretty relaxed beside him at 6 a.m., when we pop in a gang bang tape. One man after another spreading a single woman open and pumping into her.

"This is so gross," I whisper to Jonah. "They're using her like a garbage can."

"But there's somethin' in it that's exciting too, isn't there?" he says.

I make a face. "No."

"There's just no foreplay in this one," he says, his voice pulling over me like a thick, warm cloak. "No romance. This one is pure fucking. There's a time and place for this kind of thing too. When it's right, fucking is a lot of fun. But I know what you mean. Slowing down and gettin' to enjoy a body from head to toe…" he lets out a sensuous, throaty moan, "there's nothing in the world better than that, Silver Spoon."

He drops my hand and the warmth vanishes from my skin instantly.

"It's getting late…well, early," he says with a soft laugh, but the thought of him leaving aches. "I best get movin'. I wouldn't want you to git in trouble with Lavina for me sittin' in here." He stands up, stretching his arms high over his head with a wide yawn. He finishes by pulling a hand down over his brow and rubbing his eyes.

"I don't know how you're still awake. I hardly ever stay awake all night." I smile sheepishly. "But don't tell Lavina that."

"I'd never," he says, shaking off another yawn. "I just gotta wake up, so I can drive."

"Maybe you shouldn't drive," I say. The options send a wire of excitement speeding through me. I'm usually tired at the end of my shift, but I'm wide awake from watching the movies, having my hands massaged, and the conversations that tickled thoughts between my legs.

"Maybe not. I can probably go down the street and get a room."

"Why don't you just stay here?" Wow. My voice sounds deep and silky, partly from being up all night and mostly from the thoughts running through my head.

"There aren't any rooms." He lifts his hand toward the key board, then cocks his head. "Are you asking me to stay with you?"

I think of him lying beside me, filling up half my bed, talking in his soft, mellow tone. But I've never gone all the way with anyone, and I haven't known Jonah that long. I think of Jonah kissing my neck, the way he says he likes to, as he leaves his lemon scent on sheets. What am I thinking? The thousands of lightening bugs in my stomach spark with a mix of excitement and anxiety over the thought and nearly burn holes in the lining to get out. I can't stop smiling, partly from excitement and mostly from terror.

"I'd invite you to stay," I say softly. "But I don't want to give you the wrong idea."

I couldn't have even said that sentence two hours ago without the skin burning off my face.

"I'm too tired to expect anything, but a pillow," he says.

I lean back and pull the spare key for my room off the board. I hand it to him. "If you're tired, you can go up. I've got to wait for Lavina."

"You sure?" he asks, taking the key from me.

"As long as we're just sleeping," I say.

193

My broken jewelry box crosses my mind and of course I consider it for a half second longer than I probably should. I should trust people more, especially Jonah. He's bought me breakfast and dinner and stood up for me with Ned. And we've just spent most of the night together in the cage, talking about every intimate detail of my life—right down to the burning center of my legs.

He flashes me his beautiful smile before slipping out of the cage and up the stairs to wait for me in my room.

Jonah's eyes open when I finally get up to my room.

He's lying on the side of the bed closest to the door, on top of my bedspread, shoes off, socks on, clothes on. He's on my bed, where other things could happen besides sitting. It throws me into a sudden light terror.

I mean, I just coaxed a lion into a cage without any intention of giving him any real food. I wanted to, but now that he's here, I don't know that I can go through with it. It's very possible that I could throw up or pass out. I start thinking of alternate escapes.

"You want something to drink?" I ask. "We could go downstairs and make coffee. Or get pop."

"I'm good," Jonah says. "Thanks for letting me stay. You tired?"

I nod.

He pats the bed beside him. "Why don't you come lay down with me, then."

I walk around the edge of the bed, closest to the window, sit, and take off my shoes first. It's weird to lay down beside Jonah, even though I stay in my clothes. He doesn't ask why. He stays on top of the covers even after

I slide under the sheet. He doesn't ask why about that either. He closes his eyes. I turn on my side, with my back to him, looking at the hotel sign outside through the slits of my eyes.

We lay there a few minutes, me listening to him breath and afraid to move.

"Are you asleep?" he whispers.

"No."

"It's tough sleeping in someone else's bed," he says. "You care if I turn on the TV?"

"I don't mind."

The screen pops to life and I remember, the minute the moaning fills the room, what I'd been watching, and doing, last time the TV was on. I squeeze my eyes together, my back still to him, and mouth oh my God.

"Lavina must've changed the tape," he says casually. "This isn't the one I put in."

Put in. My gut clenches. "She has the longer ones that play for four hours, so she doesn't have to keep running up and down the stairs."

"That makes sense," he says. "Wow. Look at that right there. Now that's a limber woman."

I open my eyes to see a red head with her legs flanking her face like a picture frame. Her wrists are bound with silver handcuffs.

"What do you think of that?" Jonah asks.

"I don't know," I say. We were talking about porn all night, laughing and critiquing, but now that we're lying in my bed and I can feel his heat near my back, I'm embarrassed all over again. "You probably already figured it out, but I haven't had sex. I have no idea what I like and what I don't."

He doesn't skip a beat. "Even if you never had sex, you still know what's interestin' to ya."

"I guess." Like my face won't just burn off if I tell him.

"You haven't confessed to what you like yet," he chides.

"I like to hear about what you like," I say. Of course he's smiling as his eyes flick to mine. His eyes are the color of dark soil, turned over in the sun. His gaze plants thoughts in my head of what his mouth tastes like, if kissing the skin beneath his ear would uproot his calm, collected nature.

"I told you already," he says.

"You just say, everything."

"It's true."

I start laughing.

"You don't mind a guy shovin' a fist up yo' butt?" I try on Lavina's accent. We saw that happen on the gang-bang tape, between the men waiting in line to get with the girl. "Remember that tape? That one dude looked like he was being stuffed like a Thanksgiving turkey!"

I turn my face toward his, and Jonah makes a funny face. I crack up even more.

"You're right," he says. "I don't like everything."

I reach for him, before I can second guess myself. I plant my hand softly on his cheek and Jonah's soulful eyes just watch me as I bring my face closer, and closer, until my lips are on his. I close my eyes and feel my way then, behind his lips, across his tongue. I kiss him the way he kissed me at the shop—deep and sure—trying to let him know I like everything about him.

I'm laying with this man in my own place. I'm an adult now. I'm a woman. The longer I think about it, the more I think, what am I waiting on? My mom would be mortified, but I'm the only one I need to please now.

Jonah's breath quickens against my cheek. His hands encircle my wrists, pulling my body even closer. He dips his tongue into my mouth, the urgency of his kiss building as he pushes me onto my back. He hovers over me.

"Do you like this?" he asks, holding down my hands.

"It's okay," I whisper. I want to tell him that I'm scared to death of what might happen next, but I don't want it to stop. I want to tell him I'm terrified of my mother's thousand and one warnings that are all shouting in the back of my head. It's a trap. Free milk. Diseases. One track minds. This is just hormones. Whore. Pregnancy. Sin.

I want assurances.

"I'm scared," I blurt out. Where it came from, I have no idea, but there it is.

"Okay." Jonah puffs out a chuckle beneath startled eyebrows. "As long as we're being honest, I'm not."

"I don't know why I said that."

Jonah shrugs. "You can say anything you want."

Jonah doesn't let go, but drops down on my earlobe, pulling it between his teeth and suckling it. He drags his lips down my neck, all the way to my collarbone.

"This okay?" he asks.

"Yes." I yank one of my hands loose from his grasp and get hold of his shirt. I pull him down on me. With everything I've got, I push him over until I'm on top of him, a calf on each side of his ribs. I push his hands back on either side of his head and hold them there.

"Do you like this?"

"I do," he says.

With one kiss, I turn to goo. He pulls me down for a deep kiss, his jaw nudging mine open wider, his fingers at my back, unhitching my bra. It comes loose, the scrap of fabric falls away and Jonah rolls me off him, tucking me beneath him again. He pulls off his shirt and tosses it on the floor.

My inhibitions fall away with my clothes. I run my hands over his smooth, dark skin, feeling the supple muscles of his arms and chest. He drops his head, his lips on my breast. The warmth of his mouth arches my back. I've had boyfriends, I've been touched before.

197

But never like this.

Jonah unbuttons my jeans and slides them off, along with my panties. This is a different story. Lying naked on my bed, the sunlight filtering through the window, I want to be what Jonah thinks of me.

A woman.

I'm not sure how to get there, but I know Jonah knows the way as he slides his legs between mine, easing them further apart.

"Tell me if you want me to stop," he says.

"No, I don't want to stop," I say. "I want to go all the way."

I thought it was supposed to be like being stabbed in the crotch.

I thought there was supposed to be enough blood to destroy the whole mattress.

And I thought if neither of those things happened, than I thought it would've felt amazing.

None of that happened. I don't know if that means there is something wrong with me.

"Everything okay?" Jonah asks when I come out of the bathroom.

"I think so," I say, and his pager goes off. He takes it off the bedside table, checks the number and exhales with a groan as he swings his legs off the side of the bed.

"I don't believe this," he grumbles, pulling on his pants. "I have to go."

"Leave? Why?"

"My sister," he says. "She doesn't have a ride home from work. I've gotta go pick her up."

"She works midnights too?"

"Yeah," he says, shrugging into his shirt. "Come e're."

I go to him and he wraps his arms around me, sweeping my face with kisses until I laugh, which is good, because I feel like I'm going to cry. This isn't the way I expected it to happen my first time.

"Do you really have to go?"

He lets go of me and pushes his feet into his boots. "Trust me, I don't want to, but she'd be pissed if I made her spend on a taxi."

"But you haven't slept all night. You shouldn't drive like this."

"I'll be alright," he says, gathering my face in his hands. "I'll be thinking of how damn good you felt."

His kiss melts me and I can't help but cling to him, his smooth muscles beneath my hands.

He pulls away first. "You're working tonight?"

"Not today. Tomorrow night," I say.

"Want me to come by tomorrow night?"

"Can't you come back later?"

He smiles. "I'm beat. I've gotta work tomorrow, and if I come back here, I'm not going to sleep at all."

"But that'd be fun, wouldn't it?"

He lifts the spare room key off the dresser that I gave him earlier. "How about if I take this and let myself in if I can make it back?"

I beam as he slips it into his pocket. With another kiss, he heads for the door.

"Can I call you?" I ask. "I'd need your number."

He turns back again. I love seeing him do that.

He flips open my sketch book on the dresser.

"Nice," he says, pointing to my last sketch. It's still not done—the picture of Grimm's King Grisly-Beard—the creepy fiddler, his beard spreading apart and the princess peeking out from beneath it. With one of my drawing pencils, Jonah scratches his digits at the bottom.

"I'll see you tomorrow," he says, pausing to drag his eyes up my naked body and ending with a slow smile that sets me on fire.

I'm so glad my first was Jonah. I just wish he wouldn't leave.

Jonah's gone for an hour and I already miss him.

I bury my face against the bed sheets and inhale Jonah. I hold the pillow he used over my face and breathe in and out until his scent seems to disappear.

I finally roll over to the phone and dial the number he left, excited to tell him I'm thinking of him, but I don't get a phone. I get his pager. I punch in my number, but after an hour, my eyelids get so heavy, I fall asleep.

Waking up is a different story. I get up at midnight. The dark makes everything seem even lonelier. I take the chain off the door, in case Jonah shows up. And I stay naked.

I page Jonah, but he doesn't call.

I eat a peanut butter sandwich on dried-out bread.

I page Jonah. He doesn't call. Maybe it's too late. He's probably sleeping.

I try to draw and can't. I scribble all over the King Grisly-Beard picture and rip it out of my sketch book and wad it up, until I remember it's got Jonah's pager number on it. I smooth it out and stick it in the corner of my mirror.

I watch channel 3, but my fingers don't come close to how it felt with Jonah. It leaves me frustrated and depressed.

I pick up the phone to page him again, but put it back down on the cradle.

By four in the morning, I can't stay awake any longer, and the next time I wake up, I know by the way the sun is blasting in through the blinds, Jonah couldn't come back. The chain on the door is still hanging free, but he's got to be next door, at work, by now.

My mood spirals into the dirt. I make up all kinds of scenarios, of Jonah using me and throwing me away, of him stealing all my money—but I check my ballerina box and it's all there. Will pounds on my door and I ignore him. Lavina calls up to ask if I'm okay, and in my most cheerful voice I tell her everything's fine and why would she ask? I assume Jonah's been in, kissing and telling, but when Lavina says, "'Cause you ain't been glued to my cart" it makes me feel missed and therefore, better.

I'm in a terrible mood when I go downstairs to relieve Ned. He leaves me with a heap of film that unraveled from a tape stuck in the machine.

"I picked it outta there, so you can rewind it back into the case," he says.

"Fine," I say tightly, glancing at the pile of film as I put the cash drawer on the desk top.

"Aww...what's the matter, Fail? You down because—"

"Shut the fuck up, Ned."

He juts his lip out. "Oh, that's a big word for you, little girl."

I can't take any more of it. I fly out of the office chair and spin on him. His eyes are wider than I expected when I punch my index finger against the center of his grungy t-shirt.

"I've had enough of your shit, Ned! You hear me? Enough!" The words spew out and it feels good to loose control. "Mind your own business! I don't get in yours—don't get in mine! And I'll rewind the tape that you were too lazy to take care of, but you're going to sit down and shut up and let me count the fucking drawer because I'm sick and tired of you ripping me off!" I scream in his face. I jab his sternum so hard, he blinks and winces every time I do it. I throw myself back down on the office chair when I'm finished. "I don't care how long it takes either!"

"Okay...just chill out, Fail," he says, but he doesn't crowd me anymore.

"You're ten short," I growl.

Ned yanks out his wallet and throws ten bucks on the counter. He leaves with a slam of the cage door.

I'm an hour into my shift when the door alarm blares and then, there's Jonah, standing in front of the payment window, an easy grin on his handsome face.

My anger melts away at the sight of him, but I can't let him know that. I look away.

"Don't be like that, baby girl," he says softly and the rest of my glacier attitude dissolves with the new nickname. "I couldn't call. The phone was out at home. Don't be mad at me...there wasn't anything I could do."

"You could've driven your car to a pay phone and let me know. I was worried about you."

"I was waitin' on the phone company to fix the phone. I thought they were gonna get it fixed right fast, but I ended up waiting all day. Fuckin' phone company's got no idea what they're doin'."

I don't want to be mad. What I want is to be upstairs with Jonah again, naked, in my bed.

He walks around to the cage door and raps softly with his knuckles, chin down, eyes up. Adorable. I open up.

As soon as he's inside, he scoops me into his arms. "I've been waiting all day for this. I've been thinking of how you look," he pauses to nip my ear and whispers, "down there."

I hide my blush by grinding my face against his shoulder as the lightening bugs bubble up inside me.

"I missed you," I say.

"Missed you too," he says. He brings his folding chair back into the cage and we settle into the seats, although I would rather be nestled in his lap.

"How's your sister?"

He observes me a moment, like he's sizing up my question. "She's good. She was mad she had to wait as long as she did for me to pick her up, but she's good."

"Where does she work?"

He squints now, folding his arms over his chest. "A bar."

I've overstepped his line, it's all over his face. "I'm just curious," I say lightly, pulling at one of his elbows, but his arms stay solid. "I just want to know about your family. Who they are. What they're like—"

"You wanna see 'em?" Jonah says. I'm grateful when his arms loosen and he reaches for his wallet. He pulls out his billfold and opens it up. From an inner slot, he pulls three pictures and lays them out one at a time on the desk. "This one's my mother. She's been gone two years now."

It's an old picture, frayed at the edges. She's not black. She's a white woman with honey hair and brown eyes. I recognize the fine bones of her face in Jonah, the shape of his eyes, maybe even the color. Everything about her is Jonah, except the color of his skin, the kink in his hair, his masculinity.

"What happened to her?" I ask.

He shrugs. "Cancer."

"I'm sorry," I say. He nods somberly, returns her photo to his wallet, and taps the second picture. "This is Nia."

"Your sister?" I pick up the photo. He nods.

She's as dark as Yolanda, with loose curls that reach her shoulders. Her nose is wider, like a little bubble on the end, smaller eyes than Jonah. Her body is small on the top and bulbous on the bottom. I wonder if she'd like me.

"She's pretty," I say.

"She knows it too," Jonah laughs, taking back the photo. "And this is Nia's son, Little Man," he says, exchanging it for the last picture. "DeAndre. He's fifteen months old. We call him De."

Nobody looks exactly alike in Jonah's family. Jonah's nephew is medium skinned, with black curls and a broad, little nose beneath bright, happy eyes. Jonah's eyes sparkle as he talks about what a handful De is, how he got stitches last week when he bumped his head on a coffee table and how he sings nonsense sounds while eating his baby oatmeal. Listening to him gush about his nephew makes Jonah even more handsome to me.

"What's all this?" Jonah asks, picking up the heap of film Ned left me.

"Ned's screw up. I've got to get it back into the case."

"I'll do it," Jonah says. He pulls out a pocket knife and lifting the case, uses the knife like a screwdriver to twist the wheel in the middle of the tape. Slowly, the case chews up the long line of film, but the heap falls on the floor at Jonah's feet. He scoops it and dumps it back on the desk.

Even though I wonder why he didn't answer my pages, as we talk about things that matter, and things that don't, I get more and more certain that Jonah and I are great together. I know we are, because there is a bubble in me that fills up when he speaks and I float. I ground myself only long enough to contribute to the conversation, and then I drift into him again.

The door alarm blares and a man in a ragged windbreaker hurries in like he's going to get stuck in the door. He weaves in, smoothing down his hair as his lips murmur wordlessly. His eyes are bugged open so wide that his pupils appear like life rafts adrift in a sea. The man's head jerks with his eyes, looking at me and then at Jonah. He walks down the length of the counter, sliding along on one elbow until he stops at the window vent.

He puts his mouth close to the vent, his crazy eyes rooted on me. "Got rooms?"

Before I can answer, he spins on a heel so he's facing the wide, transparent pane of the snack machine.

"Got rooms?" he barks at the hooked rows of cookies and chips. He presses his face against the plastic window of the machine. "Did you hear me? Do you got rooms?"

"Nah," Jonah calls out in his lovely, mellow tone. "There's no rooms available tonight, sir."

There's a whole rack of keys on the wall behind me—Monday nights aren't all that busy. The man twists around to face Jonah this time.

"Sorry, man," Jonah says. "There's nothing for you here." Jonah gives him a grin that passes as a simple smile between friends.

The man doesn't smile back, but he nods. "Ok then. Thanks. Thank you. I'll tell them." The guy turns and weaves out of the lobby, patting the pay phone, like it's a small child, before he walks out the door.

"We get a lot of characters at the oil shop too." Jonah chuckles. The film falls off the counter in a heap again. I get a surge of warmth for Jonah as he gathers it up and dumps it on the desk top for the second time. Here he is, my first, and he could've one-night-standed me, but he's sitting here winding up film and talking to me instead.

I watch his long, supple fingers work, untangling the film before winding most of it into the case, and I think of how those fingers were all over me. I close my eyes for a split second at the memory, but when a customer throws a key in the slot, I pop open my eyes and Jonah's clear gaze is the first thing I see.

"I have to go up and change those sheets on that short stay," I say.

Jonah finishes the last twist on the VCR case, the film disappearing like nothing ever happened. "I'll give you a hand."

I grab the linens, towels, and washcloths from the laundry room and we head up to the second floor together.

"Mmm, mmm!" Jonah hums behind me. I know where his eyes are as I climb the steps ahead of him.

I knock on the room door and when no one answers, I pop it open. There are wet towels on the bathroom floor and sheets twisted on the bed. Jonah helps me strip and re-make the bed and I use the soiled sheets to collect the towels off the floor. We dump it all in Lavina's cart at the end of the hall.

"I think I dropped my pocket knife in that room," Jonah says, so we return and open the door again. I follow him in and Jonah crosses the room to the opposite side of the bed we just made. Once there, he runs his hand along the bedspread, finally stopping to pat it, like an invitation, as his eyes flick up to look at me.

The look starts a shiver in my spine that spreads to my heart and drizzles down, like warm honey, into my stomach. I'm aware of every inch of my body, from the fine hairs rising up on my arms to the thump of my heart hammering in my fingertips as he reaches for me and I reach back. He curls his hand around my neck and pulls me into his kiss.

"I have to get back to the desk," I murmur.

"Fuck the desk," Jonah whispers back as he lays me down on the bed. He grabs hold of my waist, his breath racing across my cheek. He yanks down my jeans and then Jonah pushes my legs back, my knees to my chest. He pulls a condom from his pocket and rolls it on. He spits in his hand

and rubs the lubrication between my legs.

It's hard, and fast, and I guess it's exciting because this isn't the way we've had sex before. His tongue jams into my mouth and then he pushes into me, shoving me across the bed with each thrust. My hair gets trapped under Jonah's hand and tugs my head sideways. Jonah buries himself so deep inside me, I wince. It hurts more than it did yesterday. I hold onto his shoulders and he scoops my rear into his hands, pulling me closer as he drives himself into me.

I suck in a sharp breath.

Jonah doesn't even slow down.

And then it is over with one heavy moan. He falls down on top of me, pulsing out the last of his passion. A tiny drip of sweat runs down my chest between my breasts, but he doesn't see it since my shirt is still on. Jonah pulls away, the rubber hanging from him, wet and filled with his white milk. He goes into the bathroom and flushes it away.

I pull on my pants. It's way more awkward to do it like this, so rushed. I'm not sure what to say or do when he comes out of the bathroom, but Jonah just swats the wrinkles we made off the bed cover.

"Looks like we were never even here," he says triumphantly as we leave the room.

As soon as we're in the hall, the door alarm sounds and I scuttle away, rushing down to the lobby alone, in case it's Clive.

Jonah brings change for Lavina on Tuesday morning. He comes in just as I'm getting off work.

"Time for breakfast?" I ask hopefully.

"Not this mornin'. I've got inventory to do at the shop," he says. He loops an arm around my shoulders and jiggles me. "No time for foolin' around today."

I giggle and when I look back, Lavina gives me a long, studying look. Jonah hasn't even kissed me, but Lavina knows. I can tell. Her eyebrows hike up, but she doesn't say anything. I watch Jonah walk out, hoping he looks back at me, but he doesn't. Probably for the best. He said he didn't want to spread our business around and have everybody in it. Me looking after him is probably verifying what Lavina's already thinking.

"Ain't you gonna folla' me 'round and hassle me while I clean?" Lavina asks as I float toward the stairs.

"No, I'm beat. I'm going to go up to bed," I say. Really, I'm going to grab a shower and lay in bed, hoping Jonah will use the room key I gave him on his break.

He doesn't.

I wake up after the oil shop has closed and Jonah's already gone home. Will asks me to read him fairy tales that night, but I tell him I don't feel like it. There's no such thing. There's just crap that happens. Will doesn't ask me anything else.

But on Wednesday, Jonah knocks on my door at lunch time. He's got a big sandwich.

"Sorry, I couldn't make it yesterday," he says as I pull him into the room. The door slams behind him.

"It's okay, you're here now," I tell him between kisses. "And you don't have to knock anymore. You've got a key."

"I forgot about that," he says, dropping the sandwich on the dresser. "I'll be using it though."

We do it, even though I feel like I'm half asleep. It's great. The whole thing feels like the most beautiful dream. I float above him and we make love, all slow and sensual, like we're in the movies. Cinema ones, not the ones on channel three. My whole body starts to quiver and I squeeze my eyes shut. My muscles take over as the tingle explodes through me.

I fall asleep beside him, before we even eat the sandwich. I may never need to eat again.

I wake up alone to the sound of a man in the neighboring room, moaning. I turn on my TV to some redneck talk show and jack up the volume.

There's no note from Jonah, no sign that he was here, except the soggy sandwich on the dresser. It feels really weird. It's also past the time when the oil shop closes, so I know Jonah has gone home for the day.

I page him. Five long minutes later, the phone rings.

"Wha's up, Silver Spoon?" he says.

It's hard to be angry when he sounds so upbeat. "It was weird waking up without you," I tell him. "I was hoping you'd come back after work."

"I couldn't make it. I had stuff to do, and my mama said she was makin' her famous spaghetti tonight. She'd kill me if I didn't come home." Then he gets all business-like, "But I'll be there bright and early tomorrow morning, ahright? I've got the last of the inventory to finish, so I'm getting an early start."

"Well, I miss you, and I can't wait to see you," I whisper into the phone. "Maybe you can bring me some of Nia's spaghetti."

"I'll see what I can do. See ya tomorrow, early."

Zing.

Jonah brings over Lavina's change in the morning. Every time I look at him, he's staring at me. We're both waiting for the same thing. I hang around in the lobby long after Lavina's counted the drawer. I buy a pop, and look in the lounge fridge, and fill up a bucket of ice, until Lavina finally disappears up the stairs and leaves us alone. I dump the ice.

"You wanna go up and lay down for a little?" Jonah asks.

Like I'd say no.

My stomach jumps as we climb the stairs. I just want to get him to my room and get naked.

Jonah follows my eyes to Will's ledge between the second and third floor. There is a pile of fast food toys in the corner with a dirty sock draped over them. No matter how Lavina gets after him, he won't stay off the ledge. Every now and then, she clears off his stuff though. He has to pull it all out of her cart trash can. I know he removed the fake plant from the tacky gold pot and stuffed his Superman costume, that he wears like pajamas, into the bottom. I'm kind of relieved that Will is nowhere around now, since I'm on a mission.

"Who does that kid belong to?" Jonah asks.

"He and his mom live here. Third floor, opposite end of the hall from me," I say as we trudge up the last set of stairs. We step off the landing into the hall and I swing a finger toward Will's door.

"They're in 36."

"A little kid living in a motel should be against the law," Jonah says, shaking his head.

We hold hands as we walk down the hall toward my room. We're walking so close that the static should be visible between us, sparking as our shoulders brush every couple steps.

"Do you like living here?" he asks.

"It's okay," I say. "Why are you asking?"

"Just wonderin'," he says. "I don't like you livin' here much. It's dangerous for a pretty white girl in a place like this. You been lucky."

"It's not so bad," I say as I unlock the door and we go in.

I stand silently at the edge of my dresser, hands behind me, impaling my palm on the corner every time I sway backward. As Jonah spins slowly, checking out the contents of my room.

It was such a strange thing to say, but it lit me up with little sparks of wondering. Maybe he's thinking about what it would be like to move in with me. I don't know how I'd do it, since Clive pays me in rent and peanuts on top of that, but if I had more time with Jonah, I'd find a way. I push my hand against the edge of the dresser again, waiting for him to say more.

"So why do you live here?" he asks. "How come you're not in an apartment someplace?"

What would it be like living with Jonah? I haven't known him that long, but— "Nobody's going to want to rent to me until I'm older."

"When's your birthday?"

"The 22nd..." I say and he cocks an eyebrow. "of June."

His eyebrow falls. It's only the end of September, after all. "That would technically make you closer to sixteen than to eighteen. It would be tough to get a landlord to rent to you."

"Where do you live?" I ask.

"Downtown." He cocks his head to one side with a lazy smile. "Why are we still talking about living arrangements when we could be layin' in that bed? C'mere." He pats the bed beside himself. "I won't bite. At least, not hard."

"It'd be nice if we could do this all the time," I say.

Jonah's smile blasts away my thoughts like a hose on tissue-paper flowers. I climb across the bed and into his lap. He wraps his arms around me and kisses my head before easing me down onto my back.

"I might've lied," he warns me.

"I think I'm falling in love with you," I whisper. I want to test the waters, dip in a toe.

He takes my face in both hands and kisses me, long and slow. "Then I might bite hard after all," he says.

THIRTEEN

"Your boy still** want to kill me?" Ned asks with a smirk as I count the drawer.

He and Jonah have kept their distance since that night with Yolanda a few weeks back. Jonah has kept his promise to me. When he comes over to see me, he doesn't even look in Ned's direction. Ned has kept his mouth shut too, and the drawer has been pretty accurate, so I'm not complaining.

"I think he might, if you call him a boy," I say.

What I don't mention is that I haven't seen Jonah since the day before yesterday, and his car was gone from the parking lot across the street when I came down for work. He admires me so much for being independent, I don't want him to see me being needy. At first, I tried paging him, but after that initial page, he's never answered another. He says he hates the thing and since he groans every time it goes off, I believe him.

"I only got it for Nia, if she needs me to get her from work or to watch De," he told me when I asked. "Otherwise, I ignore it. I ain't a dog on a leash."

I don't want him feeling like that with me, but I don't know why he bothered giving me the number. There's a hundred times a day that I think it would be nice to be able to get ahold of him and hear his voice.

The front door opens and Santa, the old bum, comes shuffling in. I haven't seen him since Clive caught him leaving one morning and just about threw the old man out the door.

Santa is wearing what he always does- his salmon, fine-knit woman's pullover with stains all over the belly that remind me of popped soap bubbles. His feet are stuffed into his army boots; the tongues hang with the laces missing.

He pauses at the pay phone to swipe a dirty finger through the coin return. When he comes up empty, he shuffles to the pop machine, sucking in his bottom lip and chewing on his bristly whiskers. He checks the returns of each of the vending machines.

"Hey," I stand up to shout at him through the vent. "You can't sleep on the couch anymore."

Ned grabs my arm. "What are you doing?"

"Clive caught that guy sleeping on the couch and he said he'd fire me if I let him stay again!" I wrench my arm loose. Santa acts like he's deaf and continues on, hobbling into the lounge, but Ned grabs hold of me again before I can get a grip on the office door.

"Clive ain't gonna fire you," Ned scoffs. "How often do you let him stay?"

"Whenever he wants," I say, jerking loose for the second time. "But I'm not losing my job over it!"

"You risk your job every time you let that fuckwad across the street sit in here," Ned grumbles, but he pushes past me out the cage door.

"Hey, I didn't sign off on the drawer yet—"

But Ned's not on his way out. He goes across the lounge, to the couch where Santa's bedded down to sleep.

"Hey man," Ned says. I've never heard him speak like this before.

Respectful. "You gotta wake up. You can't stay here tonight."

Santa burbles, jolting upright the moment he sees Ned beside him.

Ned stays hunkered down at the man's knees. "Sorry about waking you."

Santa blinks up at the lights and rubs his beard. He stands, pulling his dirty bag from the end of the couch. Ned watches, still crouched on the floor.

"I just wanted to know...if you remember James...James Guernsey? He used to hang out at the Catholic church about two miles down from here...Saint Peter's. He's about my height. He likes to be called Jesse James sometimes." A laugh trembles across Ned's lips.

"Why?" Santa checks the piece of rope that keeps his bag shut.

"He always thinks he's in a gun fight...and he's my dad," Ned says. Santa hauls the bag over his shoulder by the rope. Ned stands. "Do you know him?"

Santa shakes his head. "Dead," he says. He hobbles away from Ned, down the length of the lobby and out the door.

I'm frozen inside the cage door, watching.

Ned puts his hands on his waist and kicks the floor with the toe of his shoe. He stifles a short, unhappy laugh and then he brings up his eyes and sees me watching him.

"What're you lookin' at?" he barks, the tenderness is gone.

"Nothing." I say.

"Don't be so fuckin' nosey." He saunters toward me. "What's the big deal? My dad's a homeless turd. He's been in the nut house a million times. He walks around shooting people with his fingers...he's a fuckin' freak show."

"I'm sorry he's dead." I say. Ned just grunts.

"He ain't dead. He ain't around, but he ain't dead."

"I'll throw that guy out if he comes in again," I say. It's the least I can do. For me and for Ned, I think.

But Ned shakes his head. "No, don't." His head falls. "Just let the poor bastard sleep on the couch if he needs to." Ned pokes the cash drawer on the desk top. "Jesus, is the drawer squared yet, Fail? You're so goddamn slow."

One o'clock in the morning happens with a car roaring down the boulevard and the cops chasing after it. Once the lights and sirens have disappeared, I pick up the desk phone and do what I was determined not to. I page Jonah.

"You're always so boring," Will says from overhead. He's been on the ledge for the last hour watching me draw and erase, draw and erase, in my sketch book. It seems like nothing I draw looks right anymore.

"Then go find something else to do," I say.

"It takes you forever to make one pi'ture," he groans. "And it don't even look like nothin'."

"It's a cottage." I roll my eyes.

He scrunches up his face. "What the hell's a cottage?"

"Quit swearing."

"You swear all the time now."

"I'm an adult."

"So am I," he argues. "What's a cottage?"

I sigh. This kid's impossible. "A little house in the woods."

"Who'd want to live in a hunka wood?"

"Not a hunk of wood...woods. You know, a bunch of trees? Haven't you ever seen woods?"

"I know what wood is, retard," he snaps. He jerks his head out of the

216

hole. That's what he does when he's embarrassed, but I didn't even mean to embarrass him. I just forget how Will doesn't know about things I think everyone knows about. Like woods. It's an exotic, fairytale place to him, and super weird to me that he's never even seen a place like the one I grew up in. Especially when it's only about a half hour drive from here. Or maybe he's lying.

Either way, he's a little kid—a pain in the butt one, but a kid all the same—so I cut him some slack.

"You want me to read you the story about this cottage?" I ask him. "It's kind of creepy."

It takes a minute, but his head finally pops back through the hole. His hair is a mess. "You can do whatever you want."

That means yes. I flip back to the first page of Hansel and Gretel and start reading. Will leans his cheek on the edge of the hole in the ceiling, listening.

The alarm over the door goes off half-way through and Will jerks up, hitting his head. He's still cursing when Yolanda peeks in, peering around all wide-eyed. I thunk the book closed.

"Clive here?" he asks from the threshold.

I shake my head.

He comes all the way in then, smoothing his fake hair away from his face. It's a weird, black wig tonight with blunt bangs. Yolanda keeps shaking his head and blowing the strands out of his eyes as he walks past the counter to the stairs. He's wearing my skirt and my bracelet. That he still hasn't paid for.

"You don't have a room, do you?" I call to him.

He stops at the bottom stair, turning so the skirt flares.

"I do, darlin'. Lavina checked me in. You kin look in the book if ya don't believe me. I'm under Dawn Smitty."

I grab the ledger and flop it open on top of the counter, giving Yolanda a sour stare until I drop my eyes to look for his name. He's there, just like he said. I clap the book shut again.

"You mad 'bout somethin', lamb?" Yolanda asks.

"Yeah," I say. "You still owe me fifteen bucks, for that skirt and that bracelet."

"They're my favorites!" Yolanda says, swirling on the runner. "It's jus' that I been so broke, sweetie. I been meanin' to bring ya the money, but I ain't seen ya when I got money, and then when I don't got it, here ya are!"

"You know my room number, you can drop it off," I tell him. My money's been disappearing so quick—all of it sucked up in groceries and stupid stuff, like deodorant and tampons and toothpaste. There's nothing left for nail polish or magazines or any new clothes. Considering I'm dead broke until payday, four days from now, fifteen bucks seems like a thousand.

"I'll come an' see ya before I leave," Yolanda says, his hand over his heart like he's a boy scout. I just close the ledger and dump it on the desk.

"Whatever," I say.

Yolanda frowns. "Nah, nah, nah, baby girl...you think I'm lyin' to ya and it ain't like that."

"I don't know if you are or not, but I know you said I'd have my money almost a month ago."

Yolanda throws his manicured hands in the air. "And I been tryin' to get it for ya!"

"Ahright." I throw a bit of Lavina's accent in my words. It makes me feel strong. I add one of her little shrugs too.

"Don't you doubt me now, honey," Yolanda says. "That would break mah heart."

"Ahright," I say again.

He finally goes up the stairs. I change the movie and settle back down onto the office chair in a worse mood, thinking of how I just gave him my stuff without getting the money for it. Just like Ned and the drawer all over again.

I tip back my head. "Will?" I call. "You still up there?"

No answer.

I open up my sketch book and stare at the page, trying to get back in the mood, but Yolanda's ruined everything. And Jonah did too, since he hasn't called me back and I haven't seen him. Even Will let me down, disappearing when I'm so irritated with everyone else and could use someone to annoy me. I want to come out of my skin.

I hear a familiar tread coming down the steps. I don't know how I can identify Samson's footsteps, but I can, and I want to sink down beneath the desk when I do. He trots down to the lobby and when he sees me, a grin leaks out across his face like an oil spill.

He stops in front of the payment window, takes out his wallet, and fishes out a couple dollar bills. He drops them over the middle lip, but his fingers don't linger like his eyes do.

"How you been, Lael?" he asks. His dark eyes would be handsome if they didn't look like he was going to rip me to pieces the first chance he gets.

"Good," I say, giving him two dollars worth of quarters. I don't drop them so they roll away like Ned would.

Samson takes them and turns his back to me, popping them into the Coke machine. He gets two cans and turns back to the vent in the glass.

"You thought any 'bout what I said the last time we talked?"

I shudder. He can't be serious. I swallow hard. "I've got a boyfriend."

"Well, we ain't gotta tell him nothin'." Samson says thoughtfully, rubbing a finger on the countertop. "'Sides, every man like his woman to bring in a little income, don't they?"

"Not mine," I say. I'm positive Jonah would have something to say about that.

"Oh, you'd be surprised," Samson says. He turns sideways, glancing between me and the snack machine. "What kind of treats you like?"

"No thanks, I'm good," I say.

"C'mon now, this one's on me," he purrs.

My legs quiver beneath the desk. "No really, I'm alright. Honest."

"C'mon, girl, I'm trying to make amends, here! Let me get you some sweets."

No way am I opening the office door. "No thanks," I say.

Samson's polite grin dissolves. "This how you gonna be?"

I'm sitting behind a wall of bulletproof glass and a counter so substantial a car couldn't crush it. Sure, the door has a glass window and it's probably hollow in the middle, but it's locked. But at some point, I'm probably going to run into Samson in the hall again.

"I appreciate it, but I'm not hungry," I say. "Thanks anyway."

He rolls his tongue in his cheek. "That boyfriend you got...where he at? In a place like this...you gonna run into trouble sometime. Where's 'e gonna be then?"

"He'll be there for me," I say, but all the unanswered calls to Jonah's pager definitely crosses my mind.

"We'll see." Samson's eyes are dark as metal and they seem to throw sparks when he speaks. He raps his knuckles on the counter and pushes away. "Ahright, well, if ya ev'a git lonely, ya let me know. I'll send a friend by."

I let out a deep breath when he finally goes up the steps, but it doesn't relax me. I never want to meet any of Samson's friends.

Saturn throws open the door around five in the morning. Thank God I'm not sleeping at the desk, because Clive rolls in right behind her, laughing like I've never seen. His gold tooth glints beneath the fluorescent lights of the lobby.

"Which floor are you on, baby?" Saturn asks. I stare at her, waiting for her to see me and wave or something, but her eyes are glued on Clive.

"Second floor," he says, handing her the room key. "You go on up and I'll be there in a minute."

She drops a little kiss on his cheek and starts up the steps. She goes up slowly, maybe because her heels are ridiculously high and the width of carpenter's nails, or it could be because her broken ribs are still healing. Or maybe she just wants Clive to stare at her butt. Whichever it is, Clive doesn't seem to notice. He comes around to the cage door and I open it up for him, speechless. How did he meet her? Does he know what she is?

"How's b'iness tonight?" he asks.

"Uh...good," I say. I open the cash drawer. "Do you want to count the drawer?"

"Nah, Lavina'll do it when she come in." He reaches in and takes out a handful of twenties. I have no idea how many. Clive waves a hand at the TV. "Keep them movies runnin', eh?"

"Yup. I do," I say. He goes out, slamming the cage door behind him. He jogs up the stairs.

What just happened?

I can hardly wait for Lavina to show up and let me off my shift, but now I'm worried about the drawer. Clive just took a fist full of bills without counting them. I can probably figure out how many, by the number of rentals subtracted from Ned's drawer, but Clive's still got to okay it. And what if this is the one night I actually made a mistake?

I sit back on the office chair, pulling up my legs. I need Jonah. I really,

221

really, need Jonah.

And I keep on needing him until Lavina bustles in at eight o'clock, catching her lunchbox and purse strap on the door.

"Halleluiah, Jesus!" she shouts. It's not a prayer. She jerks her straps loose from the edge of the door handle and keeps on coming, only pausing once to pluck a scrap of paper off the runner and grumble about it under her breath. I open the door before she gets to it. "Who been in here? A herd'a livestock?" she asks as she walks in. "Them runners got to be cleaned now!"

"Clive came in with Saturn," I blurt.

"Saturn? Who she?" she asks, putting her lunch on the desk.

"That girl...you know." I swivel my hips, but Lavina's not paying attention.

"No, I don't know," she snaps. I should've known from the purse straps, she's in no mood for guessing.

"The girl upstairs," I whisper to her. "The one I gave the money to. The weed?"

"She got weed?" Lavina leans back, peering at me.

"No! That hooker we talked to out in the hall about Samson?"

"Ohhh, her—girl wit' the as'prin," Lavina says. That's as much as she cares. She takes the cash drawer out and sits down on the protesting office chair.

"Before you count that, Clive was in here and he took a handful of twenties out. But he didn't count them or tell me how much he took."

"Well, he owns the place," Lavina mumbles. "But *Lawd*, I hate when he do dat. He up in his room?"

I nod as she picks up the phone and punches in his room number.

"Boss man...yeah, don't mean to interrupt, but ya took a withdraw? Uh huh. How much? Ahright." She hangs up.

I hope he told her the right amount, or I'm screwed. I hold my breath until Lavina's done counting the drawer.

"It square," she says, putting it back. She peeks over her shoulder through the blinds at the oil shop. "How's you an' Jonah doin'?"

"Good," I say, but I can't lie to Lavina. I have to tell her everything, whether she wants to hear it or not. Lavina does that to me. "But I'm worried about him. He was over here every day, but then, sometimes he doesn't show up and he won't call me back when I page him."

"Ahhh...you one of them needy girls."

I draw back, stung. "I'm not needy!"

"He don't call ya back for a day and you all worried? You white girls is all da same."

I bristle at that. All of it.

"Are you saying that black girls don't worry if the guy they're seeing goes missing? He just wanders off, and you all are like, out of sight, out of mind?"

"We all?" Lavina hooks her head around at me. When she gets her neck going, it's not good, but I'm annoyed too.

"You said all you white girls!"

"'Cause you is!" she laughs, as if that makes everything okay. She stands up and lifts the blind behind the desk, looking across the street again. "Look like he ova' there now," she says. "Why don't ya g'won ova' an' ask 'im where he been?"

"No thanks," I say as I grab my stuff and go out of the cage. "'Cause I'm not needy like that."

"Oh, da's new." Lavina's teasing follows me up the stairs.

I tromp past Will on his ledge. "You want me to spit on her?" he whispers.

"No," I say, because Lavina would kill him. But I kind of wish he wouldn't listen to me this one time.

Saturday...still no Jonah and now I'm stubborn about it because of what Lavina said to me yesterday about being needy. I ignore Will all night and don't read him stories. I don't draw, but I doodle an entire page of question marks.

"Lael?" Jonah's deep voice rumbles through the door, just as I'm drifting off to sleep. He must've lost the key. I stumble out of bed and open up.

I realize my mistake immediately.

The man outside isn't Jonah. He's a white guy, about the same height but wafer thin, and this man is bald with scabs on his face. He lays his hand against the door and flashes a jack o' lantern smile.

I grab the edge and try to slam it shut on him, but the man stuffs his boot in the opening.

"Hey...Lael, right?" he says, flashing me a fifty dollar bill. His voice rushes over my spine like Novocain. Even my shiver is paralyzed. "Kin I come in? I jus' wanna talk wich you a minit." "

I choke out the one word that should save me. "No."

I feel the pressure of his hand from the other side. "A friend tole me ya live here all 'lone and ya wouldn't mine some company ... I got money."

"No," I say. I already know what's happening. Samson's words clang in my memory, *I'll send a friend by.*

I throw my weight against the door.

It's useless.

The guy shoves his way in. The door slams behind him.

"Samson said fifty." The guy throws the bill on the dresser and it falls down behind the furniture. "Steep, but I can see you might be worth it. He said you got a fresh pussy that ain't been popped. Where'd he find you?"

The words, *I'm not a hooker* go round and round my brain, but they don't find an exit. I just stand there, bracing for a fight and trying to figure out how I can get past him and out the door.

The guy smiles. "He said you like 'em aggressive."

I'm too terrified to scream. I want to, but while my mouth hangs open, the sound is stuffed in my throat like a sock.

The guy rushes forward, pressing me back toward the bed. He hooks my ankle, jerking my feet out from under me as he pushes me backward onto the mattress. I land on my back and he jumps on top of me, his boney frame falling against me like sharp, heavy sticks. He exhales a stale breath over my face; his dirty fingers claw at my pajama bottoms, ripping them free. Whichever way I move, his knee digs into my crotch. His chest is a vice pressing me flat.

My vocal cords come loose, but he slaps a filthy hand over my mouth. I taste the grime on his skin as I scream through his fingers. The sound comes from deep in my throat, but settles in the room like dust. He jams his knee up between my legs again, hitting me so hard, a red hot shot of pain rifles up from my pelvis and knocks the air out of me.

He fumbles with his zipper, but he can't get himself free with me twisting and biting. His breathing flashes in my nose in hot, sour bursts as we struggle and grunt. He shoves his fingers between my legs, but I'm so locked up, he can't get in. His fingernails cut into me. I don't know how long I can keep fighting like this.

I never hear the scrape in the lock.

But I do hear my door handle punch a hole in the wall.

"WHUCH YOU DOIN', NIGGA?" Jonah roars as he drags the guy off me sideways. The pain between my legs is incredible.

I roll onto my side as Jonah throws the guy on the floor. Clutching myself, I have to get further away. I shove off the opposite side of the bed, hunched and still clutching myself, as Jonah kicks the man on the floor over and over again. Jonah winds back his steel-toed work boot again and again, cussing at the guy as he sinks his boot into the man's gut. The groan from the floor is excruciating to hear. I think Jonah is deaf. He lands another kick and I hear a sick crunch. I shriek, backing up and knocking over my coat rack piled with clothes.

Jonah glances up, spots me, and the expression on his face shifts down from boiling rage to fury.

"Whuch you doin', man?" Spit flies from Jonah's mouth.

The man's hands shoot up over the side of the bed in surrender as Jonah's leg swings back and he shoots his heavy boot out at the man again. There's a horrific crack and the man's hands fall with a pitiful cry.

The only sound in the room is Jonah panting and the man softly crying and begging Jonah to stop.

"Get out!" Jonah shouts. He backs up, thrusting a finger toward the door, but the man on the floor only continues to cry. "GET OUT!" Jonah roars.

The man's head bobs up as he pushes his legs under him. He clutches his bleeding and broken face with one hand and his chest with the other. Jonah grabs hold of the man's shirt along the guy's spine and drags the stumbling man to the door. Jonah gets it open, shoves the guy into the hall, and slams the door shut behind him.

He turns to me, his expression so flat, I'm frightened of him too. I'm still folded down, mostly naked.

"Come 'ere," he says, motioning me over. He's still breathing hard.

I stay where I'm at, stunned. Shocked. My crotch is throbbing.

"You okay?" he asks.

I know he's talking, but suddenly my brain scrambles his words.

226

"Are you okay?" he asks again, his mouth moving slowly this time, his voice louder. He takes a step forward and I take one back, but I stumble and smash into the coat rack again. It scrapes a scar into the wall.

Jonah raises both palms toward me, as if he's a lion tamer. I try to cover myself with my hands, but I don't have enough hands to do it.

I nod at him. What I even mean, I don't know. But I keep nodding, like my nodder is stuck. I nod so he doesn't talk again. I nod so he stays away from me. I nod, I nod, I nod. *Fuck* if I know why. I just keep nodding.

It doesn't help. Jonah says things, but I don't understand the words. It's just sound, and his voice is too big for the room. It's the sound of the wood cutter. He's roared at the wolf but he's still dragging his ax overhead, letting it fly.

I think Jonah's trying to cut me out of this moment.

Get me loose.

I have to get out of the way.

He backs up. Flattens up against the door.

I step forward.

I want to peel off my skin and put on a new one.

I skitter past Jonah into the bathroom, slamming the door behind me. Locking it. Fast.

"You okay?" Jonah asks from the other side of the door. I understand the words. His voice wavers like he's going to cry, his question moving in jagged waves. I wonder if the woodcutter cried.

I turn on the shower and wait for the steam to erase me from the mirror. I step into the shower, the water scalding my skin. I scrub until I can't tell what hurts most or why.

When I finally emerge, I am deep pink instead of white.

My skin stings so much, I can't feel myself inside it.

Jonah taps on the door. "Lael," he says, "it's gonna be okay."

I want to tell him he has no right to say that to me.

The man's fifty dollar bill is still sitting on the dresser. That's the biggest violation of all.

Jonah is perched on the edge of my bed when I come out of the bathroom, a towel tied around me tighter than a noose. It's been an hour. He doesn't move, doesn't speak, but his brow is wrinkled, like a messy rug.

I fantasized, way before this happened, about how sexy it was when Jonah took care of me. I loved every time he fussed over me, or gathered me in his lap, or brought me food. Now, I just want him to leave me alone.

His worry makes me feel even more naked than I already am. It makes me think of his boots and his roar. Jonah became a man I didn't know.

"What can I do for you?" he asks.

I want my cool sheets. I want silence. I want nothing, but him to be *gone*. I need time inside my head to sort this all out.

"I'm alright," I say woodenly.

"You look sunburned."

I want him to stop looking. My nerves are scoured as raw as my skin by his gaze.

"I'm alright," I say again. "You can go."

He ignores that. "Do you want to lay down?"

"Yes." I go to the other side of the bed and slide between the sheets, the damp towel still wrapped tight around me.

"Do you want something to eat?"

"Yes," I say, only because I think he'll have to walk down to Red's to get it. He'll be gone for a half hour, at least. I can close my eyes then and try to forget the man. The smell of his breath. The finger gouging between my legs.

Jonah walks over to the edge of the dresser and starts poking around in the cardboard box full of cans. He holds up my bag of bread.

"Looks like it's molded," he says.

"I'd really like some hash browns," I say.

He perks up. "You want eggs too?"

"Yes. All of it." The more I order, the longer it will take for him to bring it back.

"Alright," Jonah says. "I'll be right back."

"Don't hurry," I whisper as he goes out the door. I am expecting to be able to exhale and close my eyes. But the man is there, pushing his way in, kneeing me between the legs over and over again. His fingers. His stink. The towel around me scratches and burns. I get up and put on my long pajamas.

The key scrapes in the door knob way too soon. He couldn't have gone to Red's and gotten back that fast. I draw my legs up, clutching the wadded blankets, my stomach turning over even as my throat closes. I choke on little gulps of air. There's nowhere to hide.

"It's me," Jonah says, walking into view. With one look at me, the wrinkles appear across his brow again. "It's just me," he says. "I got Will runnin' down for some food for us."

I wanted him gone, but now that I thought the man might be coming back, I don't want Jonah to leave.

"What can I do for you?" he asks.

"Lay here with me," I say. But don't touch me.

"Sure," he says, lying down on top of the blankets, beside me.

He reaches out for my hand and I stiffen, even with the sheet layered beneath his touch. He doesn't let go. Instead, he reaches for the remote with his free hand and turns on the TV, quickly shifting away from

Channel 3. He turns on a talk show. Turning his face to me, he raises his eyebrows in question.

I give his fingers a light squeeze. "It's okay."

He turns down the volume, kicks off his boots, and lays back on top of the covers. He doesn't let go of my hand under the sheet.

We lay there like that until Will knocks on the door with the food.

"Lael's okay?" I hear Will ask. I'm touched by the worry in his voice. Who knew that Will cared about anything?

"She's fine, little man. Did you get yourself somethin' to eat?"

"Pancakes," Will says. "Can I have money for pop?"

I hear some rustling, along with the squeak of the Styrofoam food trays, and then Will says, "Thanks!" His footsteps speed away as Jonah closes the door. The gust brings the stink of the food, heavy with butter.

"Food's here," Jonah says.

I don't sit up. "I don't think I want to eat."

"Ahright," Jonah says, but I can tell he's disappointed, after having bought all the food. He sets the trays down on my dresser and climbs back onto the bed, taking my hand through the sheet again.

"Don't you have to go back to work?" I ask.

"Nope. Marco's gonna cover the rest of my shift so I can stay here with you. He knew I wasn't comin' back by the way Will came tearin' into the shop."

"Will?"

"Yep," Jonah says. "He said he saw a man breakin' into your room."

Will. My eyes prickle. I have a gush of love for the kid who never wants to do anything but spit on me and steal my pop. I have to remember to get Will a six pack.

"How are you feelin'?" he asks softly.

"I just want to go to sleep," I say.

"Then g'won to sleep," Jonah says. "I'll be right here. Nothing's gonna happen to you now. I'll be watchin'."

"Alright," I say, closing my eyes. I believe him. For the first time, I exhale completely. My body relaxes. The sting becomes something like white noise to my nerves.

Jonah's hand is heavy on mine as I drift off.

FOURTEEN

My *mother calls* before my shift.

"How are you?" Her tone is as rigid as my nerves. "And how's that person you were seeing?"

"Jonah is fine," I answer. Thinking of him sends a warm glow through my heart. He's a *man* who protected and watched over me after I was attacked.

My mother never once told Bob to stop shoving me around. I don't want to talk to her about any of it. So much has changed since I last spoke to her.

I'm a woman now.

I'm a victim.

I've started narrowing my eyes and looking over my shoulders.

I don't smile at anybody I don't know anymore.

And the new me trusts my mom even less than the old me does. The only people in the world I trust right now are Jonah and Will. Maybe Lavina.

"I thought about what you said," my mother says, but there's that nasally sound in her voice, the one that means she hasn't thought at all about what I said, except to think about how she can spin it in a different direction and attack me for it. I don't think there's a road we haven't been down yet, and none of them lead out of where we're at. But I listen as she takes a deep breath, the one that means she's being patient with me. "I've come to terms with the fact that you're gone," she says and I frown on my end of the phone. "I know you're not coming back and I think that's for the best."

She thinks? "I *know* it is."

"Yes, well," a tiny, annoyed laugh escapes through the line. I'm sure it's grinding her to bits that this whole thing wasn't her idea. She wants to be the one doing the rejecting. "We are in agreement, at least, but as your mother, I still want things to work out for you."

I'm caught off-guard. It's not her words...she's said a million sentimental things to me that have meant absolutely nothing...but it's her tone. Her tone is fragile and so real, it brings a lump into my throat. If she's just being melodramatic, then, she's got me fooled.

"Thanks, Mom."

"I want to make sure you're safe and making the best choices for yourself. It's almost impossible to see what's at stake and how to handle it properly at your age." And the lump dissolves.

"That's why I'm making the choices," I tell her, "instead of anyone else."

"I know you are," she says softly and the lump returns. "We have to decide what you're going to do about school and how you're going to support yourself and pay your bills."

School. How can I think about school when I hardly work enough to afford groceries? School isn't anywhere near the top of my leader-board of worries and she should know that. She's done everything she could do to make just surviving harder for me.

But maybe she's rethinking it all. Maybe she's going to try helping. I melt a little at the thought of her helping rather than continually trying to prove to me that I can't.

"If you could put the insurance back on my car, it would make things a lot—"

"Oh no." There's that little laugh again. "You're on your own, remember? That's what you wanted, and I'm supporting it. I just want you to start thinking of the rest of your life...not just the next five minutes."

So, this was a guerilla warfare conversation. She got my guard down first, so she could lob in the grenade. This call is all about working me up and reminding me that I'm fucked. Grinding it in.

My mother called to remind me that I don't have the luxury of thinking ahead, because I can barely keep up with what's happening right now.

She's clueless. She wants to talk about school, and how hard it's going to be to return and how much I need to...but she has no idea what my life is like now. She doesn't realize that getting attacked by strangers is easier than living under the thumb of a mother whose love is so conditional, I've lived the first seventeen years of my life feeling like I was the worst child on the planet.

Figuring out how to fit in with the jocks and preps and stoners is laughable, compared to figuring out how I'm going to make it another week at the hotel. She wants me to take time to writing papers to please some teacher, when every ounce of my energy now is dedicated to earning money to eat, keeping my eyes on the cage door, and watching my back with every person who walks past me. Getting A's is the last of my worries when I have Samson watching my every move. She wants me to worry about being a fucking scholar, when I'm more concerned over whether or not I'm going to get sick, or if Jonah is going to show up, or if a cop is going to pull me over and impound my car.

"You're delusional," I snap at her.

"You need an education," she shrills. "I don't even thing you can flip burgers without your high school diploma anymore! You won't get anywhere in your life without finishing school!"

"I'm nothing if I'm dead," I tell her flatly. "I got bigger problems than learning another useless history date, or memorizing a bunch of algebra problems. None of that is going to get me grocery money right now. What I need is to make money. And I need to do that right now. Not next year, after I graduate. I won't last that long."

"Then just come home if you can't handle it," she says.

Of course. There it is. That's what she's really been after. Her point.

"I can handle it here just fine," I tell her. "I just can't handle you not knowing what you're talking about, and not having a clue about real life."

"Oh, I don't know about real life?" she says. Here we go. "I've been doing real life for the last seventeen years, I'll have you know."

"And look how good you've been doing," I fire back. "You raised a high school drop out and a runaway. But Bob's been a great catch! Where is he? I don't hear him. Oh wait...is it almost time to go drag him off a bar stool? Or is he just going to drive home drunk tonight?"

"Bob has a disease," she growls.

"Bob is a disease," I tell her. "You just don't know you can get rid of it."

My mother sniffs, not a sad sniff, but an indignant one. She's trying not to cry because she wants to show me how much stronger she is than me. How much more the adult. The line is silent for a hundred heart beats.

"I didn't call tonight to discuss Bob," she starts again in a more gentle, measured tone. "I called to discuss a game plan with you. To help you."

"Uh huh," I say, picking up a pen from the desk. I scratch out a doodle of angry eyebrows over rocks that are supposed to be eyes on the corner of the room ledger page. The inkling of trust at the beginning of our conversation has been utterly annihilated in the last few comments. She's not going to catch me without my weaponry at the ready again.

"Lael, I'm your mother," she says all softy and buttery, but I'm immune now.

"And I'm your daughter," I clip each word short.

Her plan hasn't changed. She's going to break me down so I'll come home.

That will never happen now. Not when I know it means she'll have me dangling on the ends of her strings, and not when she'll be yanking on them every minute she can, having me kick myself in the ass with my own feet.

"I'm only trying to tell you how you can help yourself," she says.

"I think I've got it covered, but thanks." I sit back on the chair. "Listen, Mom, I'm at work. I've got to go."

"Alright," she says, all full of sorrow and melodrama, like she really, really tried, and she just couldn't reach me. At least, that's the recording I'm sure she'll play in her head every time she thinks of how this call went.

"See ya," I say.

"Call whenever you'd like to talk," she says and she waits for me to hang up. It's her other stupid game—as if my hanging up first means she's won something.

"Yup. Goodbye." I sit there.

"Goodbye," she says softly, but I think she realizes I'm not going to hang up first.

And it's killing her. Ha.

Fuck if I'll be the first one to hang up tonight. I'll lay it down on the desk and leave it for Lavina if I have to—

"I love you," she says, and then her end of the line clicks.

Wait. What?

Another spin on the usual tactics. Well, at least she got in the last words.

And they were good ones.

I guess she thinks she won this battle. She thinks she cut a huge gash in me.

I set down the receiver and go back to doodling, the ice machine kicking on in the silent lobby.

The lobby door swings open and a man, shoved from the back, comes stumbling over the threshold. He nearly falls flat, catching himself just like a runner coming out of the blocks. Once he is on his feet again, I get a glimpse of his moustache, as thick as shag carpet, but little else. He turns his face away, so I can't see him. The rest of him—he's dressed in cowboy boots and jeans, and stands under five feet tall.

"Can I help you?" I ask through the window vent.

He bustles around in a tight two step, jerking away each time he would face me. He steps toward the door and then turns back toward the machines as if he's trapped. This guy is either high, or his cheese has completely slipped off his cracker.

"Can I help you?" I ask again. Speechless, the guy continues to fidget in the bright light of the lobby—a moth on a stove.

The door alarm blasts. We both turn to focus our attention on the opening as Yolanda tromps into the lobby, the hem of his dress blowing up and revealing way too much of his holey pantyhose.

Yolanda gives me his wide, gruesome smile and a fingertip wave. I jerk my head, in warning, toward the fidgeting man, but Yolanda only winks at me and plods toward him. The man cowers as Yolanda comes near, rubbing his palms over the thighs of his jeans. Yolanda towers over him.

"Did ya pay her, Amir?" Yolanda asks sweetly.

Amir shakes his head fiercely, even though his entire body is quivering.

Yolanda's grin falls. His voice turns as solid as a linebacker. "I said...pay her...you greasy little fuck."

Amir dodges Yolanda like a frightened bunny, with a quick step in the direction of the door, but Yolanda pivots, mirroring the man's lunge and blocking his exit. He freezes, trapped.

Yolanda slides his tongue over his lips, licking off some of his blood-red lipstick and revealing his mangled smile. "You ain't goin' nowhere 'til mah lamb gits paid, Amir."

The little man rubs his neck and shuffles in a tight circle again, looking for a way out.

"Did ya hear me, ya lil' cock? Ya pay my baby lamb and then ya git to go...you gonna put two twenties in that slot there, in da window. If you wanna be on yo' way, then you gonna pay my girl like I tole ya to."

Yolanda herds Amir to the window. The guy's fear seeps through the glass and splashes across my skin like spilled blood. Yolanda's fury shoots in right behind it, barking his orders at Amir again once he's got him wedged against the counter.

Yolanda grabs Amir's cheek and jerks his face toward me. Amir struggles to press his chin against his opposite shoulder, but Yolanda holds strong, bashing Amir's resisting forehead into the bullet proof glass. I jump backward.

Amir continues to wrestle like a fish on a line, but Yolanda's too big for him. Yolanda grabs a fist full of black hair at the top of Amir's head and uses it like a handle, yanking up his forehead. The guy's panicked face leaves a sweaty smear.

Yolanda croons to him, still holding Amir's face, smashed against the glass, the guy's mouth open like a smear. I can see the hair in his nostrils.

A little bubble of steam forms on the glass.

"You pay her or you gonna feel them veins in yo' neck gush, ya little faggot. And aft'a ya done wigglin', I'm gonna take yo' wallet and I'm gonna go find yo' mama an' tell 'er how much ya liked my moda fuckin' black cock up yo' ass." Amir's eyes squeeze shut. "This da last time I say it, Amir," Yolanda says. "Give 'er the fuckin' money or I'm gonna cut ya open right here, boy."

I swallow hard behind the glass. "You can't do this—"

"Hush up now, lamb," Yolanda growls at me. "An' lemme handle this."

Sweat breaks out on Amir's face and neck. He gulps like a jammed toilet. I feel dizzy too.

"Whuch you wanna do now, faggot?" Yolanda snarls beside Amir's head.

"Pay...her." Amir chokes out each word.

Yolanda knocks his head against the glass one more time, but releases him. "Da's right, baby," Yolanda croons. "Da's all ya gotta do an' you kin go."

Amir withdraws his battered wallet, cowering in Yolanda's shadow. The man wedges a stubby thumb between the folds, pulls out two bills and works them through the window slot. They fall out on my side, fluttering down like broken wings onto the desk.

I don't want to touch them. This isn't right.

"Da's a good boy, Amir." Yolanda steps away, leaving the man a path to the door. His face flat, he growls, "Now git."

Amir bolts for the door, still clutching his wallet. He streaks out, the alarm screaming behind him.

Yolanda turns back and wiggles his fingers gingerly at me. He smiles, as if he is as clueless to what just happened as he is of the red lipstick smeared across his front teeth.

I'm speechless.

"You all paid up now, Lamb, plus interest, 'cause ya had ta wait so long. I'm sorry I forgot, baby. Really I am." Yolanda blinks back what looks like real tears. "I don't want ya thinkin' I don't pay my debts 'cause I do. I'd neva' fuck ova' a friend...neva'...and now ya know fo' sho' that you my friend, lamb. You gimme twenty and you keep twenty, ahright?"

I pick up Amir's money, lying on the desk. It's damp. I slip one of the bills back through the slot.

"So, we square, honey?" Yolanda asks.

I nod, numbly.

"Ahright then, sweetie, then whuch you got on the third floor fo' me? I wanna room for da week."

"I told my mother I'd take her to Bingo." Jonah sighs over the phone. It's lunch time, but he's across the street, eating at his desk.

"Then why don't you just come over here now?" I trace circles on my belly, thinking of him.

"Boss man's due to come in again today. It's a big inventory week," Jonah says.

"I'm having withdrawals," I say. "We went from seeing each other every day, to now I only see you once a week. I miss you."

"It's been a busy week." He chuckles on the other end of the line. "You're not gonna be my needy girlfriend, are you?"

I smile at the warmth in his tone. There's an ache in my gut as I say it. I am a needy girlfriend. The more he took care of me after the attack, the more needy I've become. We spent an afternoon with his body curled around mine, watching talk shows. He made food in my mom's skillet and fed it to me. The less he pushed me to be physical again, the more I started to want him.

"You bet I am. I need you here all night, every night," I say.

"I'd love that." His voice is velvety and I melt the same way I do every time I hear it now.

The ache transforms to a pulsing flutter in my heart, my stomach, between my legs, and then an impulse lifts in my mind.

"Would you love that?"

"What? Have you every night? You know it, Silver Spoon."

"I hate it when you call me that," I murmur, but I don't hold a grudge when my thoughts wander back to that last day he visited at lunch time.

We left the blinds open, and the rain clouds that day made the room dim. The drops tapping on the window was romantic. He sat on the bed naked, with me facing him, in his lap. He was inside me until I couldn't stand it anymore and had to lean back so I could work my hips like a slow piston against him. His hands were on the small of my back, my butt, running down my chest, over my nipples—

"You could move in with me," I whisper into the phone. "Or I could move in with you."

He pulls in a breath on the other end. "Oh."

I think of us living in Jonah's house together. Cooking dinners and watching TV. His little nephew would climb onto the couch between us with the big, beautiful smile I've seen in Jonah's pictures. Jonah's mother would teach me how to make Jonah's favorite foods and she'd hug me and tell me I'm perfect for her son. I imagine Nia and I going shopping together, laughing over family photo albums. She could be the sister I never had. I wonder what Jonah's bedroom looks like. I think of him as a slate-blue sheets kind of man, with big, fluffy pillows that he would throw me down on and kiss me until I can't breathe.

The other end of the phone is still silent.

I can't breathe now, kissed or not. "So, what do you think?"

"I can't move out," he says with a long exhale. "My family needs me at the house."

"I could move in with you," I suggest. My stomach wobbles so hard, I feel it through my shirt. I smile and picture Jonah's soft blue sheets again. "I could put in my paycheck, and there'd be two cars for everybody to use instead of just yours, and there'd be two of us to help babysit DeAndre..." It all comes rolling out, just as desperate and needy as he accuses me of being.

"Sounds like you gave this a lotta thought already," he says.

I giggle. "A little."

"It's somethin' to think about," Jonah says. "It's a lil' more complicated than jus' you an' me, but—"

My stomach jumps again. "Why don't you just come over now and we'll talk?"

"Or maybe we can do the talkin' later," Jonah says and his smile sounds like it's as wide as his face.

"That show you like's on TV," I hear Penny say to Will as she passes his ledge on her way downstairs. Any other mother would freak out and drag him off the ledge, but all Penny says is, "I'm gettin' chips, you want some?"

"Yeah!" Will answers.

"Then go on up to our room, an' I'll go get the food," his mother says. She's slurring every word.

I hear him scramble off the ledge and run up the steps to the third floor. Penny appears in the lobby moments later.

I haven't seen her in weeks and she looks different now. More awful than usual. Boney and oily, she's disappearing like Wonderland Alice inside her sweatpants and t-shirt. Her eyes can't stay focused on me either, but that's pretty normal.

It's hard for me to care though, after she accused me of wanting to be with Samson. I haven't seen him since Jonah threw the guy out of my room, but the way Penny leans up against the counter now, I'm not sure it's all water under the bridge yet.

"Can ya gimme change for the machines?" She passes me a bill and then tries to drag her fingers through her matted hair, but she gets snagged. She yanks her hand out of her hair and scoops up the money I give her, turning to the machines, but turning back to me just as quickly.

"What'd you say to Samson?" she says. *God, she's messed up.* I can tell she's trying to focus on me, but her eyes won't quite cooperate and her eyelids droop like store window shades at closing time. "Will tole me you said something to Samson and that's why he don't want to come around."

I'm not about to tell her about Samson's 'friend' that visited me—she wouldn't believe it. Will told me she thought I was trying to seduce Samson.

"Nothing," I tell her. "I never said anything to him."

"Oh," Penny says. She nods slowly like she didn't expect that answer and can't figure it out. She gets her two bags of chips from the machine and turns back to me. I think she's going to ask me more about Samson, but instead, she says, "Is your Christmas shopping done yet?"

It's October.

"No. Is yours?" I ask.

She struggles to keep her eyelids open. "Not yet." The minute the words are out, her eyelids droop.

I know Will's in their room, but in a hushed voice I ask, "Does Will still believe in Santa?"

"Of course he does." Penny sneers, but her voice is as thin as a trail of smoke. She turns toward the stairs with a grunt. "Why wouldn't he?"

FIFTEEN

I t's **Sunday night** and it feels weird because I'm usually off on Saturdays, but we had to switch because Tavon couldn't come in yesterday.

I've only seen Jonah once this week, so I'm ecstatic when he knocks on my door and says to get dressed—we're going out to Greek Town, a strip of bars and restaurants with awesome, authentic Greek food. It qualifies as a real date—something we haven't done before.

Of course, the whole date is backward right from the start.

"I thought you're supposed to fool around after the date, not before it," I say, as I fix my hair and pull on my best jeans.

"Nuh uh," Jonah says, sitting on the edge of the bed once he's dressed. "Before and after."

I put on my thick, blue, cable-knit sweater. It's got a frayed hole in it that I have to fold under since I slopped some bleach on it, but at least it's thick enough to do battle with the gusty fall weather and I won't have to carry a jacket.

"You wanna take your car? I'm almost out of gas," Jonah says.

I hand over my car keys. "Just don't get us pulled over. There's no insurance on it."

"Girl," he laughs at me, "most'a the people I know don't even got a driver's license, never mind havin' insurance on the car they're drivin'."

We head downstairs. Tavon's slumped on the chair in the cage, all three hundred pounds of him, and the volume on the porn is turned all the way up. The moans and slaps and slurps can be heard all the way up on the third floor landing and get louder as we go down to the lobby. Tavon glances up as we pass and we wave to him, but he doesn't wave back.

We get in my car and Jonah adjusts the seat. The engine whines when it turns over and keeps whistling as we leave the parking lot.

"You got a bad belt," he says, his head cocked to the side. "I could get that fixed up for you."

"I hope the whole date's not this romantic," I tease. "How much do you think it would cost?"

"Depends on which belt it is."

"Half the time, I think I should just park the car for good and get myself a bike. No insurance, no license, no big repair bills." I reach across the seat for his hand.

"Not a bad idea. Give ya some time to fix it up an' git your bills paid."

I unclick my seatbelt and slide across the seat to be closer to him. I trace the small lines shaved near his temple. I find every single thing about Jonah fascinating. "If we were living together, you could fix my car, and me and your mom and your sister could all use it."

"That's a thought," he says.

"Really? Have you thought any more about it?" He takes his hand from the steering wheel and I squeeze his fingers between mine. They are long and brown, the knuckles knobby; they're like beautifully carved, wooden flutes.

"I think about you all the time." He lifts my hand and kisses the top of it. "You are one beautiful woman, Silver Spoon, you know that?"

I grimace at the name, but lay my head on his shoulder as he turns up the radio on Gregory Abbott's Shake You Down. His pager goes off on his belt, vibrating against my hip. He shakes my hand loose, unclips it, and reads the number. He re-clips it to his belt and puts his hand back on the steering wheel.

"Who is it?" I ask.

"Just work," he sighs.

"The shop's closed, though."

"Lael," he says with a shake of his head, like I'm nagging him. "Work never stops. But, I got things ta do tonight, so they're just gonna have to figure it out on their own."

I lift his hand off the wheel and plant a kiss on top. We drive downtown, listening to the radio and kissing at the red lights. He parks in a private lot with two guys and a hand-painted sign that says for five bucks, they'll make sure nobody breaks into my car. Jonah gives them five bucks and grabs my hand when one of the guys smiles at me.

"I love you," I say when we walk out of the lot and onto the sidewalk. He steers me toward the main street.

"Do you?" he asks, looking down at me with a grin.

"You don't believe me?"

"I don't know," he teases. "Maybe. Some other guy comes along—younger, with more money—and then what?"

My smile fades and my jumpy stomach lays down, turning from airy excitement to being as heavy as any burden. He thinks that my feelings for him are that small?

"Then, nothing," I say. "You think I'd leave you?"

His pager goes off again and he drops my hand to reach down and turn it off. He doesn't pick up my hand again.

"Hey! Lael! What're you doin' here?" a familiar voice says. We turn to see Penny, standing between two white plastic buckets full of flowers, outside a sweet shop. She swings her droopy gaze to Jonah and I can't remember the last time I saw her when she wasn't completely stoned. She eyes Jonah as best she can. "Aren't you the guy from the oil shop?"

"I am," he says, flashing a smile at her and looking away. I can tell he doesn't like her already, but this is as close as I have to friends now—somebody familiar.

"What are you doing here, Penny?" I ask her. "Where's Will?"

"Will stayed home. Gotta make money somehow," she says. She picks up a dozen, wrapped red roses, holds them in the air for us to see, and then dumps them back down into her bucket with a splash. "Samson set me up with this gig a while ago. I sell all these and I've got enough for rent and stuff."

"Sounds like a good deal," I say.

Even her shrug is slurred. "It sucks. It's too slow. Nobody wants to buy no flowers tonight." An older couple approaches and Penny snatches a dripping dozen out of the bucket. She holds them up high, her depth perception awful as she nearly pokes the woman in the face. "Flowers for the pretty lady?" she says.

The woman rears back and the man pushes the flowers out of her face. "No thanks," he says.

"You ain't gonna get laid treatin' 'er like that," Penny mumbles as they walk away. She turns back to us. "What about you?" She holds up her drippy flowers toward Jonah. "You should treat Lael good. Get 'er some flowers."

"You want flowers?" Jonah asks me.

Asked like that, I know the answer. I smile. "Not really."

"C'mon," Penny chides. "Prove ya love 'er!"

He laughs. "She's gotta prove that to me."

We say goodbye to Penny and walk away, down the sidewalk toward Trapper's Alley. There aren't a ton of people out, but more than I expected for a gusty Sunday night.

"You don't think I love you?" I prod him when we're out of ear shot.

He looks away with a sigh I don't expect. I'm not sure what I've done to make him think that. When he looks back, he's got a dry grin plastered to his lips.

"Let's not start this up, okay?" he says. "My boss has just been on my ass all day, an' I need ta relax. Let's jus' have a good dinner and forget about everythin' else tonight, ahright?"

"Okay," I mumble, but now my feelings are hurt. I've never seen Jonah stressed out and he's never talked to me like that before. I'm hollowed out with loneliness as we walk along in silence, bumping elbows, and letting strangers pass between us.

"You wanna eat here?" Jonah tips his forehead toward a restaurant door as he tucks his fingers into his pockets.

"Sure," I say, as a sharp gust of wind blows up the sidewalk and into my face. I follow him inside, coughing dust out of my mouth.

The entry has old, broken tiles pressed into the floor and a heavy, wood podium for the hostess to stand behind. She shivers with the gust that follows us in and asks how many before taking us to a window booth. It's a great seat—we can watch the people walking by outside.

Jonah immediately buries his face behind the menu, but his pager, which he laid on the table top, buzzes across the table toward me like a broken-winged bee. It must be work again, because with one glance, Jonah hits the button to silence it.

"Can you just turn it off so it doesn't bother you all night?" I ask.

"It ain't botherin' me," he says.

A waiter stops at our table and Jonah orders us both water.

A white guy, maybe a little younger than Bob, walks past the window where we're seated. He glances in at Jonah as he walks down the sidewalk, but his stare lingers too long on my side of the table.

Jonah reaches up and raps his knuckles sharply against the window. "Whuch you starin' at?" He barks at the man outside.

The two couples at the table beside ours turn to look. The man outside just looks away, shaking his head as he continues on down the street. My cheeks are so hot, I think they light more of our table than the candle in the center.

"You see how white people think?" Jonah says, turning back to me.

"White people? I'm white!" I laugh, to lighten the mood.

But Jonah's expression is so hard, it looks carved, and it kills anything I think I could say to soothe him. "You want to move in with me, but don't you see what happens? People think there is no way a black man should be sitting with a white woman. They can't stand it."

"I don't think that's what anybody's thinking."

"They're staring!" he says, gesturing to the window. A couple walking by look in, but I don't know if they would've noticed us if Jonah didn't look so angry. They stare as they walk past, which just makes everything worse. Jonah turns back to me with wide eyes. "See? That's what they're all thinkin', Lael! Ain't no way a black man and white woman should be together!"

The waiter returns, puts a bread basket between us, and asks for our order.

"You want the Chicken Lemonato? It's good," Jonah says flatly.

"Sure," I say. Jonah says yes to rice and house salads, no to appetizers. His mood has crashed and I would do anything to restore it to the funny, happy Jonah again. "You know, I'd probably stare too," I say with a smile. "I'd stare just because you're so handsome, and we're so unusual. You don't usually see a black guy and white girl, so people might swear. So what. If I was them, I'd be wondering what our relationship is like and what we see in each other." I say dreamily.

"What we see in each other?" The muscles in his jaw jump. We sit in silence. We don't touch the bread basket. The waiter returns and leaves our salads. We eat those without a word and then the waiter brings our plates of lemon chicken. It seems like this whole date is going to happen in complete silence.

"I don't get why you're so mad," I whisper once the waiter leaves. "It doesn't matter what anybody thinks, but us, right?

Jonah sits back in his chair, arms straight out on the table, his gaze meeting mine like a fist. This is not Jonah. This is someone I don't know, with hard eyes that won't let me in.

"Let me ask you somethin', Silver Spoon ... how do you describe me to other people?" His hostile tone pounds the words out of me. I don't know where this is coming from or why he's angry with me. His pager buzzes on the table top again. He presses the button down hard to stop it. He picks up his fork and knife, ripping into his chicken. He spears a chunk, shoveling it into his mouth as he swings his brass-knuckled glare back at me. "When somebody asks you what I look like, what do you say?"

"I say, Jonah. Everybody I would tell already knows you."

"But if they didn't," he says. "Would you describe me as tall, dark haired, dark eyed? No. You'd say he's a black guy."

What's happening? I put my fork and knife down, feeling wild inside. The skin around my eyes pulls back as I stare at him. "You are a black guy!"

"That's all you see?" he fires back. "My skin? That shouldn't be the first thing you think to tell people about me."

"It's not! But if they're asking me what you look like and they're a bunch of white people, that's the first thing that stands out! If you wore

251

a bone in your nose, I'd say, he's the guy with the bone in his nose..."

He glares across the table. "That's where you're gonna take this? To my African heritage?"

"Jonah," I try to calm down. I don't know how we got from one stranger's stare to this. Him against me, this table-sized battlefield between us. Weapons drawn. "I was just trying to make a point. If you were a fat guy, I'd say he's a big guy."

"That's real sensitive," Jonah says. The waiter passes by and Jonah waves him away with two fingers.

"I'm not trying to be insensitive," I say, "I'm just trying to explain why—"

"Why you don't have to think before you speak?" he asks.

"Whoa," I say.

I still don't know why we're fighting, but Jonah pulls the napkin off his lap and throws it on top of his chicken. He looks out the window at another white couple passing by, huddled together and laughing, obviously in love. Jonah scowls. "White people all think they ain't responsible for nothin'."

"What?" My whisper explodes across the table.

"You know it's true."

I throw my napkin down too. "So all the white people in the world are my fault? Forever? Does that mean all the black people are your fault?"

"Just stop talking," he says. "You sound like every ignorant white woman I've ever met right now."

"Ignorant? What is happening right now?" I fire back. "Why are you so angry with me? We were having such a great time until your pager started going off, and now every single thing I say, you're picking a fight over it! What is going on?"

I can see we're aimed at each other like a gun fight at high noon and I'm getting less willing to put down my gun. But then Jonah drags his hand over his face and by the time it's reached his chin, his expression has smoothed out to the old Jonah, the one I know, the guy I've fallen in love with. He sighs, sits up, leans forward.

"You're right," he says and his gaze puts me back into the center of his universe. I lean in too, eager for this weird fight to be over, eager to hear what's happening and find a way to ease him. "Somethin's botherin' me is all, an' I shouldn't be gettin' on you for it."

"What's happening?"

"I'm worried about my sister," he says. "Well, my nephew. He's been sick all night and she don't know what's wrong with him. I thought it would get better, but she's a wreck. If she's calling me this much, it can't be good."

The weight of our argument falls off me. There's something really wrong and I hate that he's been keeping it bottled up, probably so I would have fun on our date. His pager buzzes on the table again. He picks it up, looks at the number, frowns.

"Is that work or Nia?" I ask.

"That's Nia. I've got to find a phone."

"No, you should go and be with them." I want to make everything right in his world.

"Can't," he says with one hard shake of his head. "We brought your car here. I'd have to go all the way back to the hotel, drop off your car, and then get mine. It's out of the way."

"I could come with you."

"I might have to take them to the hospital. We could be there all night."

"I'm used to being up all night," I say brightly. Even sitting in a hospital would be fine with me, as long as I'm sitting beside Jonah. "And I'd love to meet your sister."

My stomach whirls at the prospect of meeting someone from his family, but Jonah frowns.

"She's too busy with DeAndre. This ain't the right time. I don't think she'd take to havin' other people aroun' when she's worryin' over her baby boy neither." He casts a long look out the window and then turns back to me, his face brightening. "Hold up now. How about if I run back to my house in your car and you catch a ride back with Penny? I can go grab 'er and ask. I'll drop yo' car off and pick mine up after I check in on De and Nia."

"Yeah, sure." I drudge up a grin. I want to support him, I do, but I was hoping to do it by staying at his side, not by getting a lift home from Penny.

Jonah slides out of the booth. "Ahright," he says, throwing down a couple bills to pay for dinner. "I'll go find her. Thanks."

He's gone before I can say sure. I slide to the edge of the booth, picking up the leather book the waiter left. I open it up to slide the money in that Jonah left. The bill for dinner is $32.50.

Jonah left two bills: a ten and a five. I sit back in the booth, the food I ate churning like it's going to come up. I've got to wait for Penny to come get me.

Penny knocks on the window and does the air scoop, signaling me to hurry up and come out. I do the same on my side. I need to borrow some cash, but Penny shakes her head. She thinks I'm inviting her to eat. Shit.

I dig in my purse and pull out a sketch pencil. I scrawl a note to the waiter, telling him how sorry I am and how great a job he did and he doesn't deserve this. I say sorry in big print and then, when he walks by the table, I make a big show of putting the two bills I do have into the leather folder he left behind. After he passes by with a smile, I give him a second to get to the other side of the restaurant. I get up and rush-walk out the door. Lucky for me, it's a straight shot.

"You got any money?" I ask Penny. "Jonah didn't leave me enough for the whole bill and I just walked out!"

"Oh shit! No, I ain't got money for that!" She grabs her stack of empty white buckets and shouts, "Let's go!"

She sprints down the sidewalk and I take off right behind her. I'm no runner, but I am filled to my ears with adrenaline. I expect the waiter to come shouting after me, but we sprint down a side street, Penny's buckets clunking together. We turn a corner and another, until we're weaving through a parking lot lodged deep in the shadows.

"Where are we going?" I whisper to Penny, following the white glow of her buckets as we weave through the lot.

"To my car," she grumbles, "if I can find it. Jonah gave me five bucks to take you home, but I gotta stop at a friend's house on the way."

I'm so glad to be going home, I don't care if we have to run a week's worth of her errands. But my nerves surface the more Penny scuffles along, mumbling and unsure of which lot she left her car in.

I accidentally find her car.

"Hey Penny, isn't that it?" I ask, pointing to a lemon-yellow Honda hatchback under an overhead light.

She swings around and her entire face puckers in recognition.

"Yeah," she mumbles. "Yeah, this's it."

The doors aren't locked and they creak when they're opened. Penny throws her buckets in the back.

"Watch the floor," she says. I think she's worried about me getting it dirty until I look down. The gleam of the pavement shows right through the huge, gaping hole in the floorboard.

I get in, planting one foot near the console and the other on the edge of the door frame. I close the door. Penny slams her door shut, but it pops back open. She curses under her breath and slams it again. This time it stays shut. She jams the key into the ignition and the car sputters. She cranks the key again and the whole frame shivers as if the engine is being brought back from the dead.

"You sold all your roses?" I ask, just for something to say, as Penny steers us out of the parking lot. I hope she doesn't start grilling me about Samson.

"Huh?" She screws up her face at me. The engine's too loud for talking.

"YOUR ROSES," I shout.

"A crowd of kids got 'em all," she shouts back.

"That's great," I say.

"Huh?"

"THAT'S GREAT."

She just nods and navigates us through the streets.

I'm relieved when she turns onto the expressway ramp, even though every time I look down through the floor hole and see the road rushing by, I feel like I'm going to throw up. I don't know what's keeping my seat from falling down, but whatever it is, I hope it holds until we get back to the hotel. Tiny pebbles bounce up and sting me like hot sparks.

Cars fly by us. We're in the right hand lane, sort of, because Penny keeps veering off onto the shoulder. The first few times I squeal and then, I shout at her when we hit a rumble strip. I try to grab the wheel when she doesn't respond quickly enough. We serpentine across the shoulder and end up back in our original lane. Then into the one next to it.

A black sports car lays on the horn and weaves around us.

"Whoops," Penny says.

I just grit my teeth and take it, until Penny takes a ramp I don't expect.

"Whoa, whoa! Where are you going?" I say, but Penny doesn't hear me.

Her foot is jerky on the gas pedal and she's got a death grip on the steering wheel. She keeps her head tilted to the left, trying to focus on the ramp through only one eye. She steers us onto the curb and I shriek as a bunch of dust blows up through the hole. Penny jerks the wheel and brings us back down between the lines again. We do this three times before we even reach the end of the ramp.

"Your friends live around here?" I ask her as she downshifts the engine from a roar to a growl.

"Yeah," Penny says.

The end of the ramp spits us out on a street that is blotted with burnt-down and boarded-up houses. The ones that are not look as though they should be condemned. The structures all hunch like old men that don't have the strength to stand up anymore. Porches fall into high weeds. Roof tops droop in weird places. Shredded tar paper lays in the street.

Almost every house we pass has iron bars over the windows, pointed like spears on both ends and bolted on, preventing anyone from getting in or getting out. The windows are holed up with cardboard or wood. The ones with glass have curtains made of sheets, blankets, or newspapers. One has a dirty American flag stretched tight across it, but still doesn't manage to cover the whole window. The mustard glow from inside doesn't make it all the way to the street.

We travel along in the ominous shadows of this ruined street, jolting through potholes that are deep as graves. Street lights hang like dark coconuts over the street as we pass. The bulbs are either burnt out or shattered. The darkness is like an open mouth and we drive right onto it's tongue.

"Which street does your friend live on?" I shout over the engine as Penny takes us deeper into the catacomb of streets. It seems like a really stupid thing to do.

"Down here, I think." She turns down another street, the tires rubbing a curb. She finds her way as if the potholes are braille.

"You think?"

"Samson's been gone, so I gotta stop off myself."

So we're going to see Samson's friends. My dinner starts churning as if I've swallowed gasoline.

Penny turns down another street, and instead of a house, there is a five story, red brick building on the corner. A bare light bulb hangs over an open, wood door. The light shines on the crumbling brick and darkens the open front door by pouring it full of shadows. Whatever lies beyond the doorway is lost in the black hole. It looks haunted, but I can tell from looking at it, any screaming that might come from inside would all be real.

We turn at the edge of the building, where the brick trails off into weeds and turns into an alley, deep and dark. If there were no moon, there would be no light at all. I squint out the windows, but when I try to look directly at anything, there is nothing but black holes. The momentary blindness makes my pulse beat harder than an animal trying to escape a tight cage.

Penny brings the Honda to a halt in the middle of the alley. A brick wall is on my right and an enormous rusted dumpster, hunkered down a few feet ahead, against the fence on the left. Garbage bags puff out the top and trail down beside it.

Penny shoves the gear stick into park.

"Keep the windows up and the doors locked," she says as she throws open her door.

"Wait! Where are you going?" I ask.

She slides out of the driver's seat as the stench of garbage pours in and pounds me in the nose like a hammer. "I'll be right back."

She elbows down the lock and slams the door on any response I might be able to choke out.

I twist in the seat, gagging, as I watch her shuffle back down the alley from the direction we came. She disappears around the side of the crumbling brick without looking back. And then there is just me, the rotting smell, and the dark. I put my hands over my mouth and nose to breathe, but it doesn't help.

"Oh shit," I whisper and am instantly terrified that something might have heard me in this terrifying alley. Even the saliva going down my throat echoes. I try not to swallow again. I feel the dark trying to find me, touch me. This is where Samson comes from. I stay still. I try to be as motionless as death.

I spot movement from the corner of my eye and turn my head back to stare into the pit of the heaped garbage. There is a silent ripple as two rats skirt the foot of the dumpster, chasing after each other. I look down at the gaping, black hole in the rotted out floorboards. There's nothing to keep those rats out. I bite my lip against a shriek.

I want Penny to come back. Now. Right now.

Now.

Right now.

Now.

Now.

NOW.

I pull my feet up onto the seat and hold them against me.

The darkness eats the shadows, but holds its breath as I stare into it. I twist on the seat, looking down the alley for Penny's return. She's not coming. My back aches and I turn to sit straight in the seat again.

Two eyes of light flash in the rear view mirror, startling me. The lights flash off, but the dark lump of a car moves into the mouth of the alley. I swallow down the sour fist of the garbage smell. My breath stays trapped inside me as the car edges closer to the Honda. Headlights still off, a spotlight on the side of the advancing car pops on instead, the harsh beam exploding into the Honda. I throw my hands up in front of my face, but I'm completely blinded.

I twist away on my seat, reaching for my door handle, but my eyes meet the brick wall outside the window. Penny parked too close for me to escape. I can't breathe. I drop my hands.

The car engine pants as it approaches.

I am going to die here. Whoever is shining this light on me will be the last one to know I was here. They'll kill me in this alley, in front of the rats and plastic bags full of garbage. My mother will never know that I never meant to be here. Not even Penny is going to know what happened to me.

This is where my life ends. That's the only thing I see in the core of the spotlight sun aimed at my face.

The tires outside grind to a halt behind the Honda's bumper.

I wait for the side window to shatter as a bullet makes it's way through.

I don't bother to put up my hands.

I won't resist.

But the spotlight vanishes in a pop. I am left blind, with inky holes that seep and sparkle at the edges. The holes move with my vision, puddling and sliding and exploding as I try to blink them away. I can't see around them, but I am frantic to see if someone is coming for me. Aiming at me. I squeeze my eyes shut hard.

Open wide.

I'm blind.

I blink.

Blink.

Blink.

The purr retreats. The crush of the gravel backs away with it. I keep blinking, trying to see around the black holes as they grow smaller. Slowly, slowly, the holes curl up, tighten, and disappear.

The other car, a black sedan, backs out of the alley. It parks horizontally at the curb across from the opening to the alley. I recognize the car.

It's an unmarked police cruiser. I think.

I stay twisted on the seat, watching the cop car through the back window. All the lights turn off. It's a sleeping fish.

I am safe. The police are watching over me. I think.

Everything's going to be okay. I take a deep breath, but cough on the rancid garbage odor.

Minutes pass like hours until Penny comes shuffling around the corner of the building, into the alley. I squint to see her better, but it's so far down the alley, I can only make out fuzzy shapes. The cruiser door opens. A man gets out. Another man emerges from the passenger side.

I don't hear anything, but Penny lurches to a stop, turns, hesitates, and then shuffles back out of the alley toward the men in the street.

The three look like blurry posts from the back window of the truck. They move like ants milling over a picnic crumb, changing positions so I can't tell who is who. I get worried that the men are not really the police, or that they are, and that they're going to haul Penny away and leave me here, stranded. I think of Penny's sagging eyelids. Of course they'll be able to tell what she is.

It looks like the three of them are yelling at each other. Their arms rise and fall, Penny's shoulders slump. I think they are yelling at her and shoving her back and forth between them like a pinball.

But the argument ends abruptly.

The men get back into their cruiser and Penny slinks away from them, stumbling down the dark alley toward the Honda.

I exhale. They let her go. We can go home.

The dome light in the cab flicks on when Penny opens the door. I pinch my eyes in the glare. Penny gets in and slams the door shut. The light goes off and the tiny black holes return, but smaller this time. I can blink them away.

"Who was that?" Even though my vision returns, Penny doesn't look right. She's gotten a hold of some lipstick and has smeared it all over her mouth and chin. I wonder if someone in the building pinned her down and had a good laugh, painting her face. Maybe the police stopped her because she looks like a clown.

"Where did you get the lipstick?" I ask.

She shakes her head as she starts the engine. "It's blood," she croaks.

"Blood?" I peer more closely now.

Penny licks her upper lip and steers the car out of the opposite side of the alley and onto a ruined street. Blood streams down from her nostrils onto her mouth. Black droplets fall off her chin. She swipes at it with her arm and smears the blood across her face.

We barrel along through the potholes, with me shouting questions at Penny that she doesn't answer. She keeps wiping at the blood, so it's all over her hands and the steering wheel and smeared down the thighs of her jeans.

"Talk to me!" I shriek.

A blood bubble bursts out of one nostril as Penny steers us down a ramp to the empty expressway. The beating seems to have cleared her head, but I still think it's a miracle when we reach the main street. She wipes the blood off her nose with the back of her hand, glances at her fingers smeared with it and her lips crumble.

"They hit me!" she rasps. "Those was undercover cops! They said that's what I get for leaving a kid behind a dope house!"

I'm trying to keep my eyes on her, but Penny isn't paying attention as she steers us down the expressway ramp. The Honda veers off onto the shoulder and I throw out a hand and grab the steering wheel. It's a good thing I do, because Penny lets go.

She breaks down bawling, her hands over her face as we enter the expressway. From the passenger seat, I jerk the Honda out of the neighboring lane as a semi truck rushes by us, blasting its horn. We hit the rumble strip and I try to steer the car back between the lines as I brace my legs on the car frame so I don't fall through the hole in the floor.

"You have to steer!" I shout at her.

Penny finally drops her hands and grabs the wheel. She sputters blood and hiccups and says, "You can leggo...I got it. I got it!"

I let go, but stay rigid and ready on the seat.

"I made sure nothing was gonna happen to you, Lael," she explains in staggered sobs. "There were guys...up in the windows, watching the car down in the alley...with AK-47's. Nobody was gonna touch you! Nobody! I just had to get a little blast! Nobody was gonna do anything to you with those guys up there watching! They were watchin' out the window..."

I don't know how much they were watching, since the cops came up the alley and got close enough to shoot me themselves. I don't know if the guys in the window of a dope house would've done anything if anything happened at all.

I'm grateful it is Sunday and the traffic isn't too heavy. The cars that are on the road shoot around us and distance themselves quickly.

"You want me to drive?" I ask.

"No. I'm fine," Penny says but she's still sniffling and she's still not keeping us solidly in one lane. "Those cops called me a crack head! They hit me with their flashlights like I was a dog! They said you were scared to death in the car!" Her sobs overflow her again. I was scared to death, but I'm not now. Her chest heaves with her grief. "How could they do that to me? They beat me, Lael! They beat me!"

"Let me drive, okay?" I plant two fingers on the edge of the steering wheel as we drift to the edge of our lane.

"No, I'm okay. I'm okay. I'm okay!" Penny chants. "I'm gonna take you home, Lael. Like I promised. I wouldn't let anything happen to you. I was just stopping to see my friend."

The Honda swerves onto the shoulder, throws up a fine mist of grit into the cab, and Penny yanks us right again.

"I wouldn't'of let nothing happen to you, Lael. I didn't mean for you to be scared."

"I know you didn't mean to." I don't think she realizes I'm not the one crying.

Penny grasps the wheel, leans closer to the front window and puts all her concentration on the road. I take my hand away from the wheel, and as we pass under the expressway lights. My hand is stained with Penny's blood.

I'm not Snow White anymore, and as scary as it might be, going back isn't even a possibility now.

SIXTEEN

"Where's my car?" I think out loud, as the bottom of the Honda scrapes over the curb leading into the hotel parking lot. Jonah's car is gone, but so is mine.

It's not like I expect Penny to answer. The bleeding seems to have stopped, but the front of her shirt is soaked and her face is stained pink. She throws the Honda in park and jumps out without another word. She scuttles into the hotel, but I move a lot slower, sure I overlooked my car in the row of customer's cars. I didn't. It's not there. I squint at the oil shop across the street. Jonah's car is gone too. What is going on?

Something is wrong. Jonah was supposed to check in on his family, then drop off my car, and pick up his own. Something is wrong. Maybe Jonah had to take Nia and DeAndre to the hospital.

But Jonah's car is missing. Someone might have stolen it. Or maybe he dropped off my car and someone stole mine. Something is wrong.

I go into the hotel, blasted with the door alarm and the porn that Tavon has cranked up on the TV. He glances up, mid-bite on a candy bar, but looks right back at the TV screen when he sees it's me.

I stop in front of the window and tap on the glass. He still doesn't look up. "Tavon, did Jonah come in here and drop off my car keys?"

"Nope," he say. He keeps on munching his candy bar, leaning forward to watch some guy in the porn lick a chick's stiletto's.

I feel like I'm interrupting, but my worry is cancelling out my give-a-shit. "Did Jonah come in here at all?"

"Not that I seen."

Great. It's hard to feel like Tavon is a reliable witness to anything that goes on around him when there is porn streaming on the TV. Tavon puddles down on his chair and I head upstairs.

Penny's nowhere to be seen, and Will's not on the ledge.

In my room, I call Jonah's pager and leave my number, like always. My nerves are standing on end. I pace the room from the door to the window sill two dozen times.

I can't help myself.

I pick up the phone and call Jonah's pager again. Punch in my number.

I wonder if he's turned it off. He would, if they're at the hospital.

The phone rings and I snatch it off the cradle.

"Hey, Silver Spoon," Jonah says from the other end. "How are you?"

"Oh my God...thank God you're alright," I gush. "Is everything okay? My car isn't here, but yours is gone too..." I can't stop. The night's events spill out before he has a chance to answer or comment. "Penny stopped at a crack house on the way back here and she left me in the alley. The cops saw me and they beat her up. I think they broke her nose. But my car's not in the parking lot and yours isn't at the oil shop. What's going on? Are you at the hospital with DeAndre?"

"No," Jonah says solidly. "What a crazy night, huh? De's okay, but yo' car broke down on the way back ta the hotel. I had to call a friend ta get me back ta my car."

266

"Oh no." I can't breathe. "It broke down? Where? Oh my God. I don't have the money to fix it right now—"

"It's all good. My friend, Trevor's gonna go back and tow it ta his garage."

"But I can't afford to pay—"

"We'll work somethin' out." Jonah says softly. "But listen, Silver Spoon, I gotta go. Nia's gotta go to work, so I've got to go take care of DeAndre."

"Okay," I say. The answers are all good, but the adrenaline is still rushing through me. I wish he could stay on the phone just a little while longer. It calms me to listen to him speak. "Thank you for taking care of everything, Jonah."

"Yup, no problem," he says smoothly, easing me even more. "I gotta run. De's yellin' for me."

"Okay," I say, even though I don't hear anything but the smile in Jonah's voice. I add a quick I love you, but he's already hung up the phone.

Lavina knocks on my door at eleven in the morning. I drag myself out of bed and open the door when she knocks a second time and says my name. She's not going away.

"You want yo' room cleaned while I'm up here?" she asks when I open up. She knows I don't. She stretches up on her tiptoes, looking around me, probably trying to see if Jonah's lying in my bed. "Tavon tole me somethin' went down wich you an' Penny las' night."

I'm shocked to hear Tavon noticed anything other than the foot-licker.

"He said you lef' here wit' Jonah, but ya come back wit' Penny, an' he say she a mess."

Wow, he really does notice things. Who knew.

"But I din't see yo' car out in the lot dis mornin'," Lavina finishes. Instead of leaning in the doorframe, she walks in and I get out of her way. The door shuts behind her. "So, wha's goin' on?"

I tell her what happened with Penny, from the alley to the beating.

"She got a broke nose?" Lavina asks.

"I haven't seen her since last night."

"An' where's yo' car?"

"Jonah and I went down to Greek Town last night, but his nephew was sick and Jonah had to leave, so I had him take my car. I got a ride back from Penny. Jonah was going to come back here and drop off my car, but it broke down on him. He got a friend to pick it up and fix it."

"Huh," Lavina says, rolling her tongue in her mouth. "At leas' it ain't on da side 'a the road where it could get broke into. You got money to fix it?"

"No, but Jonah said it's his friend, and we'll work it out."

"Workin' stuff out kin sho' run up a bill." Lavina says, shaking her head.

"It's not like that," I say. "Jonah said it's a friend."

"Ahright," Lavina says. "I'm jus' sayin' it's good ta know whuch you payin' fo' up front."

She's wearing on my nerves. More so when she runs a finger along the top of my dresser and inspects it for dust.

"I trust Jonah," I tell her flatly. "And I already know what you're going to say...don't trust nobody wit' yo' stuff."

Her laugh is half way between a grunt and a hiccup. She shakes her head. "You know why I don't trust nobody, Lael?"

She's suddenly so intense and soft and direct at once that I'm disarmed. Lavina usually skirts everything I say or blows me off with a do whateva' ya want. Now, she's looking straight at me, her head inclined a little, her eyes soft, but as focused as darts. I can only shake my head.

Lavina moves to the edge of my bed and takes a seat. The frame wheezes under her weight.

"Tavon had a real daddy, ya know. I wa'n't no baby mama, if tha's what you thinkin'. I was married, in a church, to a real good, God fearin' man. Hollis Gordon Davis. That was his name.

"Five days af'er we bring Tavon home from da hospital, my husband was kill't. It was a Thursday night. Hollis was sittin' in his drawers in front'a his own TV, in he own livin' room. He was eatin' saltines 'cause he had a belly ache. He shouldn'ta been down dere at all. I tole him to take da Pepto from the upstairs cabinet, but he say crackers do it better.

"A week befo', Hollis brother, Myron, come by, needin' a place ta stay. He say he not in any trouble, 'cept wit' his girl. He family, so we give 'im da couch. He stay a whole week, sleepin' and eatin' our food, an' den, he ask Hollis fo' money. He know me an' Hollis savin' ta git outta our crib, 'cause we wanna be inna neighba'hood where our boy kin play in da street wit'out gittin' shot. Myron got pissed when Hollis say he ain't got no extra fo' 'im. Myron jus' up an' lef'.

"So, 'bout a week goes by. I was sleeping upstairs an' the baby was sleeping, so when I got woke up, I couldn't figure out if I was dreamin', or jus' hear a night sound in da house. Da soun' was loud an' quick, an' it was ahready ova' da secon' I open up mah eyes.

"Then I hear my Hollis groanin'. I jump out tha bed thinkin' maybe he fell down, or was throwin' up somewheres. I was a good wife. I went ta help 'im.

"But when I go downstairs, my eyes cain't see good 'cause all da lights is off. Hollis musta been comin' up ta bed, but I seen my sheers was blowin' in tha front window, and I couldn't make no sense of it. Dere weren't no window ta open up there, just a big ol' picture wind'a wit' my sheers hangin'.

"But dat room was icy, an' da air from outside was slicin' through it. Them curtains was billowin' up an' twistin' all 'round, doin' a white-witch dance in the dark. My husband was on the couch, lookin' calm and jus' watchin' out them curtains dat shouldn't'a been blowin' aroun' like dey was. All da time, I'm tryin' ta see better, by the gray haze that come flickering into da room from da streetlight out front.

"I hiss't his name at 'im from da stairs, Hollis! I din't wanna turn on no light, 'cause I was standin' dere in nothin' but mah night clothes. I call't ta Hollis agin, *how come it's so cold up in here?* An' den, *Hollis! What's blowin' them curtains aroun'?* I cou'n't figure out what my husban' was thinkin', lettin' in all dat cold air wit' a lil' baby upstairs.

"But mah husban' wan't lookin' at me. An' den I know some'pin was real wrong. I step't down on the livin' room flo' and mah feet gits cut up. I jump't 'cross dat floor, but da pieces got bigger an' bigger, an' dere was mo' of 'em. I start screamin', 'cause they goin' into mah toes, an' in 'tween my toes, an' straight up inta mah heels. I finally jump't on da couch b'side mah husban', an' ya know what? He don't even *blink*.

"I look at 'im, an' I seen his big, brown stomach ain't right. He threw'd up all ova' his'self, I think. But somethin' ain't right. He still don't blink.

"I put a hand on 'im, an' all he do is groan be'fo he fall over on his side, 'way from me. A car drive by in the street and lit up the room fo' a minute, and den I seen mah Hollis, full'a dem red, weepin' holes. Af'er dat, I don't 'member much but screamin' an' screamin', 'til one'a tha neighbors fin'lly come, but I jus' kep' on screamin'.

"The po-leese come, an' one of 'em asks me where da drugs is? Dat officer *sho'* mah Hollis's a dope dealer. But mah Hollis ain't dat! Neva' was. He was a goo't man, always was, an' I los' 'im 'cause we trusted his broda ta be a goo't person too. Instead, he be inta da dope, and he think if he kill Hollis, somehow, he gonna git some money. *Inher'tance.* Cops couldn't neva prove it's Myron, but he tole me it was him ... couple days befo' he kilt his'self."

I'm astounded. I sit down on the bed beside her. I want to reach out and hug her, but Lavina's not like that. I put my hand on hers and it immediately snaps her out of the moment. She brushes off my hands as she stands up.

"What I'm sayin' to ya is dat I learnt to know who I's dealin' wit'," she says. "I learnt not to trust 'em, an' ya know what, Lael? Ninety-nine pa'cent a' da time, not trustin' 'em is da right thin' ta do."

I screw up my face, confused. "Are you saying I shouldn't trust Jonah?"

"It ain't fo' me ta say who ya trus' and who ya don't," she says with a somber shake of her head, "but I'm sayin' I sho' would wanna know who dis friend is and how much it gonna cost ya, 'cause it sho' gonna cost some'pin and what if ya cain't pay it?"

"Jonah said we'd work it out," I repeat. She might be right—no, I know she's right—I should know who the guy is, how much it's going to cost, where the car even is ... but there's nothing I can do about it now. The details just tie up my guts in knots. My car is with Jonah's friend. I don't know where. But this is Jonah we're talking about. He'll take care of it and why shouldn't I trust him? "I believe Jonah. He's my boyfriend."

Lavina throws up her hands. "Do whateva' ya want. You a grown woman, an' I got mah own problems ta deal wit'... like gittin' Clive to git me some damn help up in here. I don't know how he think I kin keep on doin' alla my work an' alla his."

Her snapping at me doesn't help. I get her point—she doesn't have to jam it through my ear. So, I retaliate the only way I know how—my mother taught me well.

"Ahright...I's a grown up afta' all," I say snidely, drawing out her thick, black accent.

Lavina stops dead in her tracks and comes back to stand toe-to-toe with me. "Don't you go disrespec'in me like dat, lil' girl," she says, her index finger a millimeter from my nostrils. "I like you jus' fine, but I ain't da one you wanna fuck wit'."

My spit wells under my tongue like a glass of water. I gulp it down the moment Lavina drops her finger from my face. She turns and goes out of my room and I'm glad when the door slams behind her.

Yolanda isn't going away. He keeps calling my name and tapping on the door. I finally open up. Yolanda gives me a spoiled-brat smile as he shoves his copper wig back a little on his forehead. His eyes sweep over me and he frowns.

"Well, Will was right! You do look like death done gochya, lamb," he says.

I drag my hand over my unwashed hair. In three days, a lot has changed. Jonah's been too busy to see or even talk to me. I even tried asking about my car, and he said his buddy is still working on it. I haven't felt like getting in the shower the last couple of days, since my fight with Lavina.

But it's kind of nice to see Yolanda. I think he might even understand everything that's going on, since he's been a guy before. Well, is a guy. I think.

Jonah's been busy at the shop and Will was the only person left who would talk to me, until last night. He started bugging me last night, asking me when Jonah's coming over.

"I don't know. Whenever he can," I said. I feel even lonelier repeating the reasons why Jonah can't come. "He's been busy doing inventory and cleaning the shop for inspection, and his mom has needed him at home."

But all of Jonah's excuses haven't explained why he brushes me off about my car, or why he doesn't come over at lunch time like he used to. I don't feel like a priority anymore and it stings.

"That's bullshit," Will said from his hole in the ceiling. That doesn't help. "Jonah's white trash fuckwad bastard scum."

"Why are you so mad at him?" I ask. "He hasn't done anything to you...he's just busy. And you should remember who took you for breakfast and bought you pancakes."

"He ain't buyin' me none now," Will grumbled.

I didn't talk to him the rest of the night. I drew instead—a whole page full of gingerbread men broken in half, in my sketchbook. What a crappy night.

Being as bored and lonely as I am, having Yolanda show up is like Christmas morning.

"You too skinny, sweetie pie. When's the last time you ate some'pin?"

I shrug. I don't even know. I usually just lie on my bed until I have to go to work. My whole body aches. I drink water from the faucet in the bathroom and eat chips and orange crackers from the vending machine downstairs.

Yolanda stumps in and I go back to bed.

"These are pretty nail polishes," he says, picking up bottles off my dresser. "I sho' wouldn't mind havin' this color blue mah-self."

"Take it," I say. I don't care if he takes all my polish, all my clothes, all my jewelry. He can have it.

I flop down on my side and pull the covers up to my shoulders.

"Lamb," he says a little sternly. "What you bin takin'?"

"Taking? Nothing. I don't take anything," I say. I've been taking deep breaths, taking the loneliness, taking the worry. "I just feel like something's wrong."

"Whut's wrong wich you? You sick?"

"I don't know," I say. Yolanda sits on the side of the bed beside me and I lay there, kind of curled around his hips. I can smell his hair gel, which reminds me of Jonah, and a few tears slip from the rims of my eyes.

"Is this all 'bout that man nex' door?" Yolanda asks softly. "Ain't he talkin' to ya no mo'?"

I shake my head a little, just twisting it against my pillow. "I don't know. It might be nothing, but it doesn't feel like nothing. Jonah's getting my car fixed—I trust him—but now he's not telling me anything. I don't know if he's mad it broke down, or if he's afraid to tell me how much it's going to cost, or—" I don't want to say the last part. He was so distant in Greek Town, and now I am only getting glimpses of the sweet Jonah I knew. He gets annoyed when I call over to the shop. He doesn't sneak over to see me.

"Oh, Lamb," Yolanda croons, rubbing his huge bear paw of a hand over my arm. "He a man...da's da prob'em. He a man. Once they git ya, they's done. Did 'e git ya?"

I cover my face with my hands and bawl. That can't be true. Yolanda rubs my back.

"Oh, baby girl, you cain't trus' nobody," he goes on.

I sniffle. "That's what Lavina said."

"An' she right, honey, she right. This sound like da same ol' story ... he jus' movin' on an' you gotta let 'im go. You a woman. You gotta learn ta say, fuck him, and move the hell along."

"Lavina's not talking to me anymore either." I choke out the words. "She thought I was disrespecting her, but I wasn't."

"How's that?" Yolanda asks and I tell him what happened. How Lavina made Jonah seem so bad, and how I said ahright in her accent just to point out how ignorant she was being, and how I shouldn't have done that. After I finish, Yolanda chuckles. "Maybe you was outta han' a lil' bit, but I don't think Lavina was that pissed. She would'a popped you if she was really that mad. An' now, that's some'pin every grown woman in a hotel oughta know. Here now, Lamb...sit up and wipe yo' face clean. Lemme teach ya how to handle a black woman when she come at ya."

I'd like to know how to handle things with Lavina. She's so powerful, and when she was mad at me, it made me feel like a dandelion after it's been crushed beneath a boot. I sit up in bed, pulling the sheets up to my chest as Yolanda stands.

"Ok," he begins, "so when a black female come at you, here what ya gonna do. White girls wanna back off and say sorry and please don't hurt me!" Yolanda covers his face and jogs back a couple steps with a squeal. His wig slips and he reaches up, slaps his palm down on it and slides it back in place as if it's a hat instead of hair. "Now, you gotta think like a black hoe, lamb." He plants a hand on his waist and slides his neck back. He jerks his head back and forth, his expression sour. "This how you gotta look—like you don't care who's standin' in front of ya. You da queen, baby—remember that. You da queen an' nobody else!"

Boy, that is Lavina.

"It's all 'bout respec'! She want you to respec' her? Then she gotta give you respec' firs'!" Yolanda struts back and forth in front of me, wobbling his hips, snapping his fingers, and flashing me his fierce, sour expression. "Now, do ya know what ta do if one of 'em bitches come at you?"

I shake my head.

"Okay, girl, this is what ya gotta do," Yolanda says. "First thang, take out ya earrings. See this?" He leans down, his ear in my face. There is an upside-down, triangle-shaped chunk missing from his earlobe. "Bitch got ahold'a mah hoop and ripped it right outta my ear." He stands up straight again. "So git them earrin's out. Secon' thing, girls like to git up in ya face.

They gonna talk trash 'bout you, yo' mama, an' yo' man. They gonna get this close to do it too." He ducks down close again, leveling his furious gaze, our noses nearly touching. His breath smells like sausage. "But don't you back off! You gotta stay right here, while she gittin' up in yer bi'ness. You gotta let 'er know you ain't movin'. Remember what I tole you? You the queen, god dammit!"

I stay where I am, staring back, determined.

"Goo't," Yolanda says, standing up again. "Now whachya gonna do, if she ain't gittin outta yo' face?"

"Punch her?"

"Giiirl," Yolanda frowns, her eyelids fluttering shut as her eyebrows peek. "You ever had three hundre't pounds'a hoe comin' achya befo'? You ain't gonna punch nothin'. That bitch gonna rip yo' hair out befo' you even get yo' fist curl't."

"So what do I do?"

"Same thing ya stopped her from doin'! Go fo' the earrin's, then the weave. If that don't work, you git hold of anythin' you can. The only thin' ya betta not do—ya don't back down when she comin' at ya."

"'Cause I'm the queen," I say.

Yolanda smiles at me. "Ya got it, sista. You is da queen. You feelin' betta now?"

The phone rings and she waves her fingers at me. "You git that, lamb. I jus' stopped by to check in on ya. I'm gonna go watch mah stories!"

She scoots out, with two bottles of my nail polish, as I pick up the phone. "Hello?"

"Silver Spoon? Come on down to the lobby. I got somethin' fo' you."

My heart stops.

Jonah.

The beat starts up in my chest again, crashing against my ribs.

I can't let him see me...or smell me...like this.

"I have to take a shower," I blurt.

"Nah, I ain't got time ta wait. Jus' come on down first. I got a surprise," he says.

My car. He's got my car all fixed and gorgeous, waiting in the lot.

It's the best surprise ever.

"But I look awful. I can't come down like this—"

He laughs. "You got to, Silver Spoon. I'm waitin' on ya. C'mon down."

He hangs up before I can argue some more.

I jump out of bed and tie up my hair. I douse myself in a cloud of perfume, slap on deodorant and pull on a different shirt. I dance down the stairs like a mouse running to the piper. Jonah's here and he brought me a surprise.

"Where you goin' so fast?" Ned shouts from the cage as I shoot past him. I don't bother to say a word to him. I just push open the door and burst into the parking lot, searching for my car.

"Right here," Jonah says. I turn to the left, toward the street and the sound of his voice, and my eyes land on him immediately. He's standing there, at the corner of the building, with an old, green, ten-speed bike.

I go to him, leaning in to kiss him, but the bike's between us. The curled handlebar digs into my hip, but I don't even care. Jonah's lips are as soft as my resolve to be angry with him.

"Where have you been?" I ask through my bursting smile. "I've missed you so much and...where's my car? I mean, my surprise?"

He makes the face I make when I see someone fall on cement.

"The car," he says, drawing out the words. "It's takin' longer to fix than we thought. Trevor's still workin' on it." He lifts the back end of the ten-speed. "That's why I brung you this."

"A bike?" I look at it again. It's green. The tires are bald and the chain hangs like a thirsty tongue.

"I know it ain't your car, but I figure you need somethin' to git you around, until yo' ride's fixed," he says. He takes a lock with a small, silver key from his pocket. There is a plastic-coated chain coiled beneath the seat too. "You can lock it to the parking lot fence so it don't get stole."

I step forward and throw my arms around his neck, smashing the crappy bike frame between us. He's trying. He thought of me, even though he's been busy.

"Thank you," I whisper in his ear.

"You're welcome," he says, patting me on the back.

"The smell of you reminds me of my sheets, and it's been too long since it's been the other way around," I say. "We need to fix that. Can you come up for a while?" I pull back to give him the eyes. "Please? I miss you...sooo much."

"I wish I could," he says, his gaze lingers on mine, warming me to my toes. "But my mother needs some time off from De. He's a handful and she's outta hands with him today."

"You could bring him back here." I trace behind Jonah's ear with a soft fingertip. He lets out a wisp of a groan and closes his eyes a second to savor it. Seeing that is better than getting the bike.

"If I brought him back here, we'd have to lock him in the bathroom because I need some time alone with you."

"We could lock ourselves in the bathroom and he could watch TV," I say. Then, even more softly, "We could take a shower..."

"Oh, girl," Jonah groans again. "Don't tempt me. I gotta run, but I'll try to get over to see ya tomorr'ah, ahright?"

"No...today," I beg.

"Can't," he says. He leans the bike toward me, until I take it and steady it with my own hands. There is no kick stand. "I'll see ya tomorr'ah, Silver Spoon."

"Promise?"

"Oh yeah, I promise," he says with a long stare that unwraps me from my clothes, my skin, and the depression of him being gone the last few days.

I dump the phone back on the cradle. I don't care how pissed he gets.

Jonah didn't come to see me all day and his car is long gone by the time I start my shift. Now I'm sitting behind the desk, paging him over and over and over again, just like the needy girlfriend he never wanted. He's either going to answer, or I'm going to break his pager. I really don't care which.

"Who you callin' now?" Will asks from overhead.

"Jonah," I growl.

"He's a fuckwad retard idiot bas—."

"I know."

"No ya don't," Will says.

I tip my head back to look up at him. "What do you think I don't know?"

"I seen him over at his job today, talkin' to a skinny bitch nigger."

The words hit me like keys in a sock, but I try to keep calm. Rational. "You better be careful, talking like that. Someone's going to hear you and kick your ass. Besides, just because you saw Jonah talking to a girl doesn't mean it wasn't one of his customers."

But my stomach lurches at the whole idea.

"He put his arm around her," Will adds.

My heart sputters and the torch inside it blows out. My insides go dark. I try to rekindle any light I can...it could've been a customer, it might've meant nothing, he could've been being friendly—

"Did he kiss her?" I ask Will.

"No," he says.

A spark. I exhale, fanning it with life. "Okay ... so did he do anything else?"

"I dunno. They went inside and when she come out, he stayed in there."

"And then what?"

"She got in a car and left."

I pick up the phone and dial Jonah's number again. I leave the hotel's main number, as if he hasn't called it three hundred times before. Slam the phone down.

"How's your mom?" I ask Will to change the subject. Will's already told me she's still in pain from what happened in the alley—her nose is broken, but her eyes aren't black and blue anymore.

"One'a Samson's friends finally showed up and brung her some pills. She sleeps a lot now 'cause of 'em."

I gave him my half-empty jar of peanut butter and the last of my crackers yesterday, because I still feel kind of responsible for what happened with Penny. If I hadn't been there, she wouldn't have gotten beaten up. Maybe.

"The guy that brought the pills—he bring you any food?"

"A little. Want some?" he asks.

"Yeah. What do you got?"

"He brung this. Look out below!" Will drops something through the hole and I cover my head with my arms so I don't get hit. It lands on the floor and I swing down off the chair to grab it.

It looks like a candy bar and says Double Chocolate Chunk on the wrapper. It's one of those meal bars for people who are trying to get skinny. I rip it open with my teeth.

"Thanks," I say. It's chewy and has a weird after taste, but it feels good to swallow something besides water.

I'm down to a couple bags of Ramen upstairs and only have a crappy ten speed with a chain that keeps skipping between pedals. I don't know how I'm going to bike into Royal Oak to get groceries, much less carry enough back, when there's no sidewalks and it's about a ten mile ride there and back.

Garbage blows like leaves along the sidewalk outside the back cage window. It's bad now, but I have no idea what I'll do when winter comes. I hope to God that my car will be done by then.

The front door swings open and Saturn comes in with a bag of the exact thing I was just thinking about. Groceries—beautiful groceries—bursting from the edge of the brown paper sack. In her other arm, she's holding a baby on her hip, swathed in pink. The weird thing is that even with groceries and a baby, Saturn still looks every bit a hooker, with her platform heels, tight short skirt, and the blinding glare of her deep red lipstick. With a shake of her head, she swings her silky, straight hair behind her shoulder like a gorgeous black curtain.

She scoots in, the door slamming behind her. "I hate that alarm."

"Me too. Is this your little girl?"

"Yeah," she says, "this is Boo."

She stops at the vent and leans the bag of groceries on the counter against the glass, hauling the baby up on her hip.

Boo has huge, brown eyes behind eyelashes as silky as butterfly wings. And she likes to kick. She gets a serious expression and then lets it rip, both legs flailing like an airborne ballerina on speed.

Saturn readjusts the baby on her hip before turning her attention to me. "Hey, you seen Samson 'roun here?"

I shake my head. "No."

"He ain't been here!" Will shouts down and we both look up, even though Saturn can't see him from where she's standing. "He don't come because I think he don't like my mom no more. An' he's a dumb ass nig—"

"Hey!" I shout at him.

All Saturn says is, "Good. I'm glad he's stayin' out, but somebody's gotta let me know if he comes back 'round. I don't need no more busted ribs." She leans in toward the vent, her eyes flicking upward. "That kid up there's got it right. Samson's a dumbass nigga, and if Samson was shackin' up wit' 'em, gittin' with that kid's mama? Then he knows what Samson *is* betta 'en anybody. An' he sho' don't want Samson back neida."

The door opens again and the baby jerks at the sound of the alarm, but doesn't cry. At least, she doesn't cry until Yolanda walks in. Saturn gives Yolanda a long up-and-down look and scoops up her bag of groceries as she soothes the baby with a shhh.

Yolanda flashes all of us his rickety smile. I think of it as almost beautiful now, even with purple lipstick smeared on his front teeth.

"Hey, lamb," he says with a wiggle of his claw-like nails in my direction. He continues for the stairs as the door opens and a man walks in. He takes one glance at Saturn, her baby, and I, and the man draws back as if he didn't expect to see a crowd. Yolanda notices the exchange and turns to him. "C'mon, baby, it's ahright. Ain't nobody care that you here."

I look away, but Saturn doesn't. She eyes the guy, smiles. She never has mentioned the five bucks I gave her to get home when her ribs were broken.

Yolanda stumps up the stairs and the man skitters up behind her. Once they're gone, Saturn looks back to me.

"I thought Clive don't allow them kind in here," she says. The baby's drooling and kicking again.

I just shrug. I know better than to say anything else. I can't say that Lavina rented Yolanda the room, or that I would have.

"Clive's real funny 'bout that. I don't think he wants them in here ever," Saturn says with a sly grin. "You ever babysit?"

"I have," I say slowly, glancing at the bouncing baby in her arms. "Never any kids that little, though."

"Oh, she's easy," Saturn says as she turns and starts up the stairs. "I'll tell you what ... I never seen that walk upstairs, if you kin gimme a hand wit' babysittin' Boo sometime."

"Uh..."

"An' I'll even have Clive pay ya for it," she says with a wink.

I watch her go up the stairs and once she's long gone, Will leans through his ceiling hole and says, "She can git you fired."

It's been five days without a call or visit from Jonah and it's rained every day. I haven't gone anywhere on that stupid bike. Lavina brought me some of her dinner leftovers—cold spaghetti in a re-used whip cream container. I ate it like Will ate his breakfast that morning Jonah brought him to Red's with us.

And why was he nice to Will?

Or me, if he was just going to pull the plug on talking to me like he has.

He's back to ignoring my pages, he doesn't come to see me, and he tells me he doesn't have time to talk if I go over to the shop while he's working. I don't know why he was ever nice to me at all...except I do. Of course I do.

It's the one reason my mother's always said any man will be nice to a woman. There's only one.

Just off work, I lean across my bed the long way and dial Jonah one more time. I press in the number. Hang up.

I'm fading off to sleep when there's a thud, thud, thud at my door. It sounds like someone's banging with an open hand. Probably Will. I ignore it and close my eyes, drifting the moment I do.

Thud, thud...

"Lael!" It's Yolanda's deep voice, booming as if he has his lips on my door.

I open my eyes, a sharp snap of adrenaline bringing me back down from my cloud.

"Lael, it's me! Yolanda! Open up!"

You've got to be kidding. I ignore him, but every couple seconds, he calls my name again and beats on the door.

I finally lift my head and shout, "I'm sleeping! I'll talk to you later!"

"No, I gotta talk to ya, honey! Open up!"

He's not going away. I finally get up, unlock the door and swing it wide open.

Yolanda stands in the hallway, smiling, but his eyes don't look right. They look kind of the way Penny's did the night she came down to yell at me about the movies—half open and sliding around like they're loose.

He stumps into my room in fuzzy slippers, his wig tipped over his forehead a little low, so it rides up in the back and the curls barely touch his shoulders. He's wearing panty hose that snare his leg hair in the weave, with bleach-mottled red sweats over them, and a lime halter top that doesn't cover the stubbly mat of hair on his chest.

"What's going on, Yolanda?" I ask.

"I wanted ta ask you...well, I wanted ta...no...I was goin' to..." He's got a burning cigarette between his fingers that rains ashes every time he swings his arm. The way his glassy eyes cast around, I just want him to get to the point and leave.

"What's wrong with you?" I ask.

"Huh?" He jerks his head up, the wig sliding back as he squints down his nose, as if he can't see me standing right in front of his face. The cigarette has burnt out, but he's still waving the stump of it around. "Oh, I'm a...the stories is on...and, uh, Clive's downstairs...arguin' wit' Lavina...so I'm—" He drops two finger over his lips, the fake fingernail poking his wide nose. He spits a shhh and giggles. The sound of it is so unnatural, I wince. "I'm...uh...whuch you bin doin', baby?"

"Nothing much—"

"Oh, da's good, hon," he says. He can't seem to string two thoughts together. His head keeps bobbing and his jaw working even when he isn't talking. I think of Penny again. His voice turns distinctly male. "Uh...you got any cash, baby?"

A little shiver of fear slips down my spine. Yolanda's suddenly standing too close.

"What?" I step backward.

"Oh, uh..." He seems startled, as if the words slipped out without meaning to. He takes a step back too, his meaty hand wiping across his forehead as if he just lost himself for a moment. He dumps the finished cigarette in my trash can and reaches inside his top to pull out a fresh cigarette and lighter.

I would fish the cigarette butt from the trash, but I don't want to take my eyes off him. He lights the new cig, drawing in deep and exhaling a long, dirty cloud. "I'm...sorry, lamby...I'm jus' fucked up, is all." His lips turn down and tremble as if he's going to break out in tears.

I soften. "It's alright," I say, putting a hand on his arm.

"It ain't ... I din't mean nothin'...I jus'... I wan't gonna rob ya."

The second shiver to hit me is so severe, it clunks down each of my vertebrae.

"Okay ... thanks," I say. "I need to get some sleep, so—"

"Oh yeah, da's right," Yolanda says. He presses his fingers to his lips sideways so his glittery blue talons don't spear a nostril. "Ya know...I was meanin' ta say ... jezus," he whispers. "God damn, Lael! Don' ya ever even think of doin' what I do." His eyes roll into his skull as he says it, embers dropping from the tip of his cigarette and burning a hole through the leg of his red sweats. He doesn't even flinch. Instead, his voice looses all its girliness again. "I'll kill ya myself if ya do." He pops his eyes wide open, struggling to keep them focused on me.

"I won't," I say.

He considers me momentarily, before diving forward and grabbing my shirt, fisting it in his palm as he drags me to him.

"You eva' git yo'self like this," he snarls in my face, "an' I'll kill ya. I'll beat yo' goddam white brains out! Hear me?"

I'm too afraid to answer. The smoke from his cigarette curls into my nose.

"Goddam it! Do you hear me?" he roars.

"I won't," I whisper.

He lets go, shoving me away. He turns one way, then the other, like he doesn't know where the door is, but he goes out. I shut it behind him and lock all the locks.

How am I ever going to go to sleep now.

SEVENTEEN

"Y*ou still ain't* seen Jonah?" Will whispers down from the hole in the ceiling. He knows I'm grouchy by the way I rented the last two rooms without one smile.

"No," I say flatly. I don't want to talk about Jonah. Besides, Will looks particularly peeky today. "Are you feeling okay?"

"Yeah," he says, like it's silly that I'm asking. Maybe it is. "Jonah don't call you no more either?"

"No," I growl.

"He don't like you no more."

"Whatever," I say. I wish he'd quit trying to steer everything back to Jonah. I'm tired of talking about Jonah, or, actually, the lack of Jonah.

He's been invisible for over a week and the gratitude I felt for helping with my car has boiled out and left me angry. I even stomped over to the shop and insisted on talking to him about my car, but Jonah just made me wait in the lobby with all the service guys and customers coming in and out, staring at me, until I finally raced out and ran back to the hotel in tears.

Getting dumped is bad enough, but not being sure *why* is a thousand times worse. And floating along in silence is a million times worse than that.

"You gonna read somethin' from that fairy book to me?" Will says. He always says it like it's no big deal, but I know he loves hearing the stories. He especially loves finding the matching pictures in my sketch books and knowing which story they belong to. I think it makes him feel smart.

"Yeah, sure," I say. I'm so miserable, anything would be better than just sitting here wondering about Jonah, my car, and my future. I pick up my book of fairytales and am flipping through when the alarm goes off. I put the book down as an Arab man walks up in front of the window.

Tall and thin, he's a handsome man. His hair, dark as crow wings, is slicked back over his ears, while the top is thick and brushed back, exposing his forehead, which rests heavily over his dark eyes. Something about him reminds me of Jonah. It makes me both sad and curious.

"Where's Javon at?" he asks, flicking up his chin at me. His manners subtract a little from his good looks.

"You mean Tavon? Lavina's son?" I ask.

"I mean Javon," he says, narrowing his beautiful eyes as if I mean to give him a hard time.

I smile as sweetly as I can and pick up the ledger, skimming down the check-in names with one finger. There's no Javon. "Sorry, I don't see him. What's his last name?"

"It'd just be Javon. Check it again," the guy says. The bossy tone really rubs off the rest of his appeal.

I close the ledger. No smile. "There's no Javon in the book."

"Look," he chops his hand down on the counter with a superior laugh, "I know he's here."

"There's a ton of hotels around here and that name is not in my book." I meet his glare. I've completely forgotten his tall-dark-and-handsome stature, his deep brown eyes, and his defined jaw now. Nothing about him remains except that he's a bossy ass.

His glare intensifies. "Look in the book," he demands.

"Nope," I say. It reminds me of Greek Town, sitting across from Jonah as he was detached and bossy about taking my car and leaving me with Penny. Yes, he reminds me of Jonah and how Jonah hasn't bothered to speak to me, to even tell me what's happening with my property.

And now I'm standing behind a few solid inches of bulletproof glass and a counter so sturdy it could stop a car.

I don't have to take any of this. Not from Jonah, and not from this guy.

That's what Lavina would tell me. She'd say, Why you lettin' 'im talk to ya like that?

Yolanda would say, You in the cage, lamb. You can say whateva' ya want and what's 'e gonna do 'bout it?

"Just look in the goddam book," the guy says, planting his hands on the counter.

I throw my head back and laugh. Then, I return his stupid glare and snap out my expression like a wrinkle in my shirt. "Fuck. Off," I say.

The man's eyes shoot open. "FUCK OFF?" he roars. I stagger backward. I didn't expect him to shout like that, or look like that, or to be so full of rage that he throws tiny drops of spittle against the glass.

But I can't back down now. I nail my feet to the floor and plant my hands on my side of the counter as I lean in toward the beautiful, bulletproof barrier between us.

"That's right," I growl. "And you can get the fuck out of here!"

The guy holds my stare, as if he's digging through my eyes and burrowing into my soul. Then, with a twitch of his shoulders, he backs away from the counter. He walks out the door without a look back. The adrenaline buzzes up my legs and around the heartbeat pounding in my ears. My hands are trembling, but my guts feel like they're jumping up and down inside my skin.

I sit down on the chair. There's a tap on the window behind me. I turn, pushing aside the vertical blinds. Beneath the glow of the streetlights, I see the man standing on the sidewalk outside.

Our eyes meet.

He raises a gun between us.

I stare into the dark barrel. Death sits inside it, waiting for this man's decision.

This window isn't bulletproof.

"What'sa matter?" Will asks from overhead, but I can't answer him. Can't look up. Can't look away from the gun.

I don't think about how my mother will never know what happened, even though she won't.

Instead, my eyes climb up the barrel of the gun, over the man's fist, up his arm, and scale across his face to his eyes. He could've been a handsome man. And he's young, like me.

All I can think into his eyes is why...

I think, you're going to watch me die. And when you do, it won't be my choice, but I will float on the surface of every one of your thoughts, every day, for the rest of your life.

He'll never know that in this moment, I'm thinking less about my death than his. I feel like I'm in his mind, knowing him, feeling him. And I know he's going to die a little every single day if he does this. The weight of that makes me sad for him.

His finger twitches on the trigger and the mouth of the gun clinks against the window like a wine glass.

Oh...why.

But then he takes a step back.

He drops his rigid arm, the one grasping the gun, to his side.

It's like the weight of it all got to him too. I don't exhale. I'm not sure I'll ever breathe again, even as he turns and walks down the sidewalk, disappearing around the corner onto the boulevard.

I glance across the street at the oil shop and my breath rushes out. Everything's going to be okay, I know it now. Jonah's car is in the parking lot.

I stand up from my chair, turn toward the cage door, and jump backward with a shriek. Will's face is pressed against the glass.

"What's the matter?" he asks.

I don't say anything about the man outside the window. A gun in my face a few months ago would've done something different to me. I would've thought of it every second, I would've called the cops, I would've freaked out and made plans so it would never happen again. Now, all I think is, I'm alive and Jonah's here ... I'm safe.

"Jonah's across the street," I say, my hand on the knob.

"Can I come?" he asks when I open the door.

"What? No," I say as I brush him aside and shut the door behind me. I lock it up.

"You can't just leave!" Will shouts as I make for the door. "You gotta stay in there. It's your job!"

The door swings open before I reach it and the alarm shrills as Jonah steps inside. The door closes behind him and the lobby is silent.

"Hi," I say.

His smile is warm, even though he rolls his eyes, almost like he's embarrassed for having been gone so long.

"Hey, Silver Spoon," he says. "I come to talk. Can you?"

"Yeah, sure," I tell him, even though the last thing I want to do is talk to him. I want to jump in his arms and run my hands through his hair. I want to listen to him talk; listen to him breathe. I want to lay flat on my bed, sinking into the mattress, one leg twisted around his tapered waist as he moves, rhythmic and slow, inside me.

"She's gotta work," Will says from behind me.

"Shut up, Will," I tell him. I don't take my eyes off Jonah. If I do, he might disappear for another couple weeks and I can't take any more of that.

"I need to talk with ya. Somewheres private would be good," Jonah says. He's not breaking up with me, not by the way his eyes are roving over me. He wants me.

"I've got to change the sheets in one of the rooms downstairs," I say, shocked that the quiver inside me doesn't rattle out with my words.

Jonah nods. Smiles.

"I'll help you," Will says as I push past him to get the skeleton key from the cage.

"Not you," I tell him, but he trails down the stairs anyway, staying between Jonah and me as we go to the lower level. I get the sheets and towels from the laundry room. My palms are sweating. Jonah rests his hand at my waist smoothing down a little lower on my back, as I lead him down the hall to Room 22. Will shuffles behind us, looking for a gap.

I open the door and go in. Jonah follows and closes the door behind him before Will can scoot in. Will kicks the door once it's closed. Jonah ignores it while I focus on playing it cool.

"What do you want to talk about?" I ask. I strip the sheets off the bed in a couple quick flicks. Jonah lounges at the edge of the dresser, watching me work.

"Haven't seen you in too long," he says. "Missed you."

"Where's my car?" I ask, snapping out the fitted sheet in the air over the bed. It floats down soft as a crippled angel's wing.

"Ah, now, don't start with that. It's still at the shop," Jonah says. "Trevor said it needs a new catalytic converter, so I told him to go on ahead and git it."

I pause from tucking the sheet around the bottom corner. "I can't afford all this, Jonah, and I really need my car back."

"It wouldn't do ya no good if it don't run," he says, his gaze flicking over my body. He doesn't speak like the Jonah I first met anymore, but his voice still softens me, even though it shouldn't. "B'sides, I told him I'd cover it."

I shake my head. It would solve a lot of problems to have him fix it and foot the bill, but I can't let him. He was so full of admiration before, when he called me independent. I don't want that to slip away, since I've been so needy lately.

"No, it's my car and I'll pay for it," I say. "How much is it all going to cost?"

"Little over six hundred," Jonah says.

I almost choke on the number, but then Jonah is there, pressing himself to me, warm and familiar. His lemon scent is coated over with smells from the shop—sweat, oil, and solvents.

He covers my mouth with his, his tongue moving between my lips and the tension releases like he's thrown open a door. The adrenaline of his kiss runs into my shoulders and out of my fingertips. I sigh happily into his mouth and he holds me, a hand at my nape, one around my back. I'm completely in his control.

He lays me down on the clean, scriggly bed sheet that hasn't been tucked in all the way. He doesn't let up on the kiss and I return the enthusiasm. I feel him wanting me. So there is no question. I rise up, pressing my body to his in response.

"I missed you," he murmurs, pulling up my shirt and yanking down my left bra cup. My boob spills out. He presses his mouth to my skin and I arch my back, offering him everything—right down to my heart.

"I love you," I whisper.

Will donkey kicks the door again. The sound echoes through the room and I'm about to yell at him to go away when he shout-whispers through the door, "Clive's here! He's lookin' for ya!"

I spring up, shoving Jonah away. "Oh shit!" I straighten up and yank down my shirt. Jonah grabs my arm, saying something about how it doesn't matter, but I jerk away.

"You stay in here!" I tell him. "Make the bed and hide in the closet if Clive comes! I need my job and he'll fire me if he knows I was fooling around down here with you!"

"Ahright, go," Jonah grumbles, catching his cheek between his teeth. I don't have time to argue, or to point out how important it is for him to do as I say. If Clive comes downstairs and finds out what we're doing while I'm supposed to be working, I'm dead.

"Jus' go," Jonah growls. "I'll fix up the bed an' come up when the coast is clear."

I slip out the door once Jonah's on his feet.

Clive's standing in the office with the ledger in front of him when I come up the stairs. It's impossible to look like nothing's happened when something has. I fidget with my shirt and rearrange my bra strap.

Lucky for me, Clive barely glances up when I come in.

"An' where was you?" he says.

"Changing the sheets in 22. It was a short stay, so I fixed it up again—"

"Good," Clive says. "Looks like a slow night?"

"Yeah, pretty slow." I shrug with one shoulder and press my butt against the wall beside the peg board with all the keys. I want to stay there so I can watch out the cage door and wave Jonah away if he comes up the steps, but he doesn't come.

"Saturn was in the other night and she said she seen one'a them she-its in here, but you tole 'im ta leave." He eyes me sternly now, but I'm more worried about Jonah than Yolanda right now. Besides, Lavina told me to just deny anything about Yolanda and everything will be fine. She said we can always say a guy rented the room for Yolanda if we have to.

"Uh, yeah," I say.

"Da's good," Clive says, "'cause I don't want none'a them freaks up in here."

Look who's talking. "I didn't forget."

"Good," Clive says. He opens the cash drawer and pulls out three twenties. I've got to remember to write that down. "I'm goin' up ta mah room," he says. "So if ya see any'a them she-its, you call up and lemme know. I'll take care'a it."

"Alright." I don't know why he's so fired up, but I try to stay cool as he goes past me, out the cage door. He jogs up the steps and I hear him casually say, "Hey, brother," just before Jonah comes down.

I know my eyes are wide, I feel them pulling at my skin even though I can't relax them. Jonah must've gone up the emergency staircase to the third floor from the basement in order to avoid Clive. I wave Jonah to the payment window, so he doesn't come to the cage door.

He stops in front of me with a smile. I melt. It feels like we just got away with stealing diamonds.

"Hi," I say.

"Hi." He licks his lips, his eyes traveling down my chest and back up. "I stopped up in your room."

"For what?"

"You said you didn't want me paying for the repairs, so I saved you a trip. I grabbed the hundred out of your ballet box."

"In my drawer? You mean out of my jewelry box?"

"Yeah. You said that's where you keep your cash, and I know you don't want me paying for all your car repairs, so I'll let you put in a little."

But ... he had to take all of it? I don't want to be greedy since he's paying for most of it, but I wish he'd given me a choice. Payments or something. Taking everything in the box makes me feel like there's no cushion between me and the next brick wall, and lately, it seems like there's a brick wall around every turn.

"Okay," I say, but I feel my grin wavering as much as my voice. "Can't you stay?" I ask.

"All night? Nah," he shakes his head like he regrets it as much as I do. "You're workin' anyway. Maybe I can figure somethin' out fo' tomorr'ah night. I've gotta drop this cash off at Trevor's so he can get the parts."

I do a tiny stomp with my foot. "Come back tonight. Please? It's been a week and you haven't even called me or come over for lunch or anything."

"Once I get to Trevor's, I'm just about home. It's too far to drive back. I'll come see ya tomorr'ah."

I just want some small gesture to prove I'm important. I can't believe his sister and mom need him home that much.

But he's not giving in an inch. "Tomorr'ah," he says.

"You promise?" I stick out my lip, hoping it's cute enough to sway him. It's not.

"Don't be all needy, Silver Spoon. That ain't the kind of girl you are."

"I hate when you call me that," I say.

"Needy, or Silver Spoon?" He laughs as he goes out the door.

I watch Jonah cross the street and finally drive away.

I sit back in the office chair. Will dangles his head through the hole and says, "You're stupid for fuckin' him."

"I wasn't doing that!" I fire back.

"You locked me out—"

"Because we were talking."

"I didn't hear you sayin' nothin'." He pops his head back through the hole.

"It's none of your business," I call up to him, but he doesn't reappear.

The door alarm fires off as Santa, the homeless guy, waddles into the lobby.

Oh no. Not tonight. Not with Clive here, already upset and watching for Yolanda. Why does everything have to happen tonight?

"Sorry," I say, waving to get his attention. The bum stops in front of the payment window, turning his milky blue eyes to me. He seems to look right through me, but he waits for me to speak. I didn't expect him to be polite. "You can't stay here tonight," I tell him, trying to keep my voice down. "The boss is here."

Santa nods, drops his eyes. It splits my heart in two as Santa turns to leave.

"Wait," I call to him. I grab my plastic bowl off the desk. The last of my supplies — a packet of cold cereal out of the machine with a splash of Lavina's coffee creamer in it. It's not much, but it's something to say that I'm sorry for throwing him out. "I don't know if you want this, but if you're hungry..."

I go out of the cage and hold out my bowl. Santa eyes it like it's booby-trapped. Then he reaches out and takes it from me. He turns and leaves.

"I need my bowl back," I say, but the alarm blast drowns me out. I go back into the cage and drop down on the chair. I hope Jonah didn't take all my money. There was sixty bucks in my jewelry box. I'm going to need that ten dollars when I bike down to the supermarket tomorrow, whatever the weather, and whether or not there are sidewalks to get there. But I'll worry about that tomorrow.

Right now, there's an ache in my belly, but I sit back in the office chair and try to make my good deed enough to fill the space. It doesn't. Not really. I'm glad I gave Santa something to eat, but I wish I had something too.

"You could'a gave it ta me," Will says. "That bum's fat."

"I've given you a ton of stuff. Don't you have any more of those bars up in your room?"

"Nope," he says. "I got some ketchup packets if you want 'em. I ate all the jelly."

"That's all you've got? Where's your mom?" Maybe I can borrow their car.

"Sick," he says.

"What's the matter with her now?"

"She always gits like this if Samson don't come aroun'. Samson told her she's all used up and ain't no good to 'im anymore. She sleeps all the time now. When she doesn't, she's throwin' up an' mad. I gotta leave 'er alone."

"When's Samson comin' back?"

"I don't know. I hope never." Will says and for being hungry, he sounds happy enough about it.

"He gives you money?"

"He lets us sell flowers down town."

"When do you go?"

"I dunno. My mom don't wanna get outta bed."

"How're you gonna pay your rent?"

"I dunno," he says. "Maybe we gotta move again."

"Aren't you hungry?" I ask. My throat is tight as a fist.

"Starvin'," he says. "But if you want, I can go out to the dumpsters. If you go down the alley some, sometimes people throw really good stuff in the one down there."

I rest my head in my hand. I think I'm going to cry, I'm so hungry.

EIGHTEEN

N o *Jonah.*

No Jonah.

No Jonah.

I just got paid and he took everything out of my jewelry box but ten bucks. He hasn't answered my pages. I get up around eleven in the morning, put my ten bucks in my sock, my backpack on my back, and I get on the bike Jonah left for me. I ride across the street and park it outside the door of the oil shop.

Marco—I know him by name now—sees me coming. He looks up from the newspaper he's reading on the counter when I walk into the lobby. He leans back to the office door and taps on it with the pads of his fingers.

From inside the office, Jonah says, "Whuch ya want?"

"Yo' girl's out here," Marco says.

"I'm up to my ass in paperwork," Jonah shouts back. "Tell 'er I'll come see 'er this afternoon if I kin git all this done."

Marco looks at me as if I've gotten my answer, and then he goes back to his newspaper. I don't bother to argue. It won't do any good. I leave.

It starts to sprinkle. I get on the bike, but the half-flat tires are wobbly and the pedals keep pumping forward too fast as the chain slips. I don't care what's wrong with it, at least, not until the chain falls off a couple blocks down. It falls off the gear and sags like Christmas lights in July.

I get off and walk the thing back to the hotel. I stare over at the oil shop, but Jonah's car isn't there. He probably went for breakfast.

Will must've seen me coming from his window, because he meets me in the parking lot. He walks right up to me and the busted bike. He looks different.

"Where are your glasses?" I ask.

"My mom's got 'em."

"She's gonna get them fixed for you?"

"I dunno," he says. He points to the sagging chain. "I can fix that...if you let me ride it."

"If you can fix it, I need to take it down to the grocery store."

Will squints at me. "Where's there a store?"

I'm not in the mood for this. My pant legs are greasy from when the chain came off and it looks like it's going to rain. "Royal Oak. Eleven Mile."

"People's gonna hit you with their cars, or somebody's gonna knock you off and steal your bike."

"Thanks," I snap. "Or I'm gonna starve if I don't buy any food."

"I could come with you."

"Yeah? How are you going to do that? Run along beside me? You couldn't keep up. Besides, I don't have enough money to buy groceries for you too."

"Oh," he says. Then he lights up again. "I'll still fix it, if you let me ride it."

"Do whatever you want," I grumble. My jeans are ruined and these are the only pants I have without holes in them. Now there are black grease streaks all over them. "I think it's fucked, but you can try," I say.

"I'll try it," Will says. I stand outside and watch him mess with it, but when his second attempt fails—the chain falls off the moment he pedals—I lose faith in him.

"I'm going inside," I tell him as he turns the frame upside down for the third time. "Just chain it back up to the fence when you're done. Jonah can look at it whenever he shows up."

I glance over at the shop. Jonah's car is back and there's only one car in the bays. It's a few minutes to lunch time and a tiny bubble of hope rises in me at the thought of Jonah making good on his promise to come over. But I'm getting tired of having hope.

"I'm gonna fix it," Will insists. I just shrug and go inside. I know better.

Lavina's in the cage unpacking plastic containers out of the canvas tote she uses for a lunch bag. It's bright pink with blue flowers all over it and the brightest thing in the whole hotel. She flashes a grin at me. "That bike Jonah brung ya ain't workin', huh?"

"Nope." My stomach growls as she pops open the largest container. It looks like lasagna. A thick slice of cheese floats on top of red sauce like a yellow flag of surrender. My mouth waters.

"Where you off to this mornin'?" she asks.

"The store, but my chain keeps falling off."

"Jonah ain't got yo' car back yet?" she asks.

I shake my head.

"Well, it's good ya here, 'cause I need yo' opinion on dis lasagna I made las' night. Tavon din't like it none, and I got a whole pan I made of it. I think i's jus' fine, but maybe you kin tell me whuch ya think an' settle it fo' me."

She's got a metal fork wrapped in a paper napkin beside the container. It's her lunch and I know it. I know it because it's noon, when she always eats, and I know it because Lavina doesn't ever ask for anybody's opinion on anything. Ever.

"No, that's okay," I say, even while my stomach kicks me. I'm down to whatever Will can find in the dumpster as my only option, but it doesn't feel much different on the shame scale to take Lavina's lunch. I hear my mother in the back of my head telling me I can't make it my own, she knew it, I'm just a child and what am I thinking. "I'm still too full from breakfast," I lie.

She raises an eyebrow. "Oh yeah? What'd you have? Anythin' good?"

"Pancakes," I tell her. The saliva pools under my tongue at the thought of it, but the embarrassment fills my stomach. "I made them up in my room. Didn't you smell them? Everybody was complaining, they smelled so good."

"They did, huh?" Lavina says. I can tell she's going to give up, and I wish she wouldn't. If she just insists a little more, I'll take that lasagna, run up to my room with it, and gobble it down before I even get my door closed. I can almost feel the sauce running down my chin, but Lavina's tongue rolls in her cheek. "Okay, if ya don' wanna try it, da's fine."

Oh God, I want it. My stomach is snarling, my brain is in knots. I fish the ten dollar bill out of my sock. My pride makes me slip it through the slot just to prove to her that I don't need her charity. Even though I do.

"Can I get change? I was going to grab a pop out of the machine."

She gives me the change and I can't stop staring at the container of Lavina's lunch.

"You sho'?" Lavina says, but the embarrassment overwhelms me and I turn away like a fool.

"No thanks," I tell her, slipping my precious quarters into the machine. "Once Will fixes the chain on my bike, I'm going to ride down to Royal Oak. It should be a nice ride and I need the exercise."

"Ahright, but it's rainin'," Lavina says as the pop thunks down in the chute.

"I like the rain," I say. I'm almost starting to believe it. I take the can out of the machine and start up the stairs as the door alarm sounds. Another customer comes into the hotel, looking to rent a room for just as much time as it takes.

I lay in bed and stare at the ceiling, my stomach howling.

It's six o'clock and Jonah never came.

I don't bother going to see if his car is gone. I know it is. Seeing the empty parking space will just make everything feel worse.

The phone rings around eight. I pick it up, hoping it's him. Hoping he will say he's coming to see me ... sorry he didn't come earlier ... he's bringing dinner. Any of that.

"Lael?" It's my mother.

"Hi, Mom."

"What's wrong?"

I try to make my voice more cheery. "Nothing. How are you?"

"Good," she says warily. "I just thought I'd call and see how you're doing. I miss you."

Her words hit me like cinder blocks. Miss me. Her voice is so wispy, so non-calculating, so sweet. She never sounds like that. She's usually stretched tight and annoyed that she has to say anything to me at all.

My throat suddenly clots up with how much I miss her too.

"How are things going?" she asks.

"My car broke down," I tell her.

"Oh no. What are you going to do about that?" I hear the tiny hint of hope—hope that I'll fail. I detect it, like I always do, as easily as if her disbelief in me is a hunk of metal buried beneath thin layers of sand on the beach.

"My boyfriend is having it fixed," I say coolly.

There's a pause on her end. An adjustment I'm sure. She's either sharpening one of her war tools, or willing herself not to pick them up at all.

"Jonah? That's his name, isn't it? The black fella?"

"Yes," I say, "But you don't need to say he's black."

"Isn't he?"

"Yes, but he doesn't want that to be the main thing you see about him."

My mom giggles. Not a mean giggle, but an amused giggle. "Well, I don't see anything about him, so I guess I could identify him any way he wants. How should I talk about him?"

Now I break down in a small giggle. It is all pretty stupid. "He's...tall," I say and then I bust out laughing and my mom joins me. She just wants to know if I'm still dating the same guy, that's what she wants to know.

"So, you're still dating the tall, dark, and handsome boy," she says. I don't correct the boy part. I'll just let her keep thinking he's only a couple years older. She would lose her damn mind if she knew the truth. "It is awfully nice of him to help you with your car," she adds and I melt against my chair. She said he's nice.

"Mom, you might actually like him, if you met him," I say, basking in the possibility.

"Maybe. How much is he willing to pay to get your car fixed?"

Oh, but there it is. There's that tiny edge in her voice, the one that is sharp as a metal sliver and can cut open an artery if I allow her to position it right.

"I don't know, but you don't have to worry about it, Mom," I say, readjusting on the chair. I want her to get back to liking him. That felt nice. "He's a good guy and he's helping me take care of it."

"He's helping you, or he's paying for the whole thing?" she needles. "Those bills can be expensive, you know."

I sit up straight and make my tone stiff. "Like I said, you don't have to worry about it."

"I'm not," she insists and I feel the invisible noose tightening around my neck with her every word. I blow out a frustrated breath and my mom goes silent. That alone surprises me. "Well," she starts again, "I was thinking about you. I didn't call to fight with you. I'm glad Mr. Tall is helping you with getting your car fixed. I just wanted to call and say I was thinking of you and miss you."

"Ok, thanks," I say. I don't know what to say. I'm not homesick anymore. I don't miss her, but it's good to hear her voice. I'm caught between falling into what might be a trap...her missing me could be the line of crumbs that leads straight into her pressure cooker of guilting me into coming home...that's the way it's always worked before. But something has changed. I'm not really sure how to fire back at her, because I'm not sure she's fighting at all. "Thanks for calling, Mom." The words are all awkward and tumbly, falling into the phone and probably spewing out her end of the line like the broken shield they are. "I'll talk to you soon."

And in between my words, she throws in a soft and wishful, "I love you, Lael."

The whole call has gone topsy-turvy. The world has flipped upside down. My thoughts run through the usual track, trying to choose an appropriate response, but this is a war tactic she's never used before.

If it is one at all.

Holy shit...

she's disarmed me...

"Okay," I say and toss the receiver in the cradle as if it is burning my hand.

I'm falling asleep in the office chair. It's the only thing that takes away the hunger for a while, although the pangs keep waking me up.

I've been eating whatever Will finds in the dumpster—I even went down and tried to find some stuff for myself this morning, but there was nothing. Wadded up fast food bags full of wrappers and empty, plastic tubs of mayo that smelled like feet. When Will brings me anything, I try to play pretend in my head. I cut the mold off the bread and scrape any rotted parts back into the trash as if I'm at a party and the rotted food is just the stuff I don't like.

As if there is food I don't like anymore.

I drift off into that thin layer of sleep, when a guy bangs on the payment window. I snap my head up, sending a sharp pain down my neck. The alarm didn't go off, so that means whoever is pounding on the glass is already a customer.

My eyes focus on a guy in a velvet track suit. Thank God, it's not Clive. I remember this guy checking in, licking his fingers as he peeled up bills from the wad in his palm. Lavina would've had something to say about that.

"Can I help you?" I ask.

The guy drops the key into the slot for the short stay. "Just checkin' out, but I wanna lech'ya know, you got a junkie up there knockin' on doors an' tryin' to sell some busted up glasses for a couple bucks. I'm sho' y'all don't want some crack head runnin' up an' down the halls like that. It ain't good for bi'ness."

Oh my God. Penny is trying to sell Will's glasses. "I'll go up there and stop it. Thanks for letting me know."

"Sho," the man says. He waits for a woman, speckled with meth sores and way to young for him, to come down the steps. He takes her hand as if she's royalty and they go out the door together before going their separate ways.

"Will," I tip back my head and call up toward the ceiling once the alarm turns off. Will doesn't look over the edge, but I know he's there by the thumps and bumps. "Is your mom up there trying to sell your glasses?"

"I think so," he says. He sounds grouchy.

"Well, go tell her to knock it off. Clive's girlfriend is on the second floor, and if she tells Clive, you'll get kicked out for sure."

"My mom needs her medicine," Will says blandly. Not food. Medicine. That's what she tells him. She's not a junkie—she's sick. I wonder how many times she's driven him down to the alley behind the crack house and told him it's her doctor's office.

"It's not medicine, Will, it's drugs." I don't know why I have to put it in his face, but I do. He needs to know the truth and no one else is going to say it like it is.

But Will only answers, in his little-boy-voice that makes me feel guilty, "Drugs are medicine."

There's no explaining it to him. I guess if that was my mom, I wouldn't think of it that way either. What the hell am I thinking? He's just a little kid.

"Will," I say.

"What?" he grumbles.

I'm a shit. I want to make it up to him. "Do you want to hear a story?"

"You can read one if ya want. I don't care." His mumble falls down on me like a fat, heavy fog. He hasn't put his head through the hole all night—probably because he didn't want me to know about the glasses, but now I do and he still isn't putting his head through.

"What's wrong with you?" I ask.

"Nothin'," he says.

"Then stick your head out," I say.

"Lael ... you think I might be able to come live with you a while? Just fer a little while?" His voice cracks and my gut sinks. Something is wrong. Really, really wrong.

"Look at me," I call up to him. When he doesn't appear, I get scared. My voice deepens when I command him the way my mother would, "Will. Look at me right now."

His hair comes through the hole first, wild as always, but when I see his face, I cover my mouth when one hand.

"What happened to you?" I gasp.

Will's eye is black as leather and swollen shut. A deep, ugly bruise extends toward his temple and spreads down his jaw. Even his lips are swollen. I jump to my feet, the chair clattering onto its side.

"What happened to you?" My stomach is a water balloon thrown off a skyscraper. My voice climbs. "Tell me what happened!"

I don't know what to do. Call the police? No, of course not- Will's not dead, but he's been beaten. Who do I tell? His face crumples and he begins to cry and then the tears make him breathless as he tries to wipe away the sting.

I grab the key to the cage, rush out, and lock it up as quick as I can. I bound up the stairs, two at a time, to the second floor landing. Will's still there, hunched over his knees, head down, his back bucking as he tries to stop his sobbing.

"Come here," I say softly, leaning over the spindly rail and pulling at his ankle.

It takes a couple tugs, but he finally climbs over. I pull him into my arms and we collapse together on the landing. I wrap myself around him so tight, I'm sure we're both going to suffocate. He lets loose horrible shredded wails against my shoulder that echo through my chest and wrap around my heart. I rock him on the carpeted floor. He cries and cries like I've never heard anybody cry. I hold him and he cries so long and loud that I think everyone will hear, but nobody comes. I'm the only one. I hear porn blasting from a TV somewhere down the second floor hallway.

Will and I just sit on the landing until his sobs have drained away. The door alarm sounds.

"Don't go!" Will says.

"I have to," I whisper, but he shakes his head against my shoulder. His thin, little hands are around my shoulders. I could carry him, he's so skinny.

Somebody raps their knuckles on the bulletproof glass and a man barks, "Hey! Anybody here? I wanna room!"

Will clings to me, sniffling. I can't leave him like this. Won't.

"We're full!" I yell down the stairs.

"You shittin' me?" the man answers with a psht from between his teeth. "The parkin' lot ain't even half full!"

"We're full!" I shout down again.

"Well, goddammit!" the man downstairs snarls, but I hear him shuffle to the door and then the alarm sounds and the lobby is quiet again. From one of the rooms on the second floor, I hear the gauzy, muted sound of a woman moaning and the rumble of a man's voice.

"What happened to you?" I ask Will. He smells awful—sweat, grease, urine. His sniffles are skipping beats. "Who did this to you?"

Will just shakes his head against my shoulder. He doesn't want to tell, but that's not going to work.

"Your mom?" I ask.

He shakes his head again.

"Then who?"

"Some guy. He said his name was Beauregard," Will hiccups the sentence. I've never heard the name and I don't remember any Beauregard in the guest ledger.

"Where'd he come from?" I ask.

"He's a friend of my mom's," Will sniffles, trying to get control of himself. "She called him 'cause she ain't got her medicine and Samson ain't bringin' it no more."

"But why'd he hit you?"

"'Cause I bit 'im. Hard."

"Why'd you do that?"

"*Cause he was fuckin' me!*" Will burrows into my shoulder. He pinches his mouth shut on a sound that turns into a miserable whistle.

I don't know what to say. *He was fucking me.* I open my mouth, but no words come out. *He was fucking me.* I can't catch a breath.

I should know what to say—I know exactly what it feels like to have someone force themselves on me, but I wasn't *fucked. And Will saved me. He got Jonah and saved me.*

Nobody saved Will, and his mother was right there in the room with him.

Nobody saved Will. I've failed him too. Will has saved me more than once and now, something really terrible happened to him and I didn't even know.

He was fucking me.

"Why didn't your mom stop him?" I finally squeak.

"We don't got no money and my mom said I gotta do it so we're not homeless. She don't got her medicine! I'm the man'a the house, and we ain't got no food!" He breaks down, the tears flowing into the fabric of my shirt and staining it with a sadness I'll never get out.

I want to race upstairs, use my skeleton key, and whip open Penny's door. I want to drag her into the hall and beat her until she splits open. Then I'd stomp on her heart, the same way she's done to her son. Will clings to me, like he knows what I might do. I hold him tight and we keep rocking together on the landing. He starts crying again and doesn't stop. He doesn't even slow down.

I don't know what to do.

A can of pop won't fix this.

A couple cans of spaghetti rings won't fix this.

Reading him fairy tales won't fix this.

The cops said not to call unless there's a dead body—they're not going to fix this.

All I can do is sit and hold Will and let him sob.

"You're not a man yet," I whisper, but it makes him cry harder. "It's not your fault—you're not supposed to be the grown up, Will! This isn't your fault! We got to call Lavina. Your mom can't do this to you!"

He tears out of my arms. "No!" he says, lines of spit and snot hanging off him. He wipes his ragged face with his forearm. "You call the cops and they'll take me away! I'll fuckin' kill you if you call the cops, Lael! I'll steal the key from Lavina and slit yer throat! I'll slit everybody's throat!"

He jumps up and rockets up the steps to the third floor. I hear his raggedy shoes beating down the hallway toward the creepy, emergency stairwell at the opposite end of the hall, across from my room. He hides there because he can run down to a different floor and get away before anyone can catch him.

I wish he would have done that before Penny let that Beauregard into their room.

I don't go after Will. I don't know what to say to him. All the soothing words I have ever heard—the pep talks and pats on the back, the it'll be okays, or things always get better—none of it applies. There's no way out of the mess Penny's put them in and that's his mom. I don't know what I can do.

Watching this stuff on the news, my mom would say...that's horrible. Why didn't anyone call the police?

But I already know the answer to that: I'm not calling, because there is no dead body.

I'm the one adult Will trusts and I have no idea what to do.

NINETEEN

I *am itching to* talk to Lavina about Will, but when she bustles in a little before eight in the morning, loaded down with crinkly grocery bags, all I can do is jump up and open the cage door for her.

"Thanks," she says, pushing past me and tugging her bags that get stuck on the doorframe. I am smashed against the wall until she muscles her way in and deposits her bags on the counter with a clatter.

I can see the labels of cans through the bags: canned chicken, spaghetti rings, corn, green beans, black beans, and beef stew. Another bag is stuffed with packages of Ramen and jars of peanut butter, while the one hanging on Lavina's arm has a four loaves of bread.

"Help me bring in the res'," she says. I help carry in a box with at least a dozen boxes of Spam in it, and a couple tubs of margarine and a bright bag that particularly catches my eye—candy. Licorice ropes, Dum Dum suckers, Tootsie rolls. I pinch my lips looking at it all, so the drool doesn't run out of the corners of my mouth. Lavina's got enough food for a small army.

"What's all this for?" I ask. I can't look away from it. Instead, I cross my arms and dig my fingernails into my skin so I don't snatch up the bread and tear into it right through the wrapper.

"Sit down." Lavina points to the office chair between us.

When somebody like Lavina says sit, you do it.

"Ahright," she says. "Me an' mah church, we like doin' charity work. We gather food an' clothes an' we give 'em to people who needs help. Now, before ya start squawkin' 'bout takin' charity, you listen ta me. Sometimes ya jus' need help ta git ova' dat hump in yo' life. I been there. Most all'a us has. So, when ya know somebody else is gittin' on a hump, ya help 'em. An' when ya on'a hump yo'self an' ya need help, you take it. Ain't no honor to give it an' it ain't no pity to take it. It's jus' some'pin we do fo' each other so we all get on ahright."

She doesn't have to convince me anymore. My stomach hasn't stopped growling; it's like an engine that keeps on revving, and my foot is stuck on the brake. I try to concentrate on her eyes and what she is saying, but my gaze keeps wandering back to the bags on the counter and my mind is already eating everything in every bag there.

"I asked the womens in mah church group fo' food," she says. "I think you got 'nuff clothing..."

"I do." I lick my lips.

"I brought some fo' you an' fo' Will an' Penny. I seen how yer pants is fallin' off ya lately." She reaches into one of the bags and pulls out two plastic boxes with a snap lid. "An' since I made pancakes an' eggs dis mornin' for Tavon, I brought us some to eat togeda', 'fore I gotta git ta workin'. I wan'cha ta know, it'll grieve me if ya turn 'em away."

My eyes flood with hot, prickly tears until Lavina looks like she's swimming under water. I blink, blink, blink and the tears spill out onto my cheeks.

"Now, don't do dat," she says softly. Big, blurry, Lavina reaches forward with her big, brown, blurry thumb and rubs the tears off my face.

Then, for respect sake I think, she turns away to pop off the top of the pancake and egg boxes. She fishes two silver forks out of her bags and hands me one, along with a paper napkin.

"You use sur'up?" she asks and I nod. She pulls out a bottle of it and drizzles it into the box before she lays it in front of me.

The scent of the pancakes and buttery eggs hits my face, as sticky and sweet as home always smelled. It's already better than anything I ever ordered at Red's, but I can't take a bite. First, I have to swallow down the lump in my throat three or four times. I can't even look up to thank her because I'm concentrating on keeping the tears from rolling down into the box in front of me. Lavina doesn't say anything. I think she knows.

She leans up against the counter busying herself with nothing. After a few seconds she says, "Ya know what's missin'? Coffee. We need us some good coffee to go wit' this." She scoots past me, crushing me and the chair against the desk, my face right over the top of the pancake box, as she goes out of the cage door. "You g'won an' eat an' I'll make us a pot," she says. She goes into the lobby, humming a low tune that sounds like a hymn.

I hear her pouring water into the maker as I dig into the food in front of me. By the time she's clicked the filter full of coffee grounds in place, I'm going strong. It's like my stomach opens up and I can't get it in fast enough. There's syrup on my shirt and drops of it on my pants. I can hardly will myself to slow down and chew any of it, I'm so desperate not to be hungry any more. My face is right over the box as I shovel the last of the syrup-covered eggs down my throat. My cheeks are sticky. Wisps of my hair are coated in maple syrup at the tips.

Lavina hums and hums, and when she comes back with two Styrofoam cups of coffee, she sees me sitting there, my face a gooey mess. She takes one look and chuffs a laugh as she hands me one of the cups.

"G'won and eat 'dis one too," she says, handing me her box. "What I really want is one of dem cinnamon rolls I brung." She digs out another box with glazed rolls inside. She lifts one out daintily between her two fingers and then sets the box of rolls down on the desk in front of me too.

"Well, g'won," she says when I don't dig in. "Don't make me eat all by mah'self!"

I'm embarrassed, but still want to devour everything she's put in front of me. Lavina doesn't even give me a second glance. Instead, she studies the ledger as if there's something there she needs to see. When she can't look any longer, her gaze goes straight over my head, into the lounge.

"Now how come da papers on dat door's droopin'? Ya'd think I would'a seen dat be'fo'. People be thinkin' tha maid ain't doin' her job, wit' tha advertisements all fallin' off da front windas." With that, she bustles out of the cage again, past the coffee maker and across the lounge, to the front door and windows facing the boulevard. The glass is completely covered in paper with florescent type that advertises our cheap rates, free triple X movies, and clean rooms.

Lavina busies herself with removing some of the papers that rip as she tries to reposition them. She does it long enough that I finish the second box of breakfast and two of the cinnamon rolls.

"Clive hates re-tapin' dese signs when dey git ripped up like dis," she says, heartily ripping one down. "He gonna have ta have 'em all re-printed..." *Rip.* "...but he seem ta like spendin' money on dis kinda thing..." *Rip.* "...when what he need ta do is git me some help cleanin' all dese rooms..." *Rip.* "...an' doin' his inventories..." *Rip, rip.* "An' doin' his bankin', an' runnin' his bi'ness, while he up in dat room'a his, havin' his fun wit' his lady friend." *Rip.*

I grunt my agreement through a mouthful of cinnamon roll and burn my tongue with a gulp of coffee to flush it down. Lavina clears a tractor-tire-sized space in the window and on the door before she carries back the pieces to the cage, crumpling them in her hands.

She pretends not to notice the crumbs all over me, or the way I can't stop licking my fingers.

"I need to talk to you about something," I tell her. My eyes crawl up to the opening in the ceiling and Lavina follows them.

"Li'l man?" she asks.

I nod and crook my finger for her to lean in close. "Penny tried to sell Will yesterday," I whisper in her ear. "Like sell him. To a man."

Lavina presses her lips together. "Here?"

"In their room, to a friend, I guess. I don't know what all happened, but the guy beat Will up."

Lavina doesn't gasp. Her eyes sink to the floor as she pulls away shaking her head. She lets out a heavy sigh and says, "Lawd."

"I don't know what to do," I tell her.

Lavina shakes her head, her eyes losing their spark as they move along the side window of the cage. "He kin call da cops, but I dun think he'd do dat, 'cause he know dey gonna take 'im away. He tole me social service almos' took 'im befo', but Penny ran off wit' 'im so dey couldn't. Da's why dey's livin' in hotels an' stayin' way from cops. Bet dat's why she wouldn't say nothin' when dem cops got her dat night."

I'm a tiny bit insulted to hear that Will's confided in Lavina and not me. With all the times he's been in my room stealing my stuff, you'd think he would've trusted me as much.

"He said the guy fucked him," I say. "Shouldn't we call?"

Lavina rubs her forehead. "Social services would come. Dey'd take 'im an' put 'im in a foster house. His mama'd have ta git clean fo' she could git 'im back."

"Then we should call, right?" I say.

"You kin, if ya want."

"Me? You don't think we should?"

"Ain't no we," Lavina says with another shake of her head. She puts her purse in the desk drawer, picks up the forks, the empty plastic breakfast boxes, the lids. "I learn't a long time ago, ya don't git inta other people's bi'ness. Nothin' good comes of it."

I gape at her. "Even if it's a little boy that's getting hurt?"

"You don' think dat lil' boy's gonna be hurt when dey take 'im from his mama? Or when dey put 'im someplace wit' peoples that might even do the same stuff to 'im?"

Now I shake my head. I don't know how it all works, but help has always been help in my world.

We call the fire department, they put out the fire.

We call an ambulance, they take you to the hospital.

We call the cops...

I think of Penny's broken nose and bloody face. But they were trying to protect me, weren't they? I think of the cop that told me not to call unless there was a dead body.

Things don't work here like they did at home. I should know that by now. Maybe Lavina's right and it would be worse for Will, but it's hard to imagine anything worse then his mom moving him from hotel to hotel, strung out, ignoring him, letting him starve, and selling him to get more of her medicine.

All the food in my stomach climbs toward my mouth.

There's no guarantee that anything I do will actually help.

I just want Will to be in a place where everything will be okay.

But I don't know if that place even exists anymore. It doesn't here.

"Jus' leave it be, and let the goo't Lawd handle it," Lavina says. "Some thin's jus' got ta be what dey is, 'til God figure it out." Her voice is soothing, but I am not soothed. She re-packs two bags with a mixture of everything she brought and pushes them toward me. "G'won an' take dese groceries up ta yo' room now, an' git some res'."

I pick up the phone and dial the shop. Marco answers the phone.

"Marco, hi—it's Lael." I try to smile into the phone. Marco always plays the buffer for Jonah, but it can't happen today. I've never begged before, but this will be a first.

"He's—" Marco starts, but I cut him off.

"Please, Marco," I say, "can I please talk to him? It's really, really important. I know he's busy, but I swear, this is important. Please." I feel a little bit guilty, because I'm making it sound like there is a death in the family, or worse, but I'm desperate. I haven't talked to Jonah in a week and a half, since the last time he told me he was coming over to see me at lunch. I can't take it anymore.

There's a pause and then Marco whispers across the line, "Ahright, I'll send the call to 'im, but don't go tellin' 'im I did it on purpose."

"I won't," I promise and the line clicks. Rings. Jonah picks it up. "Hi," I say.

"Hi," he says, a smile in his voice that lights me up. "Who's this?"

"Lael," I say.

The smile collapses into his words. "Oh...uh...hey there, Silver Spoon. What's going on?"

What's going on? He's so casual, as if it's normal that he doesn't talk to me anymore, hasn't been to see me, and now dodges me at every turn. The last little ember of me and Jonah, the very last spark, sputters as it tries to stay alive inside me.

"How about my car?" I ask like it's a joke between us. I'm caught between wanting to yell at him and needing him so much, that I'll do anything to keep him happy with me.

"Trevor's still got it," he says with a sigh, as if I'm a gnat buzzing around his ear. "You gotta quit askin' me 'bout it. He's givin' me a deal an' workin' on it in his garage at home, so he's gonna work on it when he's got time. I don't know why you keep buggin'! You were talkin' 'bout jus' parkin' it and leavin' it be'fo!"

"I didn't mean it," I say, a little embarrassed at my impatience. He's right—this guy, Trevor, is doing me a huge favor. "I need to get to the grocery store and I need a hair cut. I'm just feeling super trapped without my car."

"Ya gotta chill," he says.

"I know. You're right. I'm just lonely. You keep saying you're going to come over, and then you don't come. It feels like you're breaking up without actually breaking up."

"Breaking up?" There's one of those sharp edges in his tone and I can't get out of the way of it fast enough. "If I was breakin' up wich you, I wouldn't be botherin' to have a friend work on yo' car. I wouldn't be talkin' ta you right now." I hear him inhale and blow it out in a disappointed sigh that sends a hairline crack down the center of my heart. "I've gotta git back ta work. It ain't like yo' job, Silver Spoon, where ya jus' sit at a desk and shuffle movies. I got a job ta do over here. I've gotta keep this place runnin' smooth an' I don't need mo' pressure from you right now."

That stings.

"I'm sorry. I just miss you so much," I whisper, my upper lip crumbling. "But there's been a lot of pressure over here too. You took all the money I had for repairs, and then I ran out of food. The bike chain keeps falling off the bike you gave me, so I don't have any way to get to the store. I'd be starving, but Lavina brought a bunch of food today from her church. And do you know what happened last night?"

Jonah chuckles. "No, what? Tell me."

I'm talking so fast, trying to justify calling him, while also catching up on everything that's happened since he's been gone—I sound like a chipmunk. But Jonah's chuckle infuriates me. This isn't a joke.

"It's not funny," I snap. "Last night, Penny sold Will...to a guy that raped him."

"That's awful," Jonah says a little more somberly. I calm down.

"Lavina told me not to call the cops, because Social Services might take Will away, and that it might be even worse for him."

"It might," Jonah agrees. "Sometimes it's betta' ta stay outta other people's bi'ness."

"Are you serious?" I grip my forehead. The whole world—the familiar one that I have always known—has disappeared. It's like everyone is just standing at the edges, saying, yeah, it's caving in, but what can you do? "So what do I do, Jonah?" My voice climbs. "What do I do?"

"Ya figure it out," he says.

"Couldn't I come live with you?" I whisper. "Have you thought about it?"

Jonah chuckles again, a little less easy this time. "Oh, I've thought of it," he says.

It's all I need, that spark. It lands on that little ember of our relationship and whoosh! Up it goes in red hot, loving flames. I haven't allowed myself this fantasy in a while, but here it is, roaring with how I'll cook his breakfast every morning before we drive me to work together— me getting out at the hotel door with a lingering, loving kiss, before he reverses and rolls across the street to the oil shop. Never mind that it's Lavina's shift. Maybe, instead of clerking the graveyard shift, I'll be the maid Lavina wants Clive to hire. We can all eat lunch together. On days when Lavina can't make it to work, Jonah can duck over on his break for a quickie. At the end of the day, we'll go home together. Maybe we'll stop off for dinner somewhere, like Greek Town, and we'll laugh about that time that he had to leave and the car broke down and it all led to us being together forever.

It's so perfect.

"It would be so easy," I say.

"I don't know about that," he chuckles again. "Maybe I can come by after work today, Silver Spoon. You gonna be sleeping?"

"You've got the key," I remind him.

"I'll try to make it over after work," he says.

"Don't try," I tell him. "Come."

Of course, Jonah doesn't come.

The oxygen in our phone call wasn't enough. The spark has died down to a tiny prick of a glow and nothing more. I couldn't get to sleep—I didn't want to miss Jonah, like I promised him I wouldn't. I stay up and at five o'clock, I go downstairs and look out. Jonah's car is gone.

I sit on the edge of my bed and dial his pager. I pound in the digits of my number.

I dial the pager.

I pound in the digits of my number.

I dial the pager.

I pound in the digits of my number.

I dial the pager.

I pound in the digits of my number.

I dial the pager.

I pound in the digits of my number.

I dial the pager.

I pound in the digits of my number.

I dial the pager.

I pound in the digits of my number.

I dial the pager.

I throw the receiver down on the cradle. It's pointless.

Breathing hard, I sit back on the bed. I want my car back. I don't care if it isn't fixed. Maybe I can borrow some money from Lavina or Yolanda to pay off whatever repairs Trevor's finished. All I know is that I am done with Jonah.

Done.

The phone rings and I pick up.

"Hello." It's no longer a question or a greeting.

"Silver Spoon?" Jonah says, his voice buttery. "Why you blowin' me up?"

"You didn't come over like you promised," I say.

"I know, I couldn't...I..."

"Who's that on da phone?" A woman howls in the background.

I pull my ear away from the receiver. "Who is that?" I ask.

"Nobody," Jonah mumbles. I don't know if he's speaking to me or her.

"Whuch you mean, nobody, Jonah? What the hell you mean?" she screeches.

"It's none'a your business, Nia," he snaps.

I let out my breath. It's Nia. Brothers and sisters fight all the time. It still makes me tense, but even tenser when I hear DeAndre crying in the background too. It jabs at my heart. I wish this wasn't the first time I've gotten to hear them—especially when she's yelling at Jonah. I'm caught between wanting to defend him and wanting him to end it, so I can get Nia on the phone and finally say hello.

"Gimme that..." Nia shrieks. DeAndre's wail pours onto the line, but the phone hangs up with a sharp click.

What are they fighting about? I hang up and sit, waiting for Jonah to ring me back.

I get up and pace. I wait for their fight to finish. I pace some more.

After twenty minutes, I dial Jonah's pager and put in my digits.

After another twenty, I dial Jonah's pager and put in my digits.

At 10:30, I'm so antsy, I figure I'll do Ned a favor. I go downstairs and count the drawer early. I make him put in the five bucks he's short.

"Why you keep lookin' at the phone?" he asks. "Lover boy not callin' anymore?"

"Why would you say that?" I ask.

Ned grins. "He's not, is he."

"The drawer's square now, you can go."

"Hey, Fail, I heard you did somethin' last week."

"I do things all the time," I grumble. I have no idea what he's talking about and I don't care.

But Ned grabs my wrist. Not in a weird way, not in a way that makes my skin crawl. His grip is really delicate, so un-Ned like that I look him in the face, and what I see there is truly weirder. His expression is soft and serious. Ned's real.

"I heard you fed that old bum that comes in here," he says. "And you got him outta here before Clive seen him."

"Who told you that?" I ask.

"Did you do it or not?" Ned counters.

"I did," I say, narrowing my eyes, as if I'll be able to detect his trap. I know there's got to be one. This is Ned. "Why do you care?"

His expression gets a little steely again, the old Ned dragged, like a musty tarp, over this nicer version. "I was going to say thanks, but fuck it."

"Oh." I draw back, shocked. Who is this guy? "You're welcome."

"Yeah, whatever," he says, throwing on his coat. He gets out of the cage and around the counter before I can stop him.

"Ned, wait," I say and he comes to a sharp halt, swinging his sour face in my direction. "Why did you want to know if I did it?"

Ned jams his fists into his pockets.

"That guy is my dad. He's out of his head, and he's a fucking useless bum, but he's my dad." He breaks my gaze, pushing his fists down further into his pockets, so it looks like he's going to punch himself in the balls. "Thanks for lookin' out for him. And listen, Lael," he pauses. "You should get outta here. You don't belong."

I almost forget this is Ned I'm talking to, and I answer him with the unguarded truth. "Where else am I going to go?"

"I dunno," he says with a wry grin, "There's a place down the street—on Nine Mile. There's a restaurant on the corner—you probably seen it, it's right on the Boulevard—and there are apartments across the street. It's not great, but it's better than here. You could wait tables to pay your rent. I've got a friend that works there as a cook. He could put in a good word if you wanted."

I don't know why he's telling me this. I would've thought he was making some weird pass at me, but Ned lives down Seven Mile.

"Why are you telling me all this?"

Ned gives me a hard shrug, as if I've got him by the scruff of the neck. "Because you did that for my dad."

"Oh. I would've—"

"Yeah, whatever," he says and he goes out the door, the alarm screaming.

The shrieking in the hallway is real. I shoot up in bed, disoriented. Sunlight streams in through the window.

"I tole you not to come back! Who let you in?" A familiar voice shouts. I rub my eyes, trying to place it.

I can't identify the shouter, but with the second shriek, I can identify the screamer. It's Yolanda.

I rush to the door before I even think it through. I rip open the door and poke my head out, just as Clive pushes Yolanda up against the wall and thrashes her so hard, it knocks off her crooked wig. Yolanda shrieks again, but it's so loud without being muffled by a closed door that I cringe.

"One of my boyfriends got the room, jus' fo' the night!"

"What's 'is name?" Clive grabs Yolanda's face, squeezing her cheeks so hard she winces. "Gimme the name, you sonofabitch, an' I'll look it up and see who checked you in!"

"I don' know 'is name!" Yolanda says.

"Don't lie to me, ya tranny freak! Who let you in?"

Yolanda shrieks again and Clive winds his fist back, plowing it into Yolanda's face. Her bones crunch. His rings cut her cheeks. Yolanda grunts, sliding down the wall and hitting the floor. She slumps to the side, motionless, but Clive kicks her twice in the gut. She doesn't make a sound and lies there, motionless.

I gasp and Clive swings to face me. He raises his shaking finger at me.

"Was it you?" he roars. "Was you the one that let this thing in mah hotel?"

I shake my head. I'm no liar, but there is murder all over Clive's face

327

and I can't speak even if I wanted to. Yolanda's lying there, bent over on the floor, bleeding.

"Goddam alla ya!" Clive shouts, throwing his hands up in the air. He struts down the hall and rounds the corner. I don't hear him go down the carpeted steps, but I grab a shoe, wedge it in my door, and creep across the hall to Yolanda.

He groans when he sees me, but he sits up. I pick up his wig and put it on his head.

"Thank ya, lamb," he whispers. "Now see there? Da's what ya do when a crazy man's afta' ya. Ya play dead." When he smiles, his scraggly teeth look bloody.

"I can't believe he did that," I say. Tears squeeze down my cheeks.

"Oh, baby, this ain't nothin' compare't ta las' time. Don't cry, lamb. Clive jus' gotta prove he still da boss an' that ain't nobody goin' up his butt ho'e." Yolanda puts his big hand on the floor and tries to lean on it and get to his knees, but he groans. "Help me out, would ya, lamb? I gotta get out of here." He laughs. Helping him to his feet is an awkward combination of pulling and Yolanda climbing up me until he's standing. He leans on me and the weight of him hunches me down. I buckle and Yolanda grabs at the wall sconce, ripping it out of the wall. He doesn't fall though. When he lets go, the sconce dangles by the wires. He steadies his feet beneath him. "Good thing I didn't have a window room, or he'd a tossed me out."

"Where's Lavina?"

"Aw, she gone home, sick. Sick' a Clive's bullshit, I think. He won't hire nobody ta help 'er an' she done had e'nuff. Took da whole day off." Yolanda cackles, but it sounds stiff and a little breathless.

"Where are you going to go?" I ask as Yolanda sways on his feet.

"Whereva' I can." We stump down the hall toward his room, me under Yolanda's mammoth arm. "''Nuff 'bout mah drama, lamby ... how's Jonah an' you?"

His blood drips onto my shoulder like a rain drop.

"Oh ... I don't know," I say. I don't want to talk about Jonah, but it does distract me from worrying so much that Yolanda's going to pass out, fall, and crush me beneath him. We stop at his room and he fishes the key from his bra.

"Clive be too much'a pussy to reach into mah bra," Yolanda says. "At leas' it's Devil Night. Maybe somebody come along and torch this place. It'd serve Clive right," he complains as he throws the door open. "Will ya help me pack up before Clive comes storming back up here? But we gotta make it quick, 'cause that's how I loss mah teeth the firs' time. Took too long."

As we walk in, I get a glimpse of a giant woman and pull back, startled. Yolanda laughs and I realize it's not a human, but a pile of Yolanda's wigs on top of his coat tree, which is draped with his dresses and clothing. One half of the dresser top has all the girly stuff that's in my room—bottles of nail polish, brushes, drugstore perfume—but the other half is full of razors still choking on globs of hair, shaving cream, a pile of pantyhose, and an assortment of lubes.

He doesn't have a suitcase. He has a couple black garbage bags that he pulls out from beneath the bed. He pulls them out and shakes one open before handing it to me.

"Use mah pantyhoses," he says. "So the glass bottles don't break."

I start wrapping the perfume, rolling it up in the delicate nylons like he said.

"An' what was you sayin' 'bout Jonah?" Yolanda says from the bathroom. He's plugging his bleeding nose with wads of toilet paper. "Somethin' 'bout you don't know what's goin' on wit' 'im?"

"He doesn't answer my pages," I say.

"Oh no? Maybe he ain't the right man fo' ya, lamb. Maybe ya oughta be lookin' fo' somebody else who do answer 'em."

"Like who? Ned? There aren't any other men around here besides Clive, Ned, and whoever comes in to get a room."

"You too young not to be out there findin' a good one. You ain't no dope head like me. There's lotsa men who'd love you."

"I'd like to know where they are," I tell him.

There's a knock at the door and Yolanda startles. She motions to me to ask who it is and I do, but in a shaky voice. I don't think Clive will treat me any differently than he did Yolanda if he catches me in here.

"Lael?" Will says from the other side. "There's a girl down in the lobby an' she says she wants ta talk to ya right now."

TWENTY

A short, *black woman* with wide hips stands near the front
door, her back to me. She's got a baby on her hip dressed in a
shiny blue running suit with designer sneakers on his tiny,
dangling feet. The ice machine hums and I can smell the lemony cleaner
Lavina uses to wipe everything down. I step down onto the lobby floor
and catch a glimpse out the door.

My car is here ... parked in the parking lot. There's something
different about it—the hood is a different color—but it's my car!

I suck in a deep, surprised breath and the woman turns at the sound.
With one good look at her face, I recognize her instantly. I spread my
most radiant smile across my face. It's Nia, Jonah's sister, and the little
boy she's holding, chewing and drooling on his own chubby little fist, is
DeAndre, De, Jonah's nephew. I walk toward them.

"What the fuck you smilin' fo', hoe?" Nia snaps.

I stop dead. "You brought back my car." I point over her shoulder,
out the door. "I'm Lael."

"You Lael?" The woman's head snaps back and forth like a winding snake on the stem of her neck. Her lip hikes up on one side.

"Aren't you Nia?" I ask.

Her eyes narrow. "How in fuck you think you kin jus' say mah name, bitch?" she growls.

My mind scrambles to snap it all together. My car's in the lot, and I know Nia and De from Jonah's photos. I'm still in my pajamas, and maybe my hair's such a mess, but she must've asked for Jonah's girlfriend. She has to know who I am. I put my fingertips on my heart. "I'm Lael. Lael Wallace. Jonah's girlfriend?"

"His girlfriend?" she roars. "If ya think ya know who I is, bitch, then ya oughta know who the fuck I is!" she fires back. DeAndre looks up at her, his little brow knit with concern. He puts a chubby hand over her heart to hold on. I shrink away from her. "I'm Jonah's baby mama! He mah fiancé, and we's gittin' married! I don't know who da fuck you is though!"

My legs go as soft as wilted flower stems. I stagger back a step. She's talking gibberish. A hand to my temple, I try to shake everything that's happening in my head into something that makes sense. "He said sister. Jonah said you're his sister, and DeAndre..."

"I ain't his sista', hoe! I jus' tole you, I his fiancé! An' don't ya even say mah baby boy's name, 'less you want me to come ova' there an' whoop yo' ass!"

I sway on my wobbly stems.

"I come up here 'cause you keep callin' mah man, an' blowin' up his pager! We gonna fig'a that out right now, 'cause if you keep after 'im, you gonna see what I'm all about!"

"He said..."

"Naw, naw, naw!" She puts her hand up to silence me. She's seething, but since she's not screaming anymore, the baby goes back to chewing his hand and looking around the lobby. "I don' care what he said, ya ugly ass hoe! Da's mah man you talkin' 'bout, an' you gonna leave 'im 'lone or I'm gonna jerk yo' hair right outta yo' head! You call 'im even one mo' time an'..."

"I didn't know any of this!" I shout back. "I've been calling him to get my car back! He said Trevor was fixing it and—"

"Trevor? Trevor's mah brother, an' yeah, he fixed up mah car that mah man got fo' me!" She throws a thumb over her shoulder at my car in the lot. The baby has settled into a bland stare, aimed in my direction, as he continues to gnaw his fist. "That car out dare ain't yo's! I's mine, so get that through yo' dumb ass cracka' skull!"

My strength returns in a gush. "It's my car, and I've got the papers to prove it! I'll report it stolen to the cops!"

But Nia grits her teeth with an open-lipped smile that scares the hell out of me. I am frozen in place as she tips down her chin and looks up at me with a brutal snarl.

"You try it, bitch," she whispers, but her words are sharper than box cutters. "You call da pigs an' jus' see what happen then. I'm'a gonna git ya in yo' sleep. You ain't worked it out yet, have ya."

I shiver and she grins at the sight of it.

"Jonah got yo' room key, don't he? He bin playin' you. He tell me everythin', you can be sho' 'a that," she says. "I know you kep' on givin' 'im money—"

"He took money for car repairs."

"An' he gave it ta me, fo' our baby diapers, *bitch*. You thinkin' he was in love w'ich you, din't ya? Yeah, ya did—that's why you wouldn't leave 'im be win he was done wich you—but ya know what? He brung yo' money home ta me, bitch. Oh yeah, he did. You was all in love wit' 'im ... wantin' 'im to git wich you ... an' he sittin' ova' there laughin', 'cause why he want some dumb little cracka' when he got a African queen waitin' fo' him at home..."

Her gaze is battery acid. Even with a baby in her arms, I already know, this girl will fight—baby or not.

I wish Yolanda would come down the stairs, but he doesn't come.

Will wouldn't be any help.

Lavina's gone home.

Nobody's coming to help.

"So da's it," Nia says, turning toward the door. "I'm leavin' in mah car an' you ain't callin' no cops, 'cause you like bein' alive. Oh, an don't go over the oil shop no more neida', you hear? Mah man don't want no stanky hoes up in there. It bad fo' bi'ness. So, if ya come 'round agin, an' I hear 'bout it, I'll be back fo' ya mah'self." Her gaze slashes at me. "An' I'll git yo' punk ass, bitch."

She turns, the force of the movement pulling the baby back. He grabs for her shirt, hanging on, as she walks out the door.

The alarm stops screaming as I watch her drive away in my car.

TWENTY
ONE

I'm still in the lobby when Yolanda sneaks out. He can't stand around and talk to me, since Clive's car is still in the parking lot. I just say goodbye as he drags out two black garbage bags, one slung over his shoulder just like Santa Claus.

Jonah's car is across the street. He knew Nia was coming over.

I drag myself up the stairs.

Will is on the ledge eating spaghetti rings out of the can, scooping them out with his fingers. He pauses and looks up as I pass.

"I tole you that asshole cock sonofabitch fucker mother was no good," Will says. The bruises still make his face look misshapen, but he's got his busted up glasses back on his face at least.

"You were right," I tell him as I plod up the steps. "I should've listened to you."

"Yup." He goes back to scooping the saucy stuff out of the can. I pause on the third step from the top and turn back toward him.

"Are you okay...you know...in your room?" I ask.

He shrugs like the bruise that's eating his face isn't there. "Yup."

"Okay," I say slowly. "If it's ever not okay, you know you can come down to my room, right?"

Another shrug. "Yeah, I know."

"Alright," I say and continue up the stairs. He turns up the can and slurps the sauce from the sharp edge.

Once I'm in my room, I go straight to the bed and pick up the phone. I call Lavina.

It rings.

Rings.

Rings.

Not even Tavon answers. I hang up.

What happened downstairs with Nia finally sinks in. It sits on me like a semi-truck.

Jonah set me up. I'm never getting my car back. Jonah has my room key and I need to switch rooms.

I drag my coat rack to the door and lean it up against it. I slide the chain into the lock.

Tomorrow, I'll tell Lavina what happened and I'll move out of my home with its hotel-sign night light. I can hear Lavina in my head already.

You been had, she's going to say.

But she knew Jonah pretty well. Did she know he had a kid and a fiancé? Was she in on the whole thing all along?

I trusted Jonah with all my heart.

I don't know if I can handle losing Lavina too. There'll be nothing left of me.

I'm asleep at the counter when the door alarm goes off. I jerk up in the chair as Lavina walks in. She shoots me a scowl, but doesn't say anything about catching me.

I've been waiting all night to talk to her, and trying to figure out how to ask her if she knew about Nia. If she set me up too.

"Good mornin'," she says, but there's a growl in her voice that stops me from asking anything right off. Lavina's brow is a hard wedge between her eyes and I can see she's already having a bad morning.

The moment she gets in the cage, I blurt, "Did you know about Jonah?"

She stops. Looks at me. Her lips form a tiny pucker. "Do I know what 'bout Jonah?"

I squirm, putting my hands behind me on the wall. "Did you know he's got a kid?"

"No. He does, huh?"

"Yes, and a fiancé."

Lavina blows out a breath and rolls her eyes. "He got a fiancé too?"

Now I exhale. "You didn't know?"

"Why would I? Who he wit' ain't none'a mah bi'ness." Her puckery frown comes off a little annoyed. "He always bin crazy 'bout da girls, I knowed dat."

"Why didn't you ever tell me?" My voice climbs and my stomach quivers.

Lavina squares her no-nonsense gaze on me. I press my fingertips against the wall behind me, smashing my finger pads so I don't shrink away from her or start to cry. I can't do that anymore.

"I ain't yo' mama, Lael," she says flatly. "You a grown woman, wit' eyes a' yo' own. Ain't up ta me ta tell ya where ta look, an' it ain't mah fault if ya don't use 'em neida'."

When she looks away, my shoulders sink. She picks up the list of supplies Clive left for her, along with a note for her to call a repairman and get the broken washing machine downstairs fixed. She releases a laugh, harsh as a cough, and drops the piece of paper. It floats, slicing through the air on its way down to the desk.

"Ya know what, Lael?" Lavina says, turning to me. "Da whole ride in ta'day, I was agitated. I kep' thinkin' to mah'self, I don't know a damn thing this mo'nin'. I don' know what I'm doin' here, or why I been puttin' up wit' Clive's bullshit fo' so long." She takes her ring of skeleton keys from her purse and tosses them on the counter. They clatter on top of Clive's note. She shakes her purse, a strange smile quickly spreading across her face. "Dis purse feel so light wit'out alla dem keys!"

She's giddy.

Lavina. Giddy.

"Know what?" she says.

I don't know that I've ever seen Lavina this happy. "What?"

"Tell Clive, I done quit," she says.

I pump my jaw, all of my words suddenly stuck in my throat.

She can't quit. I need her.

Clive needs her. Yolanda needs her. Will needs her.

This place needs her.

Who's going to clean the rooms and make sure there's toilet paper and fresh towels? Who's going to make my home smell like lemons? Who am I going to talk to when I need real advice?

"You can't—" My words chase her as she walks back out of the cage and around the counter. "What am I supposed to do?"

She pauses, shooting me a casual shrug. "Like I tole ya be'fo', you a full grown woman, Lael. You gonna fig'a it out. Dat's whuch ya gonna do."

The front door alarm is deafening as she leaves.

TWENTY TWO

S aturn comes down the stairs with Boo on her hip. She's been using Clive's personal room as if it's her own private apartment, since Clive can't get away from his wife to be here every night.

I still haven't moved from the front desk since Lavina walked out the door. My whole world crumbled in on itself. Jonah was my binding, Lavina was my glue. Now, with both of them gone, I feel like this chapter of my life is blowing around loose, somewhere in the future.

"Hey," Saturn says.

"Hey," I answer hollowly.

She stops in front of the window. "Wha's wrong wich you? Where Lavina at?"

"She quit," I say.

"Whuch ya mean, she quit?" Saturn snaps as if she's the owner, not Clive. "We had a full house up in here last night, right?" She doesn't allow me to answer. "Who gonna clean up all these rooms?"

I just shrug. It's not her hotel or mine.

I pick up the phone and dial Clive's number. He's got a pager too. I punch in the hotel's number and the pound key, so he knows it's urgent.

"Why'd she say she quit?" Saturn asks as I hang up the phone.

I shrug again. "She didn't say, but I know she's been upset about not having any back-up to do her work when she's off or sick."

"What she want Clive ta do? Money's tight! He gave her a raise!" Saturn argues.

A raise. Oh yeah. Lavina laughed at that. It was something like a quarter extra an hour.

The phone rings and I pick up, even though Saturn continues to grill me and Boo starts to fuss.

"What's going on?" Clive says on the other end.

"Lavina quit," I say. We go over all the same things Saturn just asked. Why, how can she, who's going to clean the rooms. It's nine o'clock and my eyelids are drooping from being up all night and most of the morning now too. All I can answer Clive over and over is, I don't know.

"You wanna clean?" Clive asks.

"No. I want to go to bed," I say. "I worked all night."

He lets out a long, hard sigh. "Ahright," he says. "Ahright. I'm gonna call my cousin, Vareesha, and see if she kin come on down and help out. I'll switch ya aroun' an' give ya tonight off, but you gonna have to pick up this slack. Jus' stay at the desk 'til she shows up."

He hangs up and I drop the receiver back in the cradle. I run my hand down my face. I'm going to have to pick up the slack. I can't stop yawning.

"What'd he say?" Saturn asks.

"He's sending his cousin."

"I can't believe Lavina up an' quit 'im like this," she says. "My poor baby. He gotta be stressed. He gonna need some relaxin'."

He? She's worried about Clive, not Lavina. I lean my face in my hand and just stare at her. I couldn't care less. It just wouldn't even be possible.

"Listen," she says, "I gotta run out and git some milk for mah baby." I have no idea if she means Clive or Boo now. "Clive gonna git this all straight, but he gonna need to relax when he do. If you ain't workin' tonight—"

"I'm not. This is my one day off."

"Well, if Lavina gone, Tavon might be too. That mean, Clive might need ya ta work. But if yer off ... you wanna watch Boo fo' me? I pay you good."

He might want me to work. What difference does it make? It's not like I can go anywhere or have anyone to see.

"Pay me?" I say. She nods.

"Well, Clive will, but I'll be sho' you git paid good fo' it. Six bucks a hour?"

"Sure," I say, my eyes fluttering shut. I'm exhausted. I let my words slide out. "Hey, you ever going to pay me back the five I gave you?"

An amused grin coats Saturn's lips. "I thought it was a gift."

"It was help," I tell her. "It'd be nice if you returned the favor."

"I'll see what I kin do." She turns toward the door. Over one shoulder, she says, "You betta stay 'wake 'till Vareesha git here, or Clive gonna git rid'a you too."

She goes out the door before I can remind her that Clive didn't get rid of Lavina—she quit. I put my head down on my arms...just for a minute. Just a minute.

Clive doesn't yell when he knocks on the cage door and I lift my face off the desk. It wouldn't matter if he did. I've been in the cage since last night. I stink, my butt aches, my back is stiff. The clock on the phone console says it is two in the afternoon.

Glad he was in a rush to get in here.

I stand up and unlock the door. A large, black woman with huge gold hoops in her ears and skin the color of wet potting soil pushes her way in behind Clive. A young Arab guy with sharp bones and yellow eyes saunters in right after her. I back up, near the TV, hitting the button to silence the porn.

"You sho' you need me?" the woman asks, delicately scratching the side of her wide nostril with the tip of her neon pink, fake fingernail. "Look ta me like you got help ahready, Clive."

"If I did, I wouldn'ta brung ya," he snaps. "Lael, this's mah cousin, Vareesha. An' this here's Don," he says pointing to the Arab guy. "Vareesha gonna help out cleanin' rooms fo' the day."

"Jus' today," Vareesha says with a sour frown. She looks to Clive. "A hundre't bucks ta work till five, right?"

Clive nods.

"Where you want me to start?" Vareesha asks.

A hundred dollars? For three hours? Lavina said she was getting seventy-five dollars for a nine hour day. Clive told Lavina he couldn't afford another maid, but he's throwing money at Vareesha like it's fake fingernails.

"Secon' flo'," Clive directs her with his pointer finger and Vareesha goes out and up the steps, complaining, "How many floors you got in here?" as she goes.

Clive turns back to me. "I'm gonna have ta change yo' job position ta maid, startin' tomorr'ah if I can't git Lavina back here," Clive says. "Don gonna take ova the relief shif's tonight, and then he'll take yo' usual clerkin' shif' afta Ned from now on."

"I'm no good as a maid," I say, but Clive shakes a hand in the air to shut me up.

"You as good as I got fo' now," he says. "You gonna haf'ta do, 'less you kin talk Lavina back in."

He picks up the receiver and punches in Lavina's number. Don squeezes into the cage. Don's eyes brush up and down me and it makes me want to squeegee any residue of that gaze off my skin. Clive hits the button to activate the speaker phone and the phone's ring echoes through the cage.

The phone continues to ring. It's like listening to a baby cry. Then, the ring cuts off.

"Hello?" Clive says, but there is a slam on the other end, as someone hangs up the phone. "At leas' we know she there," Clive chuckles, hitting redial. The phone starts to ring again through the speaker. Don folds his arms against his chest and leans on the counter like he owns the place too.

It feels to me like my house has been invaded and the thieves are all around me.

The phone picks up.

"Lavina, don't you hang up on me now!" Clive hollers, leaning toward the console. "I got to talk w'ich ya!"

"Whuch you want?" Lavina growls into the other end. "Our bi'ness is done, Clive. I tole Lael ta let ya know I quit. Ain't nothin' else ta say."

"Lavina," Clive says smoothly, smiling as he slides down onto the office chair. "We got to talk, girl! What's got you so work't up? You need'a day off, I'll give ya ta'day ta relax an' unwind."

"Easy fo' you to gimme anythin' I want, now that I quit," Lavina's sneer is loud and clear.

"Now listen here," Clive says, sitting up in the chair, his smile vanished. "Ya cain't jus' leave. You know this place don't run right wit'out ya. Nobody know where nothin' is, an' nobody kin keep this place lookin' like ya do—"

"I know it!" Lavina huffs on her end. "I bin doin' everythin' up in that hotel—cleanin', an' keeping da books, an' stockin'—an' doin' it fo' nex' ta nothin'! I'm done w'ich yo' disrespec'in me, Clive! I tole ya ta git a back-up maid, an' now ya done burnt me out!"

"Now, Lavina," Clive drawls. "You is a hard worker, ain't no doubt 'bout it. If we need ta talk about yo' schedule—"

"Like we done three mont's ago? Nothin' changed."

"Vareesha's here, she gonna help ya out."

"Yo' lazy cousin? She ain't good fo' nothin' an' you know it."

"She's cleanin' the rooms right now."

"Short-sheetin' da beds, ya mean."

"Well, I'm thinkin' of hirin' 'er, if yer stayin'," Clive says, leaning back in the chair, rubbing his hands down his pant legs.

"An' lettin' her quit the secon' I come back?" Lavina's laugh falls flat. "Not that it'd be any good ta let 'er stay. Vareesha soon as die 'foe she ruins 'er nails!"

I smile—Lavina's no fool. Don glances at me and I press my lips flat. Saturn walks in with Boo on her hip.

"Okay, now look, Lavina," Clive says, pressing closer to the desk as both he and Don glance up at Saturn. Saturn grins like she's giddy and Clive smiles at her. Clive continues talking to Lavina, even though both his eyes, and Don's, are glued to Saturn's ascending rear as she goes up to their room. "Look, Lavina, ya gotta come back tomorr'ah. Enuff's enuff."

"You want me back, yo' gonna gimme a raise," Lavina bargains. "Same as what ya pay Vareesha ta sit on 'er big ol' butt and talk about how hard she work. An' ya gonna gimme weekends off, wit' a back-up maid workin' 'em too. Ya do dat, an' I'll come back."

Clive thrums his fingertips on the desk. "You know I cain't afford alla that."

"If ya cain't, ya cain't," Lavina says, the shrug rich in her tone.

Clive just leans back on the chair and sighs. He's going to do it. He's going to give her everything. Lavina's won and now she'll come back. Everything's going to be okay—

"Good luck findin' anoda' job, Lavina," Clive says and he clicks off the speaker phone.

I thought I'd sleep for days, but I wake up every hour. For a second, I think of Jonah and then I remember.

And Lavina.

And Yolanda.

Will's battered, smiling face.

I go down to the snack machines for dinner.

Will isn't on the ledge—Clive would've thrown him off there if he saw it. It makes even more sense when I step down into the lobby and see Clive there, with Saturn's arm draped around his shoulders like a fox stole. Boo is still on her hip.

"I was just gonna come up," Saturn squeals when she sees me. She releases Clive and walks over to me, dumping her baby in my arms.

Boo looks up at me as if I'm a wolf and she's grandmother's basket of goodies.

"Take good care'a her." Saturn turns back to Clive as Boo leans out of my arms, reaching—straining—for her mother.

Saturn doesn't look back. "C'mon, Clive, let's go, baby."

They go out the door and when the alarm goes off, Boo jerks in my arms. Once it's silenced, Boo stares at the door a long time. When she finally glances back at me, her tiny face crumbles and she goes into the most god-awful ugly-cry I've ever seen. It's like she thinks I'm a murderer.

"Wanna go up to my room?" I ask Boo as cheerfully as I can. I put a foot on the stairs and she starts to howl.

I jog up the steps, hoping the bounce will calm her down or distract her. She squirms and I jog faster, so I can get to my room and let her out of my arms.

As I ascend to the third floor, Will is coming down.

"Wanna come play with me and Saturn's baby?" I ask him. There's snot running down Boo's face. One look at him, with his mottled bruises, and she starts howling again.

"Hell no," Will says. Then, "Maybe she's hungry. I can help ya feed her, I guess."

"You're not taking my food," I tell him over Boo's sobs. "You've got your own."

I know that's what he really wants and I have to make the food Lavina gave me last. They're not going down his throat while my stomach is rumbling all day long and I don't have any other way to get groceries but the snack machines.

Will eyes me skeptically. "What're you gonna give her to eat?"

"I don't know." I have no idea. I hadn't thought about it. I don't even have diapers. Maybe Saturn knows Boo won't poop until she comes home. "Saturn didn't give me any bottles. Or milk."

"There's creamer in the fridge downstairs that Lavina brought," Will says. He lifts one of Boo's chubby, dimpled arms. "She probably can drink that."

"Is it old creamer?"

"I drank some of it today and it tasted good."

Of course he has. Probably right out of the carton, but I can't think about that now. "Can you go get it for me?"

"Yeah!" he says and shoots off down the stairs. I go to my room, Boo trying to catch her breath between sobs, and a couple minutes later, Will's knocking at my door with the creamer. It says heavy whipping cream. I'm not sure if it's anything like baby formula, but since Will said it was good, I pour a little into one of my cups.

"She's shuttin' up," Will says as Boo watches me bring the cup to her face.

Her eyes are wide. I put the mug against her lips. She opens her mouth a tiny bit and I think she might know what to do, until I pour a dribble between her lips.

Boo sputters and coughs cream all over me and on the bed. She coughs again and again and I pat her back. Her howl is a relief, even though it nearly deafens me. Will draws back.

His lip rises on one side. "All she does is cry."

"No shit," I tell him. "She's a baby."

Will peeks into the cardboard box with my two cans in it. "You like the beef stew?" he asks.

The baby is wiggling to get out of my arms now. "Just take it," I snap at him.

He doesn't hesitate to grab a can. He shoots the baby another look. "I'm gonna go to my house now, but I'll tell ya when Clive comes back."

"Your house?" I ask. "You mean your room?"

"I don't live there no more," he says. "Not until she says sorry."

I let Boo down on the floor. She folds up and cries into the carpet. "Where are you staying, if you're not in your room?"

"In my house," he says again, reaching into my top drawer for my can opener. He cranks open the can, licks the sharp lid, and tosses it in my trash. "That place between the floors, where I always stay."

"The ledge? You can't stay there, Will. It's not safe."

Boo's crying slows just as I realize what I'm saying. It's probably safer on the ledge, out in front of everyone where a scream could be heard, then it is behind the closed door of his mother's hotel room.

"You can come and sleep on the floor in here," I offer.

"Naw," he shakes his head. "I gotta see if Samson comes back. I gotta watch out for my mom."

Like she watches out for him? I keep my mouth shut. "Okay," I tell him. Boo looks up and starts crying all over again.

"I'm goin'," Will says.

"Thanks for the help," I grumble at him. He goes out and the door clunks shut. I get up and slide the chain in the lock. I keep it locked all the time now.

I get on my hands and knees when I get near Boo. "C'mon, Boo," I say softly, trying to rub her back.

She swats at my hand and I go back through everything I have to offer—a drink of creamer, sitcoms on TV, a look into my empty jewelry box. The last one halts her crying for only a second until she reaches for the broken ballerina and pricks her finger on one of the dancer's upward-extended arms. Then she goes back to shrieking.

She shrieks like that until I want to split my head in half and rip out my eardrums.

The phone rings in the middle of my break down. I hope to God it's Saturn, so I can tell her she's got to come back and rescue me from her screaming kid.

"Lael?" It's my mother.

I jam my finger in my ear. "Hi, mom."

"Is that a baby crying?"

"Yup."

"Why do you have a baby?"

"I'm babysitting her for a friend." That last part struggles out of my mouth. It's probably drowned in Boo's wails anyway.

"She sounds unhappy." God, she's as bright as a brain surgeon tonight.

"Yup," I say tightly. "She is."

"How old is she?"

"I don't know. Little. She can walk, but she doesn't talk. At least, I don't think she does. All she does is look at me and scream."

"So she's probably around a year old."

"Sure, probably," I say sourly. I don't care how old she is. I just want her to stop screaming.

"Have you changed her diaper?"

"I don't have any."

"Her mother didn't leave you diapers? Why didn't you tell her you needed diapers?"

"Because I thought it'd be better to be totally unprepared," I say.

"Okay," my mother softens at my sharp tone and tries again. "Does she need a diaper? Just peek in the back and see if she's poopy."

I'll do anything to get this baby to stop crying. Since Boo is folded over again, I lean over and pull up the back of her diaper so I can peer down inside. All that's in there is her little brown butt.

"No poop," I report back.

"A bottle?"

"Her mom didn't leave those either. And I know—I'm stupid, but I don't have milk either. All I have is this stuff that says, heavy whipping cream."

"Okay, we can work with that," my mom says, drawing a deep breath. That's her I need to think a second inhale. I'm a lot more relaxed now that I'm not in this alone. As much as I would usually hate to say it, my mom knows things, and she's got a lot more experience with babies than I have. I've got complete faith that she will be able to help me stop Boo's crying, if I just listen to what she has to say.

It takes a while, but my mom finally says, "Okay, she might not be drinking out of a cup yet, but do you have a straw?"

"Yes," I say. I grab one off my dresser.

"Try to give her a tiny, tiny bit in the end of a straw, you know what I mean? Just a dribble."

"Yeah, I know what you mean." I dip the straw in the carton of creamer, cap the other end with my finger, and draw it out. I tap Boo and when she looks up and sees the straw, she stares at it as if it's enchanted her. I put it near my mouth and act like I'm drinking it. Then I put it near Boo's mouth.

I let it drip until she puts her lips around it. Then I let a little dribble into her mouth. The cream runs into the corners of her lips and some runs down her chin, but she swallows most of it instead of choking.

"It's working!" I tell my mom as I get another straw full.

"She's quiet," my mom says, a smile in her voice. "At least she's curious. And who doesn't like the taste of cream?"

"She does!" I say. I'm ecstatic. Boo's happiness is as good as winning an Olympic medal.

"Her mom is going to be in trouble," my mom laughs. The sound of it makes me light inside. "You're going to give her back a baby that now has much better taste than formula!"

I laugh too as Boo slurps down another straw full. She's got the hang of it now.

"So how are you doing?" my mom asks as I continue to feed the baby cream.

"I'm good," I bubble. The past two minutes has been the best I've felt in months.

"How's Jonah?" my mom asks.

I don't want to lose this magic. "Oh," I say lightly, "we broke up."

I don't want to say anything about the car, because not only would my mom lose it if I did, but this moment would end. This beautiful moment, with no fighting or trying to beat each other down.

God, I just want this to last.

"Oh, I'm sorry to hear that," my mother says in her funeral voice. "Are you alright?"

"I'm fine. Thanks."

"You're growing up so much." Her voice breaks, but it doesn't sound like sadness, it sounds like pride.

I'm so shocked, I pause, the straw in the air, and Boo has to reach up and tap my arm. I give the baby another drink.

"Thanks, Mom."

"You know, Lael, if you'd like to come back home...we could work this out. You could finish school and save a little money. You're an adult now, but I'd like to give you a hand."

I could eat.

But I look around my room as I reload the straw. My bed, my clothes, the fairytale drawings I used to make, taped around the edge of my mirror. I haven't drawn the wolves or the gingerbread houses in a while. Lately, all I've been doing is drawing numbers in lists and budgets—how much it takes to eat, how much it will take to buy another car, how much to live somewhere else.

I'm broke, but I've got a lot more than I started with. Going home would take it all out of me and I realize now that you can't put a weed back in a flower pot and expect it to grow into a rose.

The baby coos as I give her another drink. It's this soft little sigh that makes me warm inside.

"Thanks, mom, but I'm okay," I say. I hope the warmth is glowing in my mother's ear. I want her to know how grateful I am, not for the offer, but for this conversation. This is the first time she's acknowledged I'm an adult without a sneer in her voice. "I'm going to go back and finish school as soon as I can. But thanks."

Instead of attacking my rootless plans, my mother takes another deep breath.

"The door is always open for you," she says.

"Thank you," I say softly. Boo swallows the cream and claps her hands for more.

TWENTY THREE

The *screams in* the hallway wake me like I've been plunged in a bucket of ice. A human scream mixes with the wail of a siren and it is all so close, it seems like they're stuffed in my pillow. I scramble out of bed as someone pounds on my door.

A key slides in the lock and the door jerks open, catching on the chain. I scream too.

"Lael!" It takes me a second to place the desperate voice.

"Ned?"

"Open up and get out here! There was an accident, and the cops are here!"

Cops? What the hell is going on?

My mind swims. I glance at the clock. It's one in the morning. Saturn picked up Boo around eleven, an hour after the baby had fallen asleep blissfully in the middle of my bed. Saturn paid me with a fifty dollar bill and said, "See? Tole ya I'd take care'a you."

Oh my God—what if Boo got sick from all that cream.

I went downstairs after Saturn left and got some orange crackers. Will was sleeping on the ledge. What if he fell off.

"What happened?" I shriek, yanking on a pair of jeans. The light from the hallway casts a rectangular glow on the wall where the door is open, but still stopped by the chain.

"Penny jumped!" Ned's shouts through the opening. "She's fuckin' splattered on the sidewalk!"

I go to the door, shove it closed, and slide the chain out of the lock. I open the door to see Ned, wild-eyed and pale.

"What are you doing here? Clive switched our shifts," I say squinting against the light in the hall.

"Clive's at home, and his fucking replacement, Don, split!" Ned barks. "Clive told me to come in—he wanted me here to handle it, but there's a fucking lady smashed on our sidewalk out front!"

"Are you sure it's Penny?"

"Yeah, I'm sure. C'mon and look for yourself." We go down the stairs together, like we're old friends, shoulder to shoulder with each other.

"I can't believe this. I mean, I can't believe this!" Ned chants.

Will's not on the ledge. His flat Spiderman pillow is there, but he's not. I interrupt Ned's hysteria. "Where's Will?"

"No fucking clue," Ned says.

We step down onto the lobby floor and go through the lounge to the door and windows facing the boulevard. Emergency lights flash like a dance club strobe through the papers Lavina tore off a week ago, on the day she brought in all the food. The sirens and lights throb through the windows. I plug my ears with my fingers as I squint out the door.

The scramble of lights from a couple cop cars and an ambulance are blinding.

There is a small crowd of cops and EMTs on the sidewalk outside, and it takes a few minutes until I see her. Penny isn't splattered, but she's lying on the pavement on her back, her body buckles up on the sidewalk and smacks back down. I know it's her by her matted blond hair and her tiny frame. Her head throws back on the concrete and I see her face, her mouth open, her body seizing.

The EMTs slide a board under her, but she's still flopping.

"Holy shit," I say, turning away. I can't stand to look anymore.

"I know," Ned says. When I back away, he looks again. Then he turns away and paces back and forth beside me. "I can't believe it. Don didn't think she was serious about jumping."

"What do you mean? He talked to her?"

"He said she kept calling down to the desk, saying someone was out on the ledge, looking into her room. Then she told him he could come up and screw her for ten bucks. I guess he actually went up there, but she wouldn't open the door."

"Good for her," I mumble.

Two cops come in, setting off the door alarm. They ask us questions. Mountains of questions, but we didn't see anything. Ned tells them about Don and then he goes into the cage to call Clive to ask where Don lives. They take down Don's address, his phone number. Then Ned tells them about Will.

"Where is he?" one cop asks.

When the cops look at me, I say, "I don't know. He's usually up on the ledge upstairs, but he's not there."

They go upstairs and look for him, they look in the room.

They say junkie and addict and social services.

The cop who wanted to know where Will was, tells me he doesn't think Penny is going to make it. He touches my arm.

"You need to find that woman's son. A social worker has been contacted to come for him."

The ambulance pulls away, without sirens.

The cops leave.

The sidewalk is empty.

There is a stain on the sidewalk that looks like someone spilled paint.

I go upstairs, turn down the hallway and walk past my room to the emergency stairwell.

I open the door and it clunks Will, who is sitting on the top step, his head in his hands.

TWENTY FOUR

I *sit down beside* Will and put my arm around the shoulders of his
grimy shirt. He shrugs me off, jumps up, and rushes down a couple
steps, hanging onto the rail.

"Get outta here, Lael!" he growls through his tears.

"I can't," I say. "A cop sent me to find you."

"Tell 'im to fuck off!"

"Will—"

"Is she dead?" he howls.

"I don't know," I say. He sniffles, but then he dissolves in sobs that
break my soul. They are amplified in the stairwell. I'll never be able to
unremember them. "A social worker is coming to get you."

"I ain't goin'," he says. He turns to me, his face slatted with the dirty
streaks of his tears, like jail cell bars. He wipes his eye with the back of his
hand. "Can I live with you 'till she comes back, Lael? I'll run behind your

bike when you go to the store, and I'll carry everything back. I'll clean your room, and I'll do whatever you want. I can find us food. You know I can—"

"I know, Will," I say.

"I'll sleep on the floor. In a corner. Or in the bathtub, if you want. You don't even have ta give me no blankets. I got my own. You don't have to do nothin' for me. Just let me stay, so my mama can find me when she comes back."

"Will," I start softly.

"She's comin' back. You said. You said she ain't dead, and that means she's coming back."

"I said I don't know, but I don't think she's coming back for—"

"You said she wasn't dead!" he roars at me. It is a miserable, hard echo bouncing off the cinderblock walls, metal stairs, and railings. His face has changed. He doesn't look like the boy I know now. The devastation makes him look older.

I put my hands on my forehead to block him from my sight. I can't see any more of it.

"She didn't look good, Will," I start again.

"But you don't know," he argues through his streaming tears, "so jus' let me stay with you."

"I can't feed myself," I tell him, but my own tears drip off my chin and fall on the metal, mesh stairs. I can see all the way down to the bottom floor.

It feels like I'm falling the whole way, floor by floor, as I speak. "I can't do it, Will. If I could, I would. If I had a car, or money, it'd be different. But right now, it would be irresponsible if I let you stay."

"It wouldn't!"

"Listen to me," I say. "It's a lot better for you, in every single way, if you can get out of here. This is your chance, Will. You've got to take it. There's a social worker coming for you, and I think you should go."

"Fuck no! I've gotta be here—"

A surge of anger overtakes me. "What if she doesn't come back? You aren't a grown up! Clive's not going to let you stay here on the ledge! He wouldn't let you do it now, if he knew you were up there! If...when your mom gets better, she'll be able to find you if you go. They'll tell her right where you are. They're going to put you with a family that can take care of you until she's out of the hospital."

"They'll put me with stupid asshole bastards that—"

"That might not be that at all. They might be nicest people in the world and feed you real food—as much as you want to eat—and take you to doctors and get you any medicine you might need. You won't have to worry about being homeless anymore … and they'll probably fix your glasses," I say with a small laugh, but nothing about this is funny. "Look, it doesn't get any worse than this, Will. I know that's true every single time I look at the bruises on your face."

He shakes his head so hard, it seems like it will snap. "It's not! This is my home!" he insists. His head flops back, his eyes squeeze shut, and he screams.

I stand up and go down the steps to him, wrapping my arms around him as if it's anywhere near enough. His shoulder blades are sharp.

"You're gonna be alright," I tell him, burying my nose in his dirty hair. "I promise. You're a survivor, Will. You've always been that, but you deserve better, and going with this social worker might be the only chance you get to escape all this and *have better*. But you've got to be more than just a survivor now. You've got to have faith in the goodness of other people and trust that everything is going to be okay. I think your mom would want that."

His frail body releases a deep and sorrowful breath as he relaxes in my arms.

TWENTY FIVE

*S*ome days, *you* just put down the gun you've been shooting
yourself with, and there's this moment of clarity waiting.

Today's that day.

Will left with Ms. Clark this morning. She was a social worker with
emerald-colored pants and hair pulled back in a bun that was falling apart.
With one look at Will, she fished a baggie of sunflower seeds out of her
purse for him to gobble down. She promised him a stop for burgers and
he left with her, looking back over his shoulder at me as he got in her little
economy car.

I waved good-bye to him from the front door window. When I finally
went upstairs, I saw his flat Spiderman pillow still sitting on the ledge.

I've never felt so alone in my whole entire life.

I lay on my bed, staring at the ceiling, until Clive called me downstairs
to say that Penny died. He said I'd have to start cleaning rooms if I wanted

to stay.

Vareesha looked at me and said, "I heard a maid got kill't las' week down the street at the Walk In motel. Some crazy man wit' a ice pick. I'd tell Clive that front door's gotta be locked if you upstairs cleanin'. A murderer could be in the hotel, jus' as much as out, but at leas' it's somethin'."

"That was a couple months ago," is all I said to her before I came up to my room and laid down.

I hear Vareesha tell a customer out in the hall that she don't have no extra towels. She bangs the cart against the walls, pissed that she's back here working, no doubt.

I get up and pull my backpack out from under the bed. I feel around under the box spring for a particular groove and the paper stuck under the nearest slat. I slide out a fifty dollar bill and a twenty—the money that had slid behind my dresser from the man who attacked me and the money I've put away, dollar by dollar, and tried to forget about. I kept this money hidden instead of leaving it all in my jewelry box. Nobody knew about it, not even Jonah.

This was *real* emergency money ... *spinach money* for this exact moment.

I tuck half of it in the sole of my shoe. The other half in my bra. Lavina would be proud.

I try to shove my mother's electric skillet in the backpack. It's awkward and won't zip shut, so I take it back out. I put my room key inside my broken jewelry box and slide that down into the bottom instead. I take all the tiny soaps Lavina gave me and as much clothing as I can fit. Stuffed, my pack weighs as much as Boo.

I sling the backpack on my back. The weight feels good. I could carry it the rest of my life.

I might have to, because I have to leave. And I've got to leave almost everything behind.

Except the essentials.

Except me.

I walk down the stairs. Will's stuff isn't on the ledge anymore. Vareesha is in the lounge now, sitting sideways on the couch with her heels up. She's got a Styrofoam container on her lap from Red's, and a fork poised in her hand.

"Where ya goin'?" she calls to me. She stabs something in the box with her fork.

"Out," I say. "Whuch ya got?"

"Pancakes," she says, "from a place down the street. Brett's? Ret's? Somethin' like that. Guy at the oil shop next door bought me breakfast. Handsome guy, too." Her smile is sticky.

I walk out of the hotel, the howl of the alarm trailing behind me. I unlock the shitty, green bicycle Jonah from the fence. Will put the chain back on, but I don't know how far it will get me. Nobody's even tried to steal it.

I leave the lock, wedged and swinging, still stuck in the slats of the fence. Slinging my leg over the top, I take off, standing on the pedals to pump to the end of the hotel parking lot.

The bay doors of the oil shop are wide open across the street. Jonah's piece of crap car is sitting at the far end of the parking lot. I know he's there, scanning like he always does, seeing everything. There are two shadows in the last open bay, one lanky and tall like Marco, and the other is Jonah. I can tell by his walk, even the way he moves his arms. He knows I'm here and I know he's there.

He's probably betting on what I'll do next. Deciding what his escape route will be if I cross the street. He's too far from the office to retreat to his back room. I like the thought that his next move is all up to me, but it's enough that I'm the only one that is in control of mine.

With my butt still off the seat, I drive the bike pedal down hard, sailing down the sloping cement entrance to the street. A red car turns into the street from the boulevard and honks at me as I jag around it. The car doesn't slow down. Instead, it hooks into the oil shop entrance and comes to a stop in front of one of the open bays. It honks again, this time for service.

Jonah steps out of the shadows of the last bay, closest to the boulevard. In the blinding sunlight he squints, putting a hand out, palm-up, to coax the car in with a wave of his fingers, but his eyes aren't on the driver.

They're on me.

His gaze tracks the bike as I steer it onto the sidewalk that runs parallel to the shop. The whole lot is between us, a row of empty, customer parking spaces and the driveway leading to the bays. I coast along the sidewalk in the direction of the boulevard, eyes straight ahead, even though I'm scanning. I pass the first bay and Jonah is still standing outside the third. I pass the second and just as I cross in front of the last bay and am parallel to Jonah, I hit the brakes hard.

The brake lights of the car that pulled into the bay dull as it's put into park. Jonah stands in the harsh lines of the sun, staring at me. He's across the lot, but his hands ball into fists at his sides, ready.

He's afraid? Worried? Pissed? None of them fit. Jonah is none of these things. He stares out at me, daring me to confront him. I don't even recognize him now, with his hateful, hooded glare. Jonah is a man of a dozen faces and this one is completely savage.

Weeds can survive being uprooted, but not annihilated. I know now that I am a dandelion, and I've just been waiting this whole time for my wish to be made, for one of my breaths to be strong enough to catch on the right wind and float me away from all of this.

I drop my feet on the sidewalk and swing my leg over the seat. Standing there, holding the rickety, green bike between us, I face Jonah and match his heated glare.

The car in the bay honks for service. Jonah backs up one step and the shadows of the building start to swallow him. But before he retreats any further, I shove the bike toward him with everything I have.

The frame jumps sideways, away from me, on its spongy, tread-less tires and slams down on the concrete with a clatter. A piece flies off, skittering over the concrete. The mangled bike lies on its side, the back wheel circling slowly in the air. The momentum winds down … dies.

The customer in the red car rolls down his window. "Look, I ain't got all day," the guy shouts.

I hike up the strap of my backpack on my shoulder as I turn away from Jonah. I walk down the sidewalk and reach the corner of the boulevard in seconds.

Turning north, I put my back to the hotel and walk away. The restaurant and apartments Ned told me about are only a few miles away. I hope the sidewalk will reach the whole distance, but if not, I'll make my own way.

In the deep fall sunshine, I take a breath and I go.

THE END

SPECIAL THANKS

For you, God. It's always about you.

I couldn't have written this book if I hadn't lived through it first. Thank you to the people I knew who looked out for me along the way.

I wanted to mention here the kids who I met at the hotel. The little ones I had the water gun fight with (and blew out the lighting on the entire floor), the babies I held, the ones I didn't, the kids who came and went. I think of you all the time.

Thanks to Mom and Dad for answering that collect call and for coming in the dead of night. And thanks for answering all the calls ever since. Family doesn't mean flawless. It means forgiveness. I'm glad we got on with it and have ended up friends.

Huge hugs for Starla Huchton, who created this amazing cover. You nailed it. Thank you so much for sharing your awesome.

Thanks to Nadege Richards of Inkstain Interior Book Designs. I wanted this book gorgeous and knew you were the perfect chick for the job. Thanks for working under my crazy deadlines.

Thank you to Kathryn Paquette and Mindy Ruiz who did the most amazing alpha-reads. Thanks for the suggestions that made this story cleaner, clearer, and so much stronger.

Love and kisses to my beautiful family— Pook, Little Biker Boy, and Little Rocker Chick— for being mine. More than anything.

NOTE FROM MISTY

Ok, let's hit the brass tacks of this book.

I think it is important for me to mention that this is a work of fiction and in no way an autobiography. It is based on actual events in my life, but I went to hella-crazy lengths to obliterate names, faces, identifying factors and specifics to protect the innocent and the not-so-innocent. So, if you should stumble upon an uncle, or a sister, or a cousin, mother, father, brother, aunt, grandparent, spouse, girlfriend, fiancé, or neighbor in here, please know that your chances of being absolutely delusional are 100%, because any resemblance to actual persons, living or dead, is purely coincidental.

The truth of this story is that it is based on the experiences I had as a suburban teen runaway and high school dropout who took up residence at a Detroit hotel.

Some, but not all, of the similarities are:
- I worked the graveyard shift as a clerk in the office.
- The addicts I knew fed me when I was starving, and they let me know in no uncertain terms that they would end my life for me if I got into drugs.
- When I called the police or assistance with an attempted robbery, a cop did tell me not to call the police unless there was a dead body.
- I was left in a car in the alley behind a crack house.
- A person I knew was beaten for leaving me there.

- I did date a guy while I lived at the hotel, but he was not Jonah. The guy I dated never stole my car.
- Will is the conglomeration of a half dozen kids I met at the hotel.
- I've had both a gun to my face and a knife to my belly.
- My parents have been married for 50+ years to date. Neither of them are alcoholics and nobody ever laid a hand on me. My family mended fences and we are extremely close to this day.
- I did live in Room 46, the corner room with the hotel sign out my window.

I'm not pulling back the whole curtain because I don't think it's necessary. I trust you, the reader, to feel your way along and decide which events happened and which didn't.

For more about me, my Misty Provencher young adult/teen books, or my Misty Paquette new adult/adult books, please visit me at mistyprovencherauthor.com. You'll also get some free books when you join the newsletter! Enjoy the reads,

—MISTY PAQUETTE

MORE BOOKS BY
MISTY PAQUETTE

Young Adult Paranormal Fantasy
THE CORNERSTONE SERIES
(**#1 Cornerstone, #2 Keystone, #3 Jamb, #4 Capstone**)

New Adult, Contemporary Romance
THE CROSSED & BARED SERIES
HALE MAREE (Book One)
FULL OF GRACE (Book Two)

New Adult/Adult Post-Apocalyptic, Science-Fantasy
THE UTOPIA COLLECTION
THE FLY HOUSE (stand alone)
The Dimension Thieves Series (Episodes 1-12)

Adult Contemporary Women's Fiction
STRONGER

New Adult Urban Fantasy
MERCY, A GARGOYLE STORY

New Adult Retro-Romance
Careless Whisper
(Stand Alone, also included in Love in the 80's multi-author series)

Adult, Erotic Romance
THE BROWN BAG SERIES
THE RELEASE CLUB
#1 Jezebel & Daire, #2 Jezebel Joins, #3 Jezebel Surrenders

ABOUT MISTY

Misty Paquette offers readers, ranging from teen to adult, a shelf full of stories to enjoy. Paquette's genres include titles in contemporary romance, fantasy, literary fiction, sci-fi, and even erotica.

While Paquette can ride a motorcycle, knows how to karate chop, and has learned enough French, Spanish, and sign language to get herself slapped, Misty's life is dedicated to connecting with, and understanding, the people who cross her path. She is totally enchanted with the world and spends her days trying to translate her everyday muses into words.

Misty Paquette lives in the mitten. Knock on her internet door and join her newsletter at mistyprovencherauthor.com and find her wherever great coffee is sold.

Made in the USA
Charleston, SC
18 October 2016